I0672722

A SCHOOL SO GORGEOUS AND FATAL

COUNTERPART ACADEMY - BOOK ONE

SAM BLOOD

A SCHOOL SO GORGEOUS AND FATAL

CONTENTS

Edited by Alicia Lee
Development by Lara Kruszewski and Siobhan Utting

First Published by Blood Enterprises, 2025

www.sambloodauthor.com

1

Don't worry, Father, I thought achingly, as if he could still hear me. *I'm going to make them pay.*

The biting wind on Cuba Street was a physical assault, a southerly blast that funnelled through the buildings and carried the sharp, salt-crusted chill of the harbour up the pedestrian strip. Somewhere the smell of roasted coffee promised sanctuary, or at least caffeine-induced anxiety. To anyone else, it was a typical, blustery afternoon in Wellington, New Zealand. To me, it was a hunting ground.

The howl of the wind was accompanied by the rhythmic, metallic clatter of the bucket fountain. I remembered my astonishment and delight when the water had splashed on my nose as a child. Father's laughter at my expression still rang through my ears. I felt a familiar pang of longing.

I stood in the shadow of an awning, outside a boutique bookstore. I pressed my back against the brick, my gaze fixed on the people flowing by. I wasn't waiting for friends or family; I was searching for my prey. Over the last year, I'd spent countless nights treading this street and Courtenay Place, a lone girl in the dark, looking for ghosts.

My eyes swept over a group of three figures, their necks wrapped warmly in scarves, weaving through the crowd toward one of my favourite establishments: *Midnight Runner* café. They were nondescript, middle-aged. Two women and one man with fairly forgettable features, no offence intended.

They came to a stop beside two individuals who seemed to be waiting for them beside the bucket fountain, their faces obscured beneath the hoods pulled down low. To a passerby, the five of them were just classic Wellingtonians with an edge of mystique.

But I watched the lead figure of the trio pause. He didn't look at his watch or a phone; he reached up, and trailed his finger down to rest against the left side of his chest.

One of the hooded strangers repeated the gesture.

Bingo.

The mark of Shadows' Eve and its acolytes. A silent, devotional gesture to the *'Dark Father'* they served.

I felt a sickening surge of adrenaline.

I've found you, you backstabbing bastards.

One year ago, their kind had taken my father from me. But today, they were finally going to give me answers... and I was going to enjoy seeing them every bit as helpless as they'd made me.

"Crowley, what's going on?" a youthful voice piped up suddenly. It sounded mad. "Don't try to gaslight me... I read a book about that recently. Now I'm gaslight-proof."

I nearly jumped out my skin. I spun around, my hand instinctively reaching for the small of my back where my Glock sat concealed in its holster.

Harper was standing three feet away, clutching the straps of his backpack. My younger brother looked so much like our father—the same earnest brow, the same chocolate locks of hair that refused to stay flat. He was two years younger than me, still holding onto a childhood innocence that I seemed to have misplaced the night Father was killed in-front of me.

"What are you doing here?" I hissed, grabbing his shoulder and pulling him into a side-street. I waited a moment, then risked a look around the corner. The Five Musketeers didn't appear to have noticed us; they were too busy having a very intense, very *murmury* meeting.

"I told you I had important business," I said incredulously, retreating to glare at Harper. "You promised you'd stay home and play with your LEGOs or whatever it is kids do these days."

"You had that look." His voice trembled, but his face was still set with an impressive amount of judgement. "The look you get when you're staring at photos of Father. I knew you were up to something."

"I don't know what you mean."

My adorable brother looked like he was about to tear his hair out. "Crowley, you're acting like some kind of assassin. You're meant to be buying me *stationery*."

Harper shared my pale features and was two years younger than me, still waiting for that growth spurt. In contrast, I was the tallest girl in my class, an awkward, gawky scarecrow. His chocolate brown hair was closer to Mother's, though hers was darker. Mine was my father's, a blonde that was instead a shade too close to hay for my liking.

"They're acolytes, aren't they?" he demanded. He lunged toward the corner of the shop to peek. I caught him by the back of his hoodie, yanking him back into the shadows.

"Don't," I snapped, my voice softening when I saw him flinch. I reached out, smoothing a stray lock of hair away from his forehead. "Please. Just stay behind me."

"Isn't that what they call members of Shadows' Eve? Acolytes? I read it means..."

"It's a fancy word for *'follower,'*" I said. Harper's gaze moved down to the pendant held tightly in my hand; it was a tortoise carved of white bone. Father had taken it from the men who had murdered him; I'd found it clutched in his hand after the ambush. "The acolytes were traitors to the Praetory." My throat sounded choked, and I was angry with myself. I had to be strong for him. "They started their own group, Shadows' Eve, and started an invisible war on them."

"The Praetory. That's the society Father and Mother are a part of," Harper said slowly.

I subconsciously reached down to massage where my knee met its socket, phantom pain flaring.

"So, *are* those guys acolytes?" Harper pressed.

"Yes. I've been tracking them."

Harper's eyes widened, like he hadn't actually expected to be right.

"How the heck did you find them?"

"Persistence, and a general lack of hobbies. Also, I may have stolen some intelligence from Mother's office."

"Wow. She is going to *kill* you."

"Look, it doesn't matter right now," I said urgently. "You're going to turn my hair grey, kid. I need you to get to someplace safe."

"*Kid?* You're only two years older than me," Harper pointed out, glaring.

"And in those two years of self-growth, I have attained great and terrible power," I said solemnly, "and learnt of the secret wisdom from the heart of the universe."

"Oh, is that what puberty is?"

I burst out laughing.

"I wish."

"Good. I was worried I'd been doing it wrong."

I loved Harper, and he'd always looked up to me, even though I didn't feel anything close to the hero he made me out to be. We had relied on each other even more since we lost Father. Our mother had always been one for the hands-off approach, if you favoured complete understatements.

I checked again on my quarry, and felt a jolt through my chest. They were on the move, heading toward *Midnight Runner*.

"Harper, I have to go."

"I don't want to lose you too!"

Just like that; so plain and earnest from his lips.

"Let me help." He was pleading now, a single tear escaping and tracking through the dust on his cheek. "I'm fast, Crowley. I can keep watch. I can—"

"No." I gripped his shoulders, looking him dead in the eye. "If I lose you, I lose everything."

He sniffled, looking down at his sneakers.

"You couldn't lose me if you tried," I whispered into his hair, giving him a quick hug. "If I'm going in there, I need to be alert, and I can't do that if I'm worried about you getting caught in the crossfire." I looked over my shoulder, where the family car was idling. "Tell Eric to take you back straight to the estate, then scan the frequency for any local chatter. Be my eyes and ears from home, okay?"

I saw the shift in him—the way his shoulders squared

as I gave him a *'mission.'* It was a lie, a way to get him to safety, but it was a lie he needed.

"I'll have the comms open," he said seriously, wiping his eyes with his sleeve. "But Crowley? If you aren't back by dinner, I'm telling Mom you stole the files from her office."

I grinned, despite the adrenaline. "Wow. You really are a little monster."

"I learned from the best." He reached out, squeezing my hand one last time. It was a tiny, warm pressure that I felt long after he'd turned and run toward the idling family car at the end of the block.

I watched him climb into the back. Harper stared out the window at me, hiding his terror behind a brave smile as they drove away, as if he was trying to etch the image of me into his memory. I held up a hand as I watched him go.

Limping back out onto Cuba, I was just in time to see the five suspicious figures vanishing inside *Midnight Runner*. Home to some of the best and chunkiest slices of chocolate cake around.

I adjusted the fit of my prosthetic leg. The stump felt raw today; the humidity always made the titanium socket feel like a brand against my skin. It was a constant reminder that I was the one who survived.

The memories came rushing at me, of soldiers in the dark, of the inhuman sounds of something monstrous being rearing in those dark trees, something not of this world. I recalled a violet light flaring and the hot, tearing sensation that had immediately followed through my lower leg.

I was brought back to that damn night again and again, kicking and screaming, an unwilling hostage in my own mind. I could still feel the weight of Father's lifeless body in my arms.

Cautiously, I opened the door to *Midnight Runner*. The place screamed '*Wellington artsy-ness,*' and the café's walls were decorated with stars and galaxies. It had a great pinball machine, and it was famous for making coffees and hot chocolates with heavy doses of cream and molten marshmallow. Chaos for your cholesterol. Blissful chaos. Something told me however that they weren't coming to my favourite establishment just for a cuppa and a slice of cake.

How could I ever come back here for chocolatey deliciousness if this happened to be the favourite hangout spot of my worst enemy? As if those arseholes hadn't already taken enough from me.

Entering, I pivoted immediately, swerving to sit at a table occupied by four very confused looking girls my age. I angled my face away from the acolytes so all that they could see was my black beret. It looked like they were making their way to the back of the premises.

"Hello," I said to the girls genuinely, trying to sound like a normal person while my heart was doing a frantic solo.

"You're sitting at our table, weirdo," the queen of the pack said, peering at me over rhinestone sunglasses.

Making friends my age had never been my forte. After all, being from a hyper-wealthy, hyper-secretive family rumoured to be part of some weird cult didn't exactly scream '*invitation to the slumber party.*'

"Right you are," I murmured. I looked for the acolytes in the window's reflection, but they were gone. I frowned, feeling a bolt of panic that they'd somehow escaped. I knew this place like the back of my hand—there was no exit back there.

I stood up suddenly, feeling like a giraffe looming over a

bunch of zebras. "Thank you for your hospitality," I said
seriously.

"That girl talks *so* weird," I heard one of them mutter as
I limped away. "Major icky vibes. And what's up with her
leg?"

I headed to the toilets out the back. Nothing in the cubicles. I came back out, rotating around in the dark box at the
end of the cafe, UV-graffiti and artwork sprawled overhead.
I examined the blank wall in front of me, then felt around it
with my fingers. Nothing. Nothing...

There. I couldn't believe it. I felt a latch slide under the
pressure of my finger.

The wall groaned—a sound lost to the heavy bass of the
café music—and revealed a subterranean passage. I slipped
through, immediately closing it behind me.

It looked like I was in the entrance to a subway tunnel,
but the architecture was too elegant, the stone too smooth.
The ceiling arched above like the ribs of some sleeping
beast. The air smelled like rust and wet iron, and somewhere in the distance I could hear the faint sound of dripping water.

Golden signs pointed toward well-known Wellington
landmarks on the surface, like Lambton Quay, Te Papa
Museum and Courtenay Place. Others were labeled with
places that I definitely didn't recognise.

What were the acolytes doing here, creeping through
this forgotten underworld like rats beneath a cathedral?

I drew my Glock. The matte-black polymer was a cold
comfort against my palm. In the end, weapons didn't have
any intentions, any feelings about what they did. They were
entirely reliant on the will of the user... and I was prepared
to use it. I aimed into the darkness, and began the climb.

"*Listen, Crowley,*" Father had whispered to me on the

worst night of my life, his breath hitching as he pulled me into the shadow of a gnarled Pōhutukawa tree. He kept glancing toward the dark tree-line of the gardens, his voice tight with an urgency that made my skin prickle. *"The Praetory isn't just a secret club. It's a hidden nation, spread out across this entire globe. We've existed for millennia, and Wellington is our seat of power in the Pacific."*

"Here. In Wellington," I'd said, sceptically. "New Zealand?"

I supposed nothing screamed global dominion like a cinnamon flat white with oat milk.

"Of course, you've always wanted to know why the Praetory exists." Father had gripped my shoulder, his fingers digging in. *"You want to know how we came into being, and what the secret is we've protected with our own blood for generation after generation."*

"And what is it, exactly?"

Father said a word that shifted the entire axis of my world:

"Shadows."

I'd shivered, without really knowing why.

"What—"

"They're magical beings, creatures from another dimension. No two are alike—they are every fantastical thing you've ever imagined, and things you couldn't." He'd swallowed hard, his eyes searching mine. *"Every human has one. A counterpart. A reflection of your own soul on the other side. They share your emotions, your thoughts... they are the piece of you that's been missing your whole life."*

I remembered my heart hammering against my ribs. *"You're saying I have one? And Harper? Mother?"*

"Yes," he'd breathed, his eyes turning oddly misty. *"And you'll meet yours soon, Crowley. I promise."*

The tunnel sloped upward, a steep, miserable incline clearly designed by someone with a personal vendetta against anyone using a prosthetic. My stump burned in its socket, but I pushed through.

Ahead, my five little acolyte friends finally shuffled into view.

I dropped low. They were striding swiftly, and their voices were carrying to me.

"We need to move quickly," one of the acolytes was saying. He sounded young—probably my age, definitely prone to making poor life choices. His face was buried in a hood, part of that 'emotionally unstable teen' aesthetic. I suppose when you've lost a war, you couldn't exactly be too picky about the IQ of your recruits. "We can get you in or out, but the vault..."

"We know the plan," an older one snapped. "You get a gold star for effort, kid, now move."

"Then let's do this," the teenager said determinedly.

They were definitely up to something. My pace accelerated, or at least my limp got more aggressive. Were lives at stake? Should I get a drop on them now?

No. There were too many to take out on my own, and no audience to appreciate the heroism of my pointless death.

I followed them for what felt like a lifetime, the tunnel winding its way up through the bedrock of Wellington. Finally, I reached a great metal door like a bank vault, hanging slightly ajar.

Taking a deep, steadying breath, I gripped my pistol, hoping they weren't just waiting to kill me on the other side. That would have been a real bummer. Then I peeked through the gap, and stepped through.

I found myself standing in a hallway of polished white marble, illuminated by a flood of golden summer light.

Through high, arched windows, I glimpsed extensive lawns and a gorgeous stream that glittered.

I froze, my pulse thundering in my ears. I knew this place.

Praetory Academy.

Six months after the funeral, when the grief had turned into a jagged, restless needle in my chest, I had come here looking for answers. I'd figured out how to use the acolyte talisman I'd taken from Father. It had led me into the Wellington Botanic Gardens, perched high above the city... and through a shield of illusions into a school that shouldn't exist. A school which Mother and Father themselves must have once attended.

I'd thought about that night ever since. I never told Mother about what happened to me here.

But I'd only ever seen this place in the dark, when it looked like a gothic fever dream. In the daylight, it was something else entirely—elegant stone towers and polished marble that had me gaping at its majesty, wishing I could somehow drink it all in. I forced myself to focus.

Why were the acolytes *here?*

I pressed my back against the metal door I'd just come through, reluctantly returning the Glock to its holster. I didn't want to get murdered by the acolytes, but I didn't want to be shot by campus security either.

I scanned the grounds through the windows as I crept along the corridor, my eyes darting between the beauty of the gardens and the corridor of marble. No sign of the acolytes yet. If I didn't move fast, all hell was going to break loose.

A wooden door a few yards ahead creaked open. I froze, my fingers flying to the grip of my concealed weapon.

"Hello?" a voice said suddenly from the other side, and

it threw me. It was a young women's voice, curious and warm. I went very still, hesitating. Could one of the acolytes be standing there, just on the other side? Was it a trap?

Before I could formulate a strategy or even a convincing response, the voice came through the doorway again. "I'm going to come through to that side, okay? Please don't panic. I don't bite. Well, only for fun."

Charming. And vaguely worrying.

I shoved the gun into my hidden holster, smoothing my coat just as the door slid open with an eerie smoothness.

The person stalking toward me through the doorway was beautiful. Terrifying.

And 100% not human.

2

She came padding lithely on all fours.

Father gifted me an illustrated encyclopaedia of animals one Christmas, and due to my lack of a social life, I'd spent my childhood eagerly scanning its pages. One animal suddenly came back to me. It was a caracal, a wild cat found throughout Africa, Asia and the Middle East.

The large, golden-tawny feline stalking toward me could have been a splitting image. She had the exact same long tufted ears and long legs as a caracal. When she smiled, and she was actually *smiling*, I glimpsed the same long fangs. But there were some discrepancies.

Specifically, the tail. Caracals did not have long, undulating, serpentine tails covered in porcupine quills. That was a biological '*no-no.*' The same went for her eyes, which were as blue as lapis-lazuli.

No, I firmly concluded. *Definitely* not a caracal. The closest comparison I could think of was a manticore from Persian mythology; it fit the *'dangerous wildcat with a killer tail'* vibe, but she lacked the wings, mane and reportedly nasty attitude. Still, it was the best reference I had and I was working on my feet here.

Also, it seemed important to note that her front limbs resembled the arms of a monkey. She even walked on her knuckles.

If this had been the first time I'd seen a Shadow, I might have screamed, but it wasn't. Here it was, the very purpose of the Praetory: to hide the existence of beings exactly like this. To keep the world in the dark from what really lay on the other side of the veil.

The manticore smiled as I backed away from her. It almost seemed as if she were drinking in my awe, fully aware of the impact her mere appearance was creating. I considered running immediately, but that wasn't always the smartest move with wild predators. I needed a distraction, but I was hypnotised. I'd wondered what it would be like at the zoo to fall into an enclosure with a wild animal and how I'd handle the situation. Except instead it was ogling me as if I was the one in the zoo, existing solely for their amusement.

"Don't worry," the manticore said. The words came from her, from that mouth, there was no question. I'd watched her form the words, I'd seen the knowing smirk. "I'm Sephy. It's lovely to meet you...?"

I didn't respond. I'd strangely lost my voice.

"Okay, or you don't have to tell me your name. I'll have to investigate and figure it out. I like a challenge!"

Instinct kicked in. Training took over. I started scanning for exits, mentally calculating my odds of survival (low). I fought off flashbacks of what happened the last time I met a Shadow. Spoiler alert: people died.

I'd come here eight months back, chasing shadows and vengeance. Back when sneaking into secret supernatural schools seemed like a good idea. It wasn't. I'd found someone in the basement back then—bleeding, dangerous, unforgettable. I'd learnt then that not *all* Shadows could be trusted. Just like people.

There's no time to think about that, I chided myself. Nobody could ever find out about what happened that night. I hadn't told Mother. Even Harper didn't know the full of it.

Now here I was again. Round two. Different monster. Same odds. Zero sanity.

"Have you visited the Academy already?" Sephy asked, smiling a fanged smile. Absurdly, there was something almost flirtatious about it. "You look like you haven't even met a Shadow before."

"You're not my first Shadow," was all I said.

"Wow. You're mysterious, you know that?"

Sephy's eyes lit up, and her tail swept back and forth. The sharp spines scraped against stone, and I gulped.

"Wait!" She beamed. "You're one of the newbies, am I right?"

I nodded. Here I was again, deep, deep down the rabbit hole.

Be careful, Crowley. Think of Harper. You must survive.

I needed to focus. I came here for a reason. Find the acolytes. They had to be here somewhere. What if she was with them though?

"Oh, sweetie. Let me summarise: Shadows, secret hidden academies, all very new, do I suppose correctly?" the manticore queried sympathetically.

"It's still not feeling *entirely* normalised," I muttered.

"Hmm. It *is* traditional to keep those things secret until coming of age, but not many families tend to stick to that."

"Well, my mother always did love rules more than

anything else." After a moment of hesitation, I bowed to her, remembering my Praetory etiquette. "Blanche DuBois," I lied, grasping for the first fake name I could think of. "It's a pleasure to meet you."

While bending down I was surreptitiously looking around, checking the newly revealed hallway for any sign of the acolytes.

"Wonderful to meet you, Blanche. A little lost? Never fear!" the manticore declared, brandishing her spiny tail like a lion tamer's whip. "I, Sephy Nekomata, will be your guide and master. All I ask is that you submit your full allegiance to myself and my machinations."

"What...?"

"A simple *'yes'* will suffice."

"I..."

"We can work on your obedience later," she decided. "Now, follow me!"

I blinked in astonishment. Could I trust her? What here *could* I trust? I knew so little about this world at all, other than what I had gleaned from my mother's files. A lot of the basics still escaped me. If this *'Sephy'* wasn't involved with Shadows' Eve, I needed to warn her what was going on in the school right now. Except what if the acolytes weren't even here, and I got caught out having snuck in here myself? The one thing I did know about the Praetory, was that the punishments for breaching their codes and rules could be severe. They took their security very seriously. It was the only way that they'd managed to hide the existence of Shadows this long. My best path seemed to be to lose Sephy and locate the acolytes, as soon as possible.

"Thank you, Ms Nekomata," I said, surprising myself with how smoothly the words came out despite our circumstances. It was surprisingly natural talking to a feline who shouldn't possibly exist. "However, I'd just like to get back to my group, I was having a look around the school with them. Have you seen anyone else new around?"

"Oh, great! No, but I'm sure we can find them together. Shall I lead the way, or would you like to?"

Should have seen that coming.

"What do your friends look like, exactly?"

"They're wearing... hoods," I finished lamely.

She looked at me oddly.

Sephy and I set off together, and I set a manic pace. Prowling down the corridor I searched through the windows of classrooms and out at the grounds, looking for any sign of the acolytes.

Where the hell were those murderers? Did they really come here, or was I mistaken? I didn't know exactly where they were headed, just that they were trying to steal something important. And I could hardly ask Sephy what that might be without seeming incredibly suspicious. Praetory was a place of strict rules and consequences. I wasn't exactly sure what was safe to reveal.

Dammit. This place was labyrinthine. How was I going to find them?

Sephy seemed to be panting to keep up with my pace, which was amusing since she had four legs and I one.

"Wow, you have some attachment issues with your friends, huh?" she panted. She was still keeping what seemed to be her signature aggressive sunny optimism, but I thought I detected her getting a little annoyed as she padded alongside me. She definitely seemed to be perplexed by the pace I was keeping with my purposeful strides, despite my prosthetic.

I'd worry about losing Sephy later. You know—after I'd handled the minor tasks of locating a bunch of secret cultists and singlehandedly stopping them. Solid plan. Airtight. Just the right balance of heroic and suicidal.

"So am I the first Shadow you've seen?"

"No. Not that I've seen... many."

"What do you think, comparatively?" Sephy stretched languorously, almost suggestively.

"Very impressive," I said, clearing my throat.

"Oh, don't be so stiff and formal. I can see how you're hypnotised by me." She laughed as I flushed and looked away. "There's no need to be shy! You'd think no one had ever flirted with you."

"Certainly not cats from other dimensions," I murmured, dazed. I must have been in shock. "I'm sure you're a real feline bombshell." I cleared my throat and looked around at the grand hallway. "This place is... extravagant. Someone clearly misread the definition of *'boarding school.'*"

"Yeah, well... the Praetory is not short on money."

"The other things it could have been used for..." I muttered.

"So, welcome to Counterpart Academy!" Sephy beamed with pride. "Well, technically it's the Praetory Academy of New Zealand. *Bleurgh*. But almost everyone here calls it Counterpart Academy. Because it's while being schooled here that you're paired with your other half, who you can telepathically share your thoughts and dreams with, your partner for life."

"And how does the Academy stay hidden, exactly?"

"What do you mean?

"I mean, sure, we all have our moments of being unobservant. But there *is* a giant patch of land in the Botanic

Gardens filled with beings from another world that nobody has ever stumbled across."

Sephy smiled again, tail flicking back and forth.

"What do *you* think?" she questioned me innocently.

"Some kind of phenomena from the Shadow world that's being used over here? Otherwise it would have to be some kind of very advanced technology that the Praetory created themselves." I mused on this. "Perhaps through technological innovations, enabled by materials collected from your dimension?"

She smiled.

"Crowley, you *are* good. We call them Brilliance Stones. Precious stones that seemed to only appear where Rips between the worlds have sprouted up once. They're sensitive to the telepathic connection between Shadows and humans. The ancient Praetory learnt how to essentially program them to create disruptive illusions, to stop the everyday people wandering into their communities and properties, once they'd decided to go underground. And just in the last half century, they've used modern technology to build on this, creating elaborate holograms. People don't even notice their eyes sliding away from the Brilliance Stone field. They don't even realise that they can't account for the empty space on their precious maps."

I suddenly wondered what power Sephy had, or if she was too young to have discovered hers yet. As unbelievable as it sounded, every Shadow had a unique power, something close to what we could call straight-up magic. Some Shadows could shoot fire or freeze water to ice. Some could beguile and confuse, while others could pass through solid objects. Of course, most Shadows had fairly superficial abilities of little use. But a few were blessed with talents that could change the outcomes of entire battles, or be used to manipulate others.

"Don't worry, you're going to absolutely love it here," Sephy gushed. "This is the best place in the world. I'm not kidding. The parties, the pranks, the antics. Also we have top-notch facilities, staff and curriculum, if you care about that stuff too. It's going to be amazing."

Something about talking to Sephy was starting to give me the impression that Sephy was one of those popular, ultra-confident girls. She acted as if she was queen.

"So... you're a student too?"

"Yeah, I've been here over summer getting orientated, like a lot of us. This is pretty much my home now. I mean, it is for all of us, but I spend more time here than anyone else, helping run things. I work in administration part-time. So if you want to know any gossip on anyone, I'm your person."

"Isn't that an abuse of power?"

"Yes, I suppose it *is* a use of power," she said, satisfied. "A very smart one."

"I meant, is it an *abuse*...?" I shook my head. This was getting ridiculous. I'd seen no sign of the acolytes, and for all I knew I'd taken a wrong turn and they never came here at all. Sephy seemed to be who she said she was; perhaps I just had to take a leap of faith here and trust her with the truth. It might save more people than me just poking around in the dark.

Except we were already moving so fast that we didn't even see the person rushing around the corner until they ran right into us. When I saw the familiar hoody the person was wearing, my heart-rate escalated. It was the student who let the others into the Academy. The hoody covered the acolyte's features, and he deliberately turned his face away. I'd glimpsed nothing but darkness in that hood.

I moved to draw the handgun concealed in my handbag. But then I saw the student's hand brushing aside the baggy end of their hoody, revealing the holster of a gun in a flash. I hesitated. I couldn't be sure I'd get the draw on him first, not when he was this on edge.

Instead I slipped on the expression of a perplexed but innocent student. I needed to convince him we weren't a threat if we were going to get him to lower his guard.

"Hey!" Sephy said brightly. "You're a new face too, huh? Welcome to Counterpart Academy!" She padded around him curiously, trying to get a better look at his features. He kept turning away from her, to the point where it was almost a farcical game. "What's up, babe? You're shy, huh? What brings you here?"

"Just checking out the place," he said casually, awkwardly. Something was strange with his voice, like he was trying to disguise it by speaking low and gruff. "I'm starting this year."

"Oh, welcome!" I was sure Sephy must be suspicious, though admittedly she hid it well. "I'm Sephy Nekomata, pleasure to meet you. You should join in on our little impromptu tour then."

Whatever this guy and the other acolytes were so desperate to find that they risked breaking into this school, the one thing I knew was this guy did not seem keen for a school tour. He looked like a possum caught in headlights.

I was already running through possible moves the acolyte might make, and how to counter each of them.

Why hadn't he pulled his gun on us yet?

Whenever I imagined acolytes, it was in their traditional Shadows' Eve garb. Black robes, and masks in the image of the Dark Father who led them: a great horned tiger.

I wondered if there was a chance that this guy was just a scared, impressionable teenager. Someone who made a big mistake in running around with a group of fanatical mass-murderers.

Then again, perhaps he was just afraid that discharging his gun would attract further attention to their operation. Perhaps killing the two of us was a lesser concern.

"Everyone has their own pace," I said to Sephy lightly, wondering how talking to a winged, spine-tailed wildcat became the less alarming part of my situation. "If our friend here wants to explore on his own, I don't see why he should be forced to join our impromptu tour."

The first thing was to get this guy away from Sephy. She was an innocent here, and I didn't want her to be collateral in my little quest for vengeance.

"I apologise," Sephy said to the guy sympathetically, "but we can't let prospective students wander the school unattended. School policy." She didn't understand yet the threat this guy represented. How was I supposed to warn her without making this teen acolyte all trigger-happy?

The acolyte wore a backpack, and something about the way he was carrying it led me to believe whatever was within it was precious.

He made to bolt suddenly, but I was aiming my gun at him before he could blink, catching him off-guard.

"Don't even think of trying it," I said, voice shaking with hate. "Put your hands up."

It hit me. This guy was here alone, without the rest of his little cult. More than that, he was carrying something in that pack, and the way he was running felt more like he was running *from* something, rather than *toward* something. It was just an instinct, but perhaps he had already found whatever it was that he and the other acolytes had broken in here to get. Perhaps it was in that very backpack.

"What's in the bag?" I asked casually.

Then suddenly, the guy turned to look at us. I saw now why I hadn't glimpsed any of his features. He was wearing a black balaclava beneath the hoody, his dark eyes drilling into mine.

"Please," he pleaded, sounding tortured. "They gave everything for this. It can't be for nothing."

I stared at him strangely, a creeping sensation running up the back of my neck.

"Just let me past. I don't want to hurt you."

Sephy froze at the sight of the balaclava beneath that hoody. She'd finally caught onto the fact that we were in a bad, bad situation. If she were human, I think she'd be very pale right now.

"Whatever this is, it's your business," Sephy said quietly with surprising bravery and determination in her voice. "But please, not here. There are innocent people here who could be hurt. I know neither of you wants that."

Sephy was doing a remarkably good job of staying calm in the situation, but I could still see her shaking. Nothing prepares you for your first brush with death.

"You're safe, Sephy. I'm just here for this guy and his companions," I said evenly. I quirked an eyebrow. "Perhaps you should ask the acolyte what it is *he* wants."

Sephy fell deathly quiet at the word *acolyte*, the full level of my accusation sinking in.

"Look, if Shadows' Eve pressured you into doing this, we can help you," I said. "You need to tell us everything, and where we can find the rest of them."

"I'm not a pawn," he responded in a flash of anger that caught me by surprise.

"You're going to tell us what you're doing here," I said, fingers white-knuckled on the grip of my pistol, "and you're going to tell me who killed Peter Crowley."

"What?" the acolyte seemed perplexed. "I don't know who that is!"

"I'd be very careful with your words right now, if I were you," I said, sounding cavalier while feeling anything but. My finger rested against the curve of that trigger.

"I'm just... I'm going to go get someone," Sephy ventured, stepping cautiously away. I could see her trembling, and I was reminded that despite her fearsome appearance, she's just a high school student who woke up this morning with no idea she was going to be confronted with a traumatic experience like this.

"Turn around," I ordered the acolyte. "Hands behind..."

He moved with lightning speed, like a scorpion striking. His movement was a blur as he twisted back around, slapping my wrist. The impact was so hard that my fingers lost their grip, the gun sailing out of reach.

I caught the scent of the acolyte himself when he disarmed me. Like cloves, and woodsmoke.

He dropped out of sight and before I could react he was sweeping my legs. On my prosthetic I was less spry than him. I lost my footing, and I landed hard. My head hit the marble and I gritted my teeth as my head swam. The acolyte bolted down the hall.

"Stop there!" Sephy cried, clearly trying to bring her authority back to her voice as she lunged at the fleeing acolyte, closing in, claws outstretched...

The acolyte turned around as he ran, retrieving something from his hip...

"Sephy, look out!" I gasped, but my warning was too

late. There was the smell of burning fur, accompanied by an awful mewling.

3

Sephy hit the ground, crumpling with the weight of a leopard. The impact was audible.

"No!" I burst out.

The acolyte must have had some sort of taser on him. Arsehole. At least she wasn't shot.

This all happened because when he pleaded, I gave in to a moment of mercy. No more.

Seeing red, I got back on my feet as quickly as my prosthetic allowed. I looked around fiercely. *Dammit.* The acolyte was gone, and there was no sign of my gun. He must have taken it.

He's fast.

This was going sideways impressively quickly. I shouldn't have let Sephy the Manticore distract me, I dropped my guard. In my defence, she was extremely distracting.

I hesitated, blinded by a bloody haze of hatred at the acolyte. My instinct was to give chase, to find him and end them like I'd sworn to do.

But then I crouched beside Sephy, feeling for a pulse.

"Are you all right? Sephy, answer me." Her tawny fur was sleek to the touch. I could definitely find a pulse. She was breathing. She was alive. I exhaled in relief.

"Don't worry, you'll be okay," Sephy murmured to me in gentle reassurance, surprising me.

I frowned, then chuckled despite myself. It was as if I was still the newbie on her tour she was responsible for, and I was the one needing comfort.

"Stop it, you idiot, I'm protecting you," I chided her gently.

That acolyte still could have killed us. Why didn't he?

Reassured that Sephy would live, I regarded the passage before us. The acolyte had vanished so quickly, he must have ducked through a door into a classroom nearby, or surely I'd still be able to see him running the distance of the corridor.

Just then I heard voices. Making my way cautiously toward them, I pressed myself up against a classroom door. Taking a breath, I risked a glance through the window set into it.

The acolyte who had tased Sephy was lying inside, his back pressed against the teacher's desk. His black hood was lowered, and for the first time I saw that the teenager was not human at all. He was a Shadow.

His skin glowed a striking green, reminiscent of moss draping over ancient trees, while his chest was clad in rough, knotted wood. Twigs wove together in a circlet that crowned his brow like a twisted crown of thorns. He looked like a forest spirit plucked from the pages of myth. His skin shimmered like polished bark, rich with the hues of deep earth, flecked with delicate veins of gold that caught the light.

Also, his bright-green eyes were full of simmering

hatred. As a second figure stepped into view, I was suddenly shown the object of his loathing.

The man was human, and tall, with flowing blonde locks past his shoulders. His flawless skin was like alabaster, and he was certainly a pretty-boy. Except there was something undeniably cruel in that smile. His white military uniform gleamed like freshly fallen snow. Sharp and pristine, it acted as a reminder of the Praetory's unwavering resolve. Epaulettes adorned his shoulders that spoke of rank and valour. The high collar framed his neck, lending an air of regality.

The badges the man wore indicated that he was surprisingly decorated for someone in his early twenties. I'm not sure what drew my attention to it, but the man's shoes had left dark footprints across the floor of the classroom. It looked a lot like blood.

The soldier's Shadow was visible too, a two-legged dragon. A wyvern was the technical term, I supposed. Its scales were a poisonous purple, with wings too small and vestigial for flight. The reptile was covered in natural plates of armour like bone, resembling the exoskeleton of a horned beetle. A mane of hair flowed from the rear of its bony helmet like seaweed, and it was opulently decorated with gold and rubies.

Dammit. The Praetory's military was here. I could get in serious trouble for dabbling in things I shouldn't be dabbling in, and that was the best case scenario. The truth was, I had broken into a Praetory academy when I wasn't meant to, carrying a gun, coming up through the same secret passage that the acolytes had used. All signs really pointed toward me being part of their little cult. I watched through the glass as the soldier in the classroom stared calmly down the length of his pistol at the wounded acolyte.

"How many are you?" the soldier asked calmly.

"Go to hell, Kipling," the forest spirit spat back. There was something slightly off about his voice, but I couldn't place it.

"Ah. So you do know me."

There was a gunshot, and the Shadow screamed.

I nearly gasped at the brutality of it. The man, Kipling, hadn't shot to kill. This was torture by bullet, in a school classroom. Even though I hated the acolytes for taking Father, the fact that this acolyte looked so young...

"That's *Sir* Kipling to you. Remember that you're addressing the Governor's personal knight, traitor."

A *knight?* This man was really a knight of the Praetory? Of course... I noted the sword sheathed at Kipling's side, its golden hilt on display. That was the sign of a knight, both ceremonial and handy to have in close combat.

"How many are you?" Kipling repeated levelly. His voice was commanding, his words articulate. But I saw his lip curl in distaste, as if the very existence of the being before him was unsightly.

"Just me," the forest spirit coughed. I would have admired his courage, if I didn't know it was just pure brainwashed fanaticism talking. "I came in here alone."

"Well, I certainly hope that's not true," Kipling said smoothly. "Otherwise I just killed five innocents."

The acolyte's head snapped up to look at the man in shock, and I saw the pain and agony in his features.

"The others...?"

"They're all dead. I'm sorry you didn't get that little prize you were after."

Shocked, I struggled to come to grips with this information. Had Kipling and his fearsome wyvern really already slaughtered the very acolytes I came here for revenge on?

Now I may never get the answers I'd been wanting from them.

Another detail niggled at the back of my mind for some reason. I couldn't see any sign of the backpack near the forest spirit. Perhaps Kipling had just already confiscated it.

I could barge in there now but I couldn't be certain that Kipling wouldn't shoot me on sight. He seemed in a trigger-happy mood.

"Shadows' Eve is done," Kipling said. "You're all nothing but dust. Your precious leader is in a forsaken hole, a broken being."

"He's just waiting," the acolyte whispered, "dreaming of his moment of escape." It sounded like each word was a painful effort, but a strange expression came over the acolyte's features. An ecstatic, religious euphoria. "He'll reward all of his acolytes who have continued his great designs. Those who have remained loyal to him. Long... live... the Dark Father."

I felt a little shiver as I heard the name invoked.

Without warning, the forest spirit started spasming. Kipling snarled and lunged forth. The white fabric of his uniform flowed like a river of ice as he grabbed the forest-spirit, attempting to pry open his jaw... then the Shadow slumped, going still.

The Shadow was gone, all in an instant.

I just stared, numb. My ears roared.

I'd been told that when a Shadow died, their human counterpart died, and vice versa. Whether it was in an unrelated freak accident, or having a sudden heart attack, no one could survive once their counterpart was gone. It was why I was never going to have a chance to meet my father's Shadow either.

"Poison capsule," Kipling informed his own Shadow venomously, dropping the forest spirit to the ground. "I didn't expect such resolve from someone so young, Lilith. Still a coward's move. Heathens."

"It doesn't matter," the wyvern, Lilith, reassured him. Her voice wasn't a hiss, but rather a deep rumble. "That was the last of them."

If the acolytes had all been killed, that was my chance gone. I needed to get out the tunnel I entered through. If the Praetory didn't know that was the route the acolytes had used and still hadn't discovered it, it might be my best chance to get out of here. I didn't know how severe the consequences would be for my breaking into these grounds, but judging by Sir Kipling's idea of justice, I'd rather he not be the one who designed the punishment. At worst, he would suspect I was another acolyte, and I'd be killed on sight.

But before I could pull away from the glass, a door on the opposite side of the classroom suddenly opened and an imposing woman strode through it. She was followed by her magnificent Shadow, a tall, solemn anthropomorphic bird covered in black feathers, with four wings extending from their back. A crest of indigo quills splayed out from their head like a crown.

The woman came to a stop and regarded the dead acolyte with an inscrutable expression as she folded her arms. She had a strong jaw and dark hair cascaded down over her shoulders. When she regarded the knight, though, it was with undisguised contempt. "Sir Kipling Sloan." She nodded at the wyvern beside him. "Lilith."

Kipling instinctively bent down to kneel on the spot.

"General Morgaine Holloway," he intoned respectfully, bowing.

"Spare your honourifics," she snorted. "I'm general of nothing now, simply a teacher here."

"Yet your reputation shall always remain legendary," Kipling replied with grave respect.

"What in the blazes is the meaning of this?" Morgaine said in anger. "I saw the bodies. How could you do something so monstrous, on the grounds of a *school*?"

"I was handling a threat."

"That looked more like sport."

"I received intelligence from an informant that a nest of acolytes were attempting to penetrate the Academy," Kipling explained.

"Yet you didn't leave any alive for questioning?"

"I already extracted what information from them I could."

"And?"

"Disappointing. They are a small, atomised cell, and they've had little contact with other acolytes. This was yet another desperate ploy from a near-extinct breed. Still, any sickness can bring down the host, if left to spread unchecked."

"This is still extreme, Kipling," Morgaine spat. "Surely someone with your renowned skill could have handled this more delicately. I'm sure Governor Blackmore would agree."

I stirred at that name.

Wait. Did she just say Governor *Blackmore?*

"With all due respect, Morgaine, didn't they once call you the *'Bloody Queen?'*" Kipling posed. There was a polite smile in his voice. "Are you not the one who felled foreign governments, and conquered entire nations in the name of the Potentate?"

Morgaine regarded him thunderously, lifting her chin to show off that strong jawline. I could see in her bearing how some of that could be true. She had the very standing of a warrior, even if she was apparently now just a teacher at a school at the bottom of the world.

"I need to alert the Principal of these developments," Morgaine said. "Please ensure your soldiers don't allow any of our staff or students to see your handiwork. Honestly, they don't need the trauma."

She left. Kipling and Lilith silently made their way toward the door I was spying through. I quickly slipped away, a primal fear rushing through me. I crossed the hallway and opened the door to a classroom on the opposite side. I closed it just in time before Kipling and Lilith entered the hallway.

I realised too late that Sephy was still lying out there in the hallway. I felt a catching sensation in my heart.

She'll be fine, I reminded myself. *She's an actual student here—clearly a victim.*

"What... what happened?" I heard Sephy say dreamily, looking up toward the wyvern standing over her.

"Lilith?" Kipling instructed calmly.

The wyvern lunged forth suddenly, pinioning Sephy to the ground with his claw. She cried out.

Oh, no, I thought violently. *Don't you dare.*

I was unarmed. There was nothing I could do for her except get myself killed.

"Well, acolyte," Kipling said. "Perhaps we'll gain the answers we seek after all."

"I'm... not an acolyte!" Sephy cried. "I was giving a tour!"

"Shadows are to be seen and not heard. Especially those without counterparts."

I felt a wall of anger rise up in me like a tidal wave, and before I knew it I was slipping out from behind the door into the hallway.

I clapped slowly, mockingly. There were soldiers in the corridor now. Kipling's men in white uniforms with rifles at the ready, and their Shadows too. Shoot, I hadn't planned for that, but I stuck to my plan. As I clapped for Kipling, I could practically hear every soldier in the immediate corridor stop breathing.

"Wow," I said, lazily, my voice dripping with disdain. Lilith loosened her grip on Sephy, fixing her attention on me instead. I heard Sephy gasping for air. My hands curled into fists at the sound. "A performance worthy of accolades. Just... brilliant. Beating up unarmed students? So brave. So noble. Can I get a selfie with you before your war crimes tribunal?"

Lilith released Sephy, staring at me now. Sephy gasped for air. My hands clenched, but I kept the grin.

"So, I see that you're a decorated knight," I said to Kipling. "Clearly, you've mistaken that title for permission to act like a fascist hyena with a sword."

Kipling paused. Either considering shooting me, or just stunned that someone dared sass him.

If I had come out defensive or showing my fear, he might have read that as guilt. But since I strode out with all of the confidence of nobility, which Kipling seemed to hold sacrosanct, it gave him enough pause not to shoot me on sight. Then again, perhaps it was purely the shock of someone daring to challenge him.

I decided to lean into it.

"Tell me, Kipling. Who's the real coward? You, for

attacking an unarmed girl? Or the guy who lets his dragon do his dirty work?"

There were gasps from the soldiers. I received a punch for my trouble. It was pretty light, but it still sent me to the ground.

"When you insult me, you insult the very office of the Governor herself!" Kipling said, apoplectic, striding right up to me. "Who are you?"

"The Governor should never have employed someone with such little regard for the justice process," I continued. "From all I've seen so far, you're just a walking example of toxic masculinity founded on blatant insecurity."

"Insolent girl!"

Wham. This time, the blow was like a hammer. I saw stars. Constellations. I made a wish on them that I'd survive this.

But I'd developed something of an immunity to pain. It was all too easy to straighten and look at Kipling as if it was nothing.

Kipling took a step back. As if he saw something in my eyes that made him uncertain.

Right. That should do it.

"Take me to the Governor," I said. "Search me for weapons if you must. Let them decide my fate."

"I don't need her authority to execute you."

The Praetory was very Old Testament when it came to punishments.

"Even to execute nobility?" I posed.

"It wouldn't be the first time a weaker-willed noble fell to the influence of Shadows' Eve," he sneered.

"I see that you don't think anyone will call you up for making a Shadow into a punching bag. A human, however, and the daughter of a Count and Countess at that..."

Kipling's eyes narrowed.

"Who exactly are your parents?"

"My mother is Minister Asia Crowley. My father was Count Peter Crowley."

There was a ripple of recognition through the soldiers in the hallway.

I could see Kipling shaking with rage, wanting to give Lilith the order to murder me then and there. Instead the knight took out his phone.

"In respect for your parents' station, I will pass along your request. Although it may only delay the inevitable."

"You're too kind. Also, Sephy needs medical attention," I said firmly. "Now." I looked down at where she lay limply. She was panting, eyes squeezed shut against the pain. "She's just a student and has a genuine reason for being here, which I'm sure the Principal can corroborate."

Kipling didn't respond. There were some extremely tense seconds.

Then he read a response on his screen. He snorted.

"Your wish has been granted, acolyte."

He gestured to the soldiers.

"Bring her."

"Just so you know, Kipling," I said conversationally as rough hands took me, "I would very much like to be given all the information on your current investigations into the existing Shadows' Eve cells. It's classified, and I've been unable to access it."

"Do you have a death wish, kid?" the soldier on my right asked incredulously.

"Let her run her mouth," Kipling said, his voice dropping to a purr. "She insulted the office of the Governor. The two of them will likely be executed regardless." He regarded me like a shark. "And I will enjoy watching."

. . .

The inside of the limo felt like a cold coffin.

My heart wasn't just beating; it was trying to stage a violent coup against my ribs. I stared at the floor, my breath coming in shallow, jagged gasps. *Don't hyperventilate. If you pass out, they'll definitely kill you. Or worse, they'll kill you and you won't even get to say something witty first.*

We were driving along Lambton Quay; it looked like Kipling was taking me toward the Old Bank Arcade. Back in 1901, some ambitious bankers decided Wellington needed a cathedral for capitalism, so they built a limestone fortress to house the Bank of New Zealand. Now, it was an arcade full of boutique shops and a clock shaped like a golden Fabergé egg that did a mechanical dance every hour.

But I knew Kipling wasn't taking me out for a latte. Wherever we going, it was for a final judgment.

Panic flared, hot and blinding, and I closed my eyes, trying to find a single thread of calm to hold onto. My mind raced backward, desperate to escape the metal walls of the van, retreating to the last time I'd felt truly, untouchably safe.

My fingers hovered dramatically over the board, as I plotted the kind of move that would make Sun Tzu wake up in a cold sweat.

Oooh, yes, *I thought with delight.* You're going down, old man.

This was Father's latest find—a gritty twist on Risk, set during the Haitian Revolution. You played as enslaved rebels rising against the French colonial government. Foiling and outwitting an overwhelming enemy was a guilty pleasure of mine.

Standing in my bedroom in the light of the cold moon, I

twirled a lone game piece in my fingers, a small pawn armed with dreams and defiance against a sprawling empire. Rearranging my frontmost troops, I scooped up the die and rolled for attacks. For my final phase, I redistributed my forces to press the advantage over my opponent.

Chuckling as I imagined Father's reaction, I took a photo of the carnage and hit 'Send.'

A phone chimed right outside my open window. I nearly jumped out of my skin.

Then a curse came from beyond the window frame, followed by a sheepish knock.

"Pssst. Hey. Pssst. Hey. You awake, sweetie?"

I walked slowly, bare feet on carpet. Peering out the glass, I fully unlatched the window and opened it wide. I was careful to keep a hold on it in case another gale tore it from its brackets.

A face appeared before me. I took in the man's wild and unruly curls, his skinny neck and wide eyes slightly reminiscent of an ostrich.

"Why, hello Father," I said.

"Oh, why hello there, sweetie," he replied. I realised he was teetering on a recycling bin in order to reach my window.

I giggled a little bit, despite myself. Then I put my stern expression back in place, tucking a coil of hair behind my ear.

"What in the bloody hell are you doing clinging to my windowsill like an overgrown squirrel?"

"Language, Crowley. Now get out here so I can get off this sodding bastard of a bin, will you?"

His Scottish brogue always made his cursing hilarious. But I hesitated to let him in, stalling at the thought of Mother's reaction.

"No need to slay me with that last move," he said, holding up his phone to possibly fill the awkward silence. "That was uncalled for."

"Did I slay you?" I asked, studying my fingernails. "I hadn't noticed."

My father laughed, and I smiled.

Everyone loved Peter Crowley. He looked after all of the staff at the villa as if they were family, winning their absolute loyalty through warmth and familiarity, while Mother, in contrast, compelled it through fear and awe. I'd overheard it said at one of my parents 'gatherings' at the villa more than once, that as many who said Peter Crowley was mad said he was brilliant... and many said he was both.

"General Crowley, I look forward to serving under your command someday." He mimed a salute, nearly losing his balance.

I shook my head, feigning sadness.

"You're mocking me."

Father sighed.

"How many girls your age say 'mocking?' Shouldn't you be recreating dance trends from the internet, or something?" He sighed, more serious now. "I just want you to simply... live. To still be a child. Can you do that?"

"I think that train left the station around age seven," I deadpanned, "and caught fire halfway to its destination."

He knew as well as I did that I had been trained extensively every minute of my adolescence, under the guidance of private tutors on politics, economics and military strategy, and in gruelling physical training boot camps and marksmanship lessons held across the estate.

"Um... so, why are you here?"

"Because I wasn't going to miss today. You didn't think anything would keep me away, did you?"

I closed my eyes, an unbidden smile breaking out across my face.

"Father..."

"Happy fifteenth birthday, Alexandra Crowley."

"My birthday's not until tomorrow."

He checked his watch, frowning.

"Nope, two minutes past midnight. I'm definitely on time."
He saw my expression. "What is it?"

"You know what," I whispered. "Mother will end you. She's still mid-meltdown. I've never seen her like this."

"Ah, yes." His face twisted with pain. "We're going through a slight rough patch."

"No kidding, you're standing on a recycling bin for f—"

"Language!" Father reprimanded me, wide-eyed.

"Oh, please," I countered, not missing a beat. "Where do you think I learned these words from?"

Father laughed as he looked up at me. The pride in his eyes made me warm. I folded my arms.

"How did you even get onto the estate without tripping the hyper-paranoid security system?"

"I have my ways," he said, smugly. "I'm not just a pretty face."

I was silent for a moment. He looked so cheerful, his wiry hair askew like a mad scientist's. How could he be so cavalier about now being considered an intruder, a trespasser in his own home? I studied him, trying to figure out how much he was really hurting beneath that bravado. It must have been killing him being apart from me and Harper.

"I hate this," I said, voice dropping like a stone. "You and Mother fighting. It feels like a war that's... ripping the world apart in slow motion."

"Yes," he said, quieter now. "I know what you mean."

"Harper keeps asking when you're coming back. I don't know what to tell him."

"Tell him I love him," he said. Not a joke this time. Just truth. Quiet and sharp and heartbreaking.

"I can probably manage that," I muttered, rubbing my arm.

Father massaged the back of his neck, looking distracted for a moment. *"I know it's hard. This will all be fixed... soon. Now, do you have your runners?"*

"Excuse me?"

"Your runners. I thought you might fancy a little midnight birthday circuit." I looked at Father, taking in the running gear he was wearing.

"In this weather?"

"I thought you liked a bit of adventure. Besides, aren't you wondering what your present is?"

I smiled widely.

"You know you didn't have to get me a present, right?"

There was a gleam in his eye.

"You're going to tell me, aren't you?" I said suddenly, my voice a whisper. I felt a sudden thrill. *"It's finally happening."*

"You've asked for answers," Father agreed, *"and I can't keep the truth from you anymore. So, how about you get those cute pink joggers on?"*

"I'll be right back," I grinned.

4

Our limo pulled up behind the rear of the arcade. Kipling roughly manhandled me from the car, ensuring my cuffed hands were hidden beneath a coat. Stone steps led to an unceremonious-looking door with three padlocks. But once Kipling's guards had unlocked it and led me through, the long passageway of damp stone morphed into luxurious red carpet, and an interior that the everyday public had never seen before. It felt like the inside of a palace. I saw grand long tables set with thirty chairs covered in silverware and tall candle-holders with candles of gold and red wax, grand palms with leafy fronds potted inside, lush red carpet, columns, chandeliers and stairs, grand portrait paintings, impressive rectangle still stone pools like mirrors, and chequered tiled floors like a chessboard.

I looked around, a little slack-jawed to know that these parts of the building had been here all along. I marvelled at the marble statues and the scale of grandeur as they led me toward the office of the Governor herself.

As I was escorted up a stairway, I observed the open door to a games room, a large pool table on wooden parquet flooring, the mounted head of a stag staring out forlornly from the wall. There were portraits of what I deduced must have been famous humans from the Praetory's history and their Shadow counterparts.

Kipling was full of his usual arrogant swagger as we passed a reception desk and he knocked on a grand door. A familiar voice beyond called for us to enter.

The door opened. I was pushed through and knocked to my knees, landing on expensive carpet. I was kneeling before the Praetory Governor of New Zealand in her own personal chambers. She was one of the most powerful individuals in the Pacific.

"Crowley?" a voice said, disbelieving, in a strange mix of joy and horror.

"Hello, Jo," I smiled at my old friend.

She looked so grown up, and yet also so much like the friend I remember playing with on my family's estate. While every other person we'd passed in the building had worn a suit or at the least been very formally dressed, Governor Jolene Blackmore was wearing a gown made from a shimmering sequin fabric. It hugged her figure in all the right places. The gown had an open back and a deep plunge neckline. She looked ridiculously extra, like royalty, which I supposed was only right when everyone was waiting on her hand and foot. She was also wearing glittery blue eyeshadow. Very few would be able to carry it off, but on her it was striking.

"Tell me at once!" Jo barked, sounding livid. Her face was contorted from her outrage as she studied my marked face. "Who is responsible for this? I will have them removed from their position at once, and any titles allotted to them removed immediately!"

The colour drained from Kipling's face. He and his stooges looked to me in horror. They appeared utterly stricken.

Jo focused her full fury on Kipling and the soldiers, coming down on them like a typhoon.

"How dare you!" she cried. "This is the only daughter of Minister Asia Crowley and Count Peter Crowley! This was *you*, Kipling? Despicable."

Jo strode forward to extend a hand to me. Taking it, I rose. I turned to Kipling and his cronies so that the bruises where I'd been struck were on display.

"Your Excellency!" Kipling cried, blanching. All of his hard work climbing the food chain, gone in a moment. A single word from his Governor could have him removed from her service and placed on cleaning duty.

"Easy, Jo. It was the acolytes who did this to me," I lied, satisfied seeing the shock on Kipling's face.

Now I owned him.

Jo waved away Kipling's soldiers furiously, who seemed to be relieved to be dismissed from the situation. My old friend placed her hand on my arm.

"Babe, the *acolytes* did this to you? Those scum," Jo cursed.

I had to fight back a smile. She hadn't called me *babe* since we were basically kids, back when she was trying to act much older than she was. I was nostalgically glad to see she hadn't changed.

"The terrorists attacked me but Kipling and his people saved me. They pursued but were unable to capture them."

"How could those terrorists have the audacity? And in my own territory!"

"Hence my wish to hunt them down and exterminate them. I'd love to see what you have in your investigation."

Jo appeared troubled.

"Did I do something wrong?"

"It's not that," Jo said, nervously scratching the back of her neck. "The terrorists have... and this is classified, you understand. For the highest levels only."

Highest levels?

I inclined my head.

"Of course."

"They've stolen something from the Praetory. Something the Potentate doesn't want falling into the wrong hands."

The Potentate. The leader of the Praetory.

"Does this something require... transportation?"

"It's intelligence, stolen from a secure vault concealed beneath the Academy. But I've already told you too much. I'm trying to warn you, darling. This is dangerous, and I'd rather you weren't anywhere near it."

"Anything that's retrieved is of no consequence to me." I met Jo's gaze. "I don't need to tell you what my interest is in these people."

Jo's face hardened in understanding, and I knew I had her.

"Let me guess," Jo said. "Blood and retribution."

"Blood and retribution," I echoed. "The classics never go out of style."

She looked troubled. I could see how badly she wanted to help me, but something was holding her back. Something I didn't understand. But I needed those answers.

"Sir Kipling?" I said, and Kipling stopped in surprise. But then he nodded. Good. He knew who owned him. I could tell Jo who really assaulted me at any moment and Kipling's station, or even his life, could be forfeit.

"I can ensure we maintain the sensitivities of the case, your Excellency," Kipling said smoothly. "I can fill Crowley in, but I will insulate her from any of the particulars. You have my word."

Jo hesitated for another moment. I saw her eyes play over the bruising on the right side of my face. It seemed to have the intended effect. I felt a little guilty playing her like this, though it was nothing against her personally. I just desperately needed that intelligence, and I wasn't sure how far memories of our childhood would get me.

"Well, well. I see that you two have bonded quickly." Jo waved with a hand, surrendering. "Kipling is at your disposal for any information you may want to peruse. He was lucky to intercept the break-in today, but otherwise there's been little progress smoking the remaining acolytes from their nests. Any insights would be most helpful."

"Your Excellency..." Kipling said, surprised. Even though he had backed me up thanks to my blackmail, I could see he was shocked at the Governor simply handing over state secrets. Especially simply on the strength of an old friendship between the children of nobles.

"Don't, Kipling, you've already tried my patience. I would have trusted this case with twelve-year-old Crowley, who was a force to be reckoned with. Frankly, intimidating. Sixteen-year-old Crowley will put you to shame." Jo met my gaze. "Besides. Crowley more than anyone deserves a chance to deal a blow to the acolytes."

Kipling looked at me as if in a new light following these revelations. Then he bowed to Jo, before making to leave.

"Oh, don't go yet, Kipling. Crowley, babe, you simply must stay for tea, we need to catch up. Do you want anything? Roast duck? Tagliatelle? Port? Our chef can make, like, *anything* you ask for."

"I accept your challenge," I said with a smile. I hesitated. "I wouldn't say no to a vanilla brûlée?" I ventured. "And perhaps some creamy fettuccine. Ooh, and a mochaccino strong enough to wake the dead. Thank you, Kipling."

5

Kipling bowed stiffly over us, pouring the coffee. Of course, Jo had a servant for such things, but having a personal knight serve a guest was a mark of the highest honour. Jo was clearly elated we were reunited. It was very good to see her too. Even if she now had the terrifying capacity to demand executions between sips of espresso like she was ordering pastries.

I knew that the Praetory could be a brutal place, where nobility were treated as superior beings and the political games could be deadly. Yet it was still shocking to see my childhood friend so prepared to order executions. It required a certain level of coldness, an objective obligation to her duty. Jo seemed to have taken to her position as a Princess of the Praetory incredibly quickly. But both of us had grown up in families with the same loyalty to the Praetory's values. My mother and Jo's parents were cut from the same ilk. Regardless, Jo's ability to go from possible murder to cheerfully catching up over coffee was unquestionably bad-arse.

"So, how do you like my palace?" Jo gestured at our

presidential surroundings. "A lot of Government House is below ground, all the Ministerial Offices are down there, ooh, and also this gorgeous, meditative Taiwanese garden, one of my own designs..."

Jo's Shadow was sitting on the edge of a pool of water on one side of the office. A grinning blonde mermaid with a tail covered in black scales. For some unexplained reason, she was jauntily wearing a large pirate hat.

"That's Tempy," Jo said. "Short for Tempest. She's my rock."

Kipling bowed to Jo as he retreated, and suddenly I was seized by a longing so deep, so aching it seemed to penetrate to my very soul.

Ever since I was young, when I had only the most basic understanding of how the Praetory worked, I had wanted to be a knight: a sworn right hand. I dreamed of being the faithful number two, using the sword sheathed at my side to protect someone I believed in, upholding the honour of the Lord or Lady I served and defending them whenever required.

I'd always wanted to be someone's shield and to know that I was serving a higher calling. Yet Kipling was the one given just such an honour. Someone decorated, yes, but still... that man was nothing but blood-thirst in expensive clothing. It seemed he held a fervent loyalty to my friend, but in my opinion he didn't even deserve to pour Jo her coffee. I'd worshipped Jo as a child. I would have done anything for her. I'm sure at some level, I'd always dreamed that I would grow up to be *her* knight.

Jo always seemed like she was born to indulge in power, even if she didn't seem the wisest one to exercise it. She always stood out from the others at parties at the estate, while I was the girl who looked like a ghost. She'd been born to a Duke and Duchess, a ranking far above that of my parents in the Praetory food chain. They'd later ascended to the rank of Prince and Princess. I suppose it wasn't all that surprising Jo and I hadn't been allowed to mix socially for much longer, or that she'd ended up here.

"I should have invited you over far sooner, I hadn't intended you to go to quite these lengths," Jo joked with me in amusement, offering an ice pack. I accepted it with a rueful smile. She shook her head. "You always were the dramatic one."

"Well," I replied pointedly, regarding the overly decadent, almost theatrical interior. "Perhaps that's why we always got on so well."

Jo giggled.

"I know, right? Hey, I'm sorry we've lost touch for so many years. I was with the family in New York, and there was a lot to deal with. I should have been a better friend."

"I got your message when I lost Father," I told her softly. "It meant a lot." Then, to not bring down the mood of our entire catch-up, I smiled, nursing my coffee. "So, Governor of Aotearoa New Zealand. You've come a long way from us building traps of string to capture guests at our parents' parties. I have to say, when you came in all imperious like that, you scared me a little. I barely recognised you."

"When you're given a role like this, you have to own it. Otherwise they eat you alive."

"I had no idea you were the Governor, until I heard them say Governor Blackmore."

Jo waved a hand airily.

"I may hold the rank of Princess, but the Potentate barely wanted to acknowledge my existence. The position of Governor should have been mine by right, but let's just say it took a lot of political wrangling."

The anger in her simmering tone shocked me. It was dark, and deeply bitter. It hinted at experiences she'd been through that I couldn't guess at.

"Do you mean... just because you're adopted?" I said, incredulous.

"The Praetory has some issues with that sort of... thing. My lack of pure noble blood means that I've never quite been the Potentate's favourite, while meanwhile my brother was given a plum role in New York. There's also the fact that he's white and blue-eyed while I'm unavoidably half-Taiwanese. There are plenty of nobles who aren't white, of course, but very few Princes and Princesses. I suspected it played a role."

I sipped at my tea, troubled. My father had painted the world he was part of as something wonderful, despite its dangers. I'd somehow hoped the Praetory was above issues the outside world had. I suppose the special prejudice that Sir Kipling had for Shadows already told me things were more complex than that.

"I had to fight with everything I had to be made Governor here," Jo continued. "Though, fair to say, it has its perks."

"Wealth, excessive material possessions... raging parties?"

"Exactly."

We smiled at each other knowingly.

I noted the role of Governor did not seem to be determined by age or, necessarily, experience. Jo had always been older than me, a young woman now, and she was trained as thoroughly as I was. But surely there were still others with better experience to be governing an entire country. Being a Princess from a promising family got you a lot. I studied Jo, this girl I knew so well. Now every word of hers was obeyed by her subjects as a sacred order. This secret world had changed her. But I trusted the smile of the friend facing me; she'd done what she could to thrive in this culture. No matter my mother's other flaws, for the first time I appreciated that Mother had kept me separate from this world for so long. I hadn't been desensitised like Jo had.

"But tell me!" Jo exclaimed, "how's Harper?"

"He's good. Definitely doing better than expected," I said, already nervous about bringing him into this world of secrets and danger. Was it selfish of me to want to tell Harper the truth? To not want to hide it from him anymore?

"Good. How is he fourteen already? He must be so big now." She waved a hand around us to indicate our surroundings. "This must be all very strange for you, your mother keeping it all a mystery for you for so long."

"I'm not going to lie, Shadows were a bit of a shock."

"Well, if there's any questions you want answers to, you know I'm here to help. Now that I have your back, nothing will get in the way of our friendship," she proclaimed with grave seriousness.

"Then what do you know about my father's murder?"

The saucer and teacup rattled very slightly in Jo's hands.

"I apologise if it's indelicate," I acknowledged, studying her carefully. "But you must know how badly I need answers. And there really is no one else I'd trust to tell me the truth."

I casually plucked at my pant leg to reveal the titanium limb there, courtesy of that same night. Jo' eyes widened, as if it was something terrible. Something incomprehensible for polite conversation over insanely expensive coffee.

"I'm sorry Crowley, I don't know the specifics. But the war has been over for a year now, and Shadows' Eve have fallen. All that's left is rabble, and their Dark Father is imprisoned. That is justice."

"It's still not enough," I said, fighting back burning tears. I wouldn't let my composed mask slip. "I want to know everything I can about Shadows' Eve. Why they chose that night to attack my father and myself. Which of them gave the order, and who was there to carry it out."

Jo waved a hand unconvincingly.

"Terrible times, terrible," she mumbled. "But once we're finished interrogating the Dark Father he'll be executed, and any hope Shadows' Eve had of a comeback will surely die with him. You don't need to worry about him, Crowley. The war was... awful. So many suffered needlessly, like you and your family. But aside from a few rogue acolytes... it's over."

Jo set down her cup. She leaned forward and grasped my hands tightly. Her gaze was earnest and intense.

"I desperately hope we can be friends again," she told me. I sensed real vulnerability in her. It reminded me how I hadn't seen my friend in far too long.

I chuckled suddenly, and squeezed her hands back. Good grief, I'd missed this lunatic. Even if that hadn't been true, I was in no position not to collect allies.

"We never stopped," I reassured her, and meant it.

On the drive home, I steepled my fingers, consulting the files laid out on my lap. It made for grim reading.

"I prefer to insulate the Governor from any of the...

unpleasantries of the job," Kipling explained, his posture rigid despite the luxury of the limo. "She has enough to deal with as it is, dealing with matters of state. She expects me to handle these things without supervision."

"Of course." So that's how Kipling justified hiding his methods from Jo. I was reading reports of his attempts thus far to weed out the acolytes. He seemed to happily murder, torture and burn bridges indiscriminately in his quest to purge the remaining terrorists from their hidey-holes. He was a force you definitely wanted on your side. But despite all of his methods, he was yet to discover where the acolytes were hiding. I could empathise with the urge for vengeance on Shadows' Eve, but some of the exact monstrous acts he'd committed appeared to border on the psychopathic. Particularly his lack of caution when inno-cent civilians got in the way.

Kipling was regarding me with a cold, clinical curios-ity. It was the look of a man re-evaluating a threat. I suppose I should see it as a gift that he wasn't already stabbing me for blackmailing him in front of the Governor. Kipling zealously worshipped nobility—Jo specifically— and now that I was officially 'one of them,' it seemed he had simply moved me to a different column in his mental ledger.

"We weren't aware that passage from Midnight Runner was still in use." Kipling's voice was smooth, but his eyes remained narrowed. "With respect, you should have told us of these acolytes the moment you identified them."

"My mother, Minister Crowley, kept me at arms distance from Praetory matters." I shrugged. "I wasn't sure who to trust."

"That could be the reason," he said, with the hint of a smile too understanding for my liking, "or it was because you were hunting for revenge and didn't want anyone else to take it from you."

I pressed my lips together.

"All ended well anyhow," Kipling said with a thin, joyless smile. "You are unharmed, and the threat was neutralised."

"And you're sure all the students were dealt with?" I asked.

"I had some time with one of the acolytes before they were executed. A Shadow, filled with the pain of their human's unravelling mind,"Kipling answered. "They were most agreeable when I offered to end their mutual suffering. I'm confident we got them all."

Or, perhaps there was a chance that Kipling was more easily fooled than he believed. I recalled the tree-spirit Shadow Kipling had murdered. Something had been strange about that Shadow's voice. I could have been imagining it, I'd certainly sampled a variety of traumatic experiences in one day. However, I couldn't shake the feeling that the voice of the acolyte I'd held at gunpoint beforehand had sounded... different.

"Did you find a backpack on the last acolyte you killed?" I said, tapping my fingers on the edge of the file thoughtfully.

Kipling frowned, then shook his head.

Interesting.

"Should I have?"

"Just working on a theory," I said. "How did you find out the acolytes were going to strike the Academy in the first place? You got there very quickly."

Kipling's eyes narrowed. He appeared to find the answer distasteful.

"I had a Shadow in my employ. An adult who had not

met his counterpart. I had him scour the slum in Quietfire where his kind live for weeks, searching for Shadows' Eve. Eventually I was able to embed him in their organisation."

"And what happened to this source of yours?"

"What do you think?" Kipling said curtly. "Killed with the others."

I couldn't help it. My head jerked toward him.

"An innocent Shadow?"

"No Shadow is truly innocent, my Lady. They are wild beasts of a savage, primal realm. They're only civilised when they find the human they are a reflection of. A Shadow without a counterpart is a dangerous, corruptible thing. Brutal and violent, with no cause or honour; little better than a parasite."

Well, at least Kipling wasn't ambiguously racist, I thought dryly. He let it all hang out, along with his classism, like badges of pride. And that's because they *were* considered badges, here in this den of vipers I'd ventured into. It was views like this which ensured you were assigned as the personal knight to a Governor in your early twenties.

"Yet if the Shadow informant died, their human would have died somewhere too, isn't that correct?" I said, my hand unconsciously tracing the page of the file.

"Their human was not a member of the Praetory," Kipling said dismissively, Kipling said dismissively, already looking out the window as if the conversation bored him. "If so, the Shadow informant would have found his counterpart long ago. That is how it has always been."

I closed the file.

"Thank you for your assistance, Kipling," I said diplomatically. I kept my face a mask of noble indifference, hiding the rising bile in my throat.

"My pleasure. Anything for a childhood friend of the Governor's. Consider yourself part of the family."

He said it like a welcome, but it felt like a warning. Having him on my side would be far more useful than making another enemy. At least we had a common goal in the destruction of Shadows' Eve.

"The ways of this world are new to me," I confessed. "But as you have heard, I have a vested interest in these terrorists."

The knight inclined his head, the gesture polite but entirely devoid of warmth.

Mother had refused to tell me anything worthwhile about the Praetory after Father's death. All she had informed me was that the war had since ended, and the Dark Father was imprisoned. She somehow saw that as justice enough. I was informed the Praetory's secrets were kept precious for a reason and they 'weren't just for anyone.' She did tell me the acolytes who had escaped execution were striking deals to keep themselves out of prison, trading in the names of other acolytes. There was a fragile peace and Mother told me we were safe now, though she warned me that things were still volatile. We could not let Father's death be in vain by tipping once again into war, she warned me.

I knew it was a clear message from her not to go seeking revenge. But her cold silence and refusal to give me answers about the Praetory, Shadows' Eve or the recent war was the final straw. Even though Mother and Father had been recently separated when he'd died, I knew that she must be hurting on the inside, if she had any feelings at all. Yet I hadn't seen her shed a single tear.

. . .

I looked out the window as we drove through the opening gates. I was back at my family residence in Miramar. The central feature was a grand stone villa looking out toward the ocean. As we passed through the garden, I was seized by memories. I remembered playing among the branches with Jo, as our parents' laughter carried from the party. Jo had been the friend next door, always eager to search for hidden dragon treasure, or to explore the dark parks in the hope that we would stumble upon other magical worlds.

All that time we were playing, the adult Praetory members would conspiratorially vanish to the basement of our home. Had they been consorting with beings like Lilith and Sephy in those private meetings? Jo and I had been acting out the fantasy, while they lived the reality.

This cold estate that looked out toward the sea was my home. Since Father passed, I'd spent all of my time in the library. It reminded me of him and how he'd pore over the books up here. Shelves lined the walls stacked with dusty volumes on every topic imaginable. Of course, his favourite section was the zoological volumes. He'd shown me thick tomes with photographs of every conceivable species on the planet. Now that I thought about it, I wondered if all along he was really wanting to show me a giant book of Shadows. Just when I'd thought I had almost every single animal species memorised, I realised there was an entire dimension out there, of beings stranger than I'd imagined.

I'd always tried to maintain a perfect routine each and every day here at the house. I needed to keep up proper levels of study. I needed to prepare meals and eat. I required a proper amount of sleep to stay in an optimal state of mind. As much as I'd been training on my new leg, I couldn't rely solely on athleticism anymore. My mind was the one gift that I had. I needed to hone it like a weapon.

I hadn't read the books in our library for quite a while. My reading material had instead been replaced by all of the files on Shadows' Eve, abducted from Mother's office and photocopied. I would lie on the floor with them spread out around me, ready to hide them at the slightest sound of steps approaching.

I'd taken the office key from Mother, on one of the few nights she'd come home. I'd snuck into her room and reached down, heart hammering, for the key around my mother's throat. It was strange, seeing her in sleep. Someone so formidable, so self-possessed... now vulnerable and human. Just for that moment.

Even after Father had told me about the existence of Shadows, Mother still kept me sealed away in the house. She was rigid when it came to rules and traditions. She had an iron will and zero tolerance for anyone who cut corners.

Somehow, living in this place after Father died... it felt like someone was watching over me. It was as if the darkness in the corners of the room was listening. Breathing. Listening to my desperate desires to have him back.

Maybe that thing, that person I imagined listening wasn't Father. Perhaps it was my Shadow. Father had said that your Shadow was always there with you, even when you were apart, because they were the missing piece of you.

I tried to dismiss the thoughts. But I couldn't explain those moments when the hairs on the back of my neck stood on end.

I rushed into the house. I was met by memories of the playful antics of childhood and of a terrifying woman with black hair who called herself my mother.

"Crowley!" a relieved voice greeted me.

"Harper," I whispered, spotting my brother. He leapt off the couch from among his thick stacks of books. My mother had never been one to allow video games or television inside the house. I rushed toward Harper, embracing him in a tight hug. He didn't say anything, just hugged me back twice as tightly. I swallowed past a painful lump.

When he pulled back, he looked at me with questioning eyes far too intelligent for his age.

"Those people we saw won't trouble us again," I said.

I saw the horror in his eyes and realised he thought I'd killed them. I shook my head sharply. There was no describing how awful the sensation was, seeing him that terrified of me.

"I didn't touch them," I clarified softly, troubled. "Someone else already dealt with it."

"Miss Crowley." I turned in surprise to see Mahuika, the head of our household staff. "Your mother is here. She's waiting for you in her office."

A shiver played down my spine. I looked down at Harper and took his hand gently.

"Just stay down here, okay?" I forced a smile. "Everything will be fine."

Heart in my throat, I walked up the stairs to the darkened doorway.

6

Harper had been terrified in the months following our father's murder. I remember him following me around the house like a forlorn puppy.

"Why are you so determined not to let me out of your sight?" I'd teased him.

"Because I don't want you to die," he'd said.

Every night he came into my room, and I'd held him close, clutching one another as if we were all we had. It was as if we were orphans already.

I was glad Harper had asked for help. When I was alone, that darkness in the corners of my room was pulsating, moving... calling to me. In the dead of night, in that palace of loneliness, I would make wishes on that darkness.

One night Harper didn't come into my room. I think he'd been afraid that he'd become an imposition. I went to check on him instead, and found him crying softly into his blankets. I'd crawled into his bed and murmured to him that everything was okay, until he finally fell asleep.

. . .

Mother didn't even look up when I walked in. Classic. She was completely absorbed in her sacred paperwork, as if she hadn't even summoned me. She frowned now and then as she scrutinised the file beside her, her hand resting on it tenderly.

For so long, I'd been confused as to what Mother thought of me. Did she see me as some delicate princess that had to be protected in this castle of cold stone, as I was groomed to maintain her legacy? Or was I imprisoned here out of sight because she was ashamed of me? That would at least explain why she shied away from me as if I was a leper. Perhaps to her I really was the daughter with one leg, a constant reminder of the husband she'd lost. Then again, I'd never once seen her grieve for him.

I waited patiently, standing respectfully at attention.

Asia Kate Crowley was tall, unconventionally beautiful and unavoidably terrifying. Her suit was a grey so neutral it could have brokered peace in a war zone. Her earrings were jagged hunks of obsidian, like stalactites. Because nothing said: *'approachable maternal figure'* like shards of volcanic rock dangling from your ears.

Her eyes, though—those were her superpower. She didn't look *at* people, she disassembled them. Eye contact with her felt like an X-ray crossed with a performance review. She could look through you, figure out your unique brand of trauma, and send you the invoice, all in under ten seconds.

And the kicker? None of this should have been hers. She wasn't born into power. She married into it like a pragmatic Cinderella who skipped the ball and went straight to the prenup. The nobility talked behind her back—of course they did—but they still kept one eye on her rise. Because somehow, through sheer force of will and weaponised competence, my mother had climbed all the way up to Minister.

Anyone who underestimated her soon realised their mistake.

Finally Mother stood. She didn't just stand there to dispassionately regard me as she had so many other times. Instead she came around her desk with an urgency. I opened my mouth in surprise, but then she grabbed my arm with surprising force, twisting it.

I gasped, the pain lancing through me. But pain I could take. What made me gasp was the fact that she'd even done it.

"Don't you do anything like that ever again," Mother hissed, her lips distorted in a snarl. "Cavorting with Shadows' Eve as if you were an acolyte yourself. Associating with *terrorists.*"

"I wasn't..."

"Do you think that matters? My daughter turned up uninvited to the Academy at the same time as acolytes, using the very same tunnel they entered through. Are you trying to start rumours about this family?"

"Jo will make sure that fact doesn't get out there."

"You only know the Governor because we made sure you mingled in the right circles while you were younger. Those connections are fragile, they don't make us invulnerable."

"You're hurting me," I said through gritted teeth. I wouldn't gasp. I wouldn't show her how shocked I was.

"I have fought too long and too hard," she continued, "for you to end my career the day you enter our world."

I looked up at her, baleful. For a moment I was unable to hide the flash of hatred I felt with every fibre of my being. It even surprised me.

Mother snorted, and released me. I pulled my arm away and regarded her coolly.

"We do not have immunity from prison, Crowley," she said, more quietly. "Or from execution."

For the first time, she had truly gotten through to me. My own actions may have endangered our family, all in a single foolish miscalculation. I hadn't had the intelligence I needed to venture into the world of the Praetory. I'd been willing to risk the danger to learn more about my father's death, but I'd gambled their lives as well as my own.

"I apologise, Mother. I'll be more careful in future."

"Think on that," she said. "Think of your little brother."

That was too rich to go down smoothly. She had as little time to spend on Harper as she had on me, even if his body *was* whole. It wasn't Mother who had consoled Harper every evening over the last year, when he woke up pleading to see Father. It had been up to me to remind him of reality before smoothing him back into sleep.

If Mother and Father hadn't been so secretive, perhaps I could have gone in with eyes open that night in the forest. Maybe I could have helped Father survive, if they'd told me about the existence of beings from another universe.

"Get dressed," my mother grunted, gesturing toward an outfit folded on a chair. It was a spotless school uniform. The blazer was light grey, with gold edging.

Exhaling, I allowed myself a smile. I couldn't tell if this had been part of Mother's plan all along, or if I had accelerated things by chasing those acolytes. It didn't matter. This was what I'd been waiting for: to wear the uniform of the Praetory's Academy and make myself a part of Father's world. It was a chance to show the Praetory and Mother that I was worthy.

"Come," Mother said, departing through the doorway.

It wasn't a request. It never was with her. The power, the charisma in her tone brooked no argument. I quickly changed, then followed after her. I hated that no matter what she did, I would always be desperately seeking this woman's approval.

I slid into the back of the black presidential vehicle parked out front, alongside Mother. An escort of two unmarked vehicles escorted us, one in front, one in the rear. I resisted the urge to snort, realising it would make me too closely resemble the woman beside me. Even I was stunned by this lavish luxury, as if she were a Pharaoh. But why should that surprise me? She was part of a hidden empire who could communicate telepathically with beings from another world. What kind of power and resources did it take to keep a secret that big, a secret that could shake the foundations of the world and transform it forever... hidden for that long?

My respect for Mother, and my foreboding, only increased.

"Walk with me," Mother said as her bodyguard opened the door for her. He offered her a hand but she waved it away in derision. The man looked stricken.

The car had apparently just stopped so that my mother and I could walk down Lambton Quay together. As we did, a plain-clothes escort followed us not far behind.

I'd always loved living in Wellington. It was at the bottom of the North Island, at the mouth of Cook Strait. The city was marketed as the artsy, cool little capital of New Zealand, if beset by fierce winds and inclement weather. On days with strong gusts I'd seen people knocked over by the force of the gales. Landing in Wellington by plane was a risky business considered not for the faint-hearted.

Mother held a black umbrella, the two of us sharing its cover. Before long the drizzle of rain slowed, and new sunlight spilt out from under the cloud. It was as if we were just a normal mother and daughter walking along the Wellington main street. It was strange, walking with her like this side by side, almost in companionable silence. It was something I'd never felt with her before. I couldn't help but feel my heart lift slightly.

Perhaps this is what changes now, I thought with a rush of treacherous hope. *Perhaps now I've finally arrived on a crash course into the Praetory, Mother's own private realm, we'll have something to talk to each other about.*

Maybe she'll finally treat me like her daughter.

For a moment I had a flash of doubt. Should I have told Mother about my plan? The *'stalk the unprosecuted war criminals'* plan that had been in action even before my chance encounter with the acolytes today? Mother was the Praetory's Minister for Justice in New Zealand. So many of my own breakthroughs had, after all, come from documents I'd spied on her own desk. But she was also the one who had warned me against exactly what I am doing. Mother hated the deals acolytes were striking to reduce their sentences as much as I did, but she believed it was the only way to keep the peace.

I wondered again if our mother missed Father at all. I know they had been having a rough patch at the time, bad enough for Father to temporarily move out of the estate. I'd always convinced myself the separation was temporary. For Mother, however, it truly seemed as if her husband had never existed. Perhaps my memories of the two of them being happy together during my childhood really were just imagined after all: a survival mechanism to cope with the trauma.

I realised we were approaching the departure point for Wellington's iconic Cable Car.

"Mother," I said, defaulting back to deferential respect. "May I ask... why we're here?"

"Because it's time," Mother said without preamble. She turned to stare evenly into my eyes, her own a clear, calculating blue. They belied the brilliance behind them. "You know about the existence of Shadows," Mother said, and my heart accelerated hearing her say it, *really* say it out loud for the first time. "You know the importance of the Praetory we're part of, an ancient culture that has kept the secret of the existence of another dimension, since the very first contact."

"Yes," I swallowed.

"Well, today is a very special day," Mother said gruffly, her monotone making her momentous words almost humorous. "Despite your premature debut, tomorrow was always intended to be your first day at the Academy. Some of the first years have already moved in over the summer, but your classes will begin tomorrow."

Undoubtedly that was why the acolytes had struck today. It had been their last chance to infiltrate the school when things were still fairly quiet.

"Two tickets, please," Mother told the man in the Cable Car ticket box as we approached.

"I'm very glad to hear it," the man responded, smiling pleasantly, his arms folded behind him respectfully. Then his eyes gleamed, and he leaned forward, lowering his voice so that the throngs of people around us could not hear him. "Alexandra Crowley. The Praetory has been waiting for you for a very long time. We're very excited to see the things that you'll do."

I blinked, stunned. I didn't know what to say.

"Thank you," I managed finally, nodding my appreciation.

As Mother and I settled into the curved wooden seats of the Cable Car, away from curious ears, I murmured: "Somehow I thought the offical travel route to the Academy would be less public."

"Sometimes the best place to hide is in plain sight," Mother remarked, the corner of her mouth twitching.

She'd never said anything so whimsical in her life.

"Mother?" I queried. "You're acting... different."

It was true. Her anger from the house had faded, leaving something uncharacteristically like emotion in her eyes. She seemed... nostalgic.

"You are my daughter, Crowley. I have waited your whole life to show you the world that I really live in. Today is a sacred day, and before very long, you'll be meeting your own Shadow."

I looked down.

"I am glad I can be the one to guide you to the other side," Mother said, seeming to stumble over the clumsy words. They didn't seem to come naturally, to this parent who had always functioned as a smooth robot of deadly precision. It was as if the words got caught up in her cogs.

The two of us were unable to figure out what should be said next between a Mother and a daughter. We averted our gazes from each other, looking everywhere else.

"There is one more item you need to be informed of. When you graduate, you're to get a job at Government House," my mother informed me. "Somewhere close to the seat of power where your abilities can be of most service. You'll work your way up just as I did."

I looked at her in shock, anger flaring again at her presumption. The last thing I had ever wanted was to spend my days in the corridors of power. What I'd always really wanted to be, ever since Father described them to me, was a knight of the Praetory. One sidelong look from her, however, quelled any thought of rebellion.

Gritting my teeth, I recomposed my features into a neutral mask. Was this punishment for my actions today, or just another test of loyalty?

My father had told me all about the value of knights in the Praetory, those who made an oath to serve another individual or institution, pledging their body, mind and soul to a greater cause. The tradition harked back to a time when honour, honesty and loyalty were noble values.

The last thing I wanted to do instead was spend my days around power-hungry bureaucrats.

"And why would you want me to do that, may I ask?" I inquired politely, though I knew perfectly well: to shore up the family legacy; to build our family's name and buy us further protection against whatever the future held. As far as my mother saw it, when she and Father separated this brought irreparable shame on the family, and apparently his death hadn't been enough to expunge it. Our titles, our estate and much of our wealth had come from Father's family. Mother was worried that other opportunistic nobles would be circling our unprotected flank like vultures, just waiting to tear us apart.

"Are you questioning my judgement?" she asked in a dominating tone, turning her penetrating blue gaze on me. I ducked my head, carefully modelling obeisance.

"No, Mother."

"I expect you were hoping to enlist in the military the first chance you got," my mother said, more perceptive than I cared for. I could almost feel her eyes trying to avoid my prosthetic. Her distaste at my handicap was palpable.

That would have been my plan, yes. To prove my mettle and take a step forward on the path to being a knight. A compassionate knight of honour, the very antithesis of people like Sir Kipling.

I didn't know what to say, other than this was the furthest thing from what I wanted. I had no doubt that I could be an adept politician if I applied myself, as she had, but I'd never wanted to be one. All I'd ever wanted was to be a knight. My mother's designs for me to be her heir, wielding power from behind a bureaucratic desk and organising and hosting dazzling parties of nobility, clashed entirely with that. Her dismissal inflamed my own private fears that having a prosthetic leg would make me a liability to whoever I swore myself to. Not that I had allowed it to slow me down yet. I was filled with the aching desire to serve, to pledge myself to someone's house to defend them and finally have an anchor. To belong.

I knew my mother well enough though to know that this wasn't a request. She had her mind set on it. But until I found a loophole out of it, perhaps I could still obtain something from it in the way of a transaction. "I'll get a job at Government House when I graduate," I conceded gratingly. "But I have something I want in return."

She glared at me, but this time I matched it, staring back at her boldly. There was only one person that I was this daring for.

"I want you to tell Harper the truth," I said. "I don't want him growing up without knowing about Shadows like

I did. I want him to know all of it. He's my brother, and I'm not going to lie to him."

"Not even to protect him?"

"He can't protect himself from threats he doesn't know about." On top of that, I was already worried about him all alone with Mother and the staff while I was away at this academy now. I hadn't even gotten to give him a proper goodbye before we left. He deserved answers.

Mother studied me evenly.

"Is this what your father would have wanted?"

I felt a bolt of pain and anger shoot through me. When had she even last mentioned the man, and now she was using him to taunt me? What did that mean anyway, did Father not want me to know the full truth? Had it been his own request, which mother had honoured by continuing to keep me in the dark? The idea of her honouring a promise to the memory of someone she couldn't seem to care less about felt unfeasible.

"It's what *I* want," I said, after the briefest of pauses.

Her lip curled in amusement.

"Very well."

I cursed silently.

Is this what she wanted all along?

We disembarked the Cable Car, making our way through the gardens and past a stage that had hosted frequent musical performances and the odd Summer Shakespeare. I followed Mother toward the point where I felt my eyes subconsciously slipping to the side, as if my point of sight was caught in a visual riptide. She didn't know that I'd visited the Academy by this way once before, after Father's death. Both of us had our secrets. It was strange after breaking into this academy twice, I was finally about to have an official welcome.

I followed Mother through the thickly distributed trees. We stepped over a cluster of ruby-red flowers that bloomed amidst a nest of twisted vines. The flowers grew around the border of the Academy, though whether they were from this world, or seeds brought from the Shadow world, I did not know. Their vivid petals glistened like droplets of blood in the dappled sunlight. The rich crimson blossoms swayed gently in the breeze, releasing a sweet, intoxicating fragrance that hung in the air like a whispered secret.

To avoid being confused by the optical illusion, I focused on my mother beside me who walked boldly and assertively up the steepening slope. We moved toward that impossible point in space. A protective field, maintained by Brilliance Stones—artifacts from the Shadow world set in short stone pillars—rendered the Academy imperceptible to any who strayed too close, preserving its existence in a concealed pocket dimension.

The Academy suddenly leapt into view before us. We were first met by a vast, pristine front lawn, its radial pathways spreading outward like the rays of a rising sun, guiding us towards the grand Edwardian neo-classical main block. The East and West wings of the stately building encircled a central green divided into four immaculate squares. To the East, an artificial stream meandered.

"Welcome to the Praetory," Mother said quietly. She folded up her umbrella, then raised her chin like it was the prow of a proud ship. "Shall we?"

She allowed me to take the first step along the radial pathway. We finally marched up a series of stone steps to the tall magnificent doors at the front of the school, where two guards stood waiting.

Mother looked to me, conveying that it was up to me to give the signal.

I readied myself, then I nodded. The guards bowed, pulling the giant doors aside. I strode through first, trying to channel my mother: as if I held the entire world in my hand, and had never backed down from anyone.

I was met by blinding white lights and a cacophony of shouting. I flinched, then I calmed myself once I realised they were camera flashes. Waiting inside the foyer of Counterpart Academy for us, it seemed, was quite the reception.

"Minister," a man said in a thick Australian accent, stepping forward excitedly. He was dressed somewhat bizarrely in a cowboy hat and khaki shorts that were disturbingly tight. I detected a note of nervousness beneath his bubbly greeting. "Principal Jeremiah Faust, it's a bloody pleasure to meet ya in person at last. This is my counterpart and our one-and-only Deputy Principal, Watcher." Jeremiah was bowing so profusely I was afraid he might hurt himself. The Principal's Shadow was a stern-looking possum with orange eyes who stood upright on two legs. "We're just thrilled to have you visit." Jeremiah turned his attention to me and he beamed, bowing low once again. "Lady Alexandra Crowley. We're so very excited to see what you have in store for us."

"Smile for the camera, Alexandra!" a member of the Praetory's press shouted.

"It's Crowley," I said clearly, adopting what I hoped was a winning smile, but may have been more bared teeth. I was thrilled to be finally entering the Academy my Father had loved, though in my imagination I'd been able to fully savour the moment, without being on display to an array of cameras. Despite that, I was unwilling to show Mother I was overwhelmed. She'd trained me for this.

"Ah, now, Lady Crowley," the Principal said amiably. He seemed excited and flustered as he checked the class roll. "Let's have someone show you to your accommodations... I'd be happy to escort you myself, of course, but you may prefer to get to know some of your peers. I believe you're already acquainted with...?"

"Sephy Nekomata, sir," Watcher provided, checking the report in her claw.

"Ah. She's quite the asset, that one," the Principal winked, satisfied. "She's been working in administration. Already knows the rules and workings of the school system inside and out."

"She has to," Watcher muttered, "or she'd be expelled."

My mother made to leave.

"Please, you're welcome to stay, Minister!" the boisterous Principal insisted.

"No. I have business to attend to."

"You're leaving?" I asked, my voice catching strangely. I hadn't planned for this. I didn't know what to say to her in farewell. She'd never spoken words of affection to me. I wasn't sure we shared the language for it even now.

"Do well in your studies..."

"Yes, Mother," I said, bowing my head instinctively.

"...and make me proud."

I froze. That was not what I had expected her to say, nor how I had expected her to say it: as if it were a possibility. A storm of emotions played out inside of me.

"Yes," I said. "Yes, I will."

7

"Well, well, if it isn't Blanche DuBois," Sephy smirked when I found her. The spiny-tailed feline was waiting for me outside on one of the lawns. Her tail was swishing through the air like a house cat's. Thankfully, those deadly spines were currently flattened. "We're reunited so soon."

"Why, hello, Sephy," I smiled at her. "It's Crowley, actually."

"So I've heard. You think I didn't get that reference straight away? *A Streetcar Named Desire*. I love my black and white movies."

"I'm rather surprised to see you... up and about," I said tentatively, concerned. "Shouldn't you be in hospital? You *did* get tased." *And then crushed, by a wyvern.*

Sephy stretched her neck to stare pointedly down at a small, blackened patch on her front.

"Apart from some burnt fur, I'm starting to feel a bit more normal." She hid any trauma from being attacked in the very place she was meant to feel safe rather excellently. "They said my burn was superficial. I've been called that before, and it always hurts. So! That was a pretty rough experience for your first visit to Counterpart Academy, huh?"

"I've been here before."

The words left my mouth before I fully realised I'd spoken them. I was scanning the grounds, my gaze tugged sideways by memories that refused to stay buried. It had looked different then—shrouded in darkness, silence pressing in from all sides. The grandeur of the place had felt alien, almost infinite. Sacred. Dangerous.

"Just once," I added, voice low. "About a year ago."

I wasn't ready to talk about it—not really. Some wounds still felt too fresh, like they hadn't yet scabbed over. There had been one person I'd trusted since Father's death. One person who'd made me feel seen, understood... even safe. And then I'd learned who he truly was. That kind of betrayal doesn't dull quickly.

"It was at the end of the war when I met him," I said slowly, picking my way through the memory like stepping over glass. "I came here looking for answers—about my father, about the things my mother never told me. I slipped past the illusion guarding the perimeter. The Academy had already been evacuated."

I hesitated. Even now, the images tried to claw their way back into my mind. Blood. Silence. Stillness that didn't feel natural.

"There were bodies."

Sephy had gone still beside me, hushed. Her expression was frozen somewhere between awe and dread.

"You told me once that you'd seen a Shadow," she said. "But your parents hadn't told you anything about the Praetory. Was... was that when it happened? Here?"

I could feel the question coiling behind her eyes. What happened to you?

"You said *'him.'* Who did you meet here? Was it... a Shadow?"

I look away abruptly, embarrassed. She was too good at getting me talking. Maybe talking to a Shadow had caught me off-guard.

Luckily, Sephy got the message.

"Now!" she declared, as if I hadn't embarked on a tangent into a particularly dark moment in this academy's history. "After that mysterious and not at all intriguing tangent, the show must go on." Sephy turned and escorted me into the dorm building. She acted as if nothing had transpired since our first meeting and this was simply a reprisal of our campus tour.

"Did you know we have military training here too?" Sephy narrated enthusiastically. "That seems relatively up your alley, right? We cover everything from basic drills to simulations using cutting-edge virtual reality headsets."

"Why is the Academy training teenagers to fight exactly, when the war with Shadow's Eve is over?" I asked, unsettled. I wondered if it was a ritual leftover from the war, or if it was a darker sign.

"The schism between the Praetory and Shadow's Eve nearly tore our world apart, but that doesn't mean Shadows' Eve will be the only threat we ever face. The Praetory is always looking out for the best soldiers and leaders, so that it's always ready."

Well, that explained a little more why I was trained so ruthlessly to lead and eliminate targets from such a young age on the family estate.

"There are three dorm buildings," Sephy announced as she strode along in front. "Every student lives in a bedroom with access to a shared kitchen and lounge, sort of like self-contained apartments, you could say. I've watched a lot of human sitcoms, and I can inform you that they *always* have apartments."

"How many students to each dorm?" I asked.

"Three, usually."

I had kind of counted on having my own space. My upbringing might have been lonely at times, but I was an introvert who didn't enjoy having others up in her business when she was busy trying to hunt down an active terrorist group. "You know, I don't want to be an imposition," I said awkwardly. "I really am happy to have a room without the shared lounge and what not. Even if it's just a single cot, or in a cupboard, or something. I'm easy."

"Well, tough. This is how things operate here."

Sephy moved on to excitedly filling me in on what it had been like living here with her dormmate for the summer. Apparently a lot of first year students were given the option to move in over the summer months, familiarising themselves with the grounds and each other in preparation for their first year at Counterpart Academy. I realised that even though it was the first day of the school year here, so many of the students in my year already knew this place. They'd already started to form their own rivalries and alliances. I was clearly behind.

Why hadn't my mother wanted me to start at the earliest opportunity as well? The Praetory was her holy grail. Her everything. And yet... no golden ticket for me. Curious, right?

I knew my father had always said he wanted me to be a child for "as long as possible." Translation: bubble-wrap the kid and pray the monsters don't notice. So maybe—just maybe—Mother was playing along to honour his memory?

That would have been touching... if she'd ever *mentioned* him. At all. She barely acknowledged he'd existed. When he died, I grieved; she reorganised her bookshelves. And Father was the one who had finally told me the truth about Shadows. He was the one who had been prepared to finally tell me about the war raging invisibly all around me.

"This school is the best place in the world, it will change your life," Sephy was gushing, chin held high, striding ahead of me. "There's nowhere like it."

Oh, good. A brochure in human form. She was flouncing through this place like it was Disneyland.

I stopped suddenly, overcome with a surprising amount of hurt. There was a roaring in my ears.

Sensing my absence suddenly, Sephy turned around, confused. She saw me standing a few paces behind.

"What?" she asked, tilting her head, padding back toward me in polite bemusement. "Cat got your tongue?"

I'd waited so long for this moment. I'd longed to walk these corridors, to step into the world that my father was a part of. I'd had so much excitement, so much anticipation for when I reached this moment... and now that I was here, I felt like the ice inside me was fracturing, the crack running all the way to my heart. Because perhaps, some small part of me, some unusually illogical part, had thought that if I made it in... somehow Father would come back and he would be here to meet me.

Cue the imaginary birthday party. *'Happy fifteenth, Alexandra Crowley. Here's your Shadow, your dorm, and your resurrected dad.'*

When Father had told me about Shadows, I'd been filled with wonder. I'd spent so long afterwards imagining what his Shadow had looked like, though Mother had been determined to keep that information from me until she deemed the time was right. I'd spent just as long imagining what my own counterpart would look like; a being from another world, who felt what I felt, someone whose thoughts I could hear and who shared in my dreams. What I'd never had: a constant companion. A best friend.

But now I was thinking how Shadows had also been there in the trees the night he was killed. The Dark Father himself was a Shadow. This whole secret world that my parents were wrapped up in only existed in the first place because of the eggs that Shadows had gifted to our dimension.

Sephy, on the other hand, was amusing. But she also reminded me of every popular girl in school who had rubbed me the wrong way. Seeing her here among all of this privilege, as if this place truly was a wonderland and it hadn't partly been responsible for taking Father as well... it filled me with a strange resentment. I could feel the slow burn in my chest that quickly turned into a boil. My hands were shaking, jaw tight.

"You're just like the rest of them, aren't you?" I said. My voice was quiet, but I could hear the contempt in my own words. "You think you're superior to everyone who isn't part of the Praetory."

"Um, excuse me?" Sephy laughed awkwardly.

"Living here in this entitled luxury, keeping all of this technology, an entire other world secret... *why*? How many cures for diseases could you have made from studying the powers of Shadows?"

"We have!" she protested.

"Ah, and you used all of the profits to build some more private palace-schools and drill secret tunnel networks, is that it? Got it."

"Ooh, you are beginning to agitate me."

"All that just to maintain some vanity project," I smiled witheringly. "A secret nation hidden from sight, waging secret wars that cost real lives."

"Just to remind you, it was the *acolytes* who tried to hurt us this morning," Sephy pointed out. "You seem to be under the mistaken impression that I've tried to, I don't know, murder you or something."

I wanted to enjoy this place. I wanted to love it so badly. But being here was filling me with guilt. If my father hadn't been part of this secret world, he'd be here with me, alive. How could I just enjoy it as if that wasn't true?

"I'm just saying, do you think those acolytes just popped up just in a vacuum?" I countered.

"Um, ah-*scuse*-me, are you really blaming me for *terrorism* now?" Sephy said, incredulously. There was a slight hiss of warning in her words.

"If my father had been an accountant with a regular nine-to-five job who'd never heard of Shadows, of the Praetory, of other worlds... he'd still be here."

Sephy went still.

"Crowley," she said softly. "I'm so sorry. I didn't know."

Dammit. I hadn't meant to tell anyone, though I was sure that information was easily accessible. The plan hadn't been to draw attention to myself.

What was it about this particular Shadow that could rile me up so that I forgot myself? Were all Shadows like this?

I tried to steel myself against the sympathy in her gaze.

"You think some school is meant to make all that better?" I snorted derisively. Of course Sephy thought this school was paradise. It was an exclusive luxury getaway designed to keep everyone who wasn't Praetory out. "It's all just a joke. A fallacy. This entire place is."

"You're getting on my nerves, you know!" Sephy glared, huffing. "I'm sorry about your Dad, okay, and I usually am exceedingly polite and understanding. But you're the one who needs to check her own privilege, and you're the one coming off all high and mighty! I'm sorry if the Academy is a joke to you, but this is my home, and I love it! It may have its quirks, but it is the greatest place in the entire world, probably both the worlds. Even though, technically, I've never seen my own world..."

"Then how could you possibly...?"

"*I just know it, OKAY?* If you can't appreciate the Academy for what this place really is... I will eviscerate you. I'm sorry, I don't mean that... no, wait, I do mean that! Plus, you want to know something else...?" Sephy trailed off, indignant, her outrage swelling even further. "Hey! You're not even paying attention to me!" she commanded, clearly wounded.

When I didn't respond, she looked between me and where I was now staring. I suddenly felt the blood drain from my face, as I stared at a seat down at the end of the hall. A young boy was sitting there patiently on a bench, all alone, waiting.

Sephy leaned forward, extending her neck to get a better look past me around the corner. "Who's that small child?"

"That's... Harper," I whispered, dazed and shocked.

"Oh." Understanding seemed to dawn in those eyes. "He's your brother."

I tried to breathe.

"Yeah."

"He's not meant to be here then, is he?"

We looked at each other, then we both turned back to stare at the boy at the end of the hallway.

I'd told Mother I wanted Harper to know the truth. I didn't know that meant that she'd just... what? Just drop him in the middle of the Academy, with no one around? Had she misunderstood our conversation as me suddenly adopting him as my own son instead of hers? How could she just let him be here on his own, undefended, when terrorists attacked here just earlier today, the same scum who killed our father? A wave of wrathful fury rose in me and then crashed, leaving only fear.

"You should go to him," Sephy said gently. She sounded surprisingly adult, definitely more so than she had a moment ago when she was lambasting me. I'd thought of her as a spoiled cheerleader type, but I suppose she was right. I was the one coming off like an entitled, inconsiderate brat with my tirade. I felt the prickling of shame.

"Harper doesn't know about any of this," I said flatly. "What the hell do I say to him?"

"Well, we'll figure it out!" Sephy said cheerfully, then she turned and began marching up the corridor toward Harper. Eyes widening, I lurched after her, hoping to get to Harper before he started screaming at the nightmare predator stalking toward him.

"Hello, I'm Sephy," she greeted him.

"Hello Sephy, I'm Harper," he said, awed. "May I pat you?"

I winced, assuming that it was a rude question to ask. But Sephy considered it, then nodded, beaming.

"Sure!"

With a cute smile of shy excitement, Harper gently stroked her down the back of her neck. She turned toward me, smug.

"You're right," Sephy purred. "He seems simply traumatised."

Harper's eyes were as wide as saucers as he ran his fingers in Sephy's fur, as if confirming over and over again that she was real.

"Crowley, isn't this the most magical day ever?" he said, looking at me with tears of happiness in his eyes. "Are you aware that we seem to be at a hidden school full of impossible creatures?"

"Yes. Yes I am," I said, regarding him anxiously. "How... are you doing?"

"I suppose I'll have to wait until all this shock wears off?" he wondered aloud. "For now, I'm just going to treat it as if it's an excellent dream."

"Sounds like the best plan, really," I chuckled nervously. Everything about this was surreal. "Harper, how exactly did you even get here?"

"I was worried about you after I left," Harper said, sounding a little shaken. "Mahuika said she was allowed to give me a lift to meet you here once you'd taken the Cable Car up."

So: proof that mother had already been prepared to let Harper in on the truth before we struck our so-called deal. There was time for anger at her later. I was still trying to get my head around the fact that Harper was here, hanging out with me in a school full of Shadows, and he wasn't running screaming as I might have feared. Everything had changed in one single day.

"Well, come along then," Sephy said brusquely, and she proceeded to parade us down a long stretch of corridor.

"Where are we going?" I asked, puzzled.

"Typical, you break into my little kingdom and suddenly you want all the answers," she jested. "How does Harper put up with you?"

I'd only spent a matter of minutes with Sephy in total,

and I was already vexed by her damn pride. But I could hardly forget how she'd tried to save me from that acolyte with the gun earlier either.

"Come on, Crowley," Sephy said, turning her head so I could see her wink. "I want to show you your new home."

Smiling, Sephy led us through a door into the lounge of a surprisingly comfortable flat. I took in my new surroundings.

There was a blue couch covered in cushions that you could sink right into, as well as a generously sized television, a kitchenette and a small dining table with stools. Across from us was a latticed window with an arched top, with a little window seat that had a good view of the grounds. A small stairwell behind the couch led up to a landing and presumably more rooms.

"The bathroom's on the ground floor. There's one bedroom on the ground floor, two more up there," Sephy said, her spined tail flicking in the direction of the stairs.

"It's…" I wasn't sure what to say, feeling self-conscious. It looked like a home. I hadn't expected that. It was the opposite of the quiet, empty expansiveness that I was used to. It seemed small, worn, but cosy and lived in.

I felt a sudden undercurrent of uncertainty and vulnerability, standing here in this strange dorm that was my new home in this Academy. The ground was unsteady again under our feet. Harper and I were standing at the verge of a brand new world. Its strange rules, along with the unknowable contents of our future, left me feeling as if Harper and I were adrift in an endless sea. I put my hands on my brother's shoulders, holding onto him like an anchor against the unfamiliar new oceans beckoning before us.

While I'd been searching for something to say, Sephy had moved over to the couch and had started ruffling through a basket with her spider-monkey arms. She was inspecting the quality of the contents, which strangely appeared to be a variety of heart-shaped cards and parcels wrapped in red paper. Before I had time to question it, a voice suddenly spoke from behind me.

"Well, well, what do we have here?"

It was the first time I heard that iconic voice, one I would never forget.

I turned and time dropped away. I was utterly unprepared. He stood before me like a statue of self-absorbed beauty. Standing near him you could almost feel a heat emanating from him, as if he was powered by the force of a sun. He had his hands on his hips, assessing me, dark eyes amused.

And oh, *God help me*, he was beautiful. Gorgeous was probably a more apt word, though that didn't quite touch it either. Dangerously carved cheekbones, black spiky hair like he'd just won a swordfight and hadn't bothered to fix it. That wicked curve to his mouth that made promises without ever saying a word. And his eyes—his *eyes*. Dark, fathomless things. The way they reflected the lights, it appeared as if they held glimmering galaxies. I was falling.

Eurgh. This guy was making me all poetic. I tried to speak, except I didn't, because I almost *choked*, and hated it. What was I choking on, oxygen?

"Riley Aberdeen," he introduced himself, smirking. He had a way of smiling that made it feel he'd carefully tailored that smile entirely just for you. "But call me Aberdeen. Everyone does." *Scottish*. His accent hit like a sucker-punch to the chest. The familiarity of it stirred something old and aching in me. Looking at him, I wouldn't have guessed

Scotland. The angles of his face, the warmth of his skin—there was something there that suggested Southeast Asia, maybe the Philippines.

From his clothes and bearing, I assumed he was another child of nobility like myself. He was dressed like he'd stepped out of a fashion ad and accidentally wandered into our world. That cashmere turtleneck looked ridiculously expensive, and he wore it like armour. Not that it looked like anything could touch him anyway.

The name 'Aberdeen' rang a bell, too. Wait... yes, of course. The Count and Countess Aberdeen had attended events at our house in Miramar, though I think I'd remember if I'd ever run into their son. The irony of meeting another child of a Count and Countess who went by his surname rather than his given name didn't escape me.

The Praetory's nobility was part of what had made the society sound like a freakish cult to me when I was younger. Mother had taught me that noble titles weren't attached to land; they could be won as promotions or lost if one was seen as having dishonoured their rank. Counts and Countesses were wealthy and high up, but they were still below Marquesses. Dukes and Duchesses were even more prestigious. At the very top were those whose families directly served the Potentate. Those esteemed nobles and their children were referred to as Princes and Princesses, although they were simply titles. They didn't insinuate any genetic relation to the Potentate, the Praetory's leader who ruled from his throne in New York.

"Addie," Sephy addressed the new arrival, sounding amused, "allow me to present our dormmate."

Dormmate? I wondered, taken aback.

"How exciting," Aberdeen commented playfully. There

was something about his smile, as dazzling as it was. It felt as if it were perfected at court. It was a smile that could have meant anything. He seemed charming and intelligent, but I couldn't help but look for the double-meaning behind all his words. I sensed an arrogance that I so associated with nobles in general. But after my unwarranted outburst at Sephy, I was determined not to judge by first appearances. I held my hand out firmly to him, smiling pleasantly.

"Alexandra Crowley," I said warmly. Then, with a smile that showed the irony didn't elude me, "but call me Crowley, everyone does. Pleased to meet you. This is my brother, Harper."

Aberdeen shook my hand—warm, steady. My skin still hummed when he let go.

"An honour to meet you, Crowley, and yourself, Harper." His Praetory manners were impeccable.

"Not one for school uniform?" I asked, suddenly feeling out of place in my Academy colours.

"The uniforms are just for formal occasions," Sephy explained. "Otherwise it's a choose-your-own adventure, fashion-wise."

"Hopefully having someone else living with us will mean Sephy has a new willing accomplice for all her shenanigans," Aberdeen smirked.

"Oh, don't act like you don't love it," Sephy scoffed.

"Sephy is something of a dangerous master puppeteer," he confided in me with that smile that made me all wriggly inside. Damn him.

"Yes, I think I've gotten the measure of her quite quickly," I agreed in amusement.

"Addie's is one of the most promising military candidates we have starting here this year," Sephy added.

"There's very few who have ever beat him in the simulations."

"*Very few?*" Aberdeen glared at Sephy, as if she was deliberately trying to get a rise out of him. "Please. I've yet to meet anyone in this hemisphere who could even touch me."

"Well, you'll just have to prove it in actual classes this week," Sephy said lightly.

That got my attention. If I was going to prove myself capable to be a knight and show the true value of my training, despite the small fact that I was missing a leg, it was people like Aberdeen that I would have to beat.

With not a small amount of dread, I noticed Aberdeen's gaze reach my titanium limb. What surprised me though was that unlike most guys, his expression didn't show pity. Just calm assessment, like he was cataloguing me—every strength, every scar—and somehow finding it all fascinating.

"Have you two known each other long?" I ventured, awkward nonetheless.

"A couple months? We met because we were both here over the summer, settling in," Sephy said. "This is our first year too but they had some voluntary classes on that we've been able to try out."

"So when exactly did your parents reveal the whole... *Shadows* thing to you?" I asked Aberdeen.

He stared at me strangely.

"Like... my whole life? What about you?"

I tried to hide my shock and embarrassment.

"Recently," I muttered.

"Their family is a little more... traditional," Sephy explained to Aberdeen, then coughed. She looked at me apologetically. "Not everyone follows those old customs so much these days."

I tried not to dwell too much on the fact that my mother had been putting me through psychological torture just because she was a purist for the Praetory's old traditions, while other children like Aberdeen had secretly known about Shadows their entire adolescence. I'd brood over that one later.

"Anyway, are you ready, Addie?" Sephy asked authoritatively.

Aberdeen had been headed for our stairs but he stopped short. A suspicious look crossed his face, as if he knew that tone all too well.

"What are you...?"

"Don't you remember agreeing to help me out?"

He moaned suddenly.

"I thought you were *joking*!"

"I *never* joke about serious matters," she said sweetly. "Now get into that spandex before I make you."

Aberdeen sighed.

"The things I sacrifice for your schemes," he commented wryly. Then, without any warning, he started taking off his clothes.

I whirled around like I'd been slapped, cheeks hot enough to fry eggs. What. The Hell. Was. *Happening?*

When I finally risked a look back to see what Harper was regarding with such amusement, Aberdeen was shirtless, barefoot, and trying to shimmy into what could only be described as a very tight-fitting homemade Cupid costume. His torso was all sharp planes, his lean musculature giving him the appearance of a reluctant demigod. Sephy was attempting to help.

"Stop flapping about Aberdeen and just get it on!" Sephy scolded him. A giggle escaped her. "You look so *cute*."

Aberdeen rolled his eyes. He was clasping a bow and there was a heart at the end of its notched arrow. Sephy spluttered as Aberdeen twisted, unintentionally smashing his left wing into her face.

I quirked an eyebrow. The costume was so tight that it was nearly... indecent. "Um, what exactly is going on here?"

"Valentine's Day," Aberdeen said with a kind of tired resignation, as if this explained everything.

"I thought it would be fun to give cards and presents to everyone we knew wasn't in an exclusive relationship and wouldn't be receiving a Valentine today!" Sephy explained to me boisterously. "Aberdeen is going to shoot them with toy arrows and spread the love. Doesn't he make such a cute little cupid?"

Aberdeen rolled his eyes.

"It's very sweet of you to do this for me, Aberdeen. Think how much joy you'll bring to the students."

He just sighed long-sufferingly. "I'm going to need therapy."

"Hey, Harper," Sephy said, winking at him. "Want to help Aberdeen shoot people in the name of love?"

Harper giggled.

"Go on, then."

Harper ran over to Aberdeen. Soon Harper was trying to helpfully get Aberdeen to put his foot through one of the leg holes. Sephy sat down, smiling, seemingly content to watch their machinations.

"So... who else lives in this dorm?" I ventured.

"Just you, Aberdeen and myself."

I looked at her sharply, stunned.

"You and I, we're... roomies?"

"Is that going to be a problem?" she questioned me, sitting up straight as if just daring me to protest. "Shadows usually dorm separately from the humans in another building, but I'm an exception."

"Why?"

"I just am. Always." She licked a paw delicately. "Also, as student administrator I need minions to rope into various school activities, and this location is convenient. I tend to get what I want."

"I've noticed." I had so many questions about Shadows, but I'd been trying to hold them all in. "Do you have any siblings?" I ventured.

"Alas, no," Sephy answered, tossing back her head with a wink. "My biological parents, it seems, were wise enough to know that you can't improve on perfection." Then she frowned. "Oh wait, I forgot, I'm not talking to you."

"Why not?"

"Because you're a tyrant."

"*I'm* the tyrant here?" I spluttered.

There was a little silence. I recalled our spat from before.

"Sorry I blamed you for terrorism," I said in a small voice.

Sephy laughed.

"That's okay. Despite myself, I enjoy you, Alexandra Crowley. You're a beguiling puzzle. But something still tells me that won't be our last fight."

I blinked in surprise.

"That was some tantrum," Sephy added, her tone teasing. "I didn't know you had such dramatic flair. Have you considered signing up for the dramatic arts society?"

I glared at her in mock outrage.

"You'd make an excellent mime," she said seriously.

8

I woke, gasping for breath. Even with my eyes wide open, the lingering vision stayed with me, an indelible stain on my consciousness. A behemoth of a tiger had loomed before me. The Dark Father's horned head resembled a metal mask, the one his followers loved to imitate. His whiskers had crackled with lightning.

I'd had the same recurring nightmare many times this last year.

Drenched in cold sweat, I trembled. It disturbed me how I both feared and longed for the dreams. In some of them, the tiger had removed his mask and it was my own father staring back at me, face slicked with blood.

Why won't you leave me alone? I silently asked the darkness.

The unfamiliar layout of the room unsettled me until I remembered where I was. The dark of early morning only added to my disorientation. Remembering the events of yesterday, I felt myself starting to relax.

I'm here, I thought, dazed. *The same academy my father himself once attended.*

Harper had gone home yesterday evening, only saying goodnight after a series of fierce hugs and my promise that he could come and visit next Saturday to explore the grounds together more thoroughly. I wanted to keep him with me; I had petitioned mother to let him stay, but apparently the Academy only allowed enrolled students to stay in the dorms.

I looked past the foot of my bed and realised I was staring into a pair of shining eyes. I nearly screamed.

"Sephy!? What the f—?"

"You want to help me set up for the orientation?"

"Haven't you heard of boundaries?" I exclaimed, throwing my pillow at her. My heart was hammering all over again. The pillow flew back at me, whomping me in the face. I let out an: '*Oof.*'

"I couldn't sleep," Sephy complained, launching herself up onto the mattress. "Hang with me."

Now that the shock of waking with a spine-tailed wildcat studying me had started to somewhat ebb, I sighed. Sephy appeared demanding by nature, and didn't exactly seem like one to settle for '*no*' as an answer.

She winked at me.

"Happy First Day, Crowley. Today, you're really born. Today, you become part of the Praetory. And more than that... we are the *best* dorm there is!" she declared, sounding bloodthirsty and triumphant. "So I got a load of coffee for the new first years, because I'm trying really hard to impress them. Also, I need your help setting up some killer pranks, because hazing them is important and traditional and it builds character, but we'll discuss that later."

"Wait, what?" I said, stunned. "I feel like that's something that we should discuss *now*. Sephy... it's my first day. Let me wake up at least."

"You've wasted sixteen years, we can't wait any longer! You need to spread your beautiful wings!"

"You realise that I don't have wings."

"I see. Some Shadows have wings, but those who don't can't use metaphors? That's racist, Crowley. Look, I just want to help you bloom. Like a delicate flower."

"Well, that is what they always call me," I said dryly.

"You have a future in student leadership with me, I just know it. Together, we'll build a dynasty that will last a thousand years!"

"Aren't dynasties meant to be made up of... I don't know, people who are genetically related?"

"So? You're my sister from another mister."

She had all of the flirtatiousness of a cat, as if she was a goddess and totally aware of it.

"When *is* this orientation again?"

"Five hours from now."

"Five hours?" I blanched. "You're waking me *now?*"

"We need time to prepare so we can create a sense of community. What are people going to eat? Will we be there to greet them at the door? How can the chairs be arranged to equalise power in the room? How can we really institute powerful and fertile conversations to listen deeply and ask the important questions that will shift our education forward?"

I blinked.

"I think there's a chance that at some point your brain ascended to another state of reality," I growled.

"Yes, sweetie, I'm Sephy. Keep up. Come on, let's get some breakfast in you."

"Okay, okay," I relented, surrendering. "I'll get some clothes on."

"You're the best."

"Just give me a second to change, *s'il vous plaît*."

Sephy lounged shamelessly on the bottom of my bed, making no show of going anywhere. Her tail was in the air, waving back and forth.

"Please, go ahead," she blinked innocently, practically purring. "I've always found human anatomy an inherently puzzling conundrum."

"Out," I directed her sternly, pointing to the door. This was hardly the time for her weird cross-species flirtations.

Once she was gone I got dressed and fitted on my prosthetic. When I stood to check my appearance in my mirror, I stared at the stranger there. Was I looking at the daughter of a Minister, trying to do her mother proud? Was I looking at a Count's daughter, wishing to attend the academy that her father had apparently described as the happiest time of his life? Or was I nothing now but a creature of vengeance, intent on hunting out any remnant of Shadows' Eve who still existed?

Shadows' Eve had risked everything to break into this very Academy — which meant they wanted something badly. They were after something so highly classified I couldn't even get Jo to share it with me. That didn't make it sound as if Shadows' Eve were on their last legs, or even dormant.

They were planning something.

Did it have anything to do with the Dark Father, their illustrious leader? What if there was some chance, however small, that the acolytes could break him out from his prison and start the war all over again?

I shuddered.

Instead of interrogating him, the Praetory should have killed him when they had the chance.

· · ·

I carefully considered Aberdeen over my morning coffee. He was eating noodles, wielding his chopsticks with deft precision. Sephy was busy on the floor, poring over her spread out forms and plans for her Valentine's-themed Orientation Day.

Aberdeen, meanwhile, lounged like a prince at court: sly, irreverent, charming in a way that felt designed. There was something too perfect about it — the timing of his jokes, the arch of his brows, the calculated carelessness of his smirk. I hated that I noticed the perfection. Hated even more that I liked it.

It felt like he was trying to win me over. And I loathed that part of myself — the traitorous, fluttering part — that *wanted* to be won.

Still, I couldn't stand people who acted like what they were not. While yes, I did acknowledge my own hypocrisy. I was pretending to be an excited new student like all the others, while secretly I was here to avenge Father. The more I knew about this world, the closer I came to learning the identities of those who'd taken him from me.

Aberdeen picked up the prop Cupid bow off the dining table beside him and pulled back the string with a puckish smirk on those ethereally pleasing features, miming firing an arrow at me.

I quirked an unimpressed eyebrow, trying to pretend his looks didn't make me breathless.

"What happened to your leg?" he asked out of the blue, nodding to my prosthetic.

"Mosquito bite," I said, without blinking.

He leaned back with that same maddening smirk, as if he was toying with prey.

"Can you still fight with that thing?"

"Aberdeen!" Sephy exclaimed. She sounded very disappointed in him.

"Why don't you come over here and find out," I offered. He laughed, delighted.

"But I prefer strategy and command," I continued with a smile, keeping my cool. "I'm more of a big picture kind of girl."

"Ah. See, I lead from the front. I prefer to actually have some skin in the game."

"Sexually," Sephy agreed solemnly, clearly stirring the pot.

"I... what? No, not sexually!" Aberdeen protested, flushing. He sent Sephy a withering glare. "In the field!"

Outraged, he still managed to rise with a dignified air. He washed his bowl in the sink and then headed upstairs.

"I'm going to shower," he muttered darkly.

"We've been over this, you don't have to announce it every time you do anything in the bathroom," Sephy called up to him. Once he was out of earshot she turned to me, concerned. "Are you okay?"

I turned to her. I guess I must have looked a little shell-shocked.

"Hmm?"

"Sorry. Aberdeen can be a force of nature sometimes. I should have given you advance warning."

I had to agree, it made sense that Aberdeen and Sephy were friends and mischievous partners in crime. Sephy also always entered a room as if she were a summer storm rolling in.

"So, what's Aberdeen's story?" I asked.

"He's very exotic, isn't he?"

I gave her a questioning look.

"He's from *Scotland*," she said importantly, as if she

could only imagine such far-flung places. "Count and Countess Aberdeen moved over here from Edinburgh a few years back."

"Ah. Guessing from the fact I heard him swearing in Tagalog in the shower, he's Filipino too, right?" I ventured.

"Correct. I'm continually full of admiration for your obscure knowledge," Sephy said. Her tail flicked back and forth, as it seemed to do whenever she was chewing over juicy gossip. "You know, it's weird how Aberdeen hasn't signed up to the military yet. They're begging to have him. He's gifted, he'd be a jewel of the Praetory's armed forces... but he's turned down every offer he's had."

"Why?" I asked, intrigued.

Sephy tilted her head, her equivalent of a shrug.

Aberdeen wasn't just pretty. He was a puzzle. A contradiction. The kind of person who wore charisma like armour — but whose eyes sometimes betrayed something lonelier. And I hated how curious I was to know what he was hiding.

I tried to shake it off. *He's vain*, I reminded myself. *He likes attention like a lizard likes sunlight. He's probably still adjusting his hair in that mirror right now.*

"So, how do you feel about Addie?" Sephy said, raising a feline eyebrow. "Do you want to get all hot and sweaty with him?"

I coughed up some coffee, and a little came out my nose. I rolled my eyes at her mild victory, trying to regain my poise as I politely dabbed myself with a napkin.

"What?" Sephy said, eyes glinting. "You think I'm perverted?"

"I think you seem to have an unhealthy preoccupation with people's personal lives," I said matter-of-factly, opening up the Praetory newspaper. Sephy swatted it with her tail, her spines shredding the paper like tissue. I just sighed.

"You are my dormmates," Sephy said firmly, with feeling, "which makes you my people. I'm in charge of your wellbeing. You're my little midgets."

"Please never say that again, it's very offensive. Also, you and I are the same age..."

"You are *my* responsibility. Do you understand me?"

"So you're encouraging me to perv over hot guys?"

"Yes."

"That's creepy."

"I acknowledge this," she nodded. "But I will not back down."

"I'm not going to get started on how amazingly inappropriate this is."

"You know you love me."

"Oh, is that why you vex me so? And to your earlier question, no way. Aberdeen looks like he'd eat me alive."

Sephy opened her mouth for her next retort, looking gleeful. I just shook my head firmly. She closed her mouth, nodding.

Still, even with the shower running, I could feel him — like some echo burned into the air. That laugh, that gaze. That maddening, golden-boy arrogance.

I felt as if I was still staring into those infinite dark eyes. There was something about him, I concluded uneasily, this gorgeous walking paradox.

Something I couldn't quite put my finger on.

Good morning, Counterpart Academy!

Welcome to all of our first years! Hope you enjoyed this

morning's orientation. Gee golly gosh, these truly are exciting times.

Happy Valentine's Day, Lovers and Loners! Whether you're in a committed relationship or just committed to being fabulous, may your day be smothered in chocolates, declarations of undying affection, and mildly embarrassing poetry.

Second years, we welcome you to your final year of school. Some of you will already have found your counterpart, while for the rest of you, this should be your lucky year! Fingers crossed!

We know you must be as troubled as we are by what occurred yesterday. Counselling services have been made available in Room B12 for anyone who needs to debrief, cry, vent, or just enjoy the free mints. *All of your parents have been contacted as well* (some mildly panicked, some impressively chill), *and they have been reassured that the security breaches that resulted in yesterday's trespass have been addressed, and those responsible have been swiftly disciplined.*

So... no more worries!

PS For any difficulties with timetable scheduling, please see Sephy Nekomata, Student Administrator (that's moi!) or head to the main office.

A poster further down the school notice board read:

Smile, you're all on 'Love Academy!'

As part of my Media Studies Project, you are all being monitored! Your flirtations, your alliances and yes, your betrayals, are all being eagerly recorded for viewing as part of my Media Studies piece. Please come and see me in person if you do not want to be featured, and simply pay the $50 fee to opt-out.

PS—just remembered I need to recruit three video editors. Contact Sephy Nekomata if you are looking for work experience!

Beneath this second poster an amendment had been aggressively pinned which said:

IMPORTANT NOTE:

PLEASE DISREGARD the above notice, it is a sordid breach of privacy and Sephy has been put on notice. All of the hidden cameras have been removed. We are 99.99% positive. – Ms. Podmore

I'd helped Sephy put up the notices. As she'd laughed and jested with other students both first year and second year and introduced me, I realised how adored and looked up to she was by the other students. Sephy had only been here over the summer and she already seemed to have built a reputation for herself. Everyone was quick to fall under her spell. Sephy brushed it off when I asked about it, saying that she was a social chatterbox and that she just liked people... but what I saw in her was a leader.

I noticed printed posters along the white walls, ones of Sephy looking ambitiously out at the sky with a fetching emerald beret on her head as if ironically emulating a dicta-tor. At least, I hoped it was ironic. Each poster contained a giant word: *LOVE, PEACE* and *UNITY.* Seeing them, I couldn't stop myself grinning.

Unfortunately, Aberdeen seemed to have as many people in love with him at this school as Sephy did. He didn't court attention, didn't need to. People gravitated to him like moths to a low-burning flame: steady, alluring, a little dangerous. A tilt of his head, a flicker of interest in those unnervingly perceptive eyes, and suddenly whoever he was talking to was breathless, enchanted, hopelessly ensnared. I spotted him at lunch, holding court at a cafeteria table surrounded by a soft ripple of laughter and stolen glances. A gaggle of admirers hung on his every word. The envy came hot and fast, coiling low in my stomach. He looked like he didn't quite belong there. There was something remote about the way he smiled—something apathetic, as if his thoughts were somewhere else entirely.

I know, what an arsehole. But God help me, I wanted to know in those moments what he was really thinking about.

It had been good to meet the other first-years in orientation, anyhow. At least the early rising to assist Sephy had paid off. All of the students at Counterpart Academy were clad in the grey uniform, accented in reds and golds, and it was comforting to feel we were all in the same boat. Walking down the white opulent corridors crowded with Shadows, on the other hand, was a constant exercise in gaping and marveling at their pure, otherworldly majesty.

On my way to class, a gargoyle lumbered past me—reptilian, bizarre, half-born from some ancient, cracking egg. Bits of shell clung to its hide like fossilised armor, and its many orange eyes blinked at me with eerie fascination. Then came a mechanical sea-lion, all brass and brilliance, its mane shimmering as gears whirred and clicked—it brushed too close, knocking my books in a clatter behind it.

A centaur followed, breathtaking in her strangeness: the body of a deer, legs of velvet moss, and a head of antlers and hanging ferns, as if the forest itself had crowned her queen. Overhead, a fairy zipped by on wings like fractured crystal, scattering light as she darted above shrieking students, her skin a pastel blue.

I barely sidestepped in time as a massive panda thundered through, its presence casting long shadows across the courtyard. All around us, Shadows roamed — swimming through the rivers, soaring through the air. I caught a flash of lightning as a golden seahorse arced from the water, sparking like a storm made flesh.

It was beautiful. Unruly. Impossible. And one of these could be *mine*.

It was all as my father had described to me that night, when he spoke with such wonder and love for Shadows. I'd clung to the memory of that conversation, holding it to me as if it were a talisman warding against the sorrow of his passing. I'd vowed some day I would sleep within the walls of the same Academy that my father had slept in, that I'd walk the very same halls.

I'm here, Father. I'm finally here.

Lunchtime. While everyone else was off committing social atrocities in the cafeteria, I spent mine where I belonged: alone, in an empty classroom, cramming centuries of lost knowledge into my skull.

Each day, the weight of my ignorance pressed harder. Not all families were as rigorous with tradition as my mother was in sheltering their children, it was clear that most of my peers were well-versed in the nuances of Shadows.

As for the teachers themselves, Steven Campbell emerged as a beacon. The history teacher's presence was incongruous at first—a bald man with glasses with a frowny face that could easily suggest a stern demeanor. But whenever he strode through the classroom, his eyes lit up with a passionate intensity. A crystal orb from the Shadow world always hung suspended in the air beside him. It displayed shifting images: ancient battles, forgotten rituals, and the grand tapestry of the Praetory's history. As he spoke, gesticulating animatedly, his words wove through the images, transforming them from hologram into living narrative.

What struck me most was how he noticed the small things—the way he would pause mid-lecture to ensure a quiet student's hand was raised, or how he took a moment to explain a particularly tricky detail to a struggling student, his voice dropping to a conspiratorial whisper. Mr Campbell's genuine concern for our understanding, his ability to turn history into something both accessible and personal, made him more than just a teacher. It made him someone who truly cared, whose passion for his subject was matched only by his belief in his students.

"I don't believe in punishments for missing deadlines," Mr Campbell said when a student asked him about the cutoff for an upcoming essay. "You have the rest of your lives to have some dickhead as your boss. If we're going to try and build a world that we all want to live in together, then we have to start here."

My kind of teacher.

Then, in contrast, there was Morgaine Holloway.

"Crowley! Is this how you handle a threat?"

"No, Captain Holloway!" I shot back, my voice steady despite the sting in my shoulder. I refocused, scanning for a weakness in Aberdeen's defences.

But Aberdeen was already moving. With the grace of a dancer, he spun into a roundhouse kick that slammed into my other shoulder, sending me crashing onto the mats like a sack of potatoes. I glared up at him, only to see him coyly eating an apple he'd pulled from his pocket. He gave me that *stupid smirk* that made my knees feel like overcooked pasta. He hadn't even broken a sweat. I'm not entirely proud to admit it made me livid.

"Finished with training already, Crowley?" our teacher mocked me. Our instructors happened to be Captain Morgaine Holloway and her Shadow Deva, both of whom I'd spied that first day during my venture into the Academy.

Deva stood tall and solemn. She resembled the Egyptian god Horus, a bird merged into the body of a human. She was draped in a cloak of midnight feathers and possessed four magnificent wings that unfurled from her back. From her head, a regal crest of indigo quills fanned out like a celestial crown. She was a tapestry of shadows and whispers, a living embodiment of night.

I grit my teeth, pushing myself up and raising my fists again. My hand-to-hand combat training was solid, but Aberdeen had clearly volunteered to be my partner just to knock me down a few pegs. His technique was flawless, and he struck like a being of coiled rage.

While other students were also being knocked around, none were receiving the same harsh scrutiny from Morgaine. She criticized every stumble and questioned my commitment with a glare that could freeze fire. If I didn't know any better, I'd hazard that I'd committed some great injustice against her. The very sight of me seemed to rile her up, nostrils flaring, gazing down dictatorially at me.

Why is she so hard on me? I wondered, grappling with the conundrum. Other teachers fawned over the nobles, and I'd already witnessed how I was granted leniency as the daughter of a Count and Countess. Yet Morgaine seemed to reserve her harshest judgments for me, treating the other noble students with an almost reverent respect.

It was even more frustrating, I realised, because I'd actually taken a liking to Morgaine when I'd first seen her. I'd wanted to earn her respect badly, after seeing the dressing down she'd given Sir Kipling, that loathsome knight whose smile contained depths of violence.

"Keep your hands up, Crowley! I've seen better form from kindergarteners!" Morgaine barked, her face contorted into a fierce scowl.

A surge of anger fuelled me. I was determined to wipe the smirk off Aberdeen's face. My form was flawless, perfected over years of training, while some students were only just learning the basics.

I attacked with renewed vigour. Aberdeen responded with a flurry of counterattacks, and soon we were wrestling across the floor, locked in a fierce struggle. We fell, locked together, and he pinned me to the mat. His face was inches from mine. And in that awful, gut-twisting moment, his smirk faded. Something flickered in his eyes — confusion, curiosity — like he'd just noticed something in me.

I shoved him off before I could think. Got up, shaking. *Burning*.

"That wasn't control, Crowley. You're not a brawler in a bar fight," Morgaine snapped. "Fifteen laps around the field. Now."

Aberdeen's smirk widened, but he feigned innocence when I shot him a glare.

Morgaine refused to ease up on me in the weeks that followed. I was still held to a standard higher than any of the other students, and there were good-natured jokes from our classmates about what I must have done to piss her off. I was determined to prove her wrong. My extracurricular education through my entire childhood focused on strategy and warfare. My parents had picked up on my natural gifts and fascination for the area which led them to expose me to new exercises. Father had drawn out the movements of troops on boards, mimicking situations with guerrilla insurgents among dense urban environments. The given situations I had to navigate were surreal, fantastical. *'What if some of the troops I commanded could fly?'* Father had posited. *'What if particular individuals could move through solid objects, or rewind the perception of time?'*

Now, of course, I realised Father had been preparing me for the Praetory all along.

I'd done some research on Morgaine, trying to find any kind of clue or reason to why my existence seemed to be a permanent insult to her. She was something of a legend in the Praetory, both proud and fearless, someone so accomplished it was enough to make me shiver in her presence. Along with her feathered counterpart, Deva, Morgaine had snuck behind enemy lines and eliminated leaders within Shadows' Eve, quelling dissent and returning entire nations to Praetory control. Morgaine and Deva had been the favourite weapons of the Potentate himself.

My research told me that something had clearly gone down though, resulting in a massive falling out between Morgaine and the Potentate. As far as I knew, Morgaine hadn't failed the Potentate on an assignment; her record seemed flawless. And yet, here she was: teaching combat basics to hormonal teenagers in an inconsequential country at the bottom of the world.

It wasn't exile, not officially. But it reeked of punishment.

And still, none of that explained the *hatred* in her eyes when she looked at me.

9

Sephy had started exhibiting the bewildering behaviour of crashing on my bed at night. She seemed to find it immensely entertaining. I'd been stricken at first, all in a huff over the intrusion. But now whenever I entered to see her lying on the bed I just sighed in resignation and made sure I kept to my own side. I *did* wonder if Sephy was doing it mainly to mess with me, delighting in my awkwardness, or if she actually found it hard to sleep alone. I'd had to put up with the isolation of our family house for so long, the silence making it so hard to ignore my inner demons. Having someone else there was... unusual. Confusing. I made a mental note to have the '*boundaries*' conversation with her again. I wondered if she slept on Aberdeen's bed too.

Sephy also surprised us by announcing that she was throwing a literature-themed party for her friends among the first years. It was impressively extravagant, and made it feel as if we were hosting an entire ball in our somewhat cosy dorm room. Playing cards hung suspended on shimmering string from the ceiling, Wonderland-esque, their faces turned towards the room curiously. The dorm room, once a relatively modest space of ordinary walls and worn floors, had been transformed into an otherworldly gallery of enchantment. Gossamer drapes in hues of midnight and moonlight cascaded from the walls, their folds shimmering with the soft glow of enchanting lanterns, casting ethereal patterns upon the floor. Sephy hadn't done a half-bad job.

Piles of vintage books decorated every surface, their spines glittering with gold and silver. They served as both decoration and invitation, beckoning guests to dive into the worlds of their pages. The air was thick with the mingled scents of sweet confections and something that smelled suspiciously like spiced cider. Fantastical creatures, both costumed and real, chatted and laughed all around us.

I couldn't help but realise though that the Shadows and humans kept to distinctly different circles in a social context, except for Sephy, who effortlessly flitted between the two groups.

Aberdeen turned up in a stunning suit with a Mad Hatter's top hat and gleaming golden contacts. I had predicted that Sephy would be, playing to type, dressed as a very flirty Cheshire Cat, but should have seen it coming when she came as the Queen of Hearts. A small indoor game of croquet was set up with hoops dotted in a path through our flat and down the steps.

I improvised my own costume last minute, Sephy helping enlist some of her student minions in soft-tech class to sew me a blue and white Alice costume. Beings and denizens of other fictional worlds were allowed too, with King Arthur, Enola Holmes and Jekyll/Hyde all in attendance, as well as the monsters from *Where the Wild Things Are*.

Leaning against the banister, I stared down at the party

from the landing. Aberdeen and Sephy were socialising downstairs, schmoozing with everyone. They were both on fire, entirely in their element.

Aberdeen may have enjoyed the power of his popularity, but I got the feeling that Sephy was the only other student he counted as a friend. I'd heard snooty rumours from some people that Aberdeen thought he was too good for everyone. He was usually just hanging with Sephy or on a game on his phone, lost in its hyper-coloured world.

"Mind if I join you, Alice?"

I nearly jumped out of my skin as I turned to see Aberdeen right beside me on the landing. I cleared my throat.

"Of course not, Hatter."

His gaze moved down to Sephy below. I think he'd caught me staring.

"You know, in our first week Sephy had this sticky flooring placed in a corridor so people's shoes got stuck to it like flypaper. In the same week she masqueraded as a staff member in order to discipline some bullies who were picking on the smaller kids. She made them run embarrassing errands for her for a month."

A laugh escaped me at the Machiavellian prankster. Aberdeen and I had been bored one night so we'd gotten about half an hour through a horror movie before Sephy had leapt out from behind a curtain. Aberdeen had screamed so hard I'd thought he'd perish. Apparently Sephy had been sitting behind the curtain for like thirty minutes, just texting, to lull us into a false sense of security.

"She would have nearly gotten kicked out of the Academy completely," Aberdeen continued, "but the Deputy-Principal ordered her to start working in administration to try and teach her some structure and discipline. I

don't think she ever expected Sephy to be so *good* at it."
Aberdeen watched Sephy down below with a strangely
vulnerable smile. "She's overhauled and streamlined all of
the school's systems and processes. In no time at all she's
ensured that she's the one with all the keys to the kingdom,
the spider in the centre of the web..."

"... so everyone has to come to her for access. And basically, this gives her ultimate power?"

"Exactly. All of the students love and adore her, and the
staff suddenly can't seem to survive two days on their own
without her help. She's super popular here, and for a Shadow..." He shrugged. "That's pretty unprecedented."

There was a short, tense silence.

"How bad is it, really?" I asked quietly, my voice
hushed. "For Shadows, I mean." I had been reading everything I could about the Praetory and its history, but some
things weren't as clear on the page as lived reality. Especially when those in power were the ones writing all the
books. "I know most humans treat their Shadows as
servants, not equals..."

For some reason the emotion I saw behind those golden
contact lenses made me shiver.

"The Shadows who have never found their counterparts
are forced to live in towns like Quietfire, which is concealed
further out of Wellington City," Aberdeen murmured, his
lips pressed in a thin line. He turned his head slowly, eyes
meeting mine. The intensity of his gaze hit me like a
current. "Their existence is hidden from the public by Brilliance Stones. But the towns are overcrowded, full of sickness and poverty. The Praetory acts like the Shadows are to
blame for it."

My grip on the banister tightened.

"I just... I simply don't understand it," I said, incensed.

"Every human in the Praetory has a Shadow of their own, and they can hear their Shadows' own thoughts and feelings, right? There's a telepathic connection that's formed. So how can the humans justify having a system that oppresses the Shadows?"

"How was segregation ever justified?" Aberdeen snapped. He wore a hard, blazing expression, but his voice became deadly quiet. "How did men once spend their time trying to stop their wives having the right to vote? I *wish* meeting your counterpart magically fixed everything. The Praetory doesn't take kindly to anyone who rocks the boat, or who goes out and stages a public protest. Fighting for rights is agonizingly slow. Even if it doesn't seem like it here at the Academy, maybe." He looked down at Sephy, whose effusively told story had our guests doubled over in laughter.

"I'd be careful talking about this stuff too loudly," Aberdeen murmured, his voice softer now. "Some people might even report you if they overheard this kind of thing being said about the Praetory."

I felt a shiver run through me again. This secret world clearly wasn't the magical utopia I'd dreamed of ever since Father spoke of it so lovingly. Far from it.

"So does Sephy live in Quietfire?" I asked, changing my line of inquiry. "Is that where her parents are?"

"Sephy's a rare case. She was adopted by a wealthy human noble, the Marquis Nekomata, and his Shadow, despite them having no personal connection to her. James Nekomata is a big Shadow lover, deeply interested in preserving Shadow culture. Or at least, he claims to be."

I quirked an eyebrow at him.

Aberdeen sighed with that irritating air of superiority, as if he had to explain everything. "James Nekomata is a military advisor, or at least he was until he fell out of favour. He and his Shadow were experts on how to coach Shadows to tap into their powers and do things that were thought unimaginable. But Sephy's family has fallen from what it once was. Her father was demoted from Duke for making too many enemies in New York. Perhaps the Neko-matas chose their career out of an eccentric, tinkering love for Shadows and invention, and this is the only way they've found to make a comfortable existence for themselves pursuing ingenuity." He seemed unconvinced. "But they sure used it to score military victories."

"You don't seem to approve," I commented wryly.

Aberdeen shrugged. He seemed self-conscious, as if he was inwardly reprimanding himself for saying too much.

"I'm going to bed before Sephy decides to start playing a sophisticated party game of spin-the-bottle."

I winced at the idea and nodded. I headed for the stairs just as Aberdeen turned to his room. We bumped into each other, our faces suddenly uncomfortably close.

Aberdeen went still. So did I.

There was something about his scent, like woodsmoke and cloves. So familiar. Yet I couldn't place where... I froze.

The acolyte. The student acolyte, the one who got away. I remembered the moment that he'd disarmed me, that whiff of his scent.

It couldn't possibly be Aberdeen. The acolyte who Sephy and I ran into in that hallway had been a Shadow, I reminded myself fiercely. I had witnessed the forest spirit's death firsthand, as he refused to divulge any information to Sir Kipling. I'd seen him collapse, lifeless, before my eyes.

Except doubt began to creep in. What if it was actually *another* acolyte I'd seen Kipling murder? My memory was hazy. I could have gotten confused in that moment when I lost sight of the acolyte who had tased Sephy in the hallway. Perhaps there was still another acolyte hiding among the students of the Academy. The same one who had tased Sephy and escaped with something precious in their backpack, something they'd risked everything for.

The thought unsettled me. I tried to push it away, ambivalent about even entertaining it.

Even if that acolyte who had accosted us had managed to get away, there was no *way* in all of the coincidences that the missing acolyte just happened to be my dormmate. How could I just end up happening to be placed with the very student who was secretly one of the acolytes I was searching for, out of all the other students in the Academy?

It's Sephy who's in charge of room assignments, I reminded myself. *It's Sephy who wanted to take me under her wing, as some new personal pet project or... whatever.*

Was there the slightest chance that Sephy and Aberdeen were both part of Shadows' Eve?

I nearly laughed at the ridiculousness of the idea, though it made me equally nauseous. No, that was ludicrous. Besides, that hooded acolyte student we ran into *attacked* Sephy. I shook off the conspiratorial ideas clustering darkly in my head. Sephy and Aberdeen may not be caught up in this, but I couldn't get past the feeling that Aberdeen was keeping some kind of secret.

I realised that I still hadn't moved. I was standing uncomfortably far into Aberdeen's personal space, staring directly into those eyes. Aberdeen was frozen, his cheeks flushed. Scowling, he finally pushed past me to get to his room. I caught him muttering something about how everyone at this school but him was obsessed with sex.

It wasn't healthy to always see enemies wherever I looked. But surely I couldn't rule out the chance that there might be other acolytes within the student body here, ones that Sir Kipling hadn't yet rooted out. It had been an oversight for me not to consider the possibility sooner. If that was true, then by pursuing them into the Academy I may already have revealed my face and made myself a target... my very life could be in danger.

I'd have to watch my back.

I do *love being thrown in the deep end,* I mused.

Our first battle simulation was taking place in a warehouse-like structure with multiple levels. It was filled with barrels and ramps, much like a laser tag or Airsoft arena.

Every Shadow and human wore a vest full of sensors. The goggles created the incredibly believable illusion that our mission was taking place in a downtown shopping mall, thanks to virtual reality.

"*Are you doing okay up there?*" Aberdeen's voice crackled in my earpiece.

"Of course," I answered calmly, studying the map of the shopping complex in my hands. I was trying to not treat Aberdeen any differently after my moment of paranoia from the night before. I recalled the scent I may have imagined on him and felt my curiosity seething. If he wasn't an acolyte, what other secrets was he hiding?

The students from our class and another had been mixed and divided into two teams at random. Sephy was sorted onto the team opposite from mine, and she was chosen to lead. This shouldn't really have been a surprise to me, after what Aberdeen had told me about her family history as battle advisors. The fact that Sephy never mentioned it made it difficult to remember it was part of who she was.

What was more shocking was when Morgaine selected me to command my team.

A flip of a coin determined that my team would be playing as the attacking Praetory, while Sephy's team would be pretending to be the defending acolytes. My team's mission was to take out the acolytes before they could detonate their bomb, blowing themselves up along with the mall like the zealous cult they were.

I was currently on the first floor of the mall with some of my teammates. I'd designated this group: 'Cobalt Squad.'

"Aberdeen? You're going to be leading Gold Squad," I ordered via radio. "Take three units from the central squad and approach through the car park, then hold. You'll need some Shadows who can make as much noise as possible to disguise your small numbers."

"Crowley, trust me, I can take them," came Aberdeen's imperious voice, with a flash of temper. *"Grant me a full squad and we can cut to the top floor where they're holed up..."*

"And find the bomb all on your own?" I asked archly. "Excellent. Thank you, Captain Testosterone. I suppose we can all go home, folks." There was some laughter from the squad around me.

"You know that I can do this," Aberdeen seethed.

"Negative, I'm the commander here," I answered sharply. "Our smartest strategy is creating a diversion and you're it. Make the enemy think that we're sending our full force through the car park, but I repeat, do *not* advance."

"Understood," Aberdeen's voice came back. It was clear that he was pissed off.

"Crowley, you're using Aberdeen as bait," Maeve muttered uneasily from beside me. Her magnificent pair of wings, dusted in earthy browns and ivory streaks, were folded neatly behind her like a cloak. "That's risky *and* ruthless."

"We have to think rationally if we're going to pull a victory here," I said, keeping one eye on the map of the complex. "This way Aberdeen gets some action while still having some cover, instead of risking his entire unit going commando looking for that bomb. He's the best shot at providing a distraction to give us an opening. Fair?"

A lot of my teammates had tight friendships and alliances between them already, while I was the outsider. I had to show them I was decisive, but it was also important to show them I cared about the team and group consensus more than my own victory.

I liked Maeve. She was level-headed and mature. Most Shadows wouldn't think of speaking their minds to their human commander. Maeve was a harpy, with the legs and wings of a bird but the body and face of a teenage girl. She wore a pointed cowl of white feathers. Beneath it, tawny hair spilled down both sides of her face in long, wind-swept sheets, framing features that were sharp and intelligent.

Maeve hesitated. I waited, the adrenaline causing my fingers to drum against the rifle. I thought through the multiple contingencies for my strategy, checking and rechecking that the one I was committing us to was the most promising.

It occurred to me that Captain Morgaine could probably hear everything that we were saying, monitoring the progression of the simulation incredibly closely. It was bound to determine for her who was the dead weight who should be removed from the class, and who she may spend extra time on to cultivate as the potential star students.

Finally, Maeve nodded. That was all the mandate I needed to commence the operation. It was time to dance.

"Thank you," I said. "Shall we, then?"

I still couldn't believe how realistic this simulation was. I had to consistently remind myself that we weren't in a mall fighting for our actual lives, because every tiny detail of the world around me felt so incredibly realistic. In reality we were two groups of Shadows and humans rambling through a maze in a warehouse wearing oversized virtual reality goggles, and we probably looked utterly ridiculous.

Every Shadow had an individual power that made them unique, from poison spines to being able to create and control flame. There was nothing magical about it, just something that was born into them. Many of my class-mates had grown up knowing all about how the powers of different Shadows could be used to maximum advantage in the battlefield. Most Shadows discovered their power in adolescence. I'd learnt that Sephy, for example, had yet to figure out what her own one was.

I still knew so little about Shadows, yet somehow I was the one they were counting on to lead our team to victory. Morgaine sure was a sucker for any chance to watch me fail.

Another hope of this kind of exercise was that you might discover who your counterpart was during the train-ing. The need to communicate seamlessly with your team-mates meant that some individuals found themselves telepathically hearing their counterpart in the field.

Aberdeen had sighed when it was announced I was the one giving the orders. The bright side of having him on my team was that instead of being up against him, I had a serious asset. The major downside was trying to make Aberdeen freaking listen to me. I was learning quickly that Aberdeen was the most competitive bonehead I'd ever met. It was as if he couldn't imagine a more terrible fate than losing. He had an overwhelming need to be the best.

This simulation actually reminded me of when I had been in my early teens. To test the efficacy of my training, Mother had enrolled me in a local professional paintball tournament. I'd met my team and had only been granted two minutes to convince a total group of strangers much older than me to both like me *and* to trust me as their captain. All the while Mother had been watching remotely, assessing me. In my childhood, *everything* had been a test... and all of it had been leading to this.

I wanted to become a knight to protect people. Not to be an agent of destruction like Aberdeen, or Morgaine, according to rumours of her own bloody past.

Gunfire erupted, piercing the air with deafening cracks. Ten of my people stormed up the mall's escalators. They took the central approach, their weapons blazing. Shadows traded spitting firecrackers and spinning orbs of water in a diabolical exchange. The guns we carried were all part of the simulation, incapable of actually wounding. The Shadows' powers, however, could leave seriously nasty burns and ensure you were swiftly carted to the medical bay.

The defenders were holed up on the highest level, in the food court. Somewhere up there was the bomb they were guarding, but if my people tried to push through the centre it was going to be a meat grinder approach; at the very best, a pyrrhic victory. Plus, something told me this whole scenario was to test how we handled the minute decisions in battle scenarios which felt unwinnable.

I would ensure the centre route was reinforced, but there were multiple other paths to the top of the mall. Each an opportunity for us, but also a target for the defenders.

Aberdeen had Bentley in his squad, a mountain parrot who could control gales of wind and had a strange penchant for wearing a Viking helmet. Aberdeen also had

Grub, a large green larva with the ability to create sticky webs trapping anyone who strayed into them.

There were plenty of columns and cars to use for cover in the multi-level car park that led all the way up to the side of the building. Plenty of room for Aberdeen and the others to manoeuvre. Aberdeen could run circles around the defenders to his heart's content, with all of that flipping, diving and shooting action hero crap that he loved.

I considered for a moment.

"Come on," I said to Maeve beside me. "We're taking Cobalt Squad up the service stairwell."

She looked at me shrewdly.

"Isn't that just another chokepoint where Sephy can make us bleed?"

"If Aberdeen manages to pull their troops away that should help us carve out a path to locate and defuse the bomb. Move out!"

I was surrounded by a motley gang of armed human teenagers, an oversized spider, a raccoon with metal spines and a short tree that walked on its roots. Together our unlikely squad made for the highest floor where Sephy's team were camped out, my heart in my mouth the entire way.

I felt more conscious than ever of my limp, but I went as fast as I could to keep up with the others. I didn't care what they might think, I was determined not to let it hold me back. This was my one chance to show I could lead. I couldn't let them down, or Morgaine. Otherwise my career as a knight would be over before it began.

My earpiece crackled as another squad called in.

"Elsa, this is Aberdeen, over."

I pinched the bridge of my nose. Aberdeen enjoyed showing a blatant disregard for using the correct deference to me as his commander. I suppose being compared to the ice queen from *Frozen* was an improvement as nicknames went. As the tall, pale girl, I'd normally been referred to at my last school as Jack Skellington from *The Nightmare Before Christmas*.

"Read you loud and clear, how goes the diversion?"

"Eight enemy units already eliminated. Come on, I thought you *wanted* to give me a challenge."

Eight? Well done, Aberdeen!

I knew Aberdeen was good, but I hadn't expected him to eliminate even half that many this quickly. He was like a snake that could strike with terrifying power. Frankly, it was also a little disconcerting. I tried to not act too impressed. It would be interesting to push Aberdeen more next time, to find the limits of his frankly ridiculous skills.

"We're going to keep heading up through the parking lot, then cut through them on the top level to find the bomb," he informed me. I could hear his satisfied smirk.

"Oh no, you're not," I rebuked him sharply. "Right now the defenders will be sending multiple units toward you, thinking that you're our main thrust. That clears the way for our other squads and that was your job, but you need to dig in for the forces coming your way. Play the defence."

"That's absurd," Aberdeen said, his temper flaring. "You're just turning us into sitting ducks, when my squad could win this entire thing for you."

"Aberdeen…"

"Without us, you don't have a chance."

"This is a team exercise," I said, my tone dangerous. "Do *not* advance."

I could practically hear his scowl.

"Forget it. We have a shot and we're taking it."

I sighed inwardly. Rash, Aberdeen. Very rash.

"This is to the rest of Gold Squad," I commanded, gritting my teeth, "do *not* follow Aberdeen. Hold your position and prepare for incoming forces. Grub, you're the new squad captain."

There was a moment of hesitation. Everyone worshipped or feared Aberdeen, but Morgaine had designated me as commander. My word was law.

"Yes, Commander," Grub finally answered, uncomfortable. *"We'll keep them occupied."*

Satisfied for now, I checked in with the rest of our people. Everyone was in position at various chokepoints and service access points, the defenders still attempting to hold them. It was all proceeding as planned.

You've got this, Crowley. Now to move the bulk of our force into the food court to clean up any stragglers. Then we sweep the area to locate and deactivate the bomb.

Our own squad came to the top of the narrow service stairway. My squad-mates closed in to protect me.

There was a hush, all of us knowing that on the other side of that door there may be people waiting to bombard us with lightning bolts, bullets, etc., the minute we announced our presence. Fun. We just had to hope Aberdeen had drawn enough of them away with his loud shenanigans in the parking garage. It all relied on fooling Sephy that the garage was the main angle we were attacking from. Had she taken the bait?

"On your command," Maeve winked from beside me, raising her rifle in her talons.

This was it. This was my chance to prove Morgaine wrong about me. It was time to show her everything I had.

I exhaled. "Now!"

10

We charged out into the food court, firing at the enemy. A prehistoric deinonychus sprinted past me across the linoleum, leaping to take down the closest member of the other team. Just another completely normal day at the Academy.

Aiming down the sights of my rifle I fired, eliminating one of Sephy's soldiers from the simulation, and then another. It was quieter up here than expected, which was only good news for us. Most of Sephy's team must have gone to take care of Aberdeen and his squad, and it looked like Sephy had gone with them. She'd placed her bet on me putting all of my troops into the garage approach, just as we were hoping.

Most of Sephy's teammates on this floor were at the central escalators, shooting downward to stop our people's advance. They weren't expecting to suddenly be attacked from the side, and they quickly folded under Cobalt Squad's onslaught. From the perspective of our virtual reality head-sets, they vanished from sight completely when they were shot. Unfortunately, it meant we didn't get to watch the students sigh and slump off toward the exits in disgrace. Now we just had to locate the bomb before it detonated… and before Sephy could realise that the parking lot was just a decoy. Once she did, she would send her full force back at us to finish us off.

"Check the shops down that end for the bomb," I ordered our people coming up the central escalators, "start from the four corners and work your way in. Be on the lookout for enemy units we've missed. You folks, let's check out the shops near the bridge. Let's go!"

We were *so* close.

"*Elsa?*" Aberdeen's voice crackled through my earpiece.

"Where the hell were you, building a snowman? I thought you'd been eliminated." Secretly, I was relieved to hear his voice. In the background I could hear screaming and gunfire, then a laser whip humming and cracking, followed by a banshee's shriek. "Report."

"*I'm pinned down in the garage, I count twelve of them. Look, something just happened to Sephy's team. Their strategies have gotten even smarter, they've changed formation. They wiped out the rest of Gold Squad. Now a whole lot just made a beeline back to the food court.*"

I cursed silently. Sephy had caught onto my deceit? How? The clock was counting down closer and closer to us all being blown sky-high. If the rest of Sephy's people made it here we'd be fighting for our lives and we wouldn't have time to complete the mission.

"*This is your instructor,*" Morgaine's voice came through my earpiece, surprising me. "*I have relieved Sephy of commanding duties and I am taking charge of the defenders. Defending team, you will all be reporting to me.*"

She couldn't be serious! That was madness, absolute madness. Sephy was already putting up a more than formidable defence. I'd been highly impressed with her considering I hadn't thought Sephy was that passionate about the family business.

I tried to determine what this surprise change of events meant. The irrational part of my brain couldn't help but angrily fixate on the fact that Morgaine had done this because she had some bone to pick with me. Could her ego really not handle a young upstart possibly succeeding in their first simulation? Did someone as accomplished as herself really have to step in to teach a teenager a lesson?

Suddenly I understood why the other team had started racing back to our location. As Morgaine had been watching the match, she must have had complete knowledge of where all the troops were on the map. But surely she couldn't *act* on that knowledge? That was impossibly unfair. But it would be foolish to rely on any notions of fairness. It was simply what was happening.

This was almost over for all of us. Morgaine wasn't worried about winning with minimum casualties. Instead she'd ambush us with all the bodies she still had to slow us down at any cost. She knew we didn't have time to locate and defuse the bomb. There were only three minutes on the clock until... boom.

Someone cried suddenly through my earpiece. I checked the number of the channel.

"Aberdeen? Aberdeen!"

"*Argh! I'm hit! They're seconds away from you. I tried to slow them down but they knew I was coming somehow. NO, NO, NO, demonyo ka!*" His scream of fury cut suddenly as he was booted from the simulation.

I swore. Aberdeen had tried to take on the armed host coming back toward us, without any backup. Kudos, man, but where exactly was the line between courage and delusion?

I checked the electronic clock in the top right of my vision for what must have been the millionth time. We had two minutes left before the defenders won automatically when the bomb went off. It was going to be close.

Time for something of a gamble.

A short bridge of steel and glass connected the mall to the parking building across the road. It was the path that Sephy's team would be coming from any moment.

It's not Sephy's team anymore, I told myself. It's Morgaine's, and I'm not going to give her the satisfaction of winning.

"Throw everything you have at the bridge!" I yelled.

"Now?" Maeve said, not hiding her surprise. "There's no one there to shoot at!"

"Light that bridge up!" I repeated. "Maeve, use your hurricane power. Zaevon, you have shiny spines that explode or something, is that right?"

"Well, technically yes, but biologically I'd describe it as more of a..."

"Fire *everything* on my signal."

"Even the rocket launcher?" a green monkey Shadow called Taggi asked, her green tentacles holding up the weapon hopefully.

"Especially the rocket launcher, Taggi."

"Oh, good!" She sparkled with joy.

"*Everything* we have?" another guy from my team called Victor asked, incredulous. "What if the bomb is in one of those shops beside the bridge? If we hit it by accident, we'll blow us all to hell!"

"Just before we cleared out the squad here, I saw them looking automatically toward the other end of this floor," I explained quickly. "All their focus was on guarding something down that way, toward the supermarket."

"You're basing this on a *look?*" Victor demanded.

"It's a calculation."

"It's intuition, and you could be wrong."

"Listen, if Morgaine's people come back across that bridge to take us out there's no way that we can find the bomb in time."

The air suddenly came alive, bullets streaking overhead. We all dove madly for cover, overturning a table to cluster behind.

A slight complication. They were shooting from the other side of the bridge, which meant they were about to cross it imminently.

"Team, give cover-fire!" I ordered the rest of our people. Maeve locked gazes with me as we crouched behind our sorry excuse for cover. Her eyes were a deep, glinting gold, like polished amber, and they assessed me carefully. Then Maeve nodded.

"Make sure to land them this side of the bridge," I shouted at them. "We want to eliminate them from the game, not commit murder. In three..."

Every student was wrapped in protective armour and goggles for the mission, and our weapons were as much an illusion as the rest of the simulation. If we played this right, the other team would at most only be a little battered, scratched, and perhaps a little singed. I'd done the maths too, and all the students on the other team were accounted for. There wouldn't be anyone hiding out in those shops beside the bridge.

"...two..."

Maeve spun a miniature hurricane into existence. Zaevon arched his back and his spines glowed white-hot, emitting a strange purple aura. Little Taggi risked leaving her cover to balance the length of her rocket launcher on the top of our overturned table. She aimed down the barrel, thrilled.

"...one!" I commanded.

Maeve screamed and launched her hurricane toward the bridge in a spinning gale. We had to fight not to be pulled into the vortex. Blazing white spines fired from Zaevon's back, spinning toward the bridge with mad purple light... and Taggi gleefully fired her rocket.

There was a roar like no other, followed by a howling shockwave that smashed us backward along with our flimsy table. We cowered, and when the light faded I rose to squint at the bridge.

It was collapsing. The only connection between the two sides of the mall was now a flaming husk of warped metal, glass and flame, which collapsed down onto the fake street below. Flames tore at either side of the mall. The shops just before the bridge had been entirely wiped out in the eruption, and I felt a shiver of awe at what some of these Shadow's powers could achieve. Even if some of Morgaine's forces had avoided elimination, and I doubted it, there was no way that they could cross over to us now.

It may be a simulation that we were in, but I allowed myself to have a little swoop of vengeful satisfaction, a personal fantasy fulfilled as we watched the destruction of the 'acolytes.'

"Excellent work!" I congratulated everyone. It wasn't over yet. Checking the clock, I experienced another burst of adrenaline.

"We only have two minutes!" I shouted. "Everyone who's still active, join in on the sweep of the shops! Locate that bomb, move fast!"

My troops were still systemically eliminating all the possible hidey holes. At least the bomb blowing out five of the stores had eliminated some of the hiding-place possibilities. I was glad I hadn't been wrong about that one.

I ran with Maeve and the others to search the remaining shops.

One minute.

"All squads, keep sweeping," I ordered. Incensed, I swept a Thai restaurant, but I couldn't find anywhere that a large explosive might be stashed away. "Does anyone have eyes on it? Check for any areas out the back, a door that might have been missed..." Something else occurred to me. "Anyone in the bookshop, see if they've blocked any doors with the bookshelves!" It seemed like a Sephy kind of idea, and she was the one who had chosen the spot to hide the explosive.

Thirty seconds.

Ten.

"Commander, we've got it!" a voice suddenly shouts. "You were right, there was a bookshelf hiding the ..."

"Fantastic," I panted, "DISARM IT!"

The electronic clock froze at *0.02* remaining. We'd stolen victory just two seconds away from all dying a fiery and humiliating fictional death.

I smiled, feeling a savage rush of triumph at beating Morgaine. I'd just won my first ever simulation, and against the teacher herself.

I did it. I really did it.

Our team screamed euphorically and I laughed quietly to myself before the feed went to black. I removed my goggles, eyes blinking as they readjusted to reality. The shopping mall dropped away to reveal the ruggedness of the concrete floors and barrels around us. We were back in the training warehouse on the Academy grounds, the mission dissipating.

"Beginner's luck," I heard Victor mutter, who apparently could not be pleased under any circumstances. But he was quickly drowned out by the other more supportive voices.

"Freaking amazing, Crowley!" Taggi hollered. "You beat the Bloody Queen herself!"

I seriously doubted that Morgaine had been trying her hardest, or that I could have conquered her if she had been in control of the enemy forces from the start. This had been a test. But even when she threw everything at us to foil our chances of defusing the bomb, we'd held firm.

"Hey, arsehole!"

Oh, hello again.

"*Arsehole* is not a Disney character," I frowned. "Unless it's one of the new ones?" I turned to see Aberdeen toss his goggles aside. He strode toward me, wrathful, as if he was about to spit fire. He was radiating palpable heat. All of the students around us, our team and Morgaine's, gathered to watch the spectacle.

"You took away my whole squad!" he yelled.

"Uh-huh," I said patiently.

"Why didn't you give me support?" he demanded. "I could have been an asset, but you removed all of my backup."

Here it was, I thought, my anger suddenly rising. Strike three. This was Riley Aberdeen's true face. All of that coy playfulness and smirking cunning, the smooth manners of court, stripped away to reveal someone who was vain, selfish and would burn everything to the ground over something so tiny.

I constantly heard everyone in the school gushing

over him in the hallways: *'Riley Aberdeen invented bone structure...'* Honestly, I was sick of it. Anybody who looked like Aberdeen, anyone that intensely handsome, just had to ask for it with a smile and people would fall over their knees to give him whatever he wanted. So why did he feel this paranoid need to prove himself?

"You deliberately disobeyed me," I replied coldly. "We won as a team, that's what matters."

"Is your ego really that fragile?" I asked.

His nostrils flared. His gaze was merciless.

"You want to say that again? I dare you."

"You're the one making a scene because you didn't get your little player-of-the-day trophy," I said acidly.

"You think you're so different?" he scoffed.

I prickled at the accusation.

"You think we're the *same?*" I exclaimed.

"You did this for yourself, not for your team. You could have used me to sneak behind enemy lines and defuse that bomb without even getting caught. Instead, you lost soldiers in a front-on assault so you could show yourself off to Captain Holloway."

"Aberdeen, chill. We're *all* doing this for the glory, and that play with the bridge was genius," Maeve said pointedly, coming to my defence. "Crowley thought outside the box, and she used the environment to her advantage. Nobody's ever meant to win the first simulation, you know that. But she pulled it off. Honestly, it was cool just to be a part of it."

Aberdeen looked to Maeve for some reason, and he clamped his mouth shut. Though I could still see the fire raging behind his eyes with the sweet things he'd like to say.

Interesting. So, he'd listen to Sephy and Maeve, yet he hated me.

"You're talented, but not half as much as you think you are," he said finally.

"You think I'm talented?" I said, genuinely stunned by the admission. "Stop it, you'll make me blush."

"That was some fast thinking!" Sephy interrupted, pouncing into the conversation.

"Thanks, Seph," I grinned at her. "Hope you weren't one of the ones we took out when we blew up the bridge."

"That might have singed my whiskers a little bit," she admitted nonchalantly.

I looked back at Aberdeen. He was absolutely glowering at me. I just sighed inwardly.

"Well, well! A prodigy walks among us!" came Captain Morgaine's voice. I rolled my eyes, and Sephy hid her snort of laughter at my reaction. Turning, I saw Morgaine striding toward us, starting a slow clap.

I frowned. The sarcastic slow clap was meant to be *my* thing.

"Pleased with yourself, Crowley?"

"Rather, Captain, if I do say so myself," I answered, snapping to attention with the others.

She glowered at me.

"Is something wrong, Captain?" I asked steadily.

"Did you even pause to think before you took out that bridge?"

I felt my cheeks burning. I told myself that this wasn't personal. I wasn't about to pull an Aberdeen and let my ego spin out of control.

"Of course, Captain," I ground out, trying not to glare.

"Two words for you, Crowley," Morgaine thundered. "Innocent bystanders."

I blinked, stunned.

"The simulation didn't include any civilians," I said uncertainly.

"Was that ever explicitly stated? Or did you just assume that because you didn't have a visual?" she countered. "Seventeen civilians were taking shelter in the shops nearest to the bridge. Their path was blocked by Shadows' Eve and they couldn't escape the mall."

My stomach dropped sickeningly. It might just have been a simulation, but it had all felt so real. I'd assumed because I hadn't seen anyone that the mall had been fully evacuated.

Seventeen civilians, and I'd killed them all.

I felt monstrous.

I think Morgaine expected me to say something, but I just stood there in silence, the blood draining from my cheeks. She snorted.

"If this had been a real scenario, Crowley, you would have just murdered innocents in cold blood."

Deva turned to regard us, all the students quailing under the great bird's steely gaze.

"I understand that not everyone values non-Praetory lives as I do," she said, addressing the class herself. Her voice was like rich velvet. "But do not forget, by blowing up that bridge Crowley risked tearing away the Brilliance stone field and exposing the nature of our world to the everyday public. That, I think you'll agree, would be an unacceptable cost."

I felt cold all over. I was still reeling in shock.

"So, congratulations," Morgaine glared at me. But there was something else behind her stare. Something... troubled? "You've won the unwinnable scenario. I hope it has been worth it."

. . .

I headed back to the dorm to fit in some study before fourth period. I was so preoccupied with the virtual war crimes I'd just committed that I nearly tripped over a manticore wearing roller skates.

Sephy was sprawled dramatically across the hallway floor, her usually well-groomed golden-tawny fur slightly ruffled, limbs akimbo. Bright pink roller skates were strapped not just to her hind paws, but also to the knuckles of her monkey-like arms. She was attempting, unsuccessfully, to remove them.

"Strange," I commented with a wink, "how sights like this are becoming way more normalised for me."

Her lapis-lazuli eyes darted toward me with relief, framed by her large tufted ears, which twitched in mild embarrassment. Behind her, her long, sinuous tail — lined in those quill-like spines — lay curled like a question mark.

"Thank God, looks like my lucky day," Sephy beamed. "I've been stuck in these things for ages."

"Need some help?"

"Much appreciated," she said demurely, proffering a limb. She must have gotten someone to put the skates on her, because they were on both her feet *and* her hands. "*Whoever you are, I have always relied on the kindness of strangers.*"

That quote won a smile out of me.

"You weren't lying," I said, "you really are a fan of *A Streetcar Named Desire.*"

As I removed her skates, she studied my prosthetic in open curiosity.

"What's it like, having one?" Sephy asked, tilting her head inquisitively. "Sorry. Is that rude to ask?"

"It's quite difficult to use at first," I said evenly. I angled the prosthetic to show it off to effect. "It feels like you're walking on a boot with a ridiculously thick sole."

"Can you *feel* it?"

"Only when I'm running, or if I stomp down with it, when there's higher impact. Then I can feel the ricochet through my body. Since it doesn't have any toes I have to stabilise myself with my hip, since it's an above-knee prosthetic."

"How's the stump feel? Does it hurt?"

I pursed my lips. Personally I'd always felt there should be a sexier word than *'stump.'*

"It can get hot and sweaty. There are layers over it and sometimes it can feel like wearing a wet suit to be honest. When it fits, it really fits, like it's a part of me. On the other hand, if there's like the slightest kink in the sock it feels like there's these weird pressures there."

"Sort of like a princess and the pea situation."

"Ah, so you know your human fairy tales too. Yeah. Also, the volume of the stump actually changes throughout the day. So the prosthetic feels different in the morning and evening, depending what the temperature and weather is doing."

"Wowww," Sephy said, apparently awed.

Oddly, my leg—or lack thereof—wasn't an uncomfortable topic with her. She seemed to have zero judgement, but I still didn't like being defined by my injury and I didn't want to talk about it any further. Sephy seemed to catch onto that.

"Everyone's talking about your performance in the simulations," she stated, manoeuvring the conversation with great tact. "You know they've started to call you *'Our Undefeated Queen?'*"

Flattered, I made a show of considering the new title.

"It's not particularly poetic."

Sephy rolled her eyes, but then examined me carefully.

"They're not wrong. You're good, you know."

"A queen, apparently," I agreed, chipper.

She scuffed me over the head with her tail. Thankfully she'd flattened the spines so that it amounted to a slap with a bundle of twigs. But I still flinched as the spines rattled against me.

"Hey!"

"No one likes boasting, Crowley, it doesn't become you. I prefer you all humble and mysterious."

"Trust me, I'm not perfect," I said darkly, thinking of the civilian casualties in training.

"It was your first ever simulation," Sephy comforted me. "This is what training is for. So we don't make mistakes."

Training or not, I personally felt like I would be haunted by that for a long time. It had all been so real in the moment, as if our lives were really at risk, as if my decisions had real consequences.

"Besides," Sephy snorted, "the scenario makes no sense. If Shadows' Eve are going to act like some suicidal cult that's one thing, but if they're planning to blow themselves up along with the bomb, why have a timer on it?" She rolled her eyes. "It's hardly preparing us for a real-world situation."

"So…" I said, not at all keen to linger on the subject. "Um, Aberdeen mentioned you were adopted by humans? What was that like?"

Sephy fought a smile.

"Subtle topic change there. Well-played." She acquiesced though. "With my parents, I lucked out. They're brilliant, kind people. But... they have big expectations of me. They're a Marquess and a Marquis, and there are a lot of people who don't think a Shadow should be able to inherit a title like that. It can be... exhausting, feeling I have to prove everyone wrong."

That was interesting. I understood that Shadows were treated more as servants and bodyguards, but Sephy's parentage meant that Sephy's family actually far outranked my own. I suppose that constant pressure from parents didn't discriminate—it just slapped a different family crest on your guilt.

"My parents gifted my egg along with a lot of others through a Rip that opened sixteen years ago," Sephy continued. "A temporary tear between our worlds. So I'm first-generation, you could say. My biological parents gave me up. They made that sacrifice, knowing they'd have to spend their lives without me, because they believed I was destined for something important over in this world."

"So you never knew them?" I whispered.

I tried to imagine the weight of that, and the sense of emptiness that would leave in your identity. At least I knew my father. I knew what it meant to love him, and be loved by him. Sephy's parents had given up her egg to be raised in a strange realm, before even seeing their child hatch.

That was another thing it was hard to get my head around: that every Shadow hatched from an egg, not just the ones who appeared insectoid or reptilian. But I suppose it was hardly the most interesting thing about them.

"Your parents would be proud," I said softly. "Of who you've grown into."

Sephy smiled. There were tears in her eyes, but I didn't think she wanted me to notice, so I pretended not to.

"So wait, if you came over here as an egg... you've lived

your entire life contained in places like the Academy?" I asked her incredulously. "Concealed away from the general human public?"

"That's accurate."

"That must have been lonely."

Sephy shrugged.

"Wait, so you've never really gotten to walk down Cuba Street and seen all the buskers?" I exclaimed. "You've never leaned over the Bucket fountain, waiting until the buckets all fill to the brim and come crashing down, splashing water all over your nose?"

"You make Wellington sound really fun," she sighed with longing.

"Aw, and the food! The *food*," I gushed. "*Crêpes a Go Go* is this little hole in the wall place, and you can get the best sweet and savoury crepes. And *Midnight Runner*, that's the best place. They do these giant chunks of gourmet chocolate cake." I smiled nostalgically. "I used to want to come off as edgy and arty, and I thought hanging out there would achieve that. I had no idea there was a secret passage hidden there, of course. They put insane amounts of cream in your coffee and marshmallow that turns all molten and just melts into it. It's cholesterol hell, a heart attack in a cup."

"Now you're just torturing me, Crowley."

I laughed.

"I'm sorry, I'm sorry. But don't you ever want to, you know, feel the wind in your fur... so to speak?"

"I can feel that here. But I know what you mean. Sure, sometimes I want to stretch, to be able to walk around free. I even wonder what my real home is like. But I can choose to see this place as a cage, or as the home that keeps me safe. My family is here, and I'll do anything for my family."

"My mother always kept me insulated from the outside world," I offered, trying to relate. "The walls of our home felt a lot like a prison compound." I sighed inwardly, chiding myself. At least I'd been able to walk on streets among other humans down Cuba street and breathe the air of an outside world. I'd been able to feel the sun on my back in the botanic garden without needing an illusion to hide who I really was from the rest of the world.

"There were other Shadows around to play with. But I grew up raised by a human couple, watching your human movies. I was shown scraps of my own culture, things taken from my own world, but they were only trifles. I don't really feel like... I have a real connection to it." Sephy inspected her monkey-like hand. "You know... sometimes I feel like a human just stuck in the wrong body," she confessed, and it was the first thing I'd ever heard from Sephy that came close to shame. There was an aching in the way she said it.

"I'm really sorry you feel that way," I murmured. "It's just surprising to hear. I mean, you're so confident, and you must be the most popular student in school."

"Yes, because I've learnt to act less like a Shadow. I've learnt how to talk without humans feeling uncomfortable. And the very fact that my popularity despite being a Shadow is a talking point tells you everything. I look amazing, obviously. But sometimes it would be nice if I didn't have to worry about looking like a porcupine cat, and I could just focus on eating chocolate and dating cute people.

'I know that I'm very lucky though, to be adopted into a family that has more money, instead of somewhere like Quietfire, like other Shadow families are." Sephy hesitated. "Um, Crowley?"

"Yes?"

"There's something I've been meaning to ask you."

There were tears in her eyes again. I opened my mouth to apologise, feeling awful that I may have asked her things that were too personal.

"Oh my God, I'm sorry," Sephy muttered. She looked angry at herself. "I hate crying."

"No, *I'm* sorry! What..."

"It's just, I've been meaning to ask you about it for ages. When Sir Kipling and his soldiers took you away to the Governor, I thought for sure something *terrible* was going to happen to you. You'd risked your own life to save mine and... you barely knew me. I thought I'd gotten you killed, or at least imprisoned. But then... somehow... you just walked out unmarked, as if nothing had happened to you at all. How are you still standing here?" she burst out.

Startled, I felt a burn of shame. I hadn't even realised that Sephy had been wracked with worry that I may have died or been sentenced to prison just for standing up for her.

"I mean, thank God you were all right," she added pompously, quickly regaining her composure, "or I would have been livid." But then she scrutinised me, a darker, more intense curiosity seeming to bloom to life beneath those glimmering eyes. "How did you manage it?" she whispered.

It was my turn to avoid her gaze.

"Governor Blackmore is a childhood friend," I confessed. "I hadn't seen her in years, though."

Sephy smiled with an expression that was hard to read.

"Well, well. You continue to be full of surprises."

I slid the popcorn into the microwave as Sephy flicked the TV on, her fingers tapping eagerly at the remote. I wasn't much for screen time, but she was determined to convert me with her curated list of streaming obsessions.

A different thought tugged at me: was Aberdeen home? After what had happened in the simulation, the idea of facing him made my stomach knot. But the silence told me no. Without his usual soundtrack of moody, 1930s-style jazz covers of *'Mad World'* and *'Habits,'* the apartment felt mercifully empty.

"Hey, Sephy," I said suddenly. "I've never seen your room."

I was about to say that I've never seen a *Shadow's* room before and I was curious, but that sounded slightly racist, and I wasn't sure how else to approach the subject.

"Oh, okay," she said awkwardly. She seemed uncharacteristically shy. Embarrassed, even? "Then... would you like to see my room?"

"Yes, I would. I mean, you've seen mine."

"Fine. You're so odd sometimes, Crowley," she said, rolling her eyes.

It turned out Sephy's personal quarters was a lot like any teenage girl's room. It was more mature, more clean and tidy though. She had a collection of magazines and a laptop sitting on her bed. Some Shadows in the school had keyboards personalised for their appendages, but Sephy's monkey fingers seemed to work just fine on a human laptop. I noted the old-timey movie posters she had up on her walls, including *'An American in Paris'* and *'Some Like it Hot.'*

My attention was drawn to a wooden chest sticking out from underneath her bed.

"Do you want to tell me what that is?"

"Oh, this?" she said, surprised. She looked down as if she was just seeing it, and nodded awkwardly. "Huh. Yeah."

She drew it out for me and placed it on the bed. The intricate carvings in the wood brought to mind the ceremonial Shadow meeting house that stood at the year of the Academy grounds. The chest was coloured with different dyes, a Shadow world decorative style. Together the intricate etchings formed scenes that looked as if they were out of some kind of Shadow world myth. The carvings seemed to be alive. It was as if they pulsed.

"This is so beautiful," I said, marvelling at it. "Where's it from?"

"My father gave it to me. He loves all that old Shadow world stuff."

"You think the world of your Father. So why's this under the bed?"

Sephy shrugged, embarrassed.

I remembered what she said about not feeling a connection to it.

"What does it mean?" I asked, studying the chest in fascination. "If that's not... rude to ask."

"Um, okay," said Sephy, scoffing awkwardly. "Well, this side of the box represents darkness. The other side, light."

"Ooh. Interesting." I investigated the carvings in wonder. "This is kind of like our creation myths, isn't it?"

"Not entirely. Darkness isn't something evil for us. Just another half of a whole."

"Like... the light keeps darkness in balance?"

"No. Like..." Sephy's nose twitched, her expression dreamy suddenly. "Think of when you bury a seed, underground. All is darkness. But it's a fertile, nourishing darkness, before the plant breaks into the light of the world. It's the dark of the womb as well as the dark of the final rest." She looked embarrassed suddenly of her heritage. She turned away. "Anyway..."

I found myself deeply intrigued. From everything I'd learned, Sephy was a model daughter, loyal and dutiful, aside from the side-line of eccentric shenanigans she pursued for her own amusement. What was it like to be a Shadow who had never seen their own world?

"May I?" I asked.

Sephy nodded her permission.

Opening the chest, I stared in at the contents in awe. It was a large egg, a vivid tawny shade speckled with sparrow-egg blue, moonlight caught in sand. The egg had clearly been broken once, because the fracture lines were visible. It looked as if it had been lovingly glued back together. I shivered, then realised why, staring down at it in awe. It was Sephy's egg.

When we finally returned to the lounge, we came to an abrupt stop. There was an unexpected visitor sitting cross-legged on the couch. We hadn't even heard her come in.

Sitting on our couch was Captain Morgaine Holloway.

She surveyed us, seated on her cape. It prevented her from having to touch the couch, which was in a predictable state for student accommodation.Seeing her in our personal space was jarring, like a lightning strike. Deva stood beside Morgaine, dignified. Her hawk eyes scrutinised us, her indigo crest-feathers on display.

"Captain," Sephy said, dipping into a curtsy— impressive, for a feline. Her manners were immaculate. "To what do we owe this honour?"

"At ease, Miss Nekomata," Morgaine reassured her, surveying us with a slight frown.

As Sephy relaxed her pose to fall back in line with me, I heard her mutter less smoothly under her breath:

"Um, Crowley? We have a teacher in our apartment."

I still hadn't spoken, and there was a pregnant silence between myself and Morgaine. Sephy looked between the two of us in polite astonishment, eyes wide.

"Have we done something wrong requiring disciplinary measures?" Sephy ventured.

"Not at all, Nekomata," Morgaine replied, not unkindly. "This matter is just between myself and Crowley."

"If it's all right with you," I said, "Sephy can stay. I trust her." I looked sideways at Sephy. "Besides, I fear that otherwise she won't be able to handle the suspense."

"Well then," Morgaine said reasonably. There was a notable absence of her usual anger, as if she'd left that entirely behind in class along with her coaching persona. Instead there was something enigmatic about the way she was looking at me. "Why don't you tell us what this is about, Crowley? Since you're the one who summoned me."

It seemed like Sephy was about to explode.

A student summoning a teacher? I could imagine her thinking. *It's not done! Captain Holloway will defenestrate you! Why would you do something this positively loopy, Crowley?*

I walked until I was standing directly in front of the famous, brooding warrior who had forced me to suffer again and again through our combat sessions.

"You know why I've summoned you here," I said softly. "Or you wouldn't have come."

11

"Tell me. Why weren't you there that night?" My voice cut sharp as glass.

Morgaine didn't flinch, but her eyes locked on mine, calculating. She was trying to decide how much I already knew.

Across the room, Sephy pounced into an armchair with a bowl of popcorn, freshly nuked. She didn't speak. Just watched us as if she considered herself lucky to have a front row ticket to whatever was happening.

Morgaine seemed to make a judgement call. She shed her cool bearing like a cloak, as if it were all an act.

Suddenly there were tears in her eyes. Her features were full of pain.

Then Morgaine, who I'd associated so far with always being proud, scathing and dangerous, managed to surprise me further. She knelt down and bowed her head before me. When she spoke, her voice was full of many things. Fear, guilt and grief... but ultimately a kind of resigned acceptance.

"Lady Crowley," Morgaine whispered. "I have wronged you."

Sephy's jaw dropped. I stared at Morgaine in shock. I'd summoned her here on a hunch, unsure how to understand the information I'd discovered. But the genuine emotion of her response threw me off-balance.

"You've wronged me because you served my father," I said slowly, searching her eyes for confirmation. "Peter Crowley."

Sephy's eyes widened.

"Yes," Morgaine confessed. I realised she was waiting for my permission to rise, so I motioned for her to do so. Everything felt surreal. Slowly she took her seat again, looking uneasy. "I was just a teenager straight out of this Academy myself when I met Count Crowley," she confessed. "Deva and I were the best in our year, and your father offered for me to be his knight. The personal knight of a Count, at eighteen! As much as I wanted to taste blood and battle in the field, it was clear that my career would be made instantly. It was a great honour. Eventually your father released us from service amicably. We became the Potentate's favourite instruments, eliminating his enemies before they even saw us coming, and leading missions he'd rather no one knew about. Our subtle influence kept pushing world events in the Praetory's favour.

When I returned home, I reconnected with your father. Nothing could ever truly end the bond between a knight and her lord. As I saw it, his life would always be my duty, even if now we were both respected battle commanders in our own right. And your father was kind enough to have treated me like a friend for as long as I'd known him. That was the kind of man he was. At that time... we had conversations. Many." Morgaine hesitated.

"What kind of conversations?" I prompted. "What was my father's state of mind at the time?"

"We discussed the Potentate," Morgaine answered. "And the Praetory. Count Crowley was feeling... disillusioned, you could say. We both were. Still, I was uncomfortable with the direction of some of our conversations. It is often unsavoury, not to mention unsafe, to voice such doubts. Not that I am in any way questioning his character. He was a man of high moral standing."

I understood her hesitation about voicing this in front of another student, a school administrator at that, let alone to me. Any whiff of heresy such as this could be considered treason. My stomach tightened. Father had told me how in love he was with the wonders of this hidden realm. But I didn't know that he'd been uneasy with some of the decisions being made at the top. I could see the Praetory definitely had some issues that had to be addressed, but I'd always assumed Father had been every inch the loyal and honourable servant.

"Morgaine... what was your falling out with the Potentate about? Word has it you were his absolute favourite."

Morgaine tried to answer, but looked pained. I was surprised when Deva spoke for her.

"We had started to doubt the divine right of the Potentate, and the crimes we'd committed became too heavy to bear," she confessed, her voice heavy. "We could no longer fool ourselves that what we were doing was for the Praetory's defence, instead of just for the Potentate's own power. Your father called on our services occasionally, and one such occasion was the night of the attack near your home. We were the ones who helped your Father sneak past security to visit you. It felt slightly distasteful, using our skills to interfere in a domestic matter. But things were tense between your parents since the separation, and with the war ongoing he feared not seeing you one last..." Deva cleared her throat. "However, your father asked us to remain at the house and keep watch over Harper. Your mother was still at work. I'm sure your father must have had other guards in place, watching over you as he took you out for that run. But he didn't know when they were neutralised by the enemy."

"So it was to my great shame that we weren't there to protect him," Morgaine whispered, taking up the thread. "When I heard the commotion from the forest. We disobeyed our orders and rushed to help. So it was that I was the one to collect your unconscious body from the woods, prising your hands from your father to get you medical attention. You had lost so much blood. But Count Crowley..."

Morgaine hung her head and sank to her knees once more, down on the carpet before me. She clung to me like a lifeline.

"It is my greatest shame, and I have never slept a night's full sleep since," she whispered, haunted. "In your heart of hearts, you never stop being a knight. I failed, and I nearly turned my sword on myself many times. But it felt too light a mercy." The love for her liege-lord, and the pain in her, was hard to watch. "That was my justice, my punishment. But it is not enough." She looked up at me at long last. "I'm sorry," Morgaine told me. "I'm sorry that you lost him."

For a moment, I couldn't bring myself to speak.

"Sorry to ask," Sephy interjected. Morgaine flinched, as if she'd forgotten Sephy was there. "I know it might seem trivial, but... why have you been treating Crowley so brutally in class?"

Morgaine appeared abashed.

"I... perhaps I was trying not to treat her differently than the other students, and I... overcompensated. Something told me that you wouldn't enjoy favouritism or grovelling, Crowley. But I was also pushing you to be everything that I knew the daughter of Peter Crowley could be, if pressed hard enough. My Lady..."

"I am not your Lady," I said heavily, "and you are not my knight."

"Crowley..." Morgaine implored.

I never enjoyed the trappings of nobility. Ordering servants around, attending dinners where everyone lied and used silver cutlery—it wasn't my style. And as for politics? Apparently losing a leg made me a prime candidate for public office, now that my military career was dashed. At least, according to my mother.

I wanted to serve as a *knight*, the same role Morgaine had clearly taken so much pride in until her greatest failure. The first person to ever trust her, to ever accept her into his service, was my father. In her dreams, his blood was still on her hands.

I exhaled.

"Is that all you know? You don't know who gave the order to have my father killed?"

"I'm sorry. I've searched, but I don't have the information you're looking for. No acolyte has ever confessed to being the one to kill him in the war, or to give the order."

"Very well, then. I... I think we're done here."

"Crowley, please let me pledge my service to you," Morgaine whispered, staring down at the threads of the carpet. "I wish to atone for my failures. Your father would want me watching over you. If anything happened to you and I had the power to stop it..."

"By all accounts, you saved my life," I pointed out. "Surely your debt is already repaid."

"But as we both know, sometimes life itself is not enough."

She must have been able to see it in me as we stared at each other: that losing Father has defined my every living moment since. Just like for her, Father's death had turned existence from living into something else. Something aching and empty.

I got the vague impression that Morgaine didn't have a lot of people she could lean on either. But it didn't matter. Not anymore.

Sephy's crunching of kernels had become notably absent. She was staring between the two of us, maybe confused by my reluctance.

It wasn't fair, but when I looked at Morgaine all I saw was my father's death. She'd been important to him, a trusted friend. I wasn't about to add *'died horribly'* to her résumé. This little vendetta of mine against Shadows' Eve was a solo mission. Perhaps that was immature, emotional and irrational. But officially taking a knight into my service would be as good as admitting my mother had won, moulding me into a noble who had others fight her battles for her. Also, I could hardly be responsible for an emotionally shattered war veteran right now.

"Thank you, Morgaine," I said, deciding to keep those particular thoughts private. "I appreciate your offer of service, and I wish I could accept. Please, forgive yourself for your role that night. Without your actions, I would not be here."

Morgaine looked as if she wanted to beg one more time. But then she hung her head. My rejection was likely a crushing blow to what remnant of honour she still had. But my words didn't seem to go unappreciated. When she nodded, I could see tears burning in her eyes.

"Thank you," she said, bowing deeply. "Lady Crowley."

I tossed Kipling's report onto my desk, physically revolted. Swivelling my chair, I regarded the Academy's grounds out the window. It was eerily beautiful under the cover of night, illuminated by golden lanterns and wreathed in mist.

The meat of the material I really wanted to read in the report was so ridiculously redacted, it may as well have been printed on black paper. Though the parts I *could* read revealed Kipling and his soldiers to be little better than the terrorists themselves. I wondered at how much responsibility should be placed on Jo for the monster of a knight she had on her leash. Was Kipling really a necessary evil in order to take down Shadows' Eve? From everything I had read, Jo herself seemed to be a deft politician and a competent Governor. Surely she must have justifications for the decision to grant Kipling the title of knight. Yet, in my opinion, he was a stain on everything that the honourable title was meant to stand for. I cursed the irony that Kipling was allowed to serve, while any attempt by myself to pledge my fealty to someone would openly provoke Mother.

What the report had revealed to me was that Wellington and New Zealand at large was still very much in the grip of terrorism. Sure, the Dark Father was in a cage somewhere, probably contemplating evil Sudoku, but the rest of his fan club hadn't gotten the memo. Shadows' Eve weren't exactly flourishing here, but it was also unclear if the Governor was succeeding in driving them any closer to extinction. The picture these files painted was... frustrating.

And then there was the kicker: I had no idea how deep

the discrimination against Shadows ran in the Praetory. Thought Kipling was just the usual racist with a sword? Nope. Turned out he was the mascot. The whole place was built on the belief that Shadows should carry bags, not books; obey, not think. Beyond the walls of the Academy, the Praetory had enough subtle segregation to make 1960s Alabama look progressive. Counterpart Academy sounded like one of the few places where Shadows and humans could feel like equals; but even here the Shadows (save for Sephy, due to her adoptive parents' status) had to keep to their own dorm, had separate bathrooms, and even took some classes separately from the humans for what felt like no good reason.

That very discrimination is what allowed the acolytes to hide away in areas like Quietfire which had no great love for the Praetory. There the acolytes vanished from sight and from the Governor's radar, where Jo seemed unable to weed them out. Shadows without counterparts, considered at the very bottom of society under the Potentate's policies, were strongly in support of anyone that sought to challenge the institution. In other words, Wellington was a powder keg waiting to blow.

Kipling seemed sure the Academy was clear of acolytes, which was impressive considering he couldn't find his own moral compass with both hands and a flashlight. If there were any more of them hiding out among the student body, I was determined to find them. Whatever enlightenment might be hiding in these files, however, was still playing hard to get.

Exhaling, I stood and left my room. I needed a walk, to let all of these murky thoughts settle. That was usually the best way to find new insights. Maybe I'd wrangle a few people into a combat simulation. Sephy said a lot of students were eager to lose to me in high-definition again, and there was even a betting pool involved. Nothing like publicly humiliating the cool kids *and* making money off it, I thought brightly. Therapy, but with a scoreboard.

"Addie," I heard Sephy say emphatically from down below. "Can you even hear me?"

"Sorry, what was that?"

I paused on the landing and looked over the railing, to see Sephy pounce onto the couch beside Aberdeen. Sephy was so long that she took up almost all the available space, even with her long spiny tail trailing on the floor.

Aberdeen was lounging with his legs folded, his elbow resting against the arm of the couch. His eyes were glued to the dancing, colourful pixels on his phone screen. I'd never understand why he was so obsessed with this one child's game.

Sephy gently placed a paw on Aberdeen's shoulder. From anyone else that would result in a signature scowl, so I was surprised when Aberdeen didn't recoil from her.

"Look, I know things are hard right now," Sephy told him. "Shadows' Eve breaking into the school..."

I noticed Aberdeen clench his idle hand into a fist.

"I don't want to talk about it. You should never have gotten hurt."

Something about the tone of their voices told me that I shouldn't interrupt. Perhaps they hadn't realised I was home. I hesitated, embarrassed, uncertain if I should move away when the floor would likely creak and incriminate me for eavesdropping.

"We're all scared," Sephy pressed. "It's got everyone on edge."

"I said I don't want to—are you even listening!?"

Aberdeen glowered suddenly at Sephy, drawing back to fold his arms.

"What?" she said, surprised. "Is this about how I got tased by that acolyte? I'm *fine*, Addie."

Aberdeen looked away.

"I know," he muttered.

It was strange, but listening to them made me feel oddly jealous. I know that it shouldn't have, Sephy especially made a big effort to include me in everything as part of the group, but these two had a special connection all of their own.

"I'm just saying that we need people right now. We all need family around us for support. Even you do."

"I have plenty of friends, thank you," he said tartly.

"With all due respect, you have wannabe groupies. It's very different." Her voice became softer. "I just want to help. That's all I ever want to do. I know this is hard, but you have to stop reacting like everyone in this world is trying to burn you. You act like you'll always have time to form friendships later in life. For all we know, we could die at any moment in a freak gas leak explosion."

"I've said it before and I'll say it again, I'm pretty sure you're the one who needs therapy." Aberdeen leaned back, resting his head in his hands. He groaned.

"You're talking about Crowley, aren't you?"

I quickly drew my head back out of sight.

"I just feel like you two are going down the enemy track for the same reason that you should be going down the friend track instead: you have a heck of a lot in common."

"She's annoying," Aberdeen said, though I swore I could hear an edge of guilt in his voice.

"Exactly," Sephy teased.

I heard a sound which I think was Aberdeen swatting her.

"But she can also be kind," Sephy insisted, "and thoughtful and protective..."

"I've seen all of that. But she's also unforgiving once you cross her. She can be so... cold," he muttered. "Merciless."

"And you make it oh so easy on her. Just try to be nicer to her, okay? We could hang out more with the three of us, as a trio."

"I'll think about it," Aberdeen answered finally.

"Wonderful!" Sephy said happily. "After all, you *were* the one who first suggested she come and stay with us. Follow that heart of gold, Aberdeen."

There was a roaring in my ears. I stayed silent, concealed in my hiding place up on the landing.

"I just wanted us to claim a quiet and tidy dormmate before they were all taken," Aberdeen said tightly. "That's why."

"Right. I totally believe you."

I pulled away from the railing, my heart racing. My mood darkened utterly as I contemplated the facts before me.

I'd dismissed my theory that the teenage acolyte Sephy and I had encountered might actually still be alive, let alone that it was Aberdeen. It was too much coincidence that we'd been placed in the same dorm room as well for that to be believable. *Unless* the acolyte himself had literally asked for me to be placed in his dorm, so he could keep an eye on me, until he figured out exactly how much I knew.

Shit. No, I was basing all of this on that one whiff of cloves and wood-smoke. Aberdeen couldn't be working for

Shadows' Eve. What if it was all in my head? What if I hadn't even smelt that?

I didn't have much time, but I had to find out for sure. They were both busy downstairs but wouldn't be for long. Adrenaline flooding through me, I retrieved an item from my room then silently snuck into Aberdeen's across the hall. Tense, I slipped the goggles over my eyes. It had taken a lot to procure these goggles, and all thanks to my family's resources. They were a prototype from Cameron Technologies, and they weren't exactly the kind of thing you could just order online. But when I'd started trying to track down Shadows' Eve, I'd had a feeling that they'd come in handy.

I looked around Aberdeen's room, the space ghostly and hollow in my altered vision. The goggles were essentially a very rudimentary prototype of x-ray glasses. They allowed me to see through wood and solid matter to get a faint impression of any secret compartments that may be lurking behind them. My heart was pounding, but nothing immediately obvious jumped out at me. I spotted no secret doorways or hidden passages. Perhaps that was a little too much to ask for. I couldn't tell if I was disappointed or relieved.

We might clash with each other on a regular basis, but Aberdeen was still my dormmate and Sephy's friend. But if he really was an acolyte of Shadows' Eve, then he'd been lying to us all along. More than that, it would mean he posed a serious danger to us and every student in the Academy.

I scanned every inch of Aberdeen's room with a level of detail verging on paranoia. I tried to keep my ears alert for the sound of anyone climbing the stairs. I ran my hands across his wooden drawers and the closet, even the interior, searching for a hidden button or a hidden latch. I was searching for anything... you know... acolyte-y. But I found nothing. I opened Aberdeen's top drawer and started to rifle through his clothes. I knew it was useless. The goggles told me there was no hidden compartment in the base of the drawer, but there was a chance they were faulty.

"Oh. My. God," a voice came from behind me. I nearly had a heart-attack. Slipping the goggles off to conceal them, I straightened and turned around. Sephy stood there, framed in the doorway.

"Sephy..." I whispered, choked.

"You," she said, arching her tail at me accusingly, "were up to fetish-y high-jinks."

I blinked. I looked from her back to the drawer of Aberdeen's underwear that I'd been searching through. I felt my cheeks burn scarlet.

"This isn't what it looks like," I said urgently, pressing a finger to my lips as I implored her to be quiet.

"What?" Sephy asked with feigned innocence, padding over to me. "You fondling Addie's underwear, you mean?"

"Sephy, this is serious."

"No, I get that. It's clear you take this very seriously," she said, staring pointedly at the drawer, "*underwear-fondler*. I might have said something to you about how you should let loose a little more, but this is excessive."

"I'm not like that!"

"Like a pervert?" she exclaimed gleefully, then clapped a hand over her mouth, eyes going wide.

"Sephy!"

I slapped my hands awkwardly across her own to stifle the sound. We spun around in a kind of tousle as she continued to murmur a string of unkind words. It was like trying to wrestle with a writhing leopard. Then she froze, her ears perking up. She looked at me with big shining eyes.

"Kngffly," she mumbled.

"What?" I hissed, panicked, removing my hands.

"He's coming."

We stared at each other. Then, we both chose the least sensible action in the situation: to dive for the dumbest hiding spots possible. Mine was behind an armchair, Sephy's was behind a lamp that barely obscured her at all.

This is so damn stupid.

"Sephy?" Aberdeen said suspiciously as he entered. He'd spotted her immediately. "What are you doing in here?"

Sephy got a mischievous expression, then said cheerfully:

"Nothing. Bye!"

Aberdeen just shrugged as she departed. I suppose for Sephy, this kind of bizarre behaviour was far more run-of-the-mill.

Seriously!? She's just going to leave me here?

With Sephy now gone, Aberdeen removed his shirt, and stretched. His taut muscles were some kind of artistry all of their own. The dim light caught the play of shadows across his skin, accentuating the sculpted lines of his torso.

I swallowed.

I'm going to kill Sephy, I decided. I felt better having made the decision. At the same time, I was angry at myself.

Why didn't you just announce yourself at the same time as Sephy? I cursed myself, outraged. At least that would have been better than whatever *this* is.

Then Aberdeen caught a glimpse of me in the mirror, my lanky frame not quite hidden behind the armchair. He wheeled around, nostrils flaring. I gulped.

"What," he said, his tone merciless, "are you doing in here?"

"I'm sorry!" I blurted, extricating myself in the most

undignified way. "Sephy put me up to it! It was a... you know. A Sephy thing. Can't even remember what the plan was, really."

Then, most unexpectedly, Aberdeen's expression changed. It went from furious and calculating, to a self-satisfied, knowing smirk.

"What?" I asked suspiciously.

"If you were that curious, you could have just asked for a private show," he said lightly.

I looked around, confused. Then the burning blush set in.

"Oh! Oh, no. I mean, it was just a game," I elaborated, clearing my throat. "Sephy is... you know how she is. Her convoluted plots and all that."

"You two have been hanging out a lot," Aberdeen frowned, his mind suddenly seeming to travel in a different direction. "Do you think Sephy... do you think she's your Shadow?"

"Sephy?" I repeated, incredulous. I folded my arms, oddly feeling like the one who's exposed. "No! What? Why would you think that?"

"How do you know? Have you *found* your Shadow yet?" he interrogated me, tilting his perfect head.

"No!" I said, looking aside, self-conscious. "Not yet. But it isn't her."

"Oh."

I cleared my throat.

"So. Oh I'm just going to..."

I awkwardly tiptoed out of the room. I felt his eyes following me.

Back in my own bedroom, I shoved a chair against my door, blocking the handle. Then I put the goggles back on, switching the dials on the sides to frenetically toggle through the recorded footage. Another advantage of these was that they were capable of storing video files, allowing you to go back through long night shoots and pick up details you may have missed.

I scanned through the footage of Aberdeen's room. He hadn't seemed particularly on edge or anxious to find me in there. He didn't reek with the guilt of a man who was about to be found out. I could be wrong.

I recalled his impertinent smirk. He'd pretty much been laughing at me the whole time, like I was the pervert he'd always expected me to be. Well... screw you, Aberdeen.

I quirked an eyebrow. Something had caught my attention. I rewound the footage, fixating on the segment where I'd roughly scanned the long closet standing in the corner of Aberdeen's room.

I could see the shape of drawers and where clothes hung suspended from their hooks. But if I looked closer, I could also make out what looked suspiciously like a hidden compartment lying beyond it. I'd thought the dimensions had felt off when I'd felt around inside.

"No," I whispered.

You've been hiding right in front of me the entire time. You made me question my own instincts.

Suspended from a hook in Aberdeen's hidden compartment hung a long set of dark robes—and beside them, a mask shaped like the snarling face of a horned tiger.

12

There couldn't be *that* many explanations for why my dormmate had the mask and robes of a mass-murdering cult in his closet. Other than, obviously, that one of the very terrorists I'd been hunting had been sleeping in a bed only metres from my own.

I smiled at Aberdeen over breakfast, trying not to openly shake with hatred. Somehow, the extent of my loathing made it easier to perfectly play my part as Aberdeen slurped his noodles. I was eagerly anticipating the moment I'd bring his world crashing down.

Aberdeen glared at my smile, then looked away. I worried he was onto me, then realised he was probably still traumatised by my alleged late-night underwear reconnaissance mission through his room. Good. Let him marinate in the awkward. It kept him from noticing I'd discovered his little House of Horrors.

Over the next week I tried to keep track of him at all possible times. I figured the worst that could happen was that I'd come off looking like something of a stalker. As other girls ogled Aberdeen with desire in the hallways, I plotted how I was going to kill him.

What made this stalking much easier, though I was certainly not proud of it, was when I secretly logged into the cameras that Sephy had hidden all around the Academy. They were the ones she'd been using for her totally immoral 'Love Academy' media studies project. It was kind of disturbing just how *much* of the school she managed to cover, and how few of the hidden cameras the teachers had discovered when they were removing them. I wondered if Sephy possibly had some kind of dirt on every single member of the staff, just in order to continually avoid suspension for antics like this.

For days, I didn't see Aberdeen doing anything suspicious. No shady exchanges, no secret acolyte handshakes, not even a suspicious side-eye. Disappointing. I was expecting *something*—a clandestine note, a dramatic whisper, anything short of him holding up a sign saying '*EVIL HERE.*' But no. Aberdeen was playing it cool, which made sense. After all, you didn't watch your cult buddies get shredded like confetti and then immediately start recruiting again. Even villains need a grace period.

After a few days of stalking, one thing stood out in particular. Aberdeen would often vanish into the infrequently used West block toilet, sometimes for *hours*. I wondered at first if he was just wagging class, playing that inane action game he loved on his phone—*Alien Hominid,* I think?—in one of the cubicles. Either that, or there was something seriously wrong with his insides.

I waited until Aberdeen had a double-period class on Thursday afternoon, of what I assumed was Advanced Brooding and Smouldering 101, before I headed to the toilets in question. I kept an eye out for any acolytes keeping watch, masquerading as normal students. I made my way down the corridor toward the toilets...

...when Sephy slid out from an adjoining corridor, her long spiny tail flicking behind her. She padded smoothly out to stand directly in front of me.

"Crowley," she said, with a bow that was slightly mocking. Her sandy fur shimmered gold under the flickering lights.

I stared, caught off-guard.

How much exactly does she know?

"How long were you waiting there to come out and surprise me?" I asked, cautious.

"Oh, now you're talking to *moi*? So this is what existing feels like."

I sighed long-sufferingly.

"You've been avoiding me all week, *and* Aberdeen," Sephy accused me. "Don't act like you haven't." From her sour expression, the avoiding hadn't been too subtle, nor had it gone well. "You're going to tell me what's going on. Now."

"I don't know what you're talking about," I answered cheerfully, but my hand curled into a fist. If she checked my satchel right now, it would be damning. She would find an acolyte robe and mask, a pair of goggles and a new handgun that I'd sourced with great difficulty. At the very least, it looked like I was not taking my academic studies seriously.

She was right that I'd been avoiding her too since my discovery in Aberdeen's room. I felt like Sephy would somehow sniff out what I was up to, so I'd been trying to keep her at arm's length. Sephy seemed to be one of the few who could see through my own mask to try and glimpse the real Crowley operating beneath. So perhaps I hadn't been necessarily speaking to Sephy for the last few days. It had seemed easier to avoid her than to lie to her face.

I was going to root out any remainder of the Shadows' Eve network and get my answers, before destroying them all. Even if that included Aberdeen. I'd hidden a note in case anything happened to me, though I planned on coming home whole to Harper. If I just called Jo to tell her what I knew so far, there was a chance Kipling would whisk the acolytes away to a prison in a classified location before I could wring the answers out of them that I wanted. I wanted to know what really happened to Father, and so far Aberdeen was the one lead I had.

I was preparing myself for what was just ahead, and what I would have to do to avenge Father. I'd taken a life once before, to defend myself. I knew that when you killed someone, it could take a piece of you. It *should* take a piece of you. And you had to be willing to give that piece up.

To kill, you had to mean it.

The fewer people I involved in this, the better. I didn't want to bring Sephy down with me if my vigilante actions got me sent to prison, or worse.

I tried to move past her, but she swept her tail into my path like a line of barbed wire, the spines fully extended. I stopped.

"What?" I asked, my nostrils flaring. "I'm kind of a little busy."

"Oh. With what?"

I stared at her.

"Look," she continued in a rush, "I know you're up to something. I know you, Alexandra Crowley. You didn't just take a chill pill after you went off at me about terrorism during our tour of the school, or after you pressed Morgaine for answers. You've been planning something. It's written all over your face. You're on some private vendetta against Shadows' Eve because of what they did to your father. You want to find the acolytes who killed him, and you're wondering if there's any more of them still in this school placing all of us in danger." She grinned unexpectedly. There was a fire in her eyes. "So, I want in. What are we doing?" She lowered her voice. "Are you going after them *right now*?"

I roughly broke eye contact with her.

"*We* are doing nothing," I snapped. I needed to scare her off. I needed to be harsh. Otherwise she'd offer to risk her life as well, because she looked out for people. She was a good person like that, and I couldn't be distracted worrying about her losing her life, not when this was more important than anything.

"Okay. But you know what I think? I think things got too serious with our pyjama sleepover last week, and now you're freaking out." The twinkle in those eyes told me she was messing with me.

"The pyjama sleepover?" I repeated.

"Oh, you've forgotten it already? Damn it Crowley, I made us spiders with Coke and French vanilla ice cream. Did none of that mean *anything* to you?"

Sephy was meant to be looking out for her parents. I knew how important her family was to her, and how she was always looking out for them. How would they cope if she died? How would I ever live with the guilt?

Suddenly I was holding Father in my arms all over again, back in the woods. He was bleeding out in my arms and I was powerless to stop it, just a girl alone among the trees. When I was lying in bed weeks after, aching with emptiness, I would watch the shapes form in the darkness around my bed, begging that same darkness to creep close enough to swallow me whole.

I closed my eyes.

"I figured you weren't really perving in Aberdeen's room that night," Sephy said quietly. "Do you really think he has something to do with Shadows' Eve? Because you're wrong, Crowley. I know him. He's a good person."

I didn't respond.

"Did it never even occur to you that I might be able to help with whatever's going on?" Sephy demanded. "That I have skills which would make me a serious asset to you?"

"This isn't about questioning your abilities."

"Then what is it?"

"I work alone," I whispered, my tone deadly, "and anyone who gets in my way will be sorry."

We glowered at each other. I'd never really seen Sephy being serious like this. It was like a predator watching prey.

"If you really knew me," she said, her tone oddly terrifying, "you'll know that while I'm a powerful ally, I'm far more dangerous as an enemy."

It took me way too long to convince myself I'd finally lost Sephy—that annoying, furry stalker. I even went full hacker-mode and deactivated her creepy little 'Love Academy' reality show cams, just to make sure she couldn't track me like I was tracking Aberdeen.

When I slipped into the bathroom, nothing looked particularly out of the ordinary. Casually, I made sure that no one was about to come out and awkwardly wash their hands as I stood there. Thankfully, the stalls were empty. The only thing of any note in the bathroom was a surprisingly mundane piece of artwork at the far end. It depicted a bowl of fruit set against a dark background. Odd décor. Rather... unimaginative? Soothing, I supposed, as all good bathrooms should be. If there was a Shadows' Eve hideout here, and I felt mad for just thinking it... the acolytes would need to have a way to check they could safely exit the bathroom without anyone noticing.

If the Shadows' Eve cult had a hideout here—and yes, I might be losing it—it would have to have some way to see if the coast was clear. So I eyeballed the painting. Sure enough, behind the papaya, there was a tiny peephole, cleverly disguised like part of the art. I got as close as I could, hoping anyone watching would just assume I was a stressed student in the middle of a breakdown.

When I pulled on my goggles, I could make out a large, hollow space beyond the picture frame. Something caught in my chest. Beyond the papaya was the ghostly entrance to a tunnel.

No way. I was right.

Breathing in deeply, I slowly drew my gun from the satchel, then felt around the back of the painting until I found a hidden latch. Slowly I lifted it, pulling the mysterious oil painting ajar. I slipped into the mysterious beyond, closing the frame behind me. It seemed strange that there wasn't some kind of lock on it. It shouldn't have been this easy, surely. I felt an unease, but not quite enough to turn back. There was stone underneath my feet now, and a tunnel led before me into the dark.

The coast looking clear, I pulled out Aberdeen's mask and robes and donned the garb of an acolyte. There. I'd blend right in.

I moved forward into darkness.

The tunnel was rambling stone and bare earth under my feet. Brackets built into the tunnel walls held torches, their flames casting wild, flickering light as I moved further down into the earth.

A door finally came into sight before me. It was painted black, its surface weathered, bubbled and cracked. It reminded me of old parchment, or wood that's survived a fire. Painted on it was the horned visage of a masked tiger, with whiskers that seem to crackle with lightning. His eyes seem to tear into me, seeing into my very soul. He was a thing of terror, a visceral presence that I felt all through me. I stared back at him through the slits in my own mask, defiant, shaking as if I was staring at the real Dark Father himself.

The door required some kind of key. I cursed inwardly, feeling the carved depression in the stone. Many acolytes carried talismans around their necks, which I suspected was the only kind of key this door would respond to. Aberdeen must wear his own around his neck, because I hadn't spotted it in his room. But I was surprised when I pressed my hand hard against the door it slowly, reluctantly ground open. Strange. Somehow, the door was already unlocked.

Their lax security was my fair fortune.

I entered through the gap, following the dark, stone tunnel downward as it slowly widened. It was as if I was entering a very deep cave. I felt a creeping sensation across my skin, as I wondered what horrors lay waiting for me within.

"*Crowley?*" a voice suddenly came down the dark tunnel. I froze, my throat slowly closing up at that voice. I knew it. *"I very much hope that you never have to see this."*

The world seemed to tilt around me.

Impossible.

I struggled to comprehend what was happening. That

voice had to be fake, or if it was real, it must have been a recording. Which meant if someone was playing that recording now, they were playing it purely for me to hear.

The acolytes must know I was here and who I was. I needed to get out now.

But if I *had* strayed into an elaborate trap, it was likely my exit had already been cut off. I needed to gain command of the situation as quickly as possible.

I moved quickly around the corner, aiming down my pistol's sights. The tunnel widened further, but there was no one in sight. Just a sphere sitting on the floor of the cave, a sphere filled with light. It was a Shadow world technology, one of the artifacts that our teachers sometimes used in class; essentially a Smart TV crossed with a crystal ball. It cast a warm shimmering light over the walls of the cave. I stared into the sphere. There were two figures within it, a human and a Shadow. The Shadow was a grumpy but wise-looking tortoise, ocean-green with a great humped shell and a long, wizened beard. He had pointy ears and yellow and purple glyphs marking his shell.

The man beside him was sitting on a chair. He seemed to be staring out at me. He was wearing the black robes of Shadows' Eve.

It was a recording.

I took another step, then stopped. There was a ringing in my ears as I stared at that acolyte beside the tortoise. The man had wild grey unkempt hair almost to match his Shadow's, and dramatic, flaring eyebrows like lightning bolts.

Staring at that visage trapped within that crystal sphere, I scarcely believed my eyes. It was as if I was watching a dream, my most desperate desire being reflected back at me... but as something wrong and uncanny.

"My baby girl," Father said. *"I think it's time that I told you the truth."*

Peter Crowley was toying with a horned mask in his hands, a black ribbon falling to trace the air beneath it. My heart lurched.

Someone grabbed me from behind.

I twisted around. The trick with the sphere been used just to throw my attention, and it had worked. Enraged, I writhed, trying to break free in order to fire my weapon.

That was when I got a full view of my attacker through the slits in my mask.

It was Aberdeen. No robes. No tiger mask. Just *him*—the guy who made my blood sing with things no one should ever feel towards their father's killer. Seeing him like this, stripped of all his smoke and mirrors, was like staring down a live wire: dangerous, electrifying, impossible to look away from.

He didn't *look* like a member of a heinous terrorist cult who had wrecked my life. But my gun stayed trained on him. His eyes locked on mine, simmering with something that wasn't just anger. There was a familiar heat there.

There was a click as I removed the safety. He went still with the sound.

"Explain, now," I said, voice shaking. "If you reach for a weapon, you're dead. There's a silencer on this, so no one will know the moment you died. How many people are you working with? Who else is here right now?"

Aberdeen disarmed me, impossibly fast, the pistol flying out into the dark. I swore, recognising the move, and suddenly I *knew*. Whoever this was, it was the same acolyte who Sephy and I had run into together on my first day.

You had him! I cursed. I'd had the upper hand and I'd had the chance to pull the trigger, but I hadn't. I'd hesitated once Sephy's friend had been in my sights. Now it was going to be the death of me.

Aberdeen's face was illuminated in the light from the sphere, feral emotions disturbing his flawless features. He tried to grab for me before I could lunge for the gun. Instead I surprised him by tackling him. Together we crashed to the floor, the cavern swallowing us in darkness.

"Damn it, Crowley!" Aberdeen yelled. Father was still speaking from that sphere, but his words were bouncing off the stone around us, painting a sketchy picture of the shape of the cavern as we scuffled across the ground.

"What the hell's the meaning of this?" I challenged Aberdeen, my outrage directed toward the cruel mockery in the glass orb. I was wrestling with him, attempting to pin him down on the cavern floor, but Aberdeen managed to do it first. He'd always outdone me in hand-to-hand combat.

"Your father was an acolyte. He was one of us, the very greatest!" Aberdeen hissed into my ear. His breath was hot against my cheek. "Peter Crowley was the Dark Father's right hand!"

What? I'd murder him for even saying such a thing.

"You're wrong," I snarled, but it broke into a sob. "Shadows' Eve wanted my father dead!" Tears streamed from my eyes. I was nothing but torment and rage. "You people killed him!"

"No, Crowley," Aberdeen whispered, restraining me. He was holding me so close and tight I could barely move. Aberdeen's words didn't sound like the Aberdeen that I knew. They were strangely soft, and aching. They held... *feeling*. "We didn't take him from you. The Praetory did."

13

NE YEAR AGO

"Crowley!" Father's voice tore through the trees like a gunshot. "Run back home!"

My heart sank as if suctioned into my feet. Father was still finishing off the last of the two assassins who had tried to ambush him. Blood gleamed across his shirt like war paint. But one of the soldiers who had just emerged from the trees was raising an arm...

I saw the man aim his rifle.

"FATHER!"

I rushed forward. As I did, I suddenly became aware of a presence there in the trees. Something was moving there among the branches, some kind of creature. I heard the strange cry from before, but now its thunder was louder than ever.

Trees erupted. Earth and debris were thrown upward, crashing through the branches toward us like boulders. There *was a shrieking sound as a flare of violet light lanced through the trees, the scream of a beast who shouldn't exist filling the night.*

Humans were all through the trees now, disguised by the dark of night. All around me came the sounds of strange impossible creatures.

Then I saw Father lying there on the ground, and everything else was rendered into silence.

FATHER!

I rushed forward, just as another ray of violet light flashed. It was so swift, the burn so pure as it radiated through my left knee that for a moment I didn't know why I was falling.

Then the pain hit. It was like nothing I had felt before. I crashed to the ground, a strangled moan escaping me. A white-hot inferno tore through my nerves. My leg was gone. Just gone.

I screamed until my throat cracked.

Then I forced it out of my mind, pushing myself forwards. Belly-crawling back toward Father, even as more violet lightning crackled through the air.

I looked back to try and understand why everything felt so wrong, but all I saw was the bloody, tangled mess where my leg used to be. I forced my eyes away.

Forward, Crowley. Just forward now. Save Father.

'Run home,' he had said.

But how could I, with home bleeding out in front of me?

I was his daughter. One day I'd hoped to be his knight. But I couldn't run now, even if I'd wanted to. My home was there, lying in the dirt and pooling blood.

The forest was quiet now. A voice murmured nearby, barely distinct.

"Shit, the girl..."

"She wasn't meant to be here..."

The conversation came in muddied fragments. I was cradling my father, sobbing, smoothing his hair.

"Please don't go," I whispered, begging him. "Please don't leave..."

"We should end their line right here," someone was saying.

"That's not our prerogative. Look at her; she's broken. An invalid for life. We've already risked violating the terms."

I realised the attackers were retreating all around us, fading back into the trees. Then Father and I were alone in the silence, just as we'd been only minutes before.

I placed a hand on him but there was no response. I drew Father's phone from his pocket and dialled emergency services. I was barely aware of doing it. Whatever it was that had burned through my leg, it was unlike any weapon I knew of. It hadn't fully cauterised the wound though. It was difficult to maintain consciousness, reality cloaking itself in umber. But I had to stay awake for Father until help arrived.

His head lolled against my lap. I smoothed his hair like I used to when I was little and afraid of nightmares—only this one was real. With one hand, I pressed down on his wounds. I knew it was useless. The blood was everywhere. Too much. Far too much.

"You've got to hold on, Father," I smiled brokenly as he looked up at me in confusion. Tears ran down my cheeks. I kept smoothing his hair, even when the rise and fall of his chest finally went still, even when his eyes went glassy and dark. "You're going to be okay. I have you, Father. Don't worry. I'm going to save you."

14

How do you reconcile the possibility that the hate you've pursued so passionately might have nothing to do with reality?

I sat in a small armchair, regarding my father and his counterpart in the crystal orb. Aberdeen leaned against the far wall, arms crossed tightly, jaw clenched. He didn't look at me. Not once. Whether it was to give me time with my father's memory or out of anger or sheer discomfort, I couldn't tell. I'd never really known what went on in his head. But I could feel the tension in him—a coiled spring ready to snap. He'd told me the truth, and I'd felt something in his voice when he did. He'd been understanding. Compassionate, even.

But now? Now I got nothing but the sharp edge of a scowl—the classic Aberdeen mask.

The so-called *sanctum*—because calling it a *'hideout'* apparently didn't have enough dramatic flair—looked like someone gave a goth interior designer a Renaissance fair budget and said, *'Go nuts.'* It was all stone columns and arches. Wooden chests, bound with iron and meticulously carved, lined the walls. A richly patterned rug the red of fresh blood lay at the centre of the room, its intricate designs hinting at ancient, forgotten myths. Flaming braziers hanging from the ceiling like it was the Middle Ages? Absolutely. Because what screamed *'covert rebel base'* like an open fire hazard?

Banners of black and silver spilled down the walls, bearing the emblem of Shadows' Eve. I avoided looking at that horned tiger. So many confusing emotions were churning inside of me. Guilt, suspicion, confusion, hate... and hurt.

So I just kept staring intently into that sphere, attempting to separate the contents of my heart from the evidence that presented itself.

"This is Thames," Father's echo was saying to me now from that sphere. I hung onto his words. Listening to his deeply familiar Scottish brogue felt like coming home. *"I so wanted you two to meet. He's my Shadow, Crowley. He's the other part of me you never got to know."*

"I've wanted to meet you for so very long," the giant tortoise rumbled, his deep voice cracked with emotion. *"We are both so very proud of you, Alexandra."*

"I'm not sure what the world will look like when you see this," Father said. *"I just hope it looks better than the one that we left behind. We don't know how this war is going to end. It looks so dark right now, but perhaps that's because the dawn is near. You have to understand that the Praetory spreads terrible lies about us. This war has made both sides do unimaginable things... so many people have died who shouldn't have. I wanted to protect you from that. But the difference is Shadows' Eve have something worth fighting for. The people that we lose give their lives to a greater goal: true equality between Shadows and humans.*

'*The Praetory, the secret world that your mother and I have both been a part of, is wonderful, Crowley. But is also violent, and rife with problems. Your mother has always seen the best in it. But there's a sickness at its heart, and at long last I've found the cure. I may be a Praetory Count by day, but many years ago I swore myself in secret as a knight to the greatest person I have ever had the privilege to meet. Many call him the Dark Father, as if he is something to fear and treat with caution, and they're not wrong. But I call him by his true name: Jupiter.*"

I stared down at the horned tiger mask in my hands, unable to comprehend what was happening. Everything I knew had been turned irrevocably on its head.

"*I truly and deeply believe Jupiter is the one who can change things,*" Father said emphatically. "*He is the one who can lead us into a new era, and reshape the Praetory into a society built on peace and what's just. Jupiter is a Shadow, and that is who needs to lead the way to a new society, Crowley: those who have been marginalised and forgotten, not those who gain power from the status quo.*"

"*So we've taken everything that the Praetory say about us, that we're demons and phantoms... and we've made our own,*" Thames rumbled. The great tortoise nodded to the robes and the mask that my father was holding, a smile of wry amusement visible through his grey beard. "*The Praetory nobility lie awake in fear that the people will rise up against them. They do have something to fear, because every day they carry the guilt of what they've done to the Shadow people, who are forced to be slave labour while the rest of our world knows nothing of their plight.*

'*It's so strange, my girl, speaking to you this way,*" Father said softly. "*You were just bouncing on my knee not so many years ago, I swear. Now you're about to celebrate your fifteenth birthday. Absurd. I wanted to make this recording just in case.*

I've lost more good friends to this damn war than my heart can stand. But we're determined to keep serving at Jupiter's side. We vowed to defend him against whatever threats may come, even if it means having to give our own lives for his. If that happens, you deserve to have an explanation. I wanted this opportunity to speak to you, to the you *of the future: that grand, amazing young woman who might be able to finally understand some of the decisions and sacrifices I've had to make. I am so sorry if you are watching this..."* There were tears in his eyes, *"...because I know those sacrifices were not mine alone to make. I love you, Crowley. I always will."* He smiled. *"Your Father."*

My tears matched his own. I sat there in the sanctum, reeling.

Father had been a knight. A real pledge-your-soul, bend-the-knee, serve-the-higher-order kind of knight. Was that where that feeling came from in me, that longing to serve? Was that something I'd gotten from him?

The people I'd loathed for taking my father hadn't done so at all. Instead they'd been a kind of second family to him. Was it possible, after being determined to join the Praetory and get my revenge on Shadows' Eve, that I'd confused the poison with the antidote to our society? Was it possible that Jupiter had been a hero all along?

I felt sick. I was experiencing an existential crisis with a side of shame soufflé. I wondered if Mother knew. Was she secretly an acolyte too?

No, surely not. Asia Kate Crowley was *religiously* committed to the Praetory. She'd always abhorred Shadows' Eve with a vengeance, even before we were told that they were responsible for Father's death. She'd built her career on bringing them to justice. But then how was it that she ended up raising children with Jupiter's personal knight?

I fell to my knees, hands on the floor, and I sobbed. I didn't care what Aberdeen thought. I let the convulsions wrack through me, the angry, vengeful guilt that had been crushing and killing me for so long suddenly collapsing in on itself, and taking me with it. I felt the exhausting freedom of the truth and the pain and fury of taking this long to get to it.

I could feel Aberdeen peeking at me. He was clearly trying to avoid staring, but seemed unable to resist. His blazing eyes were narrowed, curious, as if searching for signs of the great Peter Crowley in my features.

Sir Peter Crowley, a champion for acolytes everywhere. How could I possibly come to terms with that?

"How can you be sure?" I demanded.

"I think you've seen the evidence for yourself," Aberdeen answered, sniffing.

"There's technology that can fake this sort of thing," I snorted, "and the Praetory have unlimited resources."

"Except it *feels* real," Aberdeen said. He watched me as if I was someone he felt responsible for while also a wild predator who may strike at any moment. "A lot of things finally make sense, don't they, Crowley?"

He was guessing, but he's more right than he knows.

"Shadows' Eve are fanatics," I muttered, staring into empty space. "Under Jupiter's orders, they massacred thousands."

"Thousands of *soldiers*. It was a war," Aberdeen growled. "Both sides spilled an amount of blood that was incomprehensible. Difference is, the acolytes did it to end the pain and suffering under the Praetory's reign. Unfortunately, history is written by the victors. Don't you ever wonder why, in your classes that tell you about the evils of Shadows' Eve, you never read any of the movement's *actual* writings? Because if you did, you'd realise that they weren't delusional. They were smart, filled with compassion and committed to the fight to win equality. The Potentate will do whatever he can to prevent you from reading material that plants those same kind of dangerous ideas in your mind: the ideas that him and the nobles *aren't* divinely chosen, and that Shadows' aren't destined to be nothing but servants." Aberdeen shook his head, and glared at me. "How the hell did you even *find* this place?"

I tapped the pair of X-Ray goggles hanging around my neck.

"That, and thanks to Sephy's make-out cameras. Oh, and also the fact that no one ever reasonably spends that amount of time in a toilet," I added absent-mindedly.

"I told Sephy those cameras were a violation of our basic rights," Aberdeen muttered, but a smile twitched at the corner of his lips.

"Try telling her that. So Sephy... she's not part of this?"

"No," he said firmly. "She has no idea. I've been trying to protect her."

"By protect her, you mean tasing her so you could escape rather than revealing who you were?" I accused him. "It was you we ran into in the corridor that day, right?"

"Don't act like you wouldn't have done the exact same thing in my shoes to complete your mission."

Damn. I hated to face it, but I wasn't sure that he was wrong. Maybe we were both equally toxic.

Aberdeen swallowed and turned away. In that moment, I saw the guilt torturing him.

"I've hated myself every day for hurting Sephy like that," he breathed. "Sir Kipling had just murdered my friend, and a handful of our brother and sister acolytes. They'd died trying to get whatever intelligence the Praetory had been keeping hidden in the guarded vault beneath the Academy. There was something in there for safekeeping that they were terrified of getting out, but we didn't know what. We hadn't been expecting Kipling's men, and I only managed to get a backpack's worth of files. But I had to smuggle something out of there. I had to try and make their deaths mean something." He turned back, and I saw the full torment on his face, a survivor's guilt that mirrored back my own. Aberdeen nodded down at the crystal sphere with my father and his sage tortoise companion within it, frozen in space. "This is one of the items I stole from the archive, and it's the only thing of any real importance that I found: solid evidence that your father and his Shadow were two of the greatest acolytes to ever live. Jupiter's left and right hand, although no one ever knew their secret identities. Those who worked closely with them in Jupiter's inner circle must have known, though. It's harder to hide your identity when you're a giant tortoise." Aberdeen stared daggers at me. "All of that service and sacrifice, only for Peter Crowley's own daughter to break in here trying to spill acolyte blood."

I shot a look at him that made him close his mouth abruptly.

"Wait." I leaned forward, trying to clarify my thoughts. "So the Praetory was willing to kill to protect this intelligence, the evidence that Count Crowley was secretly part of Shadows' Eve. Why?"

"It would be destructive for morale, probably," Aberdeen said, frowning. "The Praetory tries to suppress anything like that with an iron fist. Count Peter Crowley was a well-known, respected noble. Knowing that he and his Shadow were active acolytes would have lent more credence to Jupiter's cause. I suppose that he would have come out and revealed the information himself eventually for that exact reason, but perhaps he was worried about his ability to protect his family. Still." Aberdeen sounded bitter. "I'd been hoping that whatever secret had been hidden in that vault would be juicier, no offence. We'd bet our lives on finding a secret that could bring the entirety of the Praetory to its knees, and instead my friend died for *this*."

I remembered Kipling standing over the forest spirit.

"I'm sorry about your friend," I said quietly. "I saw his last moments. He was brave."

Aberdeen nodded, too choked to speak. I suddenly, ridiculously, wanted to reach out to comfort him. I ignored the instinct.

"Now they're hunting for us," Aberdeen finally managed. "They're intent on massacring anyone who's witnessed this recording. It seems extreme. Maybe there's more to this than we're seeing. For whatever reason, the Praetory thinks this information represents a massive danger to them, and they'll kill anyone they have to in order to reclaim it."

I wondered if Jo could have possibly known the truth about my father. Something in me felt if she had, I would have picked up that she was lying. Jo told me how classified the information was in the vault beneath the Academy. Perhaps that meant some secrets were above even her own clearance.

Aberdeen hesitated. After a moment, it occurred to me he may be listening to someone in his earpiece.

"Crowley, the others are here. I'm just going to go fill them in on this little situation, is that all right? Take your time."

"Other acolytes?" I queried, shocked. But he had already strode into one of the adjoining chambers, slowly closing the wooden door behind him. I imagined he must still have some way of keeping watch on me, or otherwise he'd have locked the exits. I didn't believe leaving here after what I knew would be quite so easy now.

I stood shakily, and walked around the space, trying to familiarise myself with it. I reached out to run my hand across a tapestry. My fingers passed tentatively across the horned, metal mask of the tiger depicted there.

Oh, Father. Was this really the world that you loved?

I proceeded to run my hands over the sanctum's columns of stone, thinking how every part of this place was part of who he was. Every feature, every element that I'd thought belied a greater evil... was actually something that Father had cared about deeply. This had been his home.

Shadows' Eve killed so many in the war. Still, I couldn't pretend I hadn't seen the suffering of Shadows first hand in the short time I'd been here. They were often treated as second-class citizens, even in the event they *did* find their human counterparts. As far as the Praetory was concerned, they were meant to be seen, not heard. To serve, not to lead, no matter what they really wanted.

If the acolytes weren't fanatics, if they really were just fighting for the liberation of Shadows, then I could understand why Father would see it as a worthy fight for justice. Yet despite their best efforts, Peter Crowley and Thames died before the end of the war. They weren't there to protect Jupiter when he was captured and imprisoned. Jupiter had been without his trusted knights when he needed them most.

I was going to need to watch that recording of my father many times before this would finally begin to make sense. I was at peace with that. Each time it played, it felt as if I was keeping a piece of him alive for just a little longer.

I spotted a gossamer spiderweb spun between two torch brackets. There was a struggling fly trapped within it. I felt myself drawn closer to watch while also strangely detached. A spider was moving in on the panicked fly, summoned by its vibrations, subtly crossing the strings of its meticulous trap.

I just stared, hypnotised, as the spider moved in to coldly devour its prey. I'd spent so long trying to harden myself against all of my doubts and my softer instincts. I had sternly told myself that I had to be the predator. Merciless. Calculating. Avenging without hesitation.

I remembered the night he'd died, just before the chaos had started. When it had just been him and me, serene with the night entirely to ourselves.

We had come to a stop among the trees at the top of the hill. Father had stretched his legs, clearly relishing our race up from the villa. I could see through the broken branches and across the water to where the lights of Wellington glowed beside the ocean, a small, luminescent citadel.

"Well, hey there, little friend," my father had said suddenly. He had spotted something on a branch, and I hadn't needed to look to know that it would be some kind of critter. To Father, the outdoors had been a veritable wonderland of fauna. Every stirring by a bird or an insect, or even an invasive possum, had caused him delight.

"Come on over here, Alex. Get a look at this little beauty."

"You know everyone else calls me Crowley now, right?" I had said, casually. *"School friends, Mother... the postman."*

"Ah, yes, sorry. But to me, you'll always be my wee little Alex," he had teased. *"Just as you were on this day, twelve years ago, when I held you in my arms as a wee little babe. Squealing, wrinkled, demanding attention... oh, shit, he's getting away. Quick, take a look!"*

Father had turned and offered his hand to me. I'd nearly shrieked.

"Oh my God. That's a wētā. That's a giant wētā!"

I'd taken in its spindly, spiny legs, its brown carapace shell, its grasshopper-like head with blank, dark staring eyes and antennae weaving through the air. The tree wētās around Wellington were only meant to get to six centimeters at the most, but this one had been a giant.

"It's nearly the size of your freaking hand!"

"Oh, don't exaggerate. Look at the gentle fella. Do you want to hold him?"

"I respectfully do not wish to, he is terrifying. Unless you brought my hazmat suit and anti-anxiety meds."

"Crowley," my father had reprimanded me, more sternly. *"We've been over this. Just because something looks a bit spooky, or like not what you're used to..."*

"I know, I know," I had sighed. *"We have to look deeper. But it doesn't change the fact that it's creepy as heck."*

My father had held out the wētā to me.

"Hold out your hand."

"Fatherrrrr..." I had pouted dramatically.

"Come on, now."

Taking in a breath for courage, I had held out my hand. The wētā had tentatively felt me, its antennae tickling my bare skin. Then it had obediently clambered across onto my hand, seeming a little stunned at the series of events that had beset it that evening.

I had giggled, marvelling at it. It had been kind of incredible, now that I was holding it, and it hadn't attacked me.

Now, standing in the acolyte's sanctuary, I knew what I was doing as I strummed the web, allowing the fly to break free. I watched as the disorientated insect buzzed away. It seemed unable to believe its luck.

Then it was gone.

This was Father's home, I reflected strangely. The Praetory wasn't the wonderful place I'd wanted it to be and the acolytes weren't just terrorists either. They wanted to rebuild the Praetory on a different foundation, one of equity. One of Shadows and humans living as equal citizens, without the class system that held them in an iron, suffocating grip.

I could hear the other acolytes conversing with Aberdeen from the other side of that door.

"She's a spoilt little princess," one of them protested heatedly as I near the door. I recognised the voice. It was Victor from my class. I felt chills. "We're meant to just welcome her in? She knows your identity, Aberdeen. If we let her out, she'll tell everyone about our hideout and bring them down on our heads. We already know that she has some kind of personal connection with the Governor."

"I accept the risk," Aberdeen fired back with crackling ferocity.

"Oh, gee, big surprise." I recognised that voice too. I swallowed. It was Maeve.

Just how many of my classmates were acolytes, exactly? This was ridiculous. Was being an acolyte just trendy now?

"You're distracted by her pretty looks, and it's going to get us all killed."

That theory was amusing. Aberdeen had made it pretty clear he was disgusted by me.

"She *is* pretty, to be honest," another acolyte confided conspiratorially.

"We're getting off base here," Aberdeen said derisively.

"Look, we can't keep her under watch 24/7."

"So what are you suggesting? She's Sir Peter Crowley's daughter and heir. We need to trust her."

"She came here to kill us! You can't counter that with logic. She's an angry, impulsive girl who'll get us all killed."

"I hope I'm not interrupting," I said quietly, stepping through to where the acolytes were locked in argument. Judging from their heights and builds, they all seemed to be teenagers. They must all be students here at the Academy.

Eight horned tigers were staring back at me.

"I'm sorry, Crowley," a masked acolyte said to me. I could tell it was Maeve. I could make out the bulge at the back of her robes from her harpy wings. "You weren't..."

"...meant to hear your honest thoughts? No matter. Though if you have any issues with me, I'd prefer it if you spoke them directly to my face. Aberdeen, please." I looked to him imploringly. "Don't release that information about my father. You know it won't bring down the Praetory all on its own like you want it to. Far from it."

"Our brothers and sisters in the cause died for this," he said tightly. "I'm not just going to..."

"Then my family will be brought under scrutiny, and they may lose everything. People may look into me more closely, and that will lead back to you. Just... wait, is all I'm asking. If Peter Crowley really meant anything to you all, then do this favour for me. Give me some time."

Time to make sense of all of this, if that was ever possible.

Aberdeen stared hard at me, then exchanged a glance with Maeve, deferring.

So. She was the leader of this group. It was surprising seeing Aberdeen having so much respect for someone he was actually displaying obedience.

Maeve finally nodded.

"Her mother is Minister Crowley!" another member of the team exploded. Victor. He'd never been my biggest fan. "She's sent more acolytes to prison than anyone!"

"That only makes Crowley more useful to us," Aberdeen insisted, stepping between me and the others as if to physically shield me. Perhaps it was because he was determined to avoid looking at me.

"Aberdeen, why are you really defending her?" Maeve implored him urgently. "Because she's your friend?"

"Alexandra Crowley is not my... fine, just... look. Do you think I planned to be here, fighting for her?" Aberdeen asked the room at large. "She aggravates me. Her entertainment value does not supersede her inherently infuriating qualities."

"The feeling's mutual," I heard myself say automatically.

"But I know that we *need* her, and I believe that she can change things," Aberdeen said imperiously, lashing the others with his words like fire. "She's part of this war. Whether she likes what that means or not. Also, Crowley was monitoring our break-in into the school from the start. She convinced the *Governor* to give her privileged information into the search for us, and then she did what Kipling and all the Praetory forces have failed to do for years: she located our sanctum. She's a weapon, and we'd be wasting an opportunity to use this weapon against our enemy."

"How can we just let her go now?" Maeve asked, frustrated. "How can we trust...?"

"You can't," I said. "But you trusted in my father. And I loved him. So, there's that."

Maeve stared at me, considering. I could sense the enormous weight on her shoulders. Being merciful to me meant risking the lives and freedom of her own people.

I came here to destroy a terrorist cell, I reflected. *Instead I've found a bunch of underdogs in tatty costumes.*

Nothing was as it seemed. In my mind's eye I could see Father with a prickly wētā clutched in his hands.

"Do you want to hold him?"

"I respectfully do not wish to, he is terrifying. Unless you brought my hazmat suit and anti-anxiety meds."

"Sweetie," my father reprimanded me, his voice stern. *"We've been over this. Just because something looks a bit spooky, or like not what you're used to..."*

"I know, I know," I sighed, rolling my eyes. *"We have to look deeper. But it doesn't change the fact that it's creepy as heck."*

"Maeve," Aberdeen said witheringly, "Because we didn't take bigger risks, Puck was killed. So were some of the best acolytes left in Wellington."

"They died *because* a risk was taken!" Maeve said sharply. "There was a reason I ordered our people not to get involved with that suicide mission. I'm just glad I didn't lose you too. It's my job to protect you lot."

"No, it's not. You know that any of us would gladly give our life for the cause!" Aberdeen glared imperiously. "Just like Puck did. Otherwise, what are we doing here? I thought you recruited me because I wasn't scared to do whatever it takes."

"That's enough, Aberdeen." Maeve stepped toward him, her voice softening. She didn't make an effort to hide the affection she had for him. "These people will need you," she murmured, so softly I don't think I was meant to hear it, and most of the others wouldn't have. "I can only take you so far. If we're going to grow again, if we're going to take the cause further, you'll need to take up the mantle. I'll need you leading beside me."

"I already tased Sephy to escape with that intelligence,

and I have to look her in the face every day," Aberdeen said, closing his eyes against the pain of the guilt. He folded his arms, resolute. "I'm not about to add *'murdering her new friend'* to the scrapbook." Did I detect the slightest tone of jealousy from him, admitting Sephy had another friend? "Besides, Crowley has as good a reason as any of us for wanting to join."

"Oh, and what's that?" Victor said sardonically. Apparently, he wasn't particularly bright.

"What Aberdeen means is, that if the Praetory murdered my father as you say," I smiled pleasantly, and they all turned to face me, "and if that order came from the very top, you can be sure that I'll bring the whole rotten edifice crumbling down. I will lay waste to all of the Praetory and the throne itself, and laugh as it burns."

15

Swallowing, I walked up to the door of Sephy's room. I was guiltily holding two large *Midnight Runner* mochas. My nerves increased the closer I got.

I worried that this would look like sucking up, as if I was trying to paint over how I'd treated her last week with a small bribe. Perhaps it was too blatant. Even a little weird maybe, and... I don't know, overly intense?

'*PLEASE!*' the mochas seemed to be screaming. '*I KNOW I'VE BEEN SHUTTING YOU OUT LATELY BUT I'M SORRY, BE MY FRIEND!*'

It was stupid. But I'd felt uncomfortably wretched ever since our last conversation. Even though I wasn't used to having someone constantly invading my personal space and roping me into her elaborate schemes, Sephy had... actually... been one of the best parts of entering Counterpart Academy. I'd never had much practice at having friends though, or at making contrite apologies.

Filled with anxiety, hoping she didn't mind mochaccinos with extra cream and molten marshmallows, I gently knocked.

Then I pushed the door of Sephy's bedroom open a crack, but she wasn't in her own bed. Shocker. I decided to try upstairs.

My hangs with Sephy were the only piece of normalcy I had left here. This dorm had been my little sanctuary. Watching old black and white movies in the evening after our homework had been my little bubble of normal. Not that I would ever have imagined watching *A Streetcar Named Desire* with a feisty manticore would have been a welcome afterschool activity.

I carefully balanced the coffees in their holder, climbing the stairs. Then I slowly prised open my bedroom door, peering in at the darkness...

There were two slumbering bodies on my bed. One was Sephy, curled up asleep, her body protectively encircling a smaller form as if guarding it with her very life...

Harper. Oh shit, of course. He'd told me he was coming over to visit last night, and in my pursuit of Shadows' Eve I'd entirely forgotten. I hadn't even come back to the dorm last night. After the conversations with the acolytes, trying to gain more answers and meaning, I'd walked the grounds of the school, then wandered all the way down into Wellington Central. I'd been the first morning customer at *Midnight Runner*, in a brazen attempt to buy forgiveness.

Harper whimpered suddenly, turning, caught in the throes of a nightmare. I watched as Sephy softly extended one of her monkey arms across him protectively. Sisterly, even. I'd never thought Harper would let anyone else do that.

I backed away, out of that room. It was the sweetest sight in the world, but it left me heartbroken as I thought of what might be coming next.

The coffees slipped from my numb hands, their

contents splashing and spilling out onto the carpet beside my doorway, congealed with cream and molten marshmallow. I cursed, then sighed as I went back downstairs to get a wet cloth and towels for the clean-up.

What if Sephy found out about all of this? It was as if I could feel my father's blood running through me, acolyte blood. I wasn't sure if that would make me dirty in her eyes. Worse, I already felt my lies to Sephy were putting a wedge between us, and now the revelation in the sanctum meant that Sephy and I might never be able to be close and honest with each other. *Ever*. Especially if my destiny was sending me on a path to join the very reviled rebel group I'd sworn to destroy.

Sadly, there was barely anything left in the coffee cups. I found myself in the bathroom, pouring their meagre contents down the sink. The chocolatey beverages sadly disappeared out of sight. I gripped the porcelain sink to steady myself against my spinning thoughts.

Could I really believe Aberdeen and the others? Was this all some strange hallucination? I was struggling to make sense of it, intellectually and emotionally.

I already *was* what Sephy hated. Even if I told her the whole truth now, Shadows' Eve was already in my bones. I'd been an acolyte all along, even if I hadn't woken up to it until now. Aberdeen had told me how Sephy's father James Nekomata had been a talented advisor, a man who had a great influence on Sephy as she grew up. An advisor in hunting down and killing enemies of the Praetory like Shadows' Eve... enemies like my own Father.

You could tell Sephy the truth. All of it, I told myself. Yes, I could tell her about the discovery that my father and his Shadow were Jupiter's knights. I could tell her how

Aberdeen, her dormmate and friend, had been lying to her all these months.

How would Sephy react, though? She was raised her entire life to believe that Shadows' Eve were a murderous cult, nothing more than a bunch of zealous terrorists. Just as I believed with certainty, until yesterday. But even if she knew the truth, I didn't feel Sephy was the revolutionary type politically, no matter what her rebel behaviour might suggest otherwise. She was part of the Academy staff, the type of person who believed in working inside a system to change it incrementally. She might be a Shadow, but she had respect here, power even, and she never seemed to have identified with broader Shadow issues as much.

If Sephy found out the truth about Aberdeen and me, what I was now keeping from her too... she'd feel betrayed. No, she'd be hurt, outraged, furious. She would hand Aberdeen and me over to the authorities, if she truly believed that Shadows' Eve posed a danger to the innocents in the school.

Maybe I wasn't giving her enough credit, but it was far too big a risk to take. It wasn't just my life that I'd be endangering by disclosing everything to her.

"Crowley?" I heard Sephy say, and I nearly jumped. She prowled through the doorway into the bathroom, regarding me with concern. "What is it?"

"I brought you coffees..." I said vaguely.

"Are you kidding me?" Sephy exclaims. "That's amazing, where are they? Gimme sugar!"

"I dropped them."

Sephy rolled her eyes theatrically.

"You're killing me, Crowley."

I cleared my throat. There was a lump there.

"Thanks for looking after Harper for me."

"Anytime."

"But I thought you said we were enemies?" I asked pointedly.

"Oh, absolutely," she agreed. "But I adore *him*, you know that."

I smiled at her. I couldn't help it.

"Crowley, you never came home."

"I know," I murmured.

"You forgot Harper. That just isn't like you."

"There's something going on," I confessed, my throat closing up. "I... can't talk about it yet. But you're the first I'll talk to about it when I can. I just wanted to say... sorry. About... you know." I shook my head. "I was a jackass."

It was her turn to smile.

"I'm sure you were trying to protect me, in your signature annoying fashion."

Even if I couldn't tell her the truth, I realised then and there that there was something else I wanted to tell her. Something I needed so badly to share with someone, but never had. I needed to make it real, and Sephy was the only person I wanted to confide in.

Slowly, I sat down, perching on the edge of the bathtub.

"Sephy, you asked when we first met if I'd been to the Academy before," I said, clearing my throat. "You were right."

Sephy sat, watching me. Her tail gently swept back and forth as she waited patiently.

Finally I spoke, and my voice sounded thick.

"When Father died a year ago, near the end of the war... he was bleeding out in my arms, and I found some kind of pendant on him. I didn't think much of it at the time, with everything else going on. The pendant seemed to be carved from white bone."

"That's an acolyte's talisman," Sephy said in a hushed whisper. "He must have taken it from his killers."

Yes, that's what I had thought too. But the talisman had been carved into the shape of a tortoise. Now the truth that it had been Father's own talisman seemed much clearer, and far more obvious.

"I know," I said, avoiding her eyes. "That must have been it. But back then I barely knew any specifics about the Praetory, or the war. A month after Father had died the talisman started making a signal, as if someone was calling to it."

Sephy stared, hanging on my every word.

"I followed it," I whispered. "I followed it from my house all the way up to the Botanic Gardens in the Cable Car, hoping I'd find answers to what really happened to him. I felt my way through the invisible barrier... and I found the wonderful school that he'd told me about. The academy that he used to go to." I swallowed. "This was during the final days of the war. Counterpart Academy had been evacuated. Shadows' Eve and the Praetory had fought with each other here on the grounds, and there... there were so many bodies. On both sides." I clamped my eyes shut, remembering the horror.

"Oh, Crowley," Sephy breathed gently. "You *saw* that?"

"I followed the talisman's signal," I continued, determined to get through the tale. "Deep down, to the lowest levels of the Academy, and I found a Shadow, someone who was wounded from the battle." I felt my eyes glaze over. "This great Shadow, unlike anything I'd ever seen before. He was the first Shadow I ever properly met. He didn't want my help, but he was hurt, and I told him to shut up and let me help him. He told me he was a Praetory soldier, a general hiding from the enemy. I nursed him back to health. We... I thought we had a bond. He even..."

I shook my head, and I couldn't even speak the words past the lump in my throat. I was barely aware of the room around us any longer. I was back during the war a year ago, when I had infiltrated this very academy, searching for answers...

I kept staring at the unmoving body of the Shadow I'd just killed, unable to believe what had happened. They lay there on the floor like a giant moth, their wings stretched wide.

"I shot them," I moaned, wrapping my arms tightly around myself. We were in the basement beneath the Academy. It was deathly quiet, as if the world was hushed in the wake of what I'd just done.

The blood. I couldn't look away from the blood.

"I just killed them!"

"Scarecrow," Jupiter murmured. His nickname for me. I barely heard it. "Hey! Alexandra, listen to me."

His voice, always so commanding, sounded strained now. And it was the first time he'd said my real name. That stopped me. I turned slowly to look up at the giant tiger behind me.

The great striped titan loomed like a living mountain, covered in battle-scars and bone armour that gleamed like dark steel. His horns curled skyward like a crown made for war. But it wasn't any of that I saw in that moment. It was his eyes. Ferocious, yes—but not cold. They were filled with something else. Something soft. Something human.

I moved before I could stop myself, pressing my face into his warm fur, seeking something—anything—to anchor me. His body went rigid in surprise. Then, slowly, almost tenderly, he wrapped one of those massive paws around me, pulling me close. And for the first time since all this began, I felt safe.

I didn't want to, but I forced myself to take one more look at the still, unmoving body of the moth Shadow on the floor. Someone who seconds ago had been a fully living, breathing, thinking, conscious person. Someone who might have had a family.

They had come here to hurt him. I'd just been protecting him, I reminded myself. This was my first kill, it was meant to be hard. I was meant to feel like I was the one dying as well, as if the whole world had been turned upside down.

"Why did you do that?" he demanded. "Why the hell did you do that! I had it handled!"

"Oh, I'm sorry!" I said, temper flaring. "You think I was just going to let you die?"

For a split second, his face faltered. I saw guilt. Like it cut him deeply that someone like me—small, breakable—had thrown herself between him and death.

"How about 'thank you for saving my arse, Crowley?'" I shot at him.

"You're impossible," he hissed, swiftly turning away from me. "I don't need a little scarecrow like you helping me..." He strode over toward the dead Shadow, to inspect the body...

Then he swayed, and collapsed. I felt the impact through the floor.

"Jupiter!"

I rushed to his side, falling to my knees. He wasn't going to make it much longer without help.

"We need to get you out of here," I said, afraid, tears in my eyes. "There are going to be others coming too. We can't stay here." Still nothing. I tried to shake him, but my hands were so tiny against his furred flank. "Look, maybe I'm not your human!" I pleaded with him, my heart hammering. "Perhaps

you're not my Shadow. But all we have right now is each other. I can help you, why can't you just trust me?"

He opened his eyes slowly, pain etched in every breath. But his voice was heartbreakingly gentle.

"You already lost your father. You have an entire future ahead of you, and it's going to be glorious. You don't have to lose that. Get out of here."

The kindness in his voice was more unbearable than the silence. He wanted me to live. Even if it meant dying alone.

"My full name is Alexandra Crowley, alright?" I said desperately. I could hear movement from upstairs now, rapid footfalls that echoed all the way down here. They were coming. A lot of them. "There. Most people just call me Crowley."

"Crowley?" Jupiter repeated slowly. Something seemed to change in him as he said it.

"Yes. My father was Count Peter Crowley. I was there when he was ambushed and killed, that's how I got this." I gestured at my prosthetic. "That's why I came here. I want to understand what he was involved in, and who killed him. Look, this isn't just some trick. I am on your side, and there's no way in hell I'm leaving you here."

"I know," Jupiter murmured. The striped behemoth looked down at me as if he finally believed me.

"I helped him escape the grounds," I heard myself saying to Sephy. "I risked my life to help him. But afterwards, I found out that he'd lied. He wasn't a general of the Praetory. He was the enemy. He'd been a member of Shadows' Eve all along."

I couldn't tell her it had been Jupiter, the Dark Father himself; I feared even *Sephy* would report me if I confessed that. But I'd wanted to tell her as much of the truth as I could.

"Crowley..."

"I'd needed someone so badly," I continued, "because I'd been so alone. I trusted him. Then when I found out he'd lied about who he was... I felt so betrayed that he'd just used me. I thought for just a moment, I'd had a parent again who would really look out for me." My voice quietened. "I hated that Shadow for a long time after that, thinking of how he must have been mocking me all along. The naïve girl who helped the acolyte general escape."

Now, all of that hate was for nothing. Yes, Jupiter had lied to me that fateful night I'd snuck into this Academy. I'd had no idea that in my search for answers, I would cross paths with the Dark Father himself.

Now I understood why he'd let me help him. Why he had fought so hard for me. I was his knight's daughter, and he hadn't known that until I'd told him my full name.

Nothing is as I'd thought it was. Perhaps it was my destiny, calling me to be an acolyte as my father was, which had drawn me to Jupiter's distress signal. Fate was to blame just as much as the talisman had been.

I suppose there was some relief in finally telling someone what had happened to me, if not all of it. I couldn't possibly tell Sephy that fate had crossed my path with the leader of Shadows' Eve and I had let him go, oblivious to his enormous significance at the time. But I was still afraid to look at Sephy straight away.

What I'd just told her, how I assisted an acolyte, even if I claimed it was a mistake... if the wrong person found that out, it might be enough to land me in prison. The Praetory wasn't so forgiving about such things. They didn't differentiate between acolytes and those that helped them.

Now it seemed I was both.

"I'm sorry," Sephy murmured, and there was so much feeling in those two words. "That wasn't fair of him. Manipulating a girl, just so he could preserve his own life... that was cowardly."

But that wasn't true. Jupiter had been the furthest thing from a coward I had ever met. Because he had tried to refuse my help at first, hadn't he? He hadn't wanted to place me in danger as well. The very idea had seemed shameful to him.

"You weren't to know who this general was, or which side he was really serving," Sephy said firmly.

"Sometimes I wonder," I said slowly, "about how he didn't *feel* evil. Not even... misguided, or unhinged. He just felt like another person. A *good* person. What if my instincts were right? What if Shadows' Eve aren't as violent as everyone thinks they are?"

I'd thought Jupiter had been a monster, but it turned out he might be our only chance for liberation. I'd wondered for so long why I'd trusted him so quickly and deeply, if he'd truly been such a terrible person.

My heart was beating extraordinarily quickly. When I gathered the courage to nervously meet Sephy's gaze, there was an awful look in them that I couldn't face. It broke me.

"What's *happened* to you?" Sephy said, looking at me reproachfully. "No one wants to make Shadows' Eve pay more than you. They're radicals. They ignored sacred laws, took countless lives and tried to destroy the Praetory itself. They just wanted to break things, no matter who they hurt."

"You can't believe wars are that black and white," I whispered. I was sure of it. I knew her.

"The Praetory is wonderful, Crowley. Yes, it has problems, but it brings people together from my world and yours in harmony. It stands for peace, and maybe even a future where our two worlds can work together someday. That's why my parents gave me up; so I could come to this world and serve a higher purpose. Shadows' Eve wanted to throw all of that away. Jupiter wasn't a saviour, he just wanted power."

Sephy's was uncharacteristically sombre and serious, staring out into something I couldn't see. In that silent moment, I reflected on the grace she had that made her seem older and more authoritative than her years. She often used that air of dignified maturity to gain favours from others and bring them around to helping on her crazy schemes for the school, but in this moment, I saw it more clearly than ever before.

"Sephy," I said uncertainly, "are you okay?"

She shook herself, as if just coming awake. Straightening, she studied me, her expression still distant.

"Shadows' Eve can't come back, Crowley," Sephy said, and my blood ran cold. "If they did, and if they freed Jupiter, everything we've built back up would come crumbling down. This Academy, our friends. All of it. This last year of healing from all that trauma would be for nothing. The acolytes have to be brought to justice, for all our sakes. Every last one." Sephy exhaled, as if shaking it off. "Now, come on. Let's go make Harper some pancakes."

"Of course," I said quietly, but I don't think the word was audible past the lump in my throat.

Sephy headed downstairs, leaving me with the strangest feeling that my insides had just been shredded into ribbons.

· · ·

Aberdeen and I had barely spoken since the events in the sanctum. The one time we had, he'd entered my room and lent me a book without a word. The silence between us had crackled like electricity.

It was *his* book. Jupiter's. The Dark Father in his own words—journal entries, teachings, quiet reflections before the war swallowed everything. I'd built him up in my mind as a monster, all fire and ruin. But on those pages... he was thoughtful. Kind. *Human.*

Reading it felt like hearing his voice again. Back on that fateful night, when I'd felt safe, his giant limbs coiled protectively around me. Before Mother told me he was evil. Before I forced myself to believe it.

When I wasn't reading the journal I kept it hidden in a larger book with hollowed out pages, bound in a chain and little lock as it was just a teenage girl's secret diary. Because nothing screamed: *'Don't look here'* like a diary covered in hearts.

I slid the fake diary and its treasonous contents under my mattress that night, then lay there in the dark, hollow and aching. When I finally dreamed, I entered a nightmare.

I was standing in the forest in Miramar again, where Father and I had been ambushed... the place where I lost him. But this time I didn't glimpse soldiers. Instead, there was someone else out there in the forest. Someone hunting me.

Then she emerged through the black. A prowling wildcat with monkey arms instead of front legs, and a long tail like a whip covered in deadly quills. She was hunting for the traitor. For me.

It was just a nightmare, I told myself when I woke gasping, drenched in sweat. *It was just your fear talking.*

Somehow Sephy Nekomata had gotten inside my head, and I didn't know if she would ever let me go.

16

The First Matching Ceremony of Counterpart Academy was equal parts a sacred event, a spiritual milestone, and a totally bonkers psychic wedding reception with extra glitter.

It was held in the Academy Grand Hall, which stood like an enormous theatre on the north side of the grounds by the Academy's gardens. Everyone in the school was already whispering, spreading gossip on who might be the latest Shadow and human to discover they were counterparts. Bets were being placed. Apparently, sometimes it was obvious which humans and Shadows had discovered their connection, while other times it came as a slow realisation. Some students didn't disclose that they were hearing each other's thoughts, and were therefore each other's life companion, until the public announcement at the Matching Ceremony. I imagined most of the people who would be announced must have been in their second year, as they already had the time to get to know their fellow students and figure out which one they were connected to. I wondered, oddly perturbed, if anyone in our year had already discovered who their counterpart was. I wondered what it would be like to hear the voice of that other person, the missing part of you, inside your head.

"Come on, Crowley," Sephy was urging me. She was waiting for me, sitting on the steps leading up to the hall. "We're going to be late." She was wearing eye shadow as well as a sparkly blue vest with a bowtie. A top hat sat on her head just back from her tufted ears, allowing the ears room to perk up at any eavesdropped gossip. Her outfit was striking. It also brought to mind cat fashion shows.

At times like this I missed heels. Heels may not be very practical, but they were even less so with a prosthetic.

My conversation with Sephy had been haunting me, as had the twist on my nightmares of late. I'd acted reluctant when she'd urged me to accompany her tonight, but to be honest I was glad to hide my troubles behind a smile, and to have an evening where we could just be two normal students like the ones milling all around us.

"What is it?" Sephy asked, stopping me. She was looking at me intently.

"What?"

"It just looks like... I've just never seen you quite like this," Sephy murmured. "I'm here if you need to talk."

I was stricken. I knew for a fact that I was a good liar. Even if my mother hadn't seen to it that I'd received formal training as part of my normal adolescent education, I'd always had a talent for hiding my true thoughts. I made such a concerted effort to flawlessly bring every intonation, every little tone and facial tic, carefully under control.

So how was it that she could see right through me?

When I didn't respond Sephy acted as if nothing had happened, chattering away to me about inane school topics as she gently accompanied me into the ceremony. Which was exactly what I needed.

"Maybe you can find your own Shadow here tonight," Sephy said cheerfully, startling me. "Or at least find yourself some guy at the party to make out with in a dark corner. A lot of the guys here are looking at you like they wanna be your Daddy."

"Sephy!" I choked. She laughed at me for being a prude.

"You're too easy. Now come on, Crowley, you're going to make us late," Sephy said, sliding past me.

Together, we entered the Matching Ceremony.

The Academy hall was set out like a grand theatre, with a circle of seating up above and a great stage. Sephy informed me that was where some of the most important nobles and dignitaries of the Praetory would be gathering. The first pairing of the year was an auspicious occasion, where the most important nobles in New Zealand Praetory society wanted to make sure they were seen. My heartbeat quickened.

Was Mother out there in the circle too? Was she watching right now? Surely, as a Minister, she must have been.

Mother had never even introduced me to her Shadow, the counterpart who was meant to be the other half of her. That was how much she hid of herself.

Giant black curtains hung from the walls, rendering the space infinite. The seating on the ground floor was packed away. Instead round bar tables had been spaced out, where some students were now sitting and mingling. Countless others stood talking with drinks in hand. It looked like every student in the school was in attendance, all of them dressed in their flashiest attire. Plates of fancy *hors d'oeuvres* were carried aloft by waiters. Lanterns like glowing orbs hung suspended at different heights overhead with a soft glow. If I stood under them at the right angle I could make out the Brilliance Stones gently illuminating them from within. It gave the strange impression that the intimidating hall had been transformed into a wedding reception with a dash of mystique.

I was still orienting myself when I realised I'd misplaced Sephy. Searching around, my gaze lighted on someone else who was welcomely familiar.

"Jo!" I called out in relief. She turned, and smiled broadly. The Governor of New Zealand looked like she was caught up in conversation with some other aristocrats. It looked as if she revelled in this entire affair. She was draped in an outrageously gorgeous dress of flowing sky-blue, decorated in chains and ornaments that belonged more on a fashion runway than on a member of government. And that's what I admired about her: zero concern for what a *'Governor'* was supposed to look like, only for what made her feel *good*.

"Crowley!" she welcomed me with a delighted laugh. She placed an arm over my shoulders, almost protectively, as she introduced me to the others. "Rocco, Obadiah, this is Alexandra Crowley! She's Minister Crowley's daughter. Excuse us for a moment, we get too little time together as it is..."

"Why aren't you in the upper circle?" I commented, once Jo had led me away from the others. "Why rubbing shoulders with the common rabble like ourselves?"

"I was looking for you, of course!"

"For me?"

"Yes, for *you*," she mocked me gently, as if I was being mildly foolish. "Hey, how's your first semester been going? I've seen your scores from the simulations. Seriously impressive. It's a *travesty* we haven't caught up for another dinner yet. Let me know when works and I'll totally clear a time in my schedule."

"What if you have a clashing appointment with some ambassador?" I asked, amused.

"Then I'll cancel it."

"Ah, of course."

"That's half the fun of being the Governor, babe," Jo winked. She looked around, checking we weren't being watched, then dropped her voice. "Have you found out anything more? I know you've had your own little side investigation going..."

"I'm sorry," I lied, uncomfortable. "Nothing useful has come up yet."

"I see. That's irksome."

"For you and me both."

"Well, maybe it's for the best," Jo shrugged. "I didn't want you getting too near this, to be honest. It's a sensitive matter. I'm getting a lot of heat from above as far as these acolytes are concerned, and I wouldn't want you to get burned too."

I studied her carefully. Her words seemed to confirm that my father's recording had been important to someone higher up than herself, confirming my theory that she was just as in the dark as I'd been. If Jo had known, would I blame her for not telling me? She'd probably think she was allowing me to grieve the man I knew, rather than a monster.

Jo had the potential to be a powerful ally. If I could show her Father's recording, maybe I could deprogram her from the Praetory's horror stories about Shadows' Eve. I couldn't do it though until I was sure that I could sit her down long enough to make her listen, and that she'd agree to keep my secret. As Governor, her political bias would be more deeply ingrained than mine.

She put her arm around my shoulders.

"We need to have a talk about your future, too. Your mother mentioned she wishes for you to work in my office, and I'm sure you'd be more capable than most of the staff I already have. But I wondered what *you* really want?"

I looked quickly at her, taken by surprise.

"I want to be a knight." The answer blurted out of me, unfiltered. "I want to serve."

But serve who, I wondered, and for what cause? Yes, I still longed to be a knight, but perhaps I should be pledging myself to the acolytes. Or maybe I should just give in to Mother's dream and get a job in government. Become a bureaucratic Trojan horse and attend tedious meetings while secretly plotting regime change between coffee breaks. If the Praetory truly was my enemy, everything was starting to look a lot different. What did I really believe in now, and what did true justice look like?

"You would be an excellent knight," Jo said seriously. I looked away, uncomfortable with her praise.

"That path looks a little blocked off from me right now," I muttered.

"I wouldn't say that," Jo replied mysteriously. "Any noble would be lucky to have you, Crowley. I've seen what you can do, all the way back when we were children and you were being trained on your estate. There's no one who would make a finer knight."

I looked down, my eyes burning, thinking of my father. It was absurd, but I nearly offered Jo my fealty, right then and there. I sensed right in that moment that I did have an ally in my corner. Someone who may also have what it took to untangle the complexities between the Praetory and Shadows' Eve.

"Thank you," I said quietly. When I looked back at Jo, I had a smile firmly in place. "I'd gladly try some more of that fettuccine."

Jo laughed and slapped me on the back.

"I would be honoured to make your dreams come true."

There was suddenly a deep hymn, a solemn music that came from all around us. It was followed by the beating of ceremonial drums, growing louder and fiercer. It was impossible to not feel a magical sense of awe and anticipation.

"We'll talk soon," Jo said. She pulled me into a rough hug, surprising me. "Don't worry, everything is going to be okay." She smiled as we parted, slightly emotional. "I'm Governor. I'll make sure of it."

Before I could speak, the music abruptly cut with an explosion of confetti. Cannons launched pink, green and yellow streamers up into the air above the stage, and balloons cascaded down from above, bumping into our heads and floating all around us. There were murmurs and joyful exclamations from the audience.

When I turned, Jo and her entourage had already made for the upper circle. But she smiled at me before she ascended to fulfil her formal meet-and-greet duties.

"WELCOME!" a lone, magnified voice suddenly gushed. "To the first Matching Ceremony of the year!"

The balloons parted to reveal Sephy standing there triumphantly up on stage. I stared in shock. Oh, so *that's* where she'd gotten off to. She was wearing a pop-star style microphone wired to catch her voice.

Sephy coughed slightly, as if she may have swallowed a piece of confetti. She recovered well.

"My name is Sephy Nekomata!" she announced, brandishing her tail dramatically. The spines were splayed outward like a fan. "The Matching Ceremony has officially begun!"

There was applause and cheering.

"Now, introducing the names of our new first years!"

Sephy started with the humans' names, which I assumed was the traditional order.

"First we have—Blake Ascott! He loves crafts, swing dancing, and you!" There was applause as a spotlight came up on Blake, seamlessly finding him in the crowd. "Next up is the wonderful Lucy Campion. She enjoys performing slam poetry, and burning effigies! Then we have the incomparable Alexandra Crowley, who enjoys... *studying,* oh, man."

I felt an uncomfortable tension running through me. I realised my heart rate was up, and everything felt hot. I swallowed. I was experiencing a strangely painful cross between wild anticipation and looming dread.

I wasn't ready yet, I realised, terrified. I wasn't ready yet to meet my Shadow. Your Shadow was meant to be your closest friend and confidante, sharing your thoughts and listening to your dreams. That's how Father had explained it to me, anyway. A telepathic link existed between counterparts, emotions and thoughts transmitting seamlessly between the two of them. But here was the problem. Whoever my Shadow turned out to be was about to be neck-deep in my aggressively illegal after-school activities. The cherry on top? From what I'd heard, the Praetory didn't distinguish between counterparts when handing out prison sentences. The sins of your counterpart were yours to share. As far as the Praetory was concerned, Shadows were entirely punishable for their human's crimes.

I wasn't at the Academy to find my Shadow, I reminded myself, even if having my own Shadow might help me on my path. A Shadow felt like a special gift, a wonder that Father had promised me... just before I let him die. I was too weak to save him, but I still survived when he didn't. I would never feel I'd earned my Shadow and deserved to meet them, at least not until I'd truly honoured Father and Thames by avenging them.

But despite that I still found myself tensely waiting, listening out for when the first counterparts would be matched.

"Ladies, gentleman and gentlepersons, you have your humans," Sephy announced, having finished listing the new human students. "Now, I have... your Shadows!"

All of the Shadows in the Academy had spent their lives in Praetory society, I reflected, hidden away. They were eternally unable to touch the outside world without risking exposing their existence. They'd spent their entire lives growing up, waiting to finally meet their humans, and this was the moment. I just hoped their counterparts were more like Father, someone who treated them as a friend and equal, rather than like Kipling.

Sephy was currently squinting at a scroll of paper.

"Next up we have Liero, the naughty, naughty elf..."

"I beg your pardon?" Liero demanded from the audience, outraged.

"Oops, *haughty*. Sorry, couldn't read my handwriting there. Now we have Circe. For her introduction she's written that she's simply '*attached*,'" Sephy announced mysteriously. "Read into that what you will."

"No, it's attached to the sheet," the fairy hissed up at her audibly. "I stapled it."

"Ohhhh, yeah, that makes more sense. Next up we have

Jayhar, who said he would go on a date with me, but still hasn't gotten back to me, which I can only assume is because he has LOST MY NUMBER because I am a GODDESS. Isn't that right?" she asked the crowd seductively.

"You're our goddess!" the crowd chanted back, many of the Shadows seeming to be openly salivating over her.

Sephy winked at them. "That's right."

I shook my head, smiling. She was something else. Sephy held the crowd in the palm of her hand. They didn't just follow her like she was their leader, they adored her.

"May I finally have the pleasure of introducing to you our latest pairing...?" Sephy said, magnified through the speaker. "Joshua Youssef and Vayra!"

I felt a wave of disappointment, so fierce it surprised me. I shoved it away, telling myself I was being childish.

A human and a gem-encrusted golem climbed onstage to bow sheepishly to another round of applause. Both looked flushed and happy as Sephy placed Hawaiian leis around their necks.

"Quiet, please!" Sephy instructed the audience. "Now, as all of you get to know each other, be on the lookout for the one who calls out to you as your counterpart. Someone in this very hall may be the partner for the rest of your life, and your constant companion." The ceremonial drums had started to beat again, but slowly, in and out, in and out, like a heartbeat. "Listen. Your Shadow's mind is whispering to yours. Their heart is singing to your own. Often when we come face to face with our Shadow, we don't recognise ourselves at first. We've been cut off from the other half of ourselves for so long, we don't realise what's right in front of us. Your time here at the Academy will help you to cut through that. It will help you to finally understand who you truly are.

'Now... go forth! Socialise! Get to know each other. And maybe, just maybe..." Sephy smiled, "you might figure out who your counterpart is."

The audience members turned to each other to mingle, but now there was a different kind of energy. Sephy had really convinced them of the possibility that tonight could be magic, that there was lightning to be bottled. The students finally believed that tonight could be the moment they met the missing part of themselves. To me, though, the set-up felt a little too forced and self-aware now, as if we were straight out of a scene on *The Bachelor* or some dreaded dating show.

Having a Shadow was opening up your heart and mind to someone, I reflected. It was about being vulnerable, learning to love someone and trust them with the entirety of yourself. Or at least, that was the romanticised idea. I doubt many people, including Kipling, saw it that way.

It meant accepting your Shadow, just as they accepted you for everything you were, both your perfections and your imperfections.

The very thought made me feel vulnerable. Exposed. Oddly, it made me want to cry.

I wasn't ready for that. My *soul* wasn't ready for that.

If I die trying to get my revenge, does that mean my Shadow will die too? Even if I haven't yet heard their voice in my head? I suddenly wondered. When a Shadow died, their human died, and vice versa.

The idea made me feel wretched. It was one thing playing with fire if it was only my life I was gladly gambling. I already worried I wouldn't be there for Harper. The idea that I could be endangering my own Shadow's life, who I may have only passed as a stranger in these hallways... it was a thought that could plant a crack in my carefully built up resolution, and bring all of my slowly forming plans crashing down. It was a thought that could get me killed.

So I forced it down.

My eyes met another distinctive pair across the hall. Aberdeen was making his way toward me, scrutinising me enigmatically. The candles from the table illuminated his face in flickering light, highlighting his ethereal features. Stupidly beautiful. Intensely unreadable.

"Crowley."

"Aberdeen."

"You didn't seem keen to come to this," he commented.

"I'm still ambivalent."

"More Sephy shenanigans, huh?"

"Always."

He arched an eyebrow at me, judging. He didn't even need to pose the silent question. We both knew we needed to talk, which was why I'd been avoiding him like the plague.

"I've still been working my mind around everything," I said, uncomfortable. Like how the acolytes were formed not as some kind of creepy cult, but an organisation for social justice who started a revolution for equality. Like how the Praetory called it a war, and burnt them to ash rather than concede to change their ancient, bigoted ways. Finally, like how they took my leg from me and murdered my father.

It was a lot to get my head around.

I had spent so long hating Jupiter, feeling all alone in my hurt. I didn't know how to make sense of that either. I'd spent so long hearing about what a monster he was for taking lives, while the murders committed by the Praetory were always painted in a noble light, as if they were done in self-defence.

He stepped closer, not enough to touch, but enough that the air between us grew tighter, hotter. "I've shown you the truth," he said scathingly, voice quiet but laced with fire. "It's up to you if you keep running from it. I would make my move sooner rather than later, if I was you." He leaned in close. "The longer you sit on the fence, the more paranoid my friends become that you might not fall on the right side."

And then he turned and strode away, vanishing among the throng. Just like that. Leaving the space colder. Leaving me standing there with my breath caught halfway up my throat.

Didn't he know? All I *wanted* was to finish this. To find out which member of the Praetory gave the order for my father to be removed from me and Harper's lives, and who carried it out. I wanted to end them. Shadows' Eve could help me with that. Maybe then I'd be ready for what came after.

The only thing I knew for sure was I couldn't sit on the fence any longer. I'd accepted now what Aberdeen, Maeve and the others had shown me. Now I had to accept that I was going to need to cooperate with them if I was really going to move ahead with this.

"Okay, Crowley," I murmured to myself, needing to hear it aloud. "Then let's do this."

"Cool, okay, what are we doing?" Sephy said joyfully from behind me.

"Holy crap!" I swivelled on the spot. "How long were you standing there?

"All your damn life," she said, winking. "I'm your guardian angel."

I noted she was supporting herself with only three limbs; her left hand holding a sunny yellow mimosa. Serving mimosas in the evening? I grimaced in distaste. Perhaps the Praetory really were monsters. Drinking laws seemed much more liberal in the Praetory. It was a more, ah... European vibe.

"Ah... yes," I swallowed. "Heh. Sure. Stay crazy."

"Oh, I plan to, Crowley. I plan to. What were you thinking about?"

"I'll spare you," I said awkwardly, waving a hand airily. "Save you from the drama."

"Oooh, I *LOVE* drama! You must tell me everything. *Everything*," she said slyly, eyes sparkling as she sidled closer.

"This is... personal."

"Alexandra Crowley, has anyone ever told you you're very theatrical?"

"Me? *You're* the one running the Matching Ceremony like some kind of weird game show! You certainly seem to have a way with the crowd."

"As they should, they're my people," Sephy said matter-of-factly. She stood up on her hind-legs to snag an asparagus roll from the table, resting her arms against it. Her tongue lolled out briefly as the roll vanished behind her fangs. She was a lioness with a bite of zebra. "I know how you feel."

"What do you mean?" I asked, cautious.

"*This.* Hearing your classmates paired off, two at a time, no matter whether you're listening or reading it out, is excruciating. The hoping, the adrenaline, the anticipation that you'll be meeting your counterpart any day now... only to be dashed. I can't believe we'll get one of these reminders every month for the rest of our education. I'll become that person just lurking at these tables, chowing down on comfort food." Sephy smiled at me playfully. "At least I'll have a buddy."

"You'll find your human soon," I reassured her, feeling awkward. "I'm sure."

"I know." She sighed. "Of course, there's a chance I already have."

I quirked an eyebrow.

"A certain son of an Italian Duke has made his intentions clear," Sephy said conversationally. "He believes he's my counterpart. He was supposed to be attending as a guest tonight, but he was detained by work. Nonetheless, I've no doubt our families are hashing out the details of the match."

I looked at her sharply, blindsided.

"How can some Duke's son from Italy just *decide* he's your human?"

"Isn't destiny something we choose?" she smiled mysteriously.

"No," I said wryly. "Never in my experience."

"Right. Sorry." Sephy winced, then hunched her back in the cat equivalent of a shrug. "The Duke's son claims he feels a pull toward me. Perhaps I could as well. Perhaps if we get to know each other, we'll discover we are counterparts after all. It would mean a great deal to my family. A Duke of the Praetory, having a Nekomata as his counterpart? My family's status would be restored. We'd climb up the social rankings again. But there are also some candidates here at the Academy too who are of a rank that my parents would consider worthy."

I frowned. I didn't like Sephy acting so cavalier and

nonchalant about sacrificing the course of her entire life for the sake of her family. I also wondered why on earth she'd needed me to tag along as a wingwoman for her encounters with potential candidates for her counterpart. Then the Sephy-ness of the entire situation became clear.

"Oh. So that's why you've demanded my presence," I commented, feeling an odd falling sensation. "To show yourself as an in-demand commodity. Cunning."

It made sense, I'd suspected that Sephy explicitly requesting me to come along so strongly had to have involved a motive. Still, it strangely stung that I was just here to encourage stronger bidding from other potential counterparts, like she was some kind of auction item. I was beginning to think it was a mistake to come along tonight.

Sephy turned to me, her jaw hanging slightly open, as if devastated by my words. She softly batted me with a paw.

"Respectfully *requested* your presence," she insisted. "I think a bit of jealousy is helpful in a budding new life partnership, don't you?" She had that dangerous twinkle in her eye. "It's important to remind my suitors that I'm a prize not so easily won. By the way, the samosas are delicious."

"They're called *mimosas*, Sephy."

"Can we get samosas after this?" Sephy queried.

"No."

"Why not?"

"Oh, why? Because all I want is for this night to end."

"You can't mean that," she pouted. She looked crestfallen, vulnerable, someone that you wished to cheer up no matter what. It was good. The act would have worked on four hundred and fifty other students in the student body and had them tied around her little claw.

"Why don't you jump Aberdeen's bones?" Sephy exclaimed, far too loudly for someone leaning in so close.

"Sshh! Keep your voice down!"

"Don't you think he's hot though?"

I snorted. I was missing a leg, not my eyes.

"Like that would ever be a thing." I doubted I met his lofty expectations. I was a wallflower, always had been.

"I thought you two had seemed more polite to each other lately?"

"A fragile truce," I said uncomfortably, looking away.

"This Duke's son is pretty handsome," Sephy mused aloud. "I'll probably jump him, if he's not my counterpart."

I stared at her, appalled.

"He's human. And counterparts don't... date. I'm *fairly* certain that's taboo."

"Yeah, but if he really is like the other half of me, then what a rare opportunity! There's hardly anyone I find more attractive than myself."

"I'm aware," I chuckled gently, confiscating her drink.

"I just wanted you to have a new tradition," Sephy mumbled, oddly vulnerable thanks to the mimosas. "I want you to feel like you belong here."

Sitting there, looking at her, I suddenly wished I could tell her all about the acolytes, the truth about my father, about Aberdeen, all of it. Sephy was the closest thing I had to a friend... no, she *was* the only thing.

"Let's begin a new tradition," I smiled, "just us."

"Excellent. You can MC on stage with me next year. You can be officially in charge of defending me from all my admirers."

"Not everyone here is an admirer," I noted. "Did you see Liero's face when you called her a '*naughty, naughty elf?*'"

The two of us laughed, furiously. Come to think of it, I couldn't recall when I'd had this much shameless fun. Perhaps coming with Sephy hadn't been a mistake at all.

17

The taxis waited like silent sentinels outside the Academy, their windows opaque, hiding the departing figures within. Some had no seats at all —emptied out to accommodate the unusual forms of the Shadows riding home. A quiet procession of students trickled away from the hall toward the dorms, laughter and chatter softening as the night drew in.

Sephy didn't follow them. Instead, she nudged me gently away from the hall, her pawsteps quiet against the slick stone path. I let her lead, neither of us speaking, as we moved into the hush beyond the light. We skirted the great curve of the hall, slipping past the columns into the gardens where the air felt colder, heavier.

Rain fell softly. The grass and the plants around us were slick and wet, highlighted silver by the slice of moon peeking from behind a cloud. The hedges on either side obscured us, pruned into surreal silhouettes of giant Shadows. The hedges crouched like dark, oversized gargoyles in the night.

Once we were at the very rear of the building, so that it was just us alone, Sephy casually came to a stop. Yet she didn't seem to make any move to speak. She simply regarded me. Her expression was unreadable, but I could feel it—like she was waiting for something to break.

Our night had been great company, fizzing jokes and a general floating feeling in my insides. But there was still a little something strange about how she was looking at me. As if I awed her... or broke her.

"Thanks for tonight." I smiled, but shifted self-consciously. "I didn't expect for it to be this... fun."

"Don't you give me that face," she said quietly.

"Which face?"

"That classic, heart-bending Crowley smile."

I frowned, studying her carefully. Whatever she was thinking, her thoughts were carefully obscured behind those azure eyes.

Oh no. *Dammit.*

There was a cold condemnation there, even if it was well-hidden. Behind the sparkling, brilliant facade of Sephy Nekomata was a predator, a lioness who had been wronged. For the first time in her presence, I felt fear.

Or was that just my overactive paranoia?

Then I was sure I'd been mistaken, because the moment was gone. She was simply beaming at me again.

"Come on, let's head back to the dorm," I said, unsettled. "It's time for a rewatch of *A Streetcar Named Desire*. I don't have enough Marlon Brando in my life." I turned and started to head off, to finish our loop of the hall's perimeter.

There was a *swish*, like a scythe slicing through air. I felt the prickle of razor-sharp quills, pressing into the back of my neck.

I came to a stop, careful to keep smiling.

"What game is this now?" I said lightly. "I thought you'd used up all your shenanigans for the evening."

I slowly turned to face Sephy. As I did, her tail's quills traced the vulnerable skin of my neck, never breaking contact. I hadn't anticipated how much the accusation in her eyes would hurt.

"*Acolyte*," she named me, and there it was. What's more, after all I'd learnt, I no longer wanted to vehemently deny it.

"Sephy," I responded courteously, but my heart was racing.

"I was right." She laughed, but there was no joy in it. "You're one of them."

I feigned a calm untouchability, even if her tail of knives was an inch from splitting my throat.

"You've been lying to everyone," she accused me. "That's what I can't get my head around, that's what hurts the most. You've been lying to me all along."

"Sephy..."

"I found the black robes, Crowley. After I confronted you, things still didn't sit right. You'd been to one of their little meetings, hadn't you? You're not the only acolyte in the Academy."

Aberdeen's robes, I realised. I'd stored them in my room.

"That's ridiculous."

"I told myself I was reading into nothing. Then I found your elaborate little hiding spot for your little love diary of Jupiter's writings. I hoped it was just for research, all part of your revenge quest." She laughed bitterly. "But the way you'd circled things, the questions you wrote in the margins... this isn't about revenge, is it? Somehow I misread you. You don't hate Jupiter, you're obsessed with him. You're... you're one of them."

"Sephy..."

"How could you possibly have stooped to collaborating with *Shadows' Eve*, of all people?" she asked me, her gaze hard. There were hateful tears in her eyes. "How could you betray us so easily? Your father was murdered by those terrorists."

"Exactly," I said urgently. "If that were really true, then why would I ever join them?"

She frowned, then pushed my words aside.

"Why didn't you tell me the truth?"

"Probably because I was worried about a situation like this." I'd been aiming for dry humour, but my voice came out deeply troubled. "Sephy... they didn't kill my father."

"Ah. Some acolytes just told you this, and the great genius Alexandra Crowley just took them at their word?"

"I saw a recording Father made before his death. He was an acolyte. He and his Shadow were knights to Jupiter himself."

Sephy stared at me, shocked. Those lapis lazuli eyes were torn between hate and uncertainty.

"Which would mean that... the Praetory killed your father."

"I've been told for so long that Jupiter is evil," I whispered. "Just like his followers. But the more I've seen of this place, of nobles who can have their enemies executed with a single word..."

"Jupiter and his people committed *slaughter*. Obscenities."

"Oh sure," I said, deadpan. "And the Praetory's just been running bake sales for the last few centuries. It was a *war*!" Ever since seeing Father's recording, I'd been looking at everything with new eyes, the truth crawling under my skin like a fever. "The acolytes were fighting for Shadow rights, for an entire species. By painting Shadows' Eve as extremists, the Praetory has been allowed to continue to oppress Shadows. The nobles have gathered ridiculous wealth, while so many Shadows fall into poverty, secretly labouring for the Praetory's great cause... whatever that is." I shook my head slowly in horror. "My own family's wealth must have come from Shadow labour too, Sephy. I don't think I can just be *okay* with that."

"The acolytes think spilling blood counts as a revolution, but it's just angry, chaotic violence," Sephy hissed. "They don't have control over it anymore, so they hide behind their masks."

"What if the real masks are the faces we wear every day," I retaliated sharply. "I'm tired of hiding who I *am*, Sephy. I thought the Praetory was the answer, but everyone's lying to each other and to themselves. I've finally found something true, and I'm not sure I can let it go."

"Masks make people cruel," Sephy shot back. "They make those acolytes feel they can do whatever they want without consequences." She shook her head. "I don't understand why you'd side with them. They're intent on using violence to overturn the Praetory, and you *know* the psychological damage that can do long-term to those who survive it. We need peace. All of us."

I didn't answer for a moment. I couldn't believe that she'd gone there.

"It's better than keeping the people trapped in their ignorance," I finally said, once I trusted myself to speak. "The Praetory isn't innocent, Sephy. Father was right. The Shadows need to be woken up. Maybe I'm starting to believe I can play a part in that."

"Oh then thank god we have *you*, our human saviour," she said sarcastically, her hackles rising. "All you've known is struggle and suffering, Crowley, and that's why you're drawn back toward it, over and over. But I always thought you'd have enough courage to be something more than that, something truly great. Guess I was wrong."

"You must be disappointed," I said acidly.

"You have no idea."

"Maybe you should read some of the words Jupiter's actually *written*. Aberdeen gave me some of his pieces to look over." The more I read, the more I found it easy to believe that Jupiter wasn't the monster they Praetory had made him out to be. He painted a picture of something that could replace the Praetory, where Shadows and humans lived equally.

I looked away, feeling a sharp, cold knot of guilt tighten in my chest. I had been so quick to brand Jupiter a devil, to view the Dark Father's very name as a curse. I knew there was another reason I was so desperate to believe his words now, a specific encounter months before that replayed behind my eyes every time I closed them.

But I wasn't ready to let that secret out into the air. Not even for Sephy.

"There's a poet or prophet behind every genocide," Sephy countered softly.

"I don't believe Shadows need to be brainwashed to revolt," I said heavily, thinking of Kipling shooting that tree spirit, and of Sephy crushed to the floor, mewling. "I'm beginning to think they've just been waiting for permission."

"I'm tired of you talking about how awful this world is that you barely know anything about. You're delusional."

"I might be new to much of this, but Father *wasn't*," I said heatedly. "He was resolved, and so am I. So... shall we just agree to disagree?"

"That may be pivotal, considering the number of things we disagree on. You could be executed for this! Unless we turn the other acolytes in—together—and you throw yourself on the Potentate's mercy."

"You can't be serious," I whispered, my anger snuffed out like a candle.

"Then sever all contact with Shadows' Eve. Forget all of it, Crowley. I'm only giving you this choice once."

"Sephy, you could... join us."

Sephy looked shocked.

"*Join you?*" she scoffed. "And the terrorists? I don't take lives."

"Sephy, your family built their entire fortune and legacy as war advisors. Aberdeen told me all about it. They were responsible for the fall and defeat of the only ones really fighting for justice for Shadows."

"My parents *love* Shadows," she hissed back at me.

"That doesn't mean they haven't profited from oppressing them. Am I wrong?"

"My parents have always kept the peace. They're peacekeepers."

"Or advisors on how to perpetuate a violent system."

Sephy's eyes flashed with anger.

"I don't see why I should trust anything that your silver tongue spews at me."

"Look, I know I'm a human," I said, desperately now, "and that it's hardly my place to tell you what Shadows want. But just because you believe the system can be changed from the inside, doesn't mean I won't speak up for those who are hurting too much right now to wait for change. Sephy... do you really want the Praetory to execute me?"

"*Yes*, Crowley," Sephy said, her voice dripping with

sarcasm. "I want the blood of my friend on my hands. Who the hell do you think I am? But you've just told me you want to bring the Praetory down. I can't just let you do that."

"Yes, you can. Just join me. Just say that we're going to do something about this whole mess."

"And why do you even want me to join you? You lie to me constantly, and I had to practically drag you out tonight. You can't even *bear* me half the time."

"Neither of us can bear each other half the time," I whispered. "Yet here we are. Standing in the rain."

Sephy didn't move. Then she slowly retracted her spiny tail from my throat. I relaxed. Slightly.

"This isn't the way, Crowley," she sighed. "An eye for an eye makes the whole world blind."

"Justice *is* blind," I answered.

"Tell me the other acolytes' names, and maybe you can get out of this alive."

"Sephy, I can't agree to hand myself in and offer up other acolytes as a ticket for my own survival. This isn't about just me anymore."

The Crowley from the start of the semester would hardly believe she was saying those words, I reflected.

Sephy stared at me, hard. Then she gasped.

"Oh, God." She backed away, like she was going to be sick. "No, no... *Aberdeen*? He's one of them?"

Shit. I hadn't wanted to give away Aberdeen's secret and endanger him as well. How the hell did she read that off me?

"Oh, of *course*. That's why you were so interested in him." Sephy shook her head, tears flitting out into the dark. "It ends now," she declared. "Hang up your masks and robes and call it quits. I'll be watching you both. Everywhere you go. Everywhere you move. If either of you keeps playing your little terrorist dress-up games, I'll bring you both down."

I believed her. "Understood."

"Don't doubt for a second that I haven't put measures in place to get the truth out, if either of you tries anything against me."

"Sephy! You can't possibly think…" I protested incredulously.

"I don't know what to think! So I'm thinking everything. Don't either of you contact Shadows' Eve again, either. I'll know if you do and any understanding between us will be gone."

Sephy turned and walked off away through the grounds, leaving me alone. As she did, I thought I heard her crying.

It felt as if Sephy had blown a hole through my chest. I stood there, overwhelmed by a wave of anxiety.

What was I *doing*? Sephy had threatened to expose us. We were in terrible danger, and we had no idea what she might do.

I couldn't help but suspect that the Crowley from before the Academy would have found a calm and effective way to defuse the situation and dismiss Sephy's suspicions. Instead I got in an emotional fight with her and unsuccessfully tried to recruit her to the cause.

Why was it that she found it so easy to get inside my head and mess me up? Was there a chance… even the faintest chance, that she could be my…?

Dammit, Sephy, I'm coming apart.

I stood alone in the garden for an eternity, wondering if Sephy even wanted me to come back to the dorm at all. It was only when I finally made to leave that I saw it. Movement, out there in the darkness.

I was being watched. Someone was standing out there between the hedges.

A prickle crawled down my spine.

I forced myself to move with calculated calm, pretending to just be another aimless student lost in melodramatic thoughts. My eyes, however, scanned every shadow. Every corner. Every flicker in the dark, trying to determine if there was more than one person watching me. Seeing no one else, I pivoted and followed the path Sephy had taken, circling back around the hall, heart pounding harder with every step.

I needed to get somewhere public. Somewhere with people. Witnesses.

On the surface, I looked like just another kid wrestling with post-Matching Ceremony angst. Inside, I was rehearsing how not to die tonight.

I gritted my teeth, limping faster and faster. Thankfully the paths of shells had ended and now there was wet grass underfoot, so my stalker couldn't hear my every movement.

Why the hell didn't I bring my gun with me tonight? I cursed silently.

I had to try and get within reach of assistance, before whoever was watching me decided to make their...

There were rapid footfalls from somewhere further behind me. In response I lurched forward, running openly now, striding as fast as possible.

Whipping out my phone, I thought of calling Sephy, but she might not even answer in her anger. I could try my new acolyte friends, but Aberdeen was known not to pick up when he was mad at me.

There was only one person I know who was still in the

hall, one lifeline who might pick up immediately. She'd told me as much when she gave me her number. But would she hear my call over the music of the Celebration, or be able to get here in the short moments it took my pursuer to close in?

I dialled and pressed the receiver to my ear.

The phone rang. It rang again. I moved off the main path, diving between two hedges, then scrambled under an iron gate dividing the gardens. I dragged my prosthetic leg behind me. Anything to slow them down a little and throw them off the trail.

"Jeremiah, is that you? I'm busy," Morgaine's irate voice came through the phone held to my ear. *"Call back later."*

"Morgaine, no!" I hissed in desperation. Back upright again, I darted past a decorative fountain in the shape of a chimera, dropping down to slide under the gate on the opposite side of the courtyard.

There was nothing but silence from the phone.

Dammit! Dammit to hell. But then I realised that the silence was a good thing. It wasn't the ring tone of a cancelled call.

"Crowley?" Morgaine asked uncertainly.

"Do you swear yourself to me?" I demanded as I wove between more hedge-Shadows. The footfalls were so close now.

"Yes," she said, almost immediately, pausing only long enough to glean my meaning.

"I accept your service," I gasped. Hopefully that oath would be enough for Morgaine to stay discreet about whatever it was I'd caught myself up in. "I'm being pursued at the very back of the hall," I filled her in quickly. I'd changed direction again, trying to lose my tail, bending my way back toward the hall itself. I sighted a window up ahead in the side of the building, but it was too high for me to climb through. "If you head to the stained window with the crest of roses, you can intercept us."

"*I understand,*" she said. "*My Lady.*"

That made one of us. I forced myself forward, hobbling. I heard the muffled shot of a silencer. No oblivion or searing pain followed. Apparently, their shot missed.

Suddenly strong hands took me. I was raised up into the air by powerful arms.

No!

I kicked futilely, trying to find purchase. Then I was thrown by someone with inhuman strength, landing hard on the grass beside the hall. Any further and my head would have cracked against the stone. I gasped for breath and finally saw my assailants.

One was tall and vampiric, with blood-red eyes staring out from the white bandages that were wrapped around his body. The other Shadow was an anthropomorphic wolf, eyes completely white as if they'd rolled backward into his head. Some of his flesh was missing, as if he'd been raised from the dead.

I didn't have time to contemplate his chilling appearance before a third figure and a fourth revealed themselves too. A strange man stepped in front of me, his pistol aimed down at me. Meanwhile, a woman knelt down beside me, her hands wrapping around my throat.

I went still. They were both wearing plain clothes, no uniform. I could see the silencer attached to the end of the man's gun.

Without warning I lunged, trying to grab the woman to use her as a shield, but she slashed at my outstretched hand with a concealed knife. I gasped in pain and she forced me back down, her grip crushing my throat. I was fighting for air.

Who the hell sent them? I thought fiercely.

"Tell us," the woman said. "What did the acolytes tell you when they made contact?"

Her voice was calm. Professional. Her hands loosened momentarily on my throat, and I coughed, dizzy with the intake of air.

Harper, I thought desperately. *Harper needs me.*

I fought for oxygen in vain, lashing out at her like a wild hellcat. I tried to channel my inner Sephy. But the woman was choking me again, and everything was going black. I felt the life being crushed from me.

I was brought vividly back to years before, just as helpless as I watched my father meet his own fate. Maybe I was going to meet him.

My head rocked back. I saw the stained-glass window up above me, the light of the hall shining through, illuminating two red roses entwined across a shield.

The stained-glass smashed open, shards flying outward. For a moment, I was sure I was hallucinating. A blur of black feathers erupted from the hall. Deva descended with the fury of a raptor, all talons and vengeance, straight for the vampire and the snarling zombie-wolf. The hands around my neck loosened, and I twisted my head away to protect my face from the falling glass.

After a moment, I risked another look—just as Morgaine Holloway leapt from the window, sailing over me. Or perhaps it was a warrior angel. A sword was held out on either side of her, and she came down slicing down at my adversaries, blood blossoming. The woman who had choked me fell back, screaming. The man's gun fired a muffled shot, but the bullet went wide; then his body hit the grass, unmoving.

Painful shudders ran through me as I gasped for air. I lay there, thinking there was a real very possibility that I was still going to die. I didn't know why, but it was Sephy who I thought of in my last moments. I kept seeing the hurt in her eyes, as if I had broken something irreparable.

18

ephy, I thought, as I came to. Why was her face the first thing I thought of?

It hurt when I breathed, and I recalled those powerful hands around my throat. My hand hurt, and I brought it up to inspect it. It was bloody from where it had been slashed, but the cut didn't seem deep. The hand vanished from sight as someone gently wrapped the wound in torn cloth.

"Crowley, are you alright?" Morgaine asked intently.

I was still lying out back of the hall, below the broken window. I must have only passed out for a minute. It didn't seem anyone had heard the commotion over the music; no one else had come rushing to our aid. Deva was keeping a careful lookout, scanning the area like something might leap out of the begonias.

I'd made peace with the acolytes... for now, at least. So who had my attackers been? There was something about the precision and the professionalism of this ambush. Who hired killers like that? Nobles with some kind of vendetta against the Crowley family, perhaps. But who would go as far to try and assassinate the eldest Crowley child, and risk the fallout that came with that?

Or perhaps it was because someone other than Sephy suspected me of consorting with Shadows' Eve. They'd demanded to know just how much the acolytes had told me. It seemed there were some people high up who were still determined to kill to keep my father's secret quiet. They may have guessed that the acolytes had confided the truth about my father. That would make me a liability too. But was the truth really worth killing a Minister's daughter over? Evidently.

Sephy. I remember what my subconscious had clicked onto, far faster than my addled consciousness. If the attempt on my life was really due to me learning my father's secret identity... what if my attackers had overheard me telling Sephy as well?

I extracted my phone and called Sephy, but she didn't pick up. Next I tried Aberdeen, but he didn't answer either. Of course not. Why would either of them do something crazy like *pick up the phone* when there's mortal danger involved? We'd mentioned Aberdeen by name in our conversation as well. I felt a sick twisting in my gut knowing they were both in possible peril and I was unable to warn them.

My pulse was wild. I knew this just might be my paranoia. But I wasn't about to chance it after nearly being murdered.

I called Mahuika at our family house to check that Harper was safe. She confirmed he was there, and told me mother was still at work. I thanked her and asked her to put all of the security team on high alert for now, then I hung up. We had to act quickly, and if I heard Harper's voice I'd be too scared to do what had to be done and risk leaving him alone.

"*EMERGENCY. Are you alright?*" I messaged Sephy and Aberdeen. "*A team of four just tried to assassinate me, you may be targets too. Get to safety, NOW.*"

Then I checked the time.

"Morgaine?"

"Yes, my Lady?"

"I fear Sephy and Aberdeen may be in danger too. We need to warn them. Sephy might be back at the dorm."

"If I may be so bold, that seems unwise," Morgaine counselled me, troubled. "There may be more of these people out there seeking to harm you. They may be waiting in your dorm for you to do just this. Keeping *you* safe is first priority. If I can help Sephy after that, I swear I will." She eyed my hand. "You need medical attention."

"No hospital," I whispered, as a thought suddenly struck like lightning. I realised I had grabbed hold of Morgaine's arm with my uninjured hand. My throat hurt from being choked, but in that moment, it barely registered against the pain in my heart.

"My Lady?" Morgaine said, frozen in confusion. Then she saw the look in my eyes.

Someone had warned me not to get too close to the truth. Someone had told me the truth of what the acolytes had stolen from beneath the Academy was too dangerous a truth.

If I were right, then I had made a terrible mistake. I told myself I was being stupid. Disloyal to even think of something so evil.

She wouldn't.

I thought of Jo and me as children, playing on the monkey bars. Sliding down a waterslide set up by Father at the back of the estate. Until very recently, we hadn't seen each other in years. Our lives had set us on different paths, but she could never be behind this. It wouldn't make sense.

But I couldn't think of any other puzzle piece that would fit.

"Why can't we go to the hospital, my liege?" Morgaine prompted me, interrupting my dark thoughts.

"I may know who sent them," I said thickly, staring at the four scattered bodies nearby. "Have you checked the bodies?"

"Not yet."

"Do it. I'm hoping I'm wrong."

My newly-minted knight moved to inspect my would-be assassins. She roughly rummaged through their pockets, while inspecting their features for any signs of familiarity.

"We're in pursuit of Nekomata," a voice crackled suddenly from the man's radio at his hip. *"She took a taxi from the celebration. We've tracked her to Quietfire."*

Morgaine and I looked at each other sharply. My heart clenched, a hermit crab retracting into its shell.

Quietfire? That was the Praetory's concealed town in Lower Hutt, built entirely to house Shadows who hadn't met their counterparts.

Sephy, why would you have gone there?

Was Sephy's anger at Aberdeen's secret really so great that she would follow after him, alone, to see what he was up to? I knew she could be impulsive, but she was also surely smarter than that.

Finally Morgaine pulled out identification from inside the jacket of the woman who had choked me. Morgaine flicked it open, then swore, turning it toward me to display the badge.

It was in the shape of a shield, with a crown sitting on

top of it. Two identical mermaids leaned into it on either side. They looked like a certain Shadow I'd met, however briefly, in Government House.

"The Crown Protection Unit," Deva murmured, staring at it. "Assigned to protect any of the Potentate's appointed officials."

I could tell she was wondering what the hell I had done to warrant this. Morgaine and Deva were fearsome warriors, but I could still see the trepidation in their eyes. This was enough for even *them* to find daunting. They had just sworn their fealty to a teenage girl. I doubt they'd expected her to be a target of the Praetory itself.

"When these four don't report back, whoever sent them won't think twice about sending the Praetory's military after you," Morgaine warned me. "This was just their attempt to do it quietly." She didn't ask the obvious: *'What did you do?'*

I wondered how far their oath of loyalty would extend, if Morgaine and Deva knew what my father had truly been.

Just then, the bandaged vampire stirred.

Gathering myself to my feet despite Morgaine's protestations, I picked up the silenced pistol from the grass.

"Tell me. Who wants to have me killed?" I asked coldly, my eyes not leaving the vampire.

"We're dead anyway," he sneered.

"True, but do you want to spend your last moments feeling your human's pain?"

I cocked the gun and aimed it at the human man instead. The man was still breathing shallowly. The fear in the vampire's features told me I had aimed at the right counterpart. "Who gave the order?"

"Crowley!" Morgaine said, shocked, "Allow me..."

The vampire glared, though I could see the pain in his eyes.

"We're the Crown Protection Unit, you fool. We're prepared to give our lives. You'll both be executed for treason."

Moments later his eyes turned glassy, and he went still. I realised his human had died as well. Another mistake. I should have acted faster.

Morgaine extracted the man's phone and used his thumbprint to unlock it. She searched through, acting completely dispassionate about the dead bodies around us.

We had to get out of here. We didn't know if any more of these people were coming for us.

I heard something coming from the phone, a familiar voice. Morgaine showed me the screen. It was a file in the voice recorder app.

"It seems we've struck lucky," she said, her tone suggesting we were really anything but. "This one made a recording. Seems like he wasn't entirely comfortable with his orders, and wanted some evidence if he had to prove he hadn't been acting alone."

Morgaine rewound it to the start, then pressed play.

"Crowley knows?" came Jo's voice, terrified. *"How could she... she wasn't meant to know."* There was a short silence. *"Alexandra Crowley,"* Jo murmured seemingly to herself, sounding dazed. Then, voice hardening: *"You know your orders."*

"Your Excellency... she's the daughter of a Countess, a Minister at that..."

"My orders come from the very top," Jo snapped, furious. Unhinged, even. *"Do you really want it to be discovered that the intelligence got out on your watch?"* Silence greeted her words. *"Take care of Sephy Nekomata too. You should have*

done it the moment Crowley confided in her. Careful with those two, there's something between them. If they're counterparts, they'll be able to communicate remotely. There cannot *be any loose ends, or your own lives are forfeit."*

The recording ended. I was cold all over.

For a moment, I said nothing. I just felt numb. The betrayal was unspeakable. How could one girl change so much over the years, she became unrecognisable?

At least this agent had a troubled enough conscience about murdering a noble's daughter to keep this recording for posterity.

"That was the Governor speaking," Morgaine said slowly, as if she wouldn't believe it unless I confirmed it.

"Yes."

She looked pale, but her face showed unwavering commitment.

"Then there's nowhere safe for you, my Lady," Morgaine said with feeling. "You have to run..."

"...and we will run with you," Deva finished.

Living on the run from the Praetory for the rest of our lives. I might never get to see Harper again, or Mother. Or...

"Take me to Quietfire," I said quietly.

"My Lady, we need to get out *now*."

"They think Sephy had a role in all this," I explained, my chest pounding. "Jo thinks that Sephy is my Shadow and that she's guilty by association. But she's not." My hand that wasn't wounded curled into a fist. "Jo's people must have followed us out to the garden and overheard. I confided in Sephy, and now I've put her in danger too. They're going after her and she's innocent. I *have* to save her."

Morgaine nodded grimly.

"My Lady," she agreed, and she and Deva bowed.

. . .

Pinpoint coloured points of light flew past us as we sped toward Lower Hutt.

"Faster," I ordered. My fingers were busying themselves peeling the car's faux leather interior. We had to make it in time. We had to.

Sephy, please be okay. I couldn't lose her from the universe. It would be a boring place without her.

I was driving shotgun. Deva was in the back, her wings taking up most of the room. The quiet of the drive at least granted me the minutes I needed to ruminate on the very restricted information available to me. There was something nagging at the back of my mind. It felt like I was forgetting something vital.

I sighed as it eluded me, gazing out the window. Dark greenery flew past as we continued along Great Harbour Way. What could I say to Sephy once we were reunited? I had placed her in incredible danger by getting her caught up in my dealings with Shadows' Eve. I really had been getting used to our pizza movie nights, but I didn't see how I could ever expect her to forgive me. There was a surprisingly tender pain at the thought.

Congratulations, Sephy. I laughed dryly. *You adopted me from my very start at the Academy as one of your secret projects. You got what you wanted. I'm not the same person inside that I was when I entered those doors.*

"What," I said suddenly, leaning forward to look in the rear-view mirror, "are *those?*"

A series of hefty armoured vehicles were rolling along the road behind us in a convoy. They were a little incongruous. They looked like something that belonged more in a war movie rather than in the streets of Wellington. The sight chilled my blood.

They were LAV's. Light Armoured Vehicles. Eight-wheeled, highly mobile on road and off road, with a mounted turret, and co-axial and roof-mounted machine guns. I suppose anyone who saw them would just assume it was that the New Zealand Army was just driving out to do a military drill somewhere outside the city limits.

What was the bet that they all contained Praetory soldiers and their Shadow counterparts with dangerous powers, being shepherded directly toward Quietfire?

This seemed beyond overkill.

Morgaine cursed.

"They're not coming for us," I said, stunned as I watched the first of them pass us by and continue on ahead. I was sure we'd been done for. They must not have known what vehicle we were in.

"This is still what I was afraid of," Deva murmured from behind us. "The Praetory military are deploying to Quietfire. They're going to surround the town to pin Sephy down."

"They're creating a military encirclement around a town... all to take out a teenager?" I asked, incredulous. I felt nauseous at seeing the exact odds we were up against.

"Her presence here just gives them another excuse to crack down on that area. They view Quietfire as little more than a slum providing cheap labour, one that also breeds rebellion," Deva clarified. "This will be taking out many little birds with one stone, providing a lesson to Shadows everywhere."

My phone rang. When I saw who it was, my heart leapt.

"Sephy?" I answered swiftly. "Oh my God, Sephy!"

Her face had appeared. Tears wet her furry cheeks. It

looked like she'd been sobbing, and it seemed she was hiding in an alleyway.

She looked traumatised, as if she'd been running for her life. It was so easy to forget with all of her vivaciousness and smarts, and the fact that she was a spine-tailed wild-cat, that she was really just a normal teenager.

"Sephy?" I demanded, fearful. "Are you all right?"

"They're armed. They're shooting at anything that moves," Sephy finally whispered, gasping, and I've never seen her so scared. "They're going to find me. Goodbye, Crowley. I hope this makes you happy." She laughed. It was a broken laugh, even though she put all of the warmth and spirit into it she could. "I'll miss causing chaos with you and driving you up the wall. Think of this goodbye as my present."

"Jeez, Sephy. You might annoy me to hell sometimes, but don't ever mistake that for me wanting you gone."

"It's frustrating trying to accommodate you sometimes, you know?" she sniffed, but I heard the smile in her voice. We were silent for a moment, just listening to each other breathe. For a moment, in the face of life and death, a ceasefire existed between the two of us.

"What the hell are you doing in Quietfire?" I asked.

"I followed Aberdeen and his little gang when they caught a taxi," Sephy confessed. "I wondered where they were going, and I figured that the people he was with might be... you know, acolytes. I was so mad at Aberdeen I didn't know what I was going to do, but I wanted to confront him. So, I followed. They went into a run-down warehouse here in Quietfire, but then I realised I was being followed myself. There were Prae-tory soldiers and... they *fired* at me, Crowley." I heard her gasp, her unsteady breaths. She must still be in shock.

"Without me doing anything to deserve it. I almost died."

"You *cannot* trust the military, do you hear me? It's Governor Blackmore who's behind all of this. Jo's making sure that anyone who learnt the truth about my father is eliminated."

"*Jo?* But she's your friend..."

"I know."

"Why is knowing that Peter Crowley was an acolyte that much of a state secret?"

"I don't know, and Sephy, you don't have time. You need to get out of there."

"I can't." I heard her helplessness. "Praetory soldiers are everywhere. I'm in the centre, I can't get out."

"Jo is having the military encircle all of Quietfire," I said heavily. "I'd hoped you would have time to escape before the trap snapped shut."

There was only one way I could think of to handle this situation and give us a chance at survival. Except that it was madness, absolute madness.

How could I not try it though, if it was the only way to save Sephy?

I quickly calculated the distances on my phone's map. Sephy was right, she may not have enough time to get out before they closed the encirclement, but we were closer. I might have enough time to enter through their lines before they shut tight.

"Sephy, you need to get back to the warehouse Aberdeen entered, and you need to make sure you're not seen. I know you pretty much said you don't want to ever see either of us again. But this is bigger than that."

"But Crowley, I don't think I can make it. The soldiers are sweeping the area..."

"You can make it. I'm en route as well."

"Excuse me, I didn't ask you to put yourself in danger for me!" she said indignantly. "Stay where you are."

"I'd like to see you try to stop me. I put you in this situation, but if we work with Aberdeen and the others, maybe we can still find a way out."

"When the *Governor* wants us dead? Are you joking? And what, your plan is to somehow convince the *acolytes* to help us escape?" she demanded, outraged.

In the rear-view mirror I saw Morgaine's eyebrows rise in surprise at the mention of cooperating with the Praetory's sworn enemies, but she didn't comment. I respected her for that. Again, they really hadn't known what they were in for when they swore their services to me. I imagine that was a difficult conversation we would save for later.

"Right now, those acolytes are the only friends we've got," I told Sephy pointedly.

"I suppose things really have gotten that bad, haven't they?" she commented, shuddering visibly.

I hesitated, wondering if I could really fulfil the promise I was about to make. After all, what was a knight really, if they broke their vows? Except I'm not a knight. Right now, they needed me to be something else.

"I need you to tell Aberdeen and the others that I can lead them out of this alive, if they follow every one of my instructions," I said.

"Crowley..."

"I know."

Sephy seemed to hear something then, her cat ears pricking up. She peered into the darkness of the alleyway, her breathing growing softer as she carefully searched for any signs of soldiers.

"You might be good in the simulations," Sephy finally

whispered to me, her voice quieter now. "You might be great, even, but this is real. It's the Governor's own military, all of their Shadows and all of their guns, and they're coming for us."

"Then I don't see that we have many other options," I responded.

"And there it is again, no matter how much you try to hide it," Sephy said wryly, and I could hear the smile in her voice. "You know what I hate about you?"

"Do tell. Your scorn is soothing."

"Your ruthless pragmatism. I loathe it, utterly. Yet at times like this, I can't help but admire it too."

Sephy was still deeply angry and hurt, I could hear it in her voice. She was still mistrusting of me, now that I was a somewhat conflicted acolyte newbie. We could hardly pretend that we hadn't had a massive falling out outside the school hall within the last hour.

"Sephy…"

"*Pause*," Sephy whispered.

"What?" I blinked.

"*Pause*. We're still having our fight, but right now we're pausing. There are bigger things afoot."

"So… '*pause?*'"

"I saw them do it on a sitcom."

"Ah. Still, Sephy… I should have told you the truth."

"You've barely known me for that long at all." I saw her tilt her head in the equivalent of a shrug. "Of course you didn't trust me with something that big. I get it."

"I should have. You know asking for help isn't one of my biggest strengths." I hesitated. "No matter how ridiculous it sounds, I'm afraid these acolytes, these people are my family." I swallowed. "Whether or not I want that to be true." *But you're my family too.* "I'm sure Aberdeen never wanted to lie to you either, he was just trying to protect you from situations like this. Sephy... I can't lose you."

"That must be unimaginably annoying for you."

"Shut up. Shut up. Just live."

She took a deep breath, peering around a stack of crates. Her fear was plain.

"You can make it," I told her. "I know you can."

"Okay. Here goes."

Sephy ended the call. I pressed the phone to my lips in silent prayer.

"She'll make it," Morgaine said. "She's a damn capable student."

"Apparently, she takes issue with my ruthless pragmatism," I remarked.

"I do not," Morgaine answered. "It shows me you truly are your father's daughter. Not that I needed another sign."

I sat with this for a moment, unable to speak.

"Morgaine, Deva, you both made a vow to me but you didn't have all of the information," I said finally. "I'd understand if you're against the idea, and you must be reeling from the revelations of the last few minutes... but you may have to cooperate with Shadows' Eve here too for the sake of our own survival. No matter your personal feelings."

Morgaine looked preoccupied, as if she was still trying to digest this new information. But she surprised me with her calm.

"Governor Blackmore has already declared war on you," she responded. "You need all the allies you can get."

"You're okay with working with *acolytes?*"

"I've seen enough of war to know that every side has its own story. I've sworn to protect *you*, no matter what."

"Deva? You didn't swear. You're still free to make your own choices."

"But I have, my Lady. It's right here."

I smiled in relief, though I also felt a nagging thought turning over in my mind.

Why was Jo doing this? Was the fact that Count Crowley was secretly a member of Shadows' Eve really enough to murder an entire community of Shadows over, or was I still missing something?

I remembered playing with Jo in a tree on the Miramar estate as children. We would build traps out of wool to trip up any guests who tried to leave, in the hope we would never have to stop playing. How could that girl grow into a woman who was so cavalier about mobilising an army to kill two students? For a moment, I could barely breathe.

Morgaine and Deva were my knights now. I should have accepted their fealty in the very first place. They were both powerful tools, and Morgaine had begged me to utilise them. Not doing so had been an entirely emotional decision. I wasn't going to make the same mistake twice.

But I tasted bile at the thought of the command that I was about to give.

"Morgaine... Deva. You have skills," I said, keeping my voice steady. "Abilities that made you the Potentate's favourite weapons of choice for many years."

"What do you want us to do, my Lady?" Deva murmured.

"You'll do anything I ask?"

"We will," Morgaine consented. "But be warned, you may not be able to take it back."

I nodded heavily, and I gave the order that might damn me forever.

19

Somewhere north of Wellington—past the hipster cafes, and the slight fog of cultural superiority—was a town. Most people drove past it without noticing, which was fine, because Quietfire wasn't exactly gunning for a tourism award. It was a secret community protected by several layers of magical gaslighting in the form of Brilliance stones around its perimeter.

It was a town populated entirely by Shadows.

I made my way deeper into Quietfire under the cover of night, keeping my footfalls quiet. Morgaine had been loath to let me go in alone, but she and Deva had their own job to do. Morgaine had dropped me off close enough that I was able to sneak through before the Praetory's blockade had closed. Now any chance of escape for me was cut off.

Offence was our best defence now. If we didn't tilt to attack, if we attempted to withdraw instead... we'd be killed. I decided to treat our current nightmare like a puzzle, and scheduled my betrayal-induced emotional breakdown for later. Feelings were for when you weren't being hunted.

Quietfire seemed like just a normal Lower Hutt suburb at first... or it did until a night market came into view. The streets were a lively cacophony of every kind of creature imaginable. A giant scorpion darted after its raucous escaping children, passing an electric blue praying mantis who was buying vases from a stone golem. Meanwhile a group of friends resembling fairies flitted overhead, pulsing with light like will o' the wisps as they wove between bizarre birds and multi-coloured dragons. The very air above felt as if it was alive. The tunes, scents and colours of the festivities overwhelmed me at first. A giant octopus was cutting up raw sushi there on the streetside, and a fluffy yeti bumbled past my hiding place. He was holding a massive cluster of balloons in the shape of characters from human cartoons like SpongeBob SquarePants and Mickey Mouse.

There was a shift in the air. Some of the Shadows started running, collecting their children and gapping it to the safety of their homes. I quickly moved on, skirting around the market before chaos broke out. When I next looked over my shoulder, a torrent of Shadows was flooding out from the marketplace, dispersing in panic as news began to spread.

Even if I hadn't already known that something bad was coming, I would have from the throngs of families rushing to make their escape. A young, harried elven mother wearing a wizard hat and cloak stumbled and fell to her knees not far from me, the young sprite who was holding her hand falling over beside her as well. I stepped forward, gently helping the two of them back to their feet.

"Are you okay?" I asked, concerned. The elven mother looked up to meet me with frightened eyes. *Untrusting* eyes.

Because I was a human? Or because she could see the Prae-tory nobility in my bearing?

"Excuse me," I asked, extracting a wad of cash from my wallet. "But can I have that cloak before you leave?"

The mother stared numbly down at the hundred-dollar bills in her hands. Then she promptly shrugged off the hooded cloak and gave me her pointy hat as a bonus.

I'd turned off my ringtone so as to not tip off any soldiers hunting for me nearby, but I still had the device clutched tightly in my hand. When it vibrated, I answered straight away.

"Sephy?" I questioned.

"*WAHOO! Hahahaha!*"

"Sephy!" I hissed. "Are you okay? Is someone hurting you?"

"*Sorry, I was just sliding down a roof. Shortcut. That was wild, do I have time to go again?*"

"You do not."

"*Oh, well. Life's joys are ephemeral and fleeting.*" She paused, her voice becoming more serious. "I'm just outside the warehouse. I can't see any soldiers nearby now. I'm going to make a beeline for it."

"*You've got this. I'm not far away.*"

Sephy kept the call open. For a long time there was no response, just ambient noise. I listened carefully, and even-tually I could pick up voices in the background. Voices both youthful and grim.

"*There must be some other way out of here. We could see if the south-west tunnel was still closed and-*"

"*Maeve?*" Sephy's voice sang out, like a dangerous

goddess. *"Don't shoot. I come bearing a message from our friend Crowley."*

I could literally hear weapons bristling through the handset, as I was left to imagine the armament suddenly poised at Sephy's face. I sighed.

Dammit, Sephy. Why give them a jump scare like that? Are you *trying* to die?

"Sephy?" I heard Aberdeen exclaim, shocked.

"No, arsehole, this message is for Maeve," Sephy responded, her voice hard. *"Not for treasonous ex-friends."*

I had to take the backstreets to avoid patrolling soldiers. By the time I came within sight of the warehouse, Sephy had already explained the basic situation to Aberdeen and the others. The warehouse must have been their base here, the equivalent of the sanctum at the Academy.

"Let me get this straight, Seph," I heard Aberdeen say faintly. *"The Governor has sent the entire military here to kill you, just because Crowley told you the truth about her father. And now, by following us here, you've put us and everyone who lives here in the firing line."*

"Oh, of course. It must be the fault of the one student in our dorm who isn't *an acolyte that the military is trying to kill us all!"* Sephy retaliated with a deadly yowl. *"You stole the information that started all of this, you filthy liar!"*

"I kept it from you to protect you from things like this," Aberdeen tried, suddenly sounding emotionally broken.

"Ooh, my hero." Sephy's fury was palpable.

"Maeve, we need to get as many civilians out as we can through the tunnels," Aberdeen said, his voice tight. *"Before they're caught in the crossfire as the military rolls in. That's all that matters now."*

"We can't," Maeve responded tersely. "The Governor's forces have caved in some of the tunnels, and soldiers are barricading the others. A lot of the residents have tried to get out underground but they can't, so they're just sheltering down there. Quietfire is locked down and entirely surrounded; anyone leaving will be shot on sight. There's no escape."

"So the military will go door to door until they find us," Aberdeen said. "Perfect." I heard him cocking his gun. "Then I suppose we'll just have to take out as many of them as we can before we meet our makers."

"They want Sephy and Crowley," another acolyte muttered desperately, but I heard the shame in his voice at even making the suggestion. "Not us."

"Don't you dare say that again," Aberdeen snapped. "Sephy is right. I put them both at risk when I told Crowley what I'd found. The Praetory have just been waiting for a good excuse to crack down on Quietfire. The military making their move was inevitable. They need to remind the free Shadows here who has the power."

"He's right," Maeve said. "They'll tear the whole town down if it means finding the rest of us acolytes."

"All right, let's assess the situation that you find yourselves in," Sephy said reasonably, as if she were a teacher at the Academy and this was her classroom. "We are all surrounded. We have no clear way out. You're trapped here, the same as us. Fortunately, our objectives and needs happen to be aligned! I don't want to die any more than you do, and we don't want anyone else in Quietfire to be hurt either. So, Crowley can lead you out of this mess, if you agree to follow every single thing we say. Is that cool?" There was a short silence. "Crowley?" Sephy noted into the phone. "Victor looks visibly enraged. Okay, now he's turning purple slightly."

Thanks for the update, Sephy.

"Crowley thinks that she can send you in here like her pet and make our resistance follow her as if she's some kind of saviour?" Victor hissed. "Forgive me, but I can't bring myself to trust the daughter of Minister Crowley!"

"You trusted my father," I said calmly into my handset.

"Oh, so you are *going to say something,"* Sephy commented. *"I wasn't sure speakerphone was working, or maybe you were just gonna get me to do this entire thing as a solo performance. Apparently there are limits to my level of persuasion, which I find absolutely unacceptable."*

"Speak for yourself, Victor," Maeve said sharply. "Crowley, you're ever amusing, but why should we trust in your plan?"

"Because I'm not all words this time." I ended the call as I entered the room. "I'm putting my own flesh and blood on the line, like every one of you."

One acolyte actually jerked backward in surprise when he saw me enter. I think he would have tripped if he'd been in his dark robes, but fortunately the acolytes were all wearing sensible streetwear.

Aberdeen whirled around to look at me, his eyes widening.

"Don't we have anyone on guard duty anymore?" he demanded of the others.

"Yes," I said. "Rosita. She's terrible."

I could feel the fear in the air. The acolytes looked panicked. Some had drawn faces. There was a kind of grief hanging over all of them, as if they already knew this day would be their last.

Looking around their secret headquarters in the upper level of the warehouse, I saw how run down and dilapidated it was. It didn't strike me as the kind of well-equipped rebel hideout you'd want to stroll into when you were about to form an alliance. I saw bags of food and provisions bundled together and stacked against a wall. There were some desks and monitors, and a table in the centre with a map of Quietfire. In the momentary silence, I heard the leaky roof dripping.

"You risked your life waltzing into an encircled active military area?" Aberdeen blazed at me. He folded his arms. "I thought you were smarter than that."

"Partner in crime," Sephy greeted me demurely. "You came for me. How sweet."

It was good to see her.

"Sephy's right," I pointed out. "Like it or not, we are all in one boat now."

We waited for the others to mull over their situation.

"Aberdeen," Sephy said quietly, with a quiet, smouldering intensity. The fact she used his actual name without any accusation in it showed she was extending the olive branch due to our extreme circumstances. "You know we have no option but to fight."

"If we do fight, we won't be able to hold out for long," Aberdeen mused. He sighed. "Just like most revolutionary groups, we've had to rely on criminal networks to get some guns into the country for our own defence. We're under-equipped as a result, while the Praetory don't have any limits on their own resources."

I assessed our team. Judging by the look of them, I was guessing they had very few experienced soldiers. The students looked more logistically-minded, if anything. Most of the humans were quite scrawny. I counted fourteen members total, composed of both adults and the teenage acolytes I met in the Sanctum. A couple were still wearing their acolyte masks, and one of them was wearing it wonky.

The Shadows didn't exactly inspire confidence either. I

recognised Grub, a green larva. A tall ginger-haired man with a grim expression had a Shadow who resembled a wacky blue jester. There was a sluggish brachiosaurus made of stone, and some kind warrior Shadow covered in bubbles. Frankly, it was the saddest ramshackle group I'd ever laid eyes on. It didn't exactly instil confidence, but I'd always had a soft spot for the underdog.

I examined them. Some of the Shadows had yet to find their counterparts, I judged, or perhaps were averse to experiencing a connection to their human. But it looked like four of the acolytes had already found their counterparts. I observed how close they stuck to their other half, and the fierce bond of love with which they looked at each other. It made me ache with longing.

I told myself sternly to bury it.

Having Shadow and human counterparts in your team made battles interesting, strategically speaking. Ideally you would have a communications person in each squad who had their counterpart back at the base, so that the two of them could communicate telepathically. It was the securest of links, one that no enemy could hack into. Then again, if someone in the field died, their counterpart back at base would too, which could be traumatising for everyone. There was a reason people in romantic relationships weren't meant to serve together in the same squad, and the same disadvantage applied to counterparts. It screwed up decision making, and it put a distorting lens on someone's priorities if they were looking out for another teammate's safety as if it were their own.

On the other hand, fighting an army of humans and Shadows meant you only needed to take out half of the enemy's forces to eliminate their entire team. It was a dark take on a *'Two for One'* deal.

Eliminate. I sickly realised that I was contemplating killing real people, but I also knew that the Praetory weren't exactly giving us many other options of how to survive this.

"But do you really think Crowley's the one to lead us out of here?" Victor demanded. Classic Victor.

Aberdeen studied me. Why did he look so angry that I was here? My cheeks flushed with heat. He was confusing. I elected to calmly stare back at him, nonplussed. I knew that was likely to infuriate him and ensure I held control of the situation.

"I hate nothing more than to admit this," Aberdeen said suddenly. "Crowley is our only hope of surviving this and finding a way out alive. We've all seen her in the simulations. We know she's the best commander in this room."

He sounded decisive, though loathe to admit it. I looked away from those piercing dark eyes, the ones that seemed to catch light and hold it. It felt strange, being the object of his praise, and I didn't know how to handle it.

"Maeve, you're our leader," Aberdeen said, inclining his head in respect. "We're your people. What do you want us to do?"

I found myself staring. I was used to the sarcastic, scowling Aberdeen, determined not to take orders from anyone. Who the heck was this?

I suppose it was due to Maeve being the one who had recruited him into Shadows' Eve and given him meaning and purpose. He looked up to her. It was kind of... sweet.

"We've been under their heel for too long," Maeve said finally. She looked around at all of her people, flaring out her wings. She looked so calm and in control standing there. I got an inkling of the charisma that had convinced so many to join her group, and why everyone looked to her as their leader. "They've been harassing the people of this town as long as we can remember. So we'll stay, and we'll fight. Just try not to get us all killed, Crowley. But if we have to die... there's no better place than right here, making a stand for what we believe in."

There were murmurs of agreement. Some of the acolytes actually cheered.

"Thank you," I said with feeling. I was thinking of all the training I'd pushed myself through growing up, and of the board games I'd played with Father, fighting off giant armies that sometimes outstripped my own. Nothing said *'quality parenting'* like teaching your kid how to destroy imaginary armies before they've hit puberty. He'd marvel at strategies I'd come out with at fourteen that he'd never even imagined, while I'd learnt so much from him.

But the game was over. This was the fight for our lives.

What I learned from Father was that even when things felt helpless, you never, ever gave up... because there were always at least six strategies to get out of your situation that you hadn't thought of.

"I'm going to split you up into three squads," I informed them. "We should avoid using our full names in case they intercept our communications. At the very least, use nicknames so we have plausible deniability later on."

"What do we call you?" Aberdeen frowned at me.

I hesitated. A memory reached up at me of the night I had broken into the Academy and encountered Jupiter.

He had refused to call me anything but *'little scarecrow'* at first. I guess he'd been throwing shade at my lanky build and straw-coloured hair. I recalled burying my face in his striped fur, overcome. I remembered how it felt as he'd slowly wrapped a paw around my back: as if I still had a parent who cared about me. My chest hurt.

Tears burned, and I fought them back. I'd spent so long

hating Jupiter. My life had been twisted by so many lies. The Praetory's misdeeds had corrupted every relationship in my life.

"Just call me *'Scarecrow,'*" I told Aberdeen firmly.

"Oh, God," whispered the acolyte standing lookout at the window. "Guys..."

We all regarded each other, then sprinted over to get a glimpse.

A stream of flame had set one of Quietfire's bakeries alight, flames licking the skyline and darkening it with smoke. The fire was already spreading to the neighbouring properties.

"What the hell are they doing?" Sephy cried in shock. "There could be people living there!"

"The Praetory are counting on it. They know that they're in hostile territory," Aberdeen said fiercely. "Shadows in the neighbourhood sympathise with us. They've always looked out for us, just as we've looked out for them. But this time the Praetory will destroy every Shadow here if they have to, all in order to weed us out. For them, they'll just be lessening the financial burden on the Praetory. They're planning a massacre."

"They wouldn't do that!" Sephy cried.

"Yes, they will, Sephy," Victor exploded at her, "that's what the Praetory is, despite all their posing, and you're the last one to figure that out. Get that into your airy *human* head."

Sephy flinched. I don't think it was the first time she'd been accused of being all human on the inside and only a Shadow in appearances, but I could see that the insult still landed. Sephy didn't grow up here, she'd been adopted by nobles. This, however, was the everyday reality for most Shadows living under the thumb of the Praetory. These were Shadows who didn't see Shadows' Eve as terrorists, but rather as freedom fighters who were the only ones watching their backs.

"Everyone, arm up with everything you have," I commanded. "We're going to stop this."

"You heard her, gang!" Maeve barked. "Now!"

I gave them all their directions. As the others were grabbing everything they needed in a flurry of activity, Aberdeen took me aside with a firm hand. As he did, I wondered if we could trust each other enough to work together against an overwhelming force, with our lives in each other's hands. It would be a far cry from what had happened in the simulations.

I realised Aberdeen was shaking. He must have been hiding it from the acolytes up until now. The ground rumbled beneath us as well, a trembling that resonated in my chest. It matched the charged energy of the air.

"Are you afraid?" I asked, my voice a soft murmur. I was suddenly aware of how close we stood. "Don't be. I'm going to try and get you all out of this."

"Me, afraid?" Aberdeen laughed, sharp and bitter, a mask over the vulnerability I sensed beneath. His defiance was fierce, but his eyes held a flicker of something deeper that pulled me in. "It's not me I'm scared for. I'm an acolyte, Crowley. I'll die for the cause, if that's what fate has in store for me." His voice became hushed, just for me. So that only I could hear the pain within it. I felt the heat radiating off him. "Maeve and I have trained these people to be soldiers, but some of us are still just kids. This is my family, do you get that?"

For the first time, I suspected that there was much more going on behind those eyes of dark infinity than I knew. The air crackled with unspoken tension, the weight of his words drawing me closer. I could see the fierce love for his people in that gaze, a raw intensity that made my heart race.

"They're my responsibility, Crowley," Aberdeen said, his gaze locking onto mine, daring me to look away. "If there's any chance I can help them survive this..."

"Then I'll see to it that they survive," I whispered back. I felt the promise hang between us like a taut string. Everything else had faded away. It was just us, two souls caught together in a moment that felt impossibly alive, aware that at any minute the air all around us could ignite.

20

Our HQ was a raucous mess. Sephy was shouting her orders at the remaining acolytes to help whip the warehouse hiding spot into order. Three of the acolytes, Taggi, Victor and Monolith, were staying here with us to manage the comms and chart the movement of the enemy troops.

"General Crowley," Sephy said, joining me at the railing overlooking the main area of the warehouse. "How are we looking?"

General Crowley. My father's voice came back to me, with the same words. I shivered, surprising myself.

"Good," I told her. "They're almost ready."

"You know, you haven't even been at the Academy for two months and you've already had a teacher try to swear herself as your vassal and the national military attempt to murder you and your friends. Do you have this polarising effect on most people?"

"Unfortunately." I glanced at her awkwardly. I cleared my throat. "You know, after our fight, I really thought you weren't ever going to speak to me again."

"Yes, but then you went and risked your life sneaking through a military blockade to try and save me. Well played." Her voice softened. "I will always come running for you too, Crowley. You're my friend. I will always hit pause on our fights. I'm still livid that you lied, I'm frustrated with you... but I can't believe what the Praetory is doing right now, endangering all these innocents. I don't understand how all of the soldiers are just... going along with it." She shuddered. "Even the Shadows in the Praetory army are prepared to use force against their brethren. What is wrong with them? This is so horrific and excessive... and all just to maintain the Praetory's public image?"

"I don't understand either. Sephy... would you have handed me in?" I asked her, looking away. I sensed her confusion. "You said you'd have to think about it, after the party," I elaborated, self-conscious.

"Of course not," Sephy said, sounding shocked.

"Why not?"

"Because friends don't do that. Not unless I really believed my silence might cost lives."

I bit my lip.

"Though for the record," she added, "I *am* still incensed with you."

I nodded in acknowledgement.

"I'm sorry," I said, surprised to realise just how deeply I meant it.

"I will be devising many humiliating and eviscerating shenanigans to bring you low, and pranks that will make you wake in a cold sweat for years afterwards."

Swallowing, I oddly experienced even more fear than when assassins had attacked me at a school event.

"Yes, Ma'am."

We looked down over the railing at the level below. The

acolytes were armed and moving out. Sephy's expression softened as she watched. We were about the same age as most of them, but some still seemed so young. It was jarring seeing kids preparing for war.

"They're not exactly the terrifying murder-cult we were picturing, huh?" I muttered.

"Not these ones," Sephy allowed quietly. "No."

I watched Maeve and Aberdeen sharing a laugh over something. Aberdeen had just finished stashing a ridiculous amount of knives on his person. I had to admire anyone who laughed in the face of imminent death. It was either bravery or a severe lack of long-term planning.

Aberdeen took a last glance up at Sephy and me. I thought Sephy might say something before he left, but her jaw stayed tightly shut. Aberdeen swallowed, but he nodded to me before he and Maeve led their people ... *our* people... out into the town. I hoped it wasn't the last time I'd see all of them. Next they would slowly and stealthily divide up into their three squads, spreading out through the streets and alleyways of Quietfire so that they were in position when the Praetory pushed in.

"I can't believe Aberdeen let me take charge here," I said.

"He's the best in the field, but you're the best at being the eye in the sky calling the shots. Aberdeen's not an idiot, he knows that just as well as Maeve does."

I looked to the flickering monitors that had been set up for us, noting the conditions. The land here was very flat, the weather calm. The well-equipped Praetory squads had started sweeping the area on foot. I watched with cold fury as the Praetory started setting entire buildings on fire, and soldiers dragged families of Shadows, even the children, into the streets. They weren't afraid of brutality, and they knew it was doing exactly what they wanted it to. It was sending a message that until we surrendered ourselves, innocents were going to die.

I recalled Morgaine raging at me in class after I accidentally murdered those civilians in my simulation debut. Now I understood she'd been that hard on me because she was determined I'd never make another error so costly... especially when the stakes were real.

The night Father died, strangers and their monsters had started coming at us through the trees, masked by the darkness. I'd thought they were acolytes, but they'd been Praetory soldiers all along. Now it was my turn to try and save my father's people, and eviscerate the side that murdered him.

"He'd be proud of you," Sephy told me softly, and I started that she always knew exactly what I was thinking. Was that just because she was observant, or...?

I hid my emotion by examining the electronic map of the battlefield they'd placed across the table.

"We can work with this," I muttered.

Then, sounding more hesitant and vulnerable than I'd ever heard her, Sephy said: "I'm a student, Crowley, not a master tactician or anything. I've done my studies, but these people are trusting us with their lives."

"It's okay, Sephy," I said. "You're a natural. You know how to read a situation, and you're one of the most organised thinkers I've ever met."

"I *am* fantastic, but what's your point?"

I felt bad asking this of her, of all of them. Her strength had always lain in bringing people together, not in taking lives. To get out of this town with our hearts still beating we were going to have to shoot to kill, and we'd need to be the ones who shot first.

"You don't have to be here, you know," I said quietly enough for only Sephy to hear. I still felt the guilt of dragging her into this. "There's probably somewhere safer to bunker down, a hiding spot to wait this out where they won't find you."

"And you'll try win this without me? Good luck with that."

Sephy turned obliquely to sit before a monitor, her deadly tail flicking back and forth.

"Very well. You're from a family of advisors, so advise me. I need you to be my eyes and ears," I instructed her. "I need you to replay commands to the squads through the comms. I'll go big picture, you break it down for them."

"Sure. I've done party planning, I'm sure those skills are transferrable." Sephy saw the look I gave her, then became serious. "I know what I'm doing. I won't let you down. Don't worry."

"I know," I told her.

We really were only working with scavenged, repurposed parts here. I stood there, surveying the screens, trying to keep all the monitors within my sights. I'd been hoping for a well-resourced resistance group, but this felt a little too much like a school AV club for my liking.

"Um, excuse me?" Sephy and I turned to see a Shadow standing beside us. She looked like a very cute and cheerful monkey, except for her mottled green skin and the wavering tentacles emerging from her back.

"Hey, Taggi," I said, "what's up?"

Now that she had our attention, she suddenly looked quite nervous. "I just... I wanted you to know, I'm not going to let you down."

I blinked, surprised.

"I know," I said gently.

"But I just... I have a little sister at home. And if I can make it out of this alive for her..."

I exchanged a look with Sephy. A silent moment where we were both saying: *We cannot fail these people. We have to figure out how to pull us all through this.*

"I can't tell you that no one is going to die," I said honestly. "But I can tell you that we're all in this together. Sephy and I aren't running, we're a team. You've met Sephy, right? You've had some simulations together."

"Oh, I know who Sephy is," Taggi said breathlessly. "She's famous. She's like... a gorgeous goddess."

Sephy blinked, then beamed.

"Well, thank you! Do you want a hug?"

Taggi nodded, apparently struggling for words, and giggled nervously. Sephy happily complied, smiling warmly.

"Um, this is a battlefield!" I said loudly, chagrined. "Why is there *hugging?*"

"Oh, have a heart, *Scarecrow*," Sephy responded, still hugging.

"I don't get why everyone falls in love with you."

"Yeah, you do." She smiled coyly once they'd parted. "It's my rugged, brooding mystique."

"Oh, my dearest Sephy." I shook my head, eyes glued to the battle map. "You have all the gravity of a cinnamon roll."

"A cinnamon roll who can be terrifying," she replied nonchalantly, and I couldn't argue with that.

"I just like how she's so optimistic and compassionate about everything," Taggi told me breathlessly. "She's the best."

"Yes, thank you Taggi," I said dryly. "Fighting for our lives here."

The acolytes each had a little chip on them that displayed their location on our screen, in the same way the Praetory's military tracked their own troops in the field. Looking at the map was like staring at a flurry of emerald fireflies, each glowing green dot tagged with a name from our team.

Unfortunately we didn't have any way of knowing the location of the enemy forces, except for when one of our people radioed in a sighting. But the reports coming in so far seemed to confirm the military was tightening their encirclement.

From our little command centre, I watched our map of the neighbourhood, giving out directions. Our people manoeuvred through Quietfire like mice through a labyrinth, avoiding the well-trained forces.

"Why '*Scarecrow*?'" Sephy asked me suddenly.

"It's what somebody I cared about used to call me."

"Oh. I thought it was because your name was Crowley. Like... '*Scarecrowley*.' You know?"

"Oh." I legitimately hadn't realised the similarity, an embarrassing oversight. "Perhaps I should have chosen a more subtle pseudonym?"

"Think it's a little too late now, Scarecrow," she teased.

Suddenly we heard gunfire.

"*Definitely* too late," Sephy said grimly.

Our people didn't change their paths of movement, so the gunfire didn't seem to involve them. It took us a moment to figure it out. When we did, I felt an awful sensation deep in my stomach.

The soldiers were firing at civilians.

"Caesar Squad, can you get a fix on the gunfire?" I asked

through my headset, terse. "There are civilians needing our help. Don't engage, though. They're trying to lure us into a trap. We'll help you draw them away."

"*Understood.*"

A voice modifier filtered everything we said through our headsets. It meant that if the enemy did listen in, they wouldn't be able to decipher our real identities.

"Napoleon Squad?"

"*Yes, Scarecrow?*" Maeve's voice crackled.

"I need you to go to the coordinates I'm sending you." I knew from the files Kipling had given me that the Praetory had their own law enforcement department in Quietfire. I also knew what they kept there. "There are some interesting items in storage the Praetory will no doubt want to use against us. I'm sure right now they'll be stacking them onto a truck for deployment, so you need to intercept them on time."

"*We're on it! Over.*"

"*Scarecrow?*" Aberdeen asked, radioing in. I zeroed in on his dot on our screen, noting his location.

"*Yes, Two?*" I said, calling him by his number designation. "*Why aren't you with the rest of your squad?*"

"There was this soldier, aiming down at this mother and her kid." Aberdeen sounded strange. Unsteady. "He was... about to kill them. And I... I..."

It took me a moment to understand it. I felt terrible when I finally realised.

Aberdeen...

Aberdeen may be an excellent fighter, he may be a member of a revolutionary cell, but he's never taken a life before. I feel guilty for the oversight.

"*I definitely killed him,*" Aberdeen breathed, his voice shaking. "*Oh God, I... I killed him. I didn't have time to tase so I shot... there was no way he survived that. I did that. Right? That was me. His Shadow just fell straight after. His heart gave out. One bullet... two lives just gone."*

"Deep breaths, Two," I said softly. "Deep breaths. You can do this. You know you can."

"Why?" Aberdeen said, sounding faint.

"I'm sorry?"

"That's what he was asking me," Aberdeen explained, voice thick with shame. *"When the soldier looked at me as he was dying, that's what I saw in his eyes. I could have shot just to injure, I should have, but I didn't..."*

"Crowley, he's losing it," Sephy hissed, incredibly tense. "We can't win this without him, and if he doesn't start moving now, he's going to get himself killed out there."

"You know him best," I said angrily, secretly panicking that I wasn't getting through to Aberdeen. "Do you want to talk to him?"

Her face clammed up, her ears flattening.

"I don't know how," she whispered.

"The soldier, he was so confused," Aberdeen's voice was coming through the headset, sounding haunted. *"So surprised that he was actually going to die. And even when he stopped moving... he was still staring at me. I feel like he's still staring at me."*

"I know," I told him, with feeling.

"How do you *know?*" he cried.

Aberdeen was asking me for comfort? He wanted *me* to make sense of this for him?

"Because that's how I felt when I killed someone for the first time," I whispered. "During the war, I found a Shadow who had been wounded. Someone tried to kill him, and I shot them." I rested my cheek against my hand, surprised to feel the wetness of a tear. "I didn't tell anyone what had happened. I spent so long wondering whether what I'd done was the lesser evil."

"*And?*" It seemed like Aberdeen was hanging on every word.

"I know that I made the right choice. It wasn't easy. It should never be easy. But if I had to do it again, I would." I shook it off, realising this was no time for meandering soliloquies. "Right now? The choice is easy," I said rapidly. "They're here to murder innocent people and us. We don't want to have to kill, but they're pushing us into a corner where we have no other choice. Because of them, you're going to have to carry that trauma with you for the rest of your life. That's not fair."

There was just static. But I could hear him breathing. I knew he was still there.

"I'm proud you put those people ahead of yourself, and for not hesitating to save them," I said softly. "I have eyes on you, you're not alone. But your people need you, and you are going to need to do this again. And again." I paused for a moment. "Can you do this for them?'

"*Yes,*" Aberdeen breathed back raggedly. "*Thank you, Cr... Scarecrow. I just lost it for a moment there.*"

"Good. Because I have an important task and I need someone I can trust. Everything relies on it."

"*I can do it,*" Aberdeen said immediately. "*Tell me.*"

"I need you to know that this is going to be a kill or be killed situation. You're going to have to shoot first."

"I understand. If I can end this faster, I want to help."

I hesitated. Was it foolish to trust Aberdeen with this, when I'd just heard him breaking? Yet who else could pull this off?

"*Scarecrow?*" he asked. "*Please. Trust me.*"

I thought of our first simulation together. He'd been

mad that I hadn't utilised him to send him behind enemy lines to defuse the bomb. Yet he'd trusted me enough to bring me into his little dysfunctional family, and enough to vouch for me to try and lead them all out of this.

"I trust you," I said. "I need access to enemy communications. Head for the Praetory field HQ they've set up here in town, and stealth your way inside. Take Xeno and Bentley with you." Both were from my class. Xeno could summon a dark mist which would be good for stealth, and Bentley could manipulate the wind to cause surprising destruction if they were cornered. "I'm sending you the coordinates. Just treat it as if it's all a simulation, all right?"

"Wait, you want me to sneak into the enemy's own *headquarters* and seize it with a skeleton crew?" Aberdeen said intensely. "All while everyone else is fighting for every inch of territory?"

"Is that too ridiculous?" I asked him.

"No, I love it. Oooh. I've got it."

My lips twitched.

"I have the faith."

"Scarecrow, we've liberated the abandoned vehicle you described," Maeve said over the radio, "it had exactly what you said it would."

"Excellent. Start laying the groundwork, I've marked the locations on your map. Update me on progress."

Aberdeen and his tiny team were making their way across town. Aberdeen was gracefully out-manoeuvring the enemy as if he was an Achilles of legend, I mused.

Show them how it's done, Aberdeen.

For a moment all my focus was on that green blinking dot. Aberdeen could be impossible, but I couldn't imagine a world in which that green light went out either. It was almost hypnotising watching him as he continued to evade capture and make a mockery of the Praetory soldiers as they chased after him. Aberdeen was a daredevil who continually defied the odds. I marvelled at it. It was as if he was damn unstoppable.

"You have a patrol coming at 3 o'clock," I shouted, and watched as Aberdeen glided precisely through a gap between two buildings, leading his team away from a group of Praetory soldiers who were firing at anything that moved.

"Scarecrow?" Aberdeen's voice came through my headset only minutes later. *"We're at the enemy's field HQ."*

"Do you have a visual on how many guards there are?"

"Eight of them."

I bit my lip.

Sephy turned to me incredulously.

"Send in more reinforcements!" she insisted.

"There's nobody else who could manage to get close enough to the area," I muttered.

"Crowley, you can't risk his life..."

"Number Two?"

"Happy to risk it," Aberdeen said. *"I'll be fine, Seph."*

"Permission to engage," I informed him.

"Yes, Scarecrow."

Even though Sephy was angry at Aberdeen, she still didn't seem to appreciate me risking her friend's life against such odds.

"If I hadn't given him permission, he may well have decided just to seek forgiveness later," I pointed out to Sephy, who was glaring at me reproachfully. "Right now he's our best hope."

We waited with bated breath for an update. I tried not to show it, but I felt positively sick. Aberdeen and the others didn't just have to take out the guards. They had to do it before anyone had the chance to sound a distress call.

Aberdeen, you arsehole... please, please don't die.

I sat there, not breathing, wondering if I'd already sent Aberdeen to his death when he'd only just started trusting me with his life.

"We have command of HQ, over," Aberdeen's voice filtered in. We exhaled, dizzy with relief.

"Are you all right?" I asked, sounding more tender than I'd meant to.

"Yes," he snapped, tetchy. "Of course, I'm fine."

Ah, good. So we were back to normal Aberdeen prickliness again. I guess that's how I knew he was going to be okay.

"Is their commander there?" I demanded.

"No. It looks like orders are being conveyed remotely."

"Is it the Governor giving commands?" I swallowed.

"No. It seems to be Sir Kipling."

I felt an icy sensation in my veins. I knew Aberdeen must have been having the same reaction. Sir Kipling murdered his fellow acolytes monstrously after they'd snuck into the Academy, including one of Aberdeen's closest friends.

"I want to kill him," Aberdeen said through gritted teeth.

"And I want to let you," I said with feeling. "But if Kipling's not here in person, then we can only hurt him by trouncing his forces and surviving. That's how we stick it to him."

Sir Kipling Sloan. The psychopathic mass-murderer and Jo's personal knight. It makes more sense now why she had someone like that in her employ. I remembered the first time I saw Kipling, his shoes wet from the blood of acolytes he'd slaughtered.

Kipling had reportedly been knighted straight out of Counterpart Academy, just like I'd dreamed of. But unlike him, I had no master to serve. Instead, everyone was looking to me. Aberdeen, Sephy, Maeve and the others; I was *their* knight now, and I have to keep all of them alive. I had to keep as many of the Shadows cowering here in Quietfire safe as I could, whether they were huddling in their houses or in the blocked tunnels beneath us.

"I'm sending you the data you asked for now," Aberdeen reported.

I exhaled in satisfaction as multiple windows blinked into life on our screens.

"Bingo!" Sephy announced, elated. We were staring at the live body-cam feeds from every single member of the Praetory army.

"Soldiers will be regularly checking in with HQ, and when they stop receiving responses they're going to start running their validation checks," I cautioned. "We have twenty to thirty minutes to make the most of this advantage."

"Time for us to pay their squads a little visit then."

I couldn't help but smirk at how the pieces were sliding perfectly into place.

Well, well. We play on the same gameboard at last. Welcome to the battle, Kipling.

Bring it.

21

The military thought they'd be playing against children, I thought, amused. *They must be worried their little mission is getting blown out of proportion.*

"My good people, we now have a fix on the enemy's positions. Sephy is going to give you your directions to ambush them. Get to them before they hurt any more innocents... and crush them."

"Yes, Scarecrow!" An excited chorus came from the radios.

I traced my lip with my finger thoughtfully as I surveyed the map.

"It's interesting, seeing you like this," Sephy said.

"Like what?"

"You look like you're... coming alive."

"Don't worry. It's probably just a temporary adrenaline boost from everyone trying to kill me."

Smiling, Sephy turned away to return a call. She was grinning like a maniac, juggling radio calls, sounding way too cheerful. The others in the warehouse were studying the bodycam footage of the enemy soldiers, then marking their positions on the map.

"Napoleon Squad," I said swiftly. They'd just successfully ambushed one of the squads through a wall. "Make sure to arm yourself with their weapons, and take their armour too. They'll hesitate if they see you in Praetory armour as well." This was a nice little opportunity to sow confusion and chaos among the enemy.

Sephy was reeling off updates.

"We have another enemy contact!" she declared. "Caesar Squad just took out an entire unit. Alexander Squad just took out those soldiers through a building. Let's give them hell, people!"

I looked sideways at her, troubled. My deputy sounded a little bloodthirsty, all loaded up on dopamine. When Sephy got truly angry, she became a dark and terrible goddess this world wasn't prepared for. Just a few hours ago, she was spitting moral outrage at me for *thinking* about hurting the Praetory. Now she was treating this bloody fight against them like a fun game of *Battleships*. Perhaps she thought treating this as a game was the only way she was going to get through it. But it wasn't the danger that broke her. Not just that. It was watching innocent Shadows getting mown down by the *'good guys'* on the Governor's orders.

Revenge used to be my niche. But Sephy? She was catching up fast—and she'd brought glitter and fire.

I was training traumatised teenagers to be efficient murderers. Sure, it was technically to *save* them, but I wondered what kind of karmic debt I was racking up.

"How exactly do you think your mother's going to feel about this, by the way?" Sephy quizzed me. "Using Shadows' Eve to destroy her beloved Praetory military."

"If she could get past her cold fury, I like to think she might even be proud of me," I commented lightly, hiding my own fear at the answer. "Maybe after she finishes throwing wine at my childhood photos." I studied the map and smiled at where our troops blinked like fireflies. I was given hope by the continued existence of that light. There was no question the Praetory still had the numerical superiority by far, but the acolytes had helpful advantages thanks to battling on their own home turf. We were making the Praetory bleed for every centimetre of territory they took.

"You can just taste their apprehension," Sephy observed. "The enemy is moving slower now. I don't think they expected our resistance to be quite so fearsome."

"Only apprehensive? Then we haven't done our job yet."

Next step: outright fear.

"I expect right now they're wondering who the hell is giving the acolytes their orders," Sephy said with a sidelong smile, "and why the Praetory are suddenly putty in our hands. Their performance so far is an embarrassment." She giggled. "You've ruined any hopes of promotion those soldiers might have. Plus, now that you've won the acolytes' awe and devotion, they're obeying you faster now and without hesitation."

"Supplying our people with an insane amount of firepower and the movement of every one of their enemies tends to have that effect," I shrugged. "Now let's be sure we don't disappoint their new expectations."

"Ooh, that's one more perfect ambush," Sephy reported, surveying the map. "Letting our acolytes be spotted on their own is working wonders, they're drawing the Praetory squads right into our traps."

Think, Kipling, think, I mocked the knight silently. He

must be furiously trying to figure out how we were suddenly omnipotent. He would be searching for any kind of surveillance that we may have set up, or any drones we'd deployed to pinpoint his troops' locations. He had yet to discover we were logged into the bodycams of his own soldiers, and that we could view the distribution of his troops just as clear as he could.

But our narrow window was almost up. When the Praetory HQ didn't respond to any of its troops' regular check-ins, it would become clear that it was compromised. Kipling would realise we'd played him.

I imagined Kipling, enjoying the mental image of his powerless fury. No doubt he was threatening to execute his lackeys left and right.

Come on, think it through, I gloated. Right on cue, our feeds of the enemy's bodycams went dark. I sighed. Unfortunate, but predictable.

So Kipling had finally noticed. He'd automatically logged everyone out from the bodycam feeds. Not ideal, but we'd humbled our enemy enough to satisfy me for now.

There was suddenly an awful sound, an eruption from the edge of town. Following it came a rumbling which shook the entire building. An explosion, I reckoned, far too close. I bared my teeth.

"Report."

"Some kind of big, shaky vibes?" Sephy suggested.

"Excellent. Thanks for clearing that up."

I rushed with the others over to the windows to look out into the darkness, still cautious not to expose ourselves to any snipers. A building two blocks over was a flaming pile of rubble, as if it had been struck by a rocket. As we watched, a building in the next street erupted into flames.

Sephy was listening to her headset intently. One of our

squads must have been reporting in. If Sephy could visibly pale, I think she would have.

"It's Lilith," Sephy whispered. I recalled Sir Kipling's Shadow: the poisonous purple wyvern. A dragon with two legs and a mane of seaweed, covered in bony armour. Her red glowing eyes had pierced deeply into my soul. "She's at the edge of town, and Sir Kipling is using her unique power to target us. She must be making those strikes in the rough area Kipling believes this base is located."

I'd done my research, I knew what Lilith was capable of. But it was still difficult to comprehend that such destructive power could be contained entirely inside a single Shadow. Lilith was a living, breathing tank, raining chaos down on the entire town. "Kipling also has humans and Shadows firing at the area he thinks our HQ is in. He's not far off. He seems determined to remove the entirety of Quietfire from the map, if that's what it takes."

"Of course he is." Nobody hated Shadows' Eve like Kipling. He also seemed to have a special hatred for Shadows who hadn't discovered their counterpart, or rather their *'master.'*

I knew it was really the Praetory's fault and not ours, but I still couldn't help but feel a deep guilt over putting the Shadows of this town in harm's way. I knew Sephy must be too.

"A lot of the townspeople are hiding in bunkers or basements below ground," she said. "But if Lilith's determined to pepper the entire area, no one will survive. Kipling will blame the casualties all on the acolytes, no doubt... oh damn, they've unleashed another artillery round." Sephy listened to her headset for a moment. There was another rumble, far too loud and incredibly close. Sephy hissed as the newest report came in. "Another building just collapsed two blocks over. They're getting closer. That one nearly hit *us*."

"They're just guessing," I muttered from across steepled fingers. "They only suspect that our HQ is somewhere in this area. They're just going off where they've encountered our troops."

"But they suspect correctly! We can't stay here. They'll be preparing another round right now. If they keep firing at us from that distance, we'll have no way to neutralise them and we won't survive. Neither will Aberdeen, the acolytes, or anyone in this town!"

"The acolytes are relying on us to be their eyes in the sky," I point out. "If we abandon position, we abandon them."

"All it takes is one blast and we're done for," Sephy stated.

"We can hardly not risk our lives like the rest of our team are."

I could practically feel Sephy rolling her eyes. Then she saw what was coming before I did. Her tone changed drastically. "Everyone *get down!*"

We threw ourselves to the floor. The entire warehouse trembled. Loose shards of stone dropped from the roof and pelted the floor. Taggi's eyes were shut tight beside us, rocking back and forth. I reached across to squeeze her arm reassuringly.

"*Scarecrow?*" Aberdeen's voice urgently crackled through the radio.

"Everyone okay?" I demanded when it stopped.

"We're still here," Sephy confirmed into the radio for all to hear. "It just missed HQ. It looks like there were multiple strikes at once."

We were lucky to have survived.

But I was staring down at our glowing map. Several emerald units had fled the bombardment, but one of those fireflies had simply flashed right out of existence.

"Maeve's transponder," I whispered. I tried her on the radio. "One?" I demanded, calling her by her assigned number. "One, come in!"

There was nothing but static. All of us were afraid to speak.

It looked like Maeve had ensured her squad had gotten to safety, but in that one instant, she herself was gone. There was an eerie silence through the warehouse and the radio waves: one of disbelief, pain, and fear.

They'd killed Maeve. She'd trusted my orders, and I'd watched as her life was snuffed out.

"Crowley?" Sephy murmured intently, leaning in close to me so that only I could hear. "Kipling's trying to force you to make an error of judgement. Don't let him. You've made it this far flawlessly. Don't let him drive you into making a mistake. Maeve believed that you could save her people. Just tell me what you need."

I might have at one point loved having such a competent opponent to try myself against, but Kipling's policy of a full-out massacre of the Shadows of Quietfire had me quaking with hate.

"We have to neutralise Lilith and anyone else firing at us from the blockade," I said through gritted teeth, resting my fingertips against my temples. "Or at the least, force them to take cover so that they're unable to keep up this bombardment. If Lilith and the others continue, they'll carve a path right through the town and our own forces.

Any meaningful ability we have to defend ourselves will be gone."

"Seven, this is HQ," Sephy called in. "Scarecrow needs a sniping team to eliminate Lilith and her support before the next bombardment. Make her pay, dearly."

"*With pleasure.*"

"Don't leave them any vehicles to escape in, understood?" I added fiercely. "I want them stranded and at our mercy."

"*Nice. That's just how I like them, too.*"

Shortly after, we heard the sniper shots ring out. Our people were in position on the rooftops now, using their rifles and the Shadows' powers to target Lilith at the edge of town, along with the LAVs and enemy units lurking there.

Sephy muted her microphone and sighed. Her monkey hands were shaking.

"*Crap,*" she muttered.

"Sephy?" I asked softly, checking in. I could see it was getting to her. We'd lost Maeve, and right now the others entrusted in our hands felt so fragile.

She grimaced. "Yeah, I'm fine."

"*We've got some good hits on the units supporting Lilith,*" one of our snipers radioed in. "*They're in tatters.*"

"Excellent work," Sephy said.

I stared at the map intently, trying to get inside the enemy's head. Kipling knew of our ability to pick them off at long range now. He also knew we'd taken out a good deal of the vehicles he'd need in order for his people to retreat unscathed. Would he still have his people attempt to retreat strategically, or push in, attempting to crush us?

"*But the bad news is we couldn't get a clean hit on Lilith,*" the sniper added. *"We've lost sight of her, and I'm afraid she's entered the town now."*

Ah. Not ideal.

"Ginagalit mo ako!" Aberdeen exclaimed over the radio, switching to Tagalog. *"Damn it, Scarecrow, they're breaking the blockade."*

So. Now I knew for sure the kind of leader Kipling truly was. One who would fulfil his mission or let his soldiers die trying. We'd driven him into a fury, and now he felt he had nothing more to lose. He couldn't return to face Jo without wiping us all out and restoring his lost honour.

"Kipling realised his blockade was too big to be a force multiplier," I mused to Sephy. "Their troops were easier to pick off out in the clear, and their infantry positioned there was wasted. So they're tightening the circle, not worrying about us slipping through the cracks. They know we haven't made a run for it yet, because we're staying here to defend this place."

"They're swapping out smaller squads for one large one, and they're coming hard for our people," Taggi said, listening to her headset. "Looks like you were right. It will be far more difficult for us to ambush such a big force. Impossible even."

"Scarecrow!" Aberdeen screamed to me through the radio. His voice sounded thick, as if his mouth was full of blood.

I was on my feet suddenly, device held in hand.

"What is it, Two?"

"It's Kipling. I can see him."

Kipling? My mind spun furiously with the possibilities. So, Kipling wasn't sending commands from afar after all then. He was here in the town, killing with his own hands. It was bold.

Aberdeen. He's in trouble.

I zoomed in on that single, vulnerable green dot with Aberdeen's identifier tag. I felt a lurching sensation inside of me as I realised he was nowhere near the rest of his squad. Aberdeen was cut off and without support.

There was another rumbling in the distance. It sounded a lot like Lilith.

"Get a sniper on Aberdeen's position, now," I said, steely.

"I'm on it," Taggi said. As she rapidly relayed directions to Maeve's team, trying to identify the nearest rooftop that may have a vantage point, I radioed Aberdeen back. "Two, what's your status?"

"Just brilliant." His breathing was unsteady. He sounded as if he had been hurt, badly. "I took a shot at Kipling and tried to take him down, but he was too far off," Aberdeen added dispassionately, reloading his gun. "Also, he has Lilith with him."

Oh, Aberdeen.

"Kipling also has a massive squad with him... and multiple LAVs."

I pinched the bridge of my nose.

"How did you get separated from *your* squad?" I demanded.

"They got separated during the last bombardment," Sephy explained. "He's been trying to link back up."

"*I'm going back*," Aberdeen said. "I *can take Kipling out, I know it.*"

"No."

"*One bullet through that monster's neck, that's all it will take to make him pay.*" I heard the quaking rage in his voice. "*Then Lilith will die too.*"

"You're more valuable to us alive."

"You know his troops will fall apart if he goes down. The military get all *weepy*, when a member of nobility dies. It's crushing for morale."

"Get out of there, Two. That's an order!" I commanded.

"*They're almost on me,*" he said calmly. "*This is it for me anyway. At least let me go out in style.*"

I turned to Sephy.

"Can you do it?" I asked.

"I really hope so."

"Two, our friend is going to give you directions to get you out of there," I said.

"*I don't need you to coddle me, Scarecrow.*"

"I'm not. If you'll allow me, I'd like to use you as bait. You just need to trust me."

I remembered the first simulation Aberdeen and I ever did together in class. I recalled his fury when I hadn't been willing to risk him in order to win. I wouldn't make the same mistake twice.

Aberdeen exhaled, his radio crackling.

"*Alright, I trust you. Although if you're lying to me, you're dead.*"

"Excellent. Two? Draw the enemy to you."

Then I heard Aberdeen yelling from his end, presumably to Kipling, Lilith and all of the troops in pursuit nearby:

"*Thanks for hanging out, I'm going now, byyyye!*"

I chuckled, imagining the expression of the soldiers as Aberdeen gave away his location before, much to their confusion, running for his life.

I watched on the map as Aberdeen dove through an alleyway. Sephy gave directions rapidly, guiding Aberdeen's glowing green dot carefully through the labyrinth. Our dormmate was moving fast through the darkness, his path only illuminated by flickering streetlamps and Sephy's directions. Still, I knew he must hurt from the fighting. Every one of those steps was a struggle, an infinite hurdle to overcome.

Come on, Aberdeen. We're so close.

A terrific explosion rocked the air. One of Lilith's flaming missiles must have detonated. I rushed to the window, where a cloud billowed into the sky like a monstrous creature awakening from slumber, each swirl kissed by the silvery glow of moonlight. Aberdeen's scream pierced through the chaos.

"They're right behind me, I'm not going to make it!"

"Yes, you are!" I shouted, panic clawing at my chest. I imagined him trapped, surrounded by the relentless enemy. What if this was the moment I failed him?

"Take the turn on your left..." I scrutinised the map. My shaking hands pressed down on it. "Now dash down that street but whatever you do, stay to the left-hand wall! I repeat, do not go anywhere near the middle of the street. Then take the street on your left and take cover when you're about half-way down."

His gasp reached me like a lifeline: *"Okay! Made it!"*

"Sephy, now!" I yelled, urgency driving each word. Aberdeen was so strong, so reckless—every move he made sparked admiration and terror in me. Would he die fighting alone, after everything? The idea twisted in my gut like a knife.

I couldn't lose Aberdeen. I hated to acknowledge it, but I cared about him too. Each beat of my heart echoed with a silent promise that I wouldn't let him down. My throat tightened. I had to focus, to push those fears aside. Aberdeen needed us, and we couldn't let him fight this battle on his own.

"You got it." Sephy pressed the controls. Nothing happened.

I quirked an eyebrow.

"Trouble?" I asked sharply.

An enormous explosion tore at the very air. The warehouse shook all around us. The windows of the command centre flared with blinding light and I shielded my eyes. When it cleared, a hellish brilliance illuminated the darkness, a fiery eruption that twisted and turned in hues of orange and crimson.

"No trouble," Sephy said cheerfully.

"What the hell was that?" Aberdeen yelped. His ears must have finally stopped ringing.

Other explosions followed from around the town, all very close to our location.

"Lilith's injured, she's down!" another acolyte reported through the headset.

"Scarecrow, what just happened?" Aberdeen demanded again.

I smiled. This time, the sound of explosions had been the sign of victory.

"I asked Maeve's squad to collect landmines from a Praetory truck they intercepted," I informed him, "then I had them place them at strategic chokepoints around the centre of town. Sephy just activated them all." Aberdeen had successfully led the enemy troops, including Lilith, right into our little trap.

You just saved us all, Maeve, I thought heavily. *Thank you.*

"As if you didn't already owe me for all the lies," Sephy said to Aberdeen matter-of-factly. "I want daily coffees from *Midnight Runner* from now on. With extra cream."

"Sephy, I'm... I'm sorry."

"Leave it to the marshmallows, sweetheart," Sephy told him sardonically. But I saw the happy tears on her cheeks.

Thanks to Aberdeen, most of the enemies' light armoured vehicles were in flaming tatters, their troops scattered and disorientated. Our other squads had been lying in wait for this very moment. Time to spring the trap.

"Finish them," I said. Tapping the arm of my chair, I felt a rush of elation unlike anything I'd ever experienced. I couldn't help it. Through sheer willpower, we'd pulled back victory from the brink of defeat. It was exhilarating.

The screams of Praetory soldiers met our ears. One of the acolytes apparently had the ability to create black portals on the ground that would drag people in with giant tentacles. The Praetory didn't seem to be enjoying that much. Not at all.

"No way," I heard Monolith whisper, the stone brachiosaurus watching out the window. "The enemy is in retreat."

With their vehicles blown up, the Praetory were stuck on foot in hostile territory, outflanked and out-manoeuvred.

"Scarecrow?" the acolyte named Kevin called in from the field. He sounded disbelieving. "We've captured the remaining soldiers. They've all surrendered."

"We won?" Taggi asked, stunned. "Can that be right?"

Shadows were slowly emerging back out onto the streets in wonder. Some were shaking their heads, as if scared to actually believe they'd survived.

Lovers hugged. Friends cried into each other. Parents sagged with relief against their doors, knowing their children were still alive and safe inside.

Taggi looked at me, then at the others. Then back to me.

"Okay, if no one else is going to say it then I will," she said in awe. "Crowley, you were *brilliant*."

"Simply incredible," Victor breathed, a maniacal gleam in his eye. "You're a miracle-worker, *Scarecrow*. May the world behold your works and tremble!"

We stared at him.

"Uh, that's certainly a change of tune," Sephy muttered.

"I was wrong," Victor confessed. He bowed his head to me. "Forgive me. We couldn't have done this without you. I still can't really believe it. Thank you for saving us all."

That meant a lot, but it also stung. Maeve's face swam before my eyes.

"I'm just sorry I couldn't save everyone," I answered.

"Maeve couldn't have had a finer commander. You pulled off the impossible and kept her people alive. She would have thought that a worthy sacrifice."

We had killed people. It had been in self-defence, and we'd had to pretend it was all some elaborate board game just to get ourselves through it. What did that make us now? Were we still normal teenage students, or soldiers?

"*Scarecrow!*" the acolytes were cheering, their words crackling through the radio. "*SCARECROW!*"

Their voices were all euphoric at having faced death, and lived to tell the tale. It was surreal.

"Crowley Victorious," Sephy murmured.

Then she padded over to the bathroom. I heard her throwing up shortly after.

I came to loiter by the door, nervous.

"Are you okay?" I risked a glance inside.

"Those were real lives Crowley!" Sephy hollered. I could make her out inside. She was shaking.

"I know."

"I wasn't ready. Maeve died, and if I'd known more, if I'd been someone better…"

"You were perfect for it," I said quietly. "That's why I didn't choose anyone else. You're a team leader. You were their guide." I fidgeted, nervous for some reason. "Sephy, you make people believe anything is possible."

"Great," she laughed, almost as if just to herself. I heard a flush before she reappeared. "Amazing."

I sat down against one of the walls, and she lay next to me. We were silent for a moment, reflecting on all of the chaos we'd just been through.

"After the thorough trouncing the Praetory's military has had, I doubt they'll be daring to set down foot in the neighbourhood for some time," Sephy murmured, with a twitch at the corner of her mouth.

"I'm sorry I didn't tell you about the acolytes. I didn't mean to hide it from you… I was just still processing it."

"It was a lot to trust me with," Sephy said, tilting her head. "I forget that really, we haven't known each other that long at all. It doesn't feel like it. But you had my back when I was in trouble. That means something."

I was the reason she'd gotten caught up in all this. I essentially gambled away Sephy's innocence as a sacrifice, and that was something I could never give her back. The idea that I may have scared her away forever when she'd discovered the truth had terrified me. I was only just realising now that I'd been so afraid because Sephy really was the closest thing I'd ever had to a best friend. She was someone I needed now more than ever.

But instead of yelling at me and coming at me with her deadly claws, Sephy simply leaned against my shoulder.

I stiffened, sitting completely still. Then I leaned my head against hers too.

"Sephy..." I whispered emotionally. I wanted to tell her how I was ashamed of how I'd acted. She'd stood by me and trusted me to pull off this defence operation despite all of that. *It meant everything,* I tried to say.

"Do you want to go get something to eat?" I asked.

Sephy considered me, poised.

"I suppose," she said, "but just so you know, you're buying for everyone."

"That's fair."

"I want the Praetory to suffer for what they did," Sephy said softly, so quietly I almost couldn't hear her. The trauma from what she'd just witnessed was clear in her features. "Not just here in Wellington, but every place in the world where people feel they can treat Shadows as... dispensable. I want the Praetory to burn. But..." she shut her eyes tightly, "...but I don't *want* to want it."

Sephy stayed there, lying next to me. Her head rested against me in sad silence as we both thought of all that had passed, and all that might still be coming for us.

The door of our HQ slammed open.

Everyone was so slow to look up. I was the first to see the great black bat emerging through the doorway. Entering right behind the Shadow was his human, a soldier in Praetory uniform. The man raised his rifle to fire.

My pistol was out in an instant and I squeezed off two shots. The bat screeched, a shockwave of sound rippling outward. My bullets ricocheted off the pulse, veering wide. The wave smashed into us like a concrete wall, knocking us off our feet and sending us crashing to the floor.

Dazed, I wiped my lip. My hand came away with blood, stained by my own mortality.

"Interesting," I murmured.

22

The soldier raised his rifle, barrel steady, finger curling toward the trigger.

I stared up at him, breath caught in my throat.

Behind the visor, the man's eyes widened in recognition as he saw that a teenager had been pulling all the strings from an acolyte hideout.

I heard two gunshots, and I thought it was all over.

The man collapsed to the floor. I blinked. The bat was lying unmoving behind him as well. Standing in the shattered doorway behind them, panting like he'd sprinted through fire, stood Aberdeen. His chest heaved, wild with adrenaline, as his gaze locked on me.

"CROWLEY!" he choked out, raw, ragged. "Crowley—!"

He was already running. I barely registered the sound of his boots before he knelt beside me, gathering me up like I might vanish. His warm, shaking hands found mine. He held them like they were the only real thing in the world.

"Stop yelling," I mumbled. "Ears hurt."

"Are you hurt?" he demanded, nearly incoherent,

cupping my face with trembling hands. He was frantic, his eyes wide. His face looked drained of blood.

Then he laughed, high and shaky. He dropped his forehead to mine for the briefest second, just long enough for me to feel how real this all was—his pulse racing, his relief crashing over him like a wave.

"You idiot," he whispered, eyes squeezed shut. "Don't scare me like that."

Without him, we'd be dead. He'd killed two armed assassins to get to me.

"Nice shooting," I murmured, gathering myself. I heard him breathe shakily with relief that I was still kicking. "Is Rosita okay?"

"She wasn't on lookout at all," Aberdeen sighed, rolling his eyes skyward. "I think she went out into the field to help clear up the stragglers."

Classic Rosita.

Aberdeen was still rather embarrassingly checking me over, as if unconvinced that I was still alive. I swatted at him half-heartedly. "You're clingy when you're worried."

"You almost died, Crowley," he snapped, but his voice was trembling with relief. "You don't get to sass me yet."

I couldn't help the smile that tugged at my own lips. I rolled my eyes as I sat up, shoving him off.

"We actually did it," he said, voice rising, breathless with joy. "Stupid Crowley. We freaking trounced them!" He laughed, triumphant, and it was so stupid and beautiful that for a moment I forgot everything else.

But only for a moment. Gently, I put my hand on Aberdeen's arm.

"What?" he asked, not frazzled in the least. He still looked positively elated from our miraculous win. His smile was luminous. "What is it?"

"Aberdeen, it's Maeve," I said slowly, my heart heavy. I felt tears on my cheeks. "I'm so, so sorry. She was hit by one of the armaments. I couldn't save her."

Aberdeen stared at me, his smile falling away. Then he looked around the room as other acolytes kept coming in, like Maeve might be coming through that doorway any moment, and I'd just made a simple mistake.

He brought a hand to his chest and held it there, going very, very still. Aberdeen looked as if he was in shock, but also as if he was waiting for something.

Then it hit me. He must have wondered, what with their close connection, if Maeve had been his Shadow.

But she was gone. And he was still here.

For a moment, I thought he was going to say something to me. He looked as if he was fighting the fear of humiliation that vulnerability could bring.

But they stayed there—unspoken, trembling in the space between us. And still, he held my hand.

Then Aberdeen's gaze found Sephy.

"Sephy," Aberdeen whispered, and he rushed over to her in a flurry. He checked her over. When he found she was alive and awake, he breathed a deep sigh of relief.

"Look, I know you're angry at me and you have every right to be," I heard him say to Sephy, his voice cracking. "But I'm going to keep trying to make it up to you, if you'll let me. Even if it takes forever."

"You're such a drama queen," she snorted. She squeezed her eyes shut, overcome with emotion, then reopened them.

"Okay," she said softly.

. . .

I walked onto the warehouse's balcony and stared out at the town, barely believing what had just taken place. The sky was lighter now. The sunrise was coming.

We won, I thought, giddy with relief. *They're alive. Their hearts are still beating.* The feeling started within me, then built and swelled until I threw my head back and laughed. The sound spilled over the rooftops, slightly hysterical.

The sun rose slowly on our dark night, promising new horizons and futures previously beyond my capacity to think of.

At long last I felt the vibration in my pocket I'd both been hoping for and dreading. I'd feared Morgaine and Deva may have failed. I answered the video call.

The phone barely rang before Morgaine connected. Morgaine's phone camera was discreetly aimed into Jo's military command room, all sleek-metal and filled with arrays of computer stations. Jo was yelling in fury at her subordinates.

"How did Crowley do this?" Jo was screaming. "How?"

"Your Excellency, I don't think a teenage first-year could have been responsible for our significant losses..."

"Do you think I'm mad? I know her style! I watched her training going up, and she was formidable just as a little girl!"

Morgaine and Deva stepped out of the darkness at the rear of the room. The feed went black and I heard a commotion as everyone was taken entirely by surprise. When the phone was held aloft again they were surrounded by dead or unconscious bodies.

I had to admire that Morgaine and Deva had managed to breach the supposed impregnable command centre, the one place Jo believed herself untouchable.

Deva dragged Jo's Shadow Tempy out of her small pool

of water. The mermaid thrashed desperately on the carpet, Deva pinning her down with one taloned foot. Jo gasped as she staggered away from her attackers, as if she could feel her Shadow's pain as her own.

"Leave Tempy alone, you sick..." Jo's voice cut off as she suddenly saw who the intruders were. *"Morgaine Holloway?"* she exclaimed, reeling. "I don't understand! Who sent you, the Potentate?"

"No," I said, hoping Morgaine had placed me on speakerphone for dramatic effect. "Worse."

I activated my video. White as a ghost, Jo stared back at me in the phone held aloft in Morgaine's hand. I knew Jo could see me when our gazes locked.

It was strange seeing Jo. Her features were the face of a friend, exactly as I remembered them, yet... changed.

"Crowley?" Jo whispered, the fear in her voice audible.

"Surprised to see me alive, *babe?*"

There it was. The shame written all over her for asking her goons to dispose of me. If the evidence hadn't already made it clear she was responsible, seeing the guilt in her eyes made it real. I could see the cogs in her head turning, as she schemed how to salvage this.

"No, Jo, you don't get to lie anymore. You don't get to play your games. Your forces were murdering innocents for sport. I don't know who the hell you are anymore, but I do know that I'm going to ask you for some answers, and you're going to give them to me."

"Crowley, there's nowhere you can run," Jo said desperately. "Please, hear me. Sephy and your little band of terrorists cannot escape either. You're only putting off the inevitable, unless you let me help you."

I stared calmly back. Her earnest mask cracked, and she seemed to swell up with rage at my impertinence.

"I'm not scared of you or this little display," Jo spat. Enraged and indignant, she swelled up to her full height, as if the very worst thing would be to show weakness. "You and your friends will be hunted to the ends of the earth! I am the *Governor*, I was appointed by the Potentate himself! You'll be nothing but echoes and dust, while the Praetory will reign eternal."

"Only a select few were told about her exact orders to kill you and your friends," Morgaine informed me, as if the Governor's prattling was inconsequential. "I am confident your identity and Sephy's are secure."

If Morgaine or Deva felt uneasy about attacking a Governor, they sure didn't show it. I think Jo's attempt to murder me had erased any of their sympathy for this figure of Praetory authority.

"Why did you come after us, Jo?" I asked, my words precise yet fuelled by my rage at all of the secrets. "Why was hiding my father's identity as an acolyte so important?"

"I'll never talk," Jo sneered.

"Oh. A bold theory. Morgaine?"

I heard Jo whimpering, calling for her guards as Morgaine and Deva moved in toward her. Muting the phone, I stared off over the rooftops of Quietfire, my entire body shaking. I took in all the devastation, all of the death that Jo Blackmore had brought upon this town. It gave me the strength I needed.

I unmuted the phone.

"Sir Morgaine?" I asked quietly. The honorific was gender-neutral for knights within the Praetory.

"Blackmore says the intelligence concealed in the vault beneath the Academy was important in some way to the Potentate himself. Knowing this, Jo had used it as blackmail against him in order to secure her position as Governor. If the Potentate found that Jo no longer had the evidence of that intelligence in her possession... her own life would have been forfeit."

"So the Potentate knows nothing about any of this," I said, relieved. "Jo was just covering her own back after the acolytes stole from her."

I thought this over. We couldn't be sure we'd eliminated everyone who'd known that we had been on Jo's personal kill list. But if this was Jo's vendetta alone, then once she was removed from power the threat against my friends and I would be ended.

"Ask her who killed my father," I said quietly.

"I already have, my Lady."

"And?"

"The Potentate himself ordered your father's death," Morgaine said heavily. "When the opportunity came to take out Jupiter's most valuable and trusted knight, the Potentate couldn't resist."

I absorbed this, feeling a measure of calm at finally knowing the truth. The Potentate himself, the highest authority in the Praetory who sat upon the throne in New York. I should have guessed that my father had made himself some powerful enemies.

Jo looked up at me darkly through the screen of my phone. There was a visceral, demented rage in her eyes.

I shook my head.

"For the sake of our friendship, I'm going to let you live. But today is your last day as Governor."

"Please, Crowley. You know how the Praetory worships nobility like gods!" Jo exploded. The dark bags under her eyes were pronounced, but her smile was filled with invincible confidence. "I'm untouchable. There are no bars that can hold me. There will be no punishment for my actions, and no one will believe your word over mine. You've already lost. You'll all be dead by morning, regardless of your efforts and not a single thing about my daily life will change."

She was right. There was no way for us to live if she survived. I reminded myself how that very voice had ordered my death, and the death of Sephy. *Sephy.*

"You were my friend. I looked up to you," I told Jo, my voice catching. Tears wet my cheeks. "But you're so selfish, and you operate entirely out of fear. I never saw it until now. How could you have thought of doing this to me?"

"Because some things are bigger than friendship."

"No," I said, feeling a breaking sensation in my chest. "You're just smaller."

I imagined what would happen if I let Jo go, and saw Sephy and Aberdeen's dead bodies in my mind's eye. I realised I could never allow that to come to pass.

Something came over me. Something wrathful.

"Morgaine?" I whispered, knowing I was leaving the old Alexandra Crowley far, far behind.

"Are you sure, my Lady? There's no going back."

"You heard Jo. She's too powerful. As long as she lives, every one of us will be running for our lives from her and the Praetory." I wanted to close my eyes, but I refused to let myself. I owed Jo that much, and nothing more. I had to protect my real friends now, the dysfunctional family that had taken me in and trusted me. "Goodbye, Jo."

It was a decision that would haunt me forever and perhaps destroy me, one that I would never come back from.

It would be the first of many.

23

It was the end of our first semester. The middle of the year was arriving in a flurry of rain and darkness, the shroud of Wellington winter enveloping us in its biting chill.

And yet—because I was clearly broken—I found it... comforting. Counterpart Academy had become something resembling a sanctuary. A weird, secretive, occasionally homicidal sanctuary, sure, but a sanctuary nonetheless. This darkness was simply a time of rest and of regeneration, of the seeds of new plans and designs growing just out of sight.

I headed back to the dorm, relishing the sound of the drizzle against glass and old stone. Students were desperately holding up umbrellas or their own jackets to shield themselves as they dove through the muddy, squelchy grounds between classes.

Unexpectedly, I collided with Aberdeen. He was clutching a pile of textbooks, and nearly lost them all. His annoyance morphed to surprise when he saw me.

"Oh, Crowley!" His cheeks reddened, probably from the cold. "Were you heading back to...?"

"Y- yes!" I stammered, trying to act casual despite a strange rush of nervous energy. "Mind some company?"

"Ah, yes. No, I mean, of course," he said, shuffling his textbooks awkwardly.

We fell into step beside each other. An awkward silence settled between us. There was a palpable, almost electric discomfort.

"So how's your little club getting along?" I asked lightly, not carefree enough with my life to risk mentioning the acolytes by name. "Now that you're leader and all."

"I'm not the *leader*," he muttered, brooding.

"That's what Maeve wanted, right?" I said quietly.

"A Shadow should be in charge. That was always *his* idea for the movement." By his tone, I knew '*his*' meant Jupiter. "Us humans are just meant to be there as allies to support their independence and autonomy."

"But until someone in your ranks steps up to the plate, it seems like they're all looking to you for answers," I pointed out. "Because you've had their backs. Because you make them come together as a team. Do you have any *extracurricular* activities planned?"

"I was actually going to ask you that," Aberdeen said candidly.

"Me?"

"Please," Aberdeen snorted. He lowered his voice, checking the coast was clear: "Do you think after our club's last outing the others aren't just hankering to find out what the great *Scarecrow* has planned next? They think you're some kind of lucky charm they want to milk for all its got."

I smiled at him.

"Oh. Well, then, maybe we can have a little brainstorming session together."

Aberdeen and I were still unsure how to be around each other. We often clashed and he was frequently infuriating. He could still come off as superior, short-tempered and fiery. He did make me want to scream.

But he'd also held me and told me the truth about my father in the depth of the sanctum, and we'd saved each other's skin again and again during our miraculous victory in Quietfire. That made things all sorts of confusing. We weren't fighting as much anymore, but calling Aberdeen a friend still felt strange. Our link had always been through Sephy. But perhaps, I hoped, we were moving in a more positive direction.

Speaking of Sephy, she was waiting for us en route. She seemed to be omniscient when it came to anything occurring in the grounds, or perhaps my suspicion that she'd planted trackers on Aberdeen and me was actually well-founded.

I walked back to the dorm with Aberdeen on one side and Sephy padding along on the other. This new life of mine at Counterpart Academy had quickly become natural and effortless. It was strange yet beautiful, I reflected, how a few nights of eating pizza and watching movies with relative strangers could change your life irrevocably. That, and outwitting and destroying an entire military regiment.

The three of us had been tense for weeks after the events in Quietfire, waiting for the moment we were hauled in for questioning or put on trial. But we hadn't heard anything. As we'd hoped, the internal investigation had concluded Governor Blackmore sent overwhelming forces to kill some high schoolers to settle an unknown personal grudge. The Governor reportedly hadn't involved anyone else in her office on the plan. Her hastiness and self-absorbed priorities had also led to devastating casualties once she'd run afoul of some local acolytes led by the mysterious Scarecrow. The Praetory was still out for blood, determined to find Scarecrow and avenge their beloved Governor. But they would certainly be much more cautious about venturing into Quietfire in future.

We passed the open door of another dorm. I saw a television playing the news inside, Morgaine and Deva's faces displayed in incredible detail. Sephy noticed as well, and rubbed up against me in comfort.

For weeks Morgaine and Deva's faces had dominated the news, accompanied by blaring updates on the hunt for them. It made for a sensational story. Morgaine Holloway, once the Potentate's favourite, had reportedly committed a crime most unspeakable: murdering a Governor. Apparently Morgaine and Deva were in league with this Scarecrow, and had taken advantage of the chaos. The Praetory had been searching for them for a couple of months now, and Wellington was still in an uproar.

I had never, ever intended for my brand new knights to take the fall for Jo's death. I was beside myself when I found out they'd used themselves to distract attention from my involvement. Morgaine had left me a way to contact her if desperately needed. After I'd called her up simply to rage at her, she'd respectfully listened to the admonishment before asking me not to call again except in case of emergency. I promised her I'd find a way to clear their names. I also told her I hoped they were safe, wherever they were.

We reached the door of our dorm and I tensed suddenly.

There were muffled sounds coming from the other side. They were voices.

"Hold up," I warned the others, suspicious. My pulse ratcheted as I slipped into survival mode.

"Oh no, Crowley, it's okay!" Aberdeen said quickly. "I invited them."

He pushed the door open.

I blinked at the people revealed inside. It was all the acolytes. I could see Taggi and Grub, Victor and Bentley... they were all just dressed casually, chatting and laughing over drinks, helping themselves to a giant bowl of fruity punch at the kitchenette. A shower of confetti was floating down from the top of the stairwell. Some of the sparkly gold strips stuck to a homemade banner stretching across the room that read: *'HAPPY BIRTHDAY HARPER!'*

I had been planning to have Harper over to hang out with Sephy and myself to celebrate. I hadn't even thought of throwing him a big surprise party like this, but spotting the guest of honour himself grinning in the middle of it all made my heart shine with joy.

"You didn't have to do this," I said to Sephy, over-whelmed.

"I didn't! Although, I'd even find it hard to improve on it myself." She smiled. "This was all Addie's idea."

I turned to Aberdeen, shocked.

"Wait, really?"

He turned away from me and shrugged self-consciously.

"Crowley!" Harper exclaimed joyfully when he spotted me. He dashed forward and slammed into me, wrapping his arms around me tightly. I laughed and squeezed him back, feeling an unexpected rush of emotion.

"So there's that," Sephy continued, "but also that you're our friend."

"Friend?"

"Yes." Sephy seemed amused. Gleeful. "You *have* had a friend before, right Crowley?"

I flushed. "Duh, of course. Numerous ones."

"Ah-huh," Aberdeen laughed. "'*Numerous ones.*' Come on idiot, let's go get some cake."

"There's *cake*?" I whispered in mock-awe.

"He spent ages making it," Sephy chimed in, grinning.

"Liar!" Aberdeen snapped. Then he remembered himself, and a sheepish smile spread across his face. "Just... just a normal amount of time."

"Aberdeen," I said seriously. "You are a damn sorcerer."

I gave him a hug. He radiated warmth.

"Wow." His face was a deep red. I'd forgotten he was pretty averse to physical touch. "You really like cake."

We enjoyed a few vigorous rounds of *pin-the-tail-on-the-Sephy* and a game of hide-and-seek in which the entire dorm filled with a dark, impenetrable mist thanks to Xeno. Afterwards, I sat down on the couch with Jupiter's journal in my hands, the absurd party antics continuing all around me.

Things were so different now from when I'd spotted the acolytes on Cuba Street and followed them here, but not *everything* had changed. I still carried Father with me. The injustice of his death was a constant, seething fuel, a red-hot lava under the surface.

I knew now that the Potentate himself ordered Father's murder. He was the one to blame for the trauma and pain of that night, which had altered my life forever. It was also clearer to me than ever that the Praetory had built itself on the oppression of Shadows. Human nobles could get away with anything, and treat Shadows as their servants and playthings.

This wasn't the end of the road for us. Quietfire was just the beginning. But how was I supposed to get my revenge on the Potentate and bring the Praetory to its knees when we were just a group of teenagers at the bottom of the world?

I closed Jupiter's book, and traced the dark binding with my fingertips. Embossed on the front was Jupiter: the giant tiger's whiskers crackling with lightning. I ran my hand across the cover reverently, even achingly. It felt like trying to touch a memory—like trying to hold onto something I'd been too young, too angry, too *afraid* to understand. Now the Dark Father—the only one who'd ever looked at me back then like I mattered—was rotting in a cell somewhere, alone. The Potentate had wrung him dry for secrets, and when the silence finally satisfied him, he'd have Jupiter killed.

I used to believe Jupiter had abandoned me.

But the truth was, I abandoned him first.

I locked gazes with Aberdeen across the room. He looked down at the book in my hands, then back up at me.

He nodded. As if he knew exactly what I was thinking, and was answering my silent question.

Jupiter's revolution nearly broke the Praetory. He inspired thousands from the ashes of despair, built a movement when no one else had the courage and gave Shadows and humans something to believe in. He made them *see* each other. He made me see myself.

And I turned my back on him.

He could have overthrown the Potentate. Maybe he was the only Shadow who still could.

If there was still time, if there was even a chance—I had to try to save him.

I was going to bring him home.

"I know that look in your eyes, Alexandra Crowley," Sephy teased, springing onto the couch beside me.

I laughed, moving to make room for her.

"Oh, really?"

She tucked her long, quilled tail carefully to one side, the barbed spines rattling softly against the upholstery. Her tufted ears flicked toward me, alert and amused.

"What are you scheming?"

"Oooh, wouldn't you love to know?" I smiled, flopping sideways and reclining against her. Despite the dangerously spiky quills decorating the long curve of her tail, I'd long since learned how to make myself comfortable without getting stabbed. Sephy adjusted to my weight with an effortless shift, propping herself upright on her long, simian forelimbs.

"Ah. Not talking about your plans yet?"

"No," I confessed. "Not just yet."

"But you'll tell me the moment you are, right?"

I smiled.

"I'll come running to you," I promised her.

Sephy seemed to have come around to Aberdeen's little club of acolyte misfits after the life-changing events in Quietfire, but I wasn't sure how to broach the treasonous act I was contemplating next. Tonight, however, was for celebrating.

"Have you thought anymore about who your own counterpart might be?" I asked Sephy casually, while feeling oddly scared. I never laughed with anyone as much as I did with Sephy. I'd carried the grief of losing Father for the last year. It was this constant, breathing darkness, as if the grief itself had a heartbeat. Our hangouts and sleepovers had become rays of sunlight piercing through that endless cloud, reminding me that there was a world beyond the sorrow. Sephy had changed everything for me.

I caught myself fidgeting and stopped myself.

"Not really," she replied.

I took a breath.

"I see. Because, because I've been wondering..."

"I mean, like I said at the ceremony, the best outcome would be if it's someone high up in the nobility," Sephy said nonchalantly. I felt a little bit like the air had been kicked out of me. "So my family can get back into the Potentate's favour. It would be great if they could hold balls at their house again, I think Mum misses that."

I knew that Sephy's family was important to her, and how deeply seriously she took her duty to her human family. But somehow I'd thought after everything Sephy and I had been through in Quietfire, after I nearly lost her, and she nearly lost me, was it really too much to hope that we might be counterparts?

I shook the thought away. Still, what if I didn't even get to see her anymore, if she moved to Italy to be the counterpart of some high-up noble?

"Right," I said, staring at my shoes. "Like the Duke's son."

"Exactly."

"I thought your plans might have changed recently, after... Quietfire."

"Oh, I strongly believe that all Shadows deserve better lives, and the chance to determine their own futures,"

Sephy said fiercely. Then she smiled. "That doesn't mean I can't also make a great trophy-Shadow for the Duke while advocating for that, though. Hey, someone made mimosas!"

With that, Sephy launched herself off the couch, leaving me behind, a painful sensation tightening in my chest. It was inconvenient, this mix of longing and fear. I just sat there, grappling with the reality of what losing her might mean.

Later on, I took Harper aside so we could have some privacy. We walked up the stairs, then came to a stop overlooking the party below.

"I need to talk to you about something," I said hesitantly.

"What is it?" he asked me, as I stared into his eyes. "Did you find out what happened to Father?"

I opened my lips, but then I looked behind Harper's shoulder and I suddenly saw Jo standing there, covered in her own viscera. I gasped. The phantom smiled ghoulishly. Beneath the blood, her skin was pale as death.

"Crowley? Are you all right?" Harper looked behind him, following my gaze, then turned back. "What happened? You said you'd tell me everything," Harper pressed. "I can keep a secret."

I tried to tell him what I'd found out about our father. I really did. I dragged my eyes from the horrific vision of Jo, back to Harper's warm, earnest features.

All I wanted was for Harper to stay happy. I was sick and tired and angry of the lies and omissions from our parents growing up, and I'd been determined to share the whole truth with him. But as I stared at the little brother who I loved so fiercely, I realised I couldn't. To tell him would be to put him in too much danger.

Perhaps that was it. Perhaps I didn't want to tell him because it would mean revealing the monstrous things I'd done in order to survive. I couldn't face the idea of him looking at me like I was a killer.

"I'm closer than ever to the answers we've always wanted to know," I told him. "But all I know for now is that Father was a good man. A great one. He believed and fought for a better Praetory until the very end, one where everyone could be equal and safe."

"I knew that," Harper said simply. "He was the best."

"Yes," I said softly, my heart raw. "Yes, he was."

My phone rang. Harper just smiled and gestured for me to answer it, drifting back down the stairs to grant me some privacy.

"Yes, who is it?" I answered.

"Crowley," a high, courteous voice said. Though constrained, it was also strangely emotional. *"It's such a pleasure to talk to you at last."*

My pulse quickened, although I didn't know why.

"I'm sorry, do I know you?" I asked in a calm tone.

"In a manner of speaking. My name is Kaethe. I am Minister Crowley's Shadow."

My breath caught in my throat. This was my mother's Shadow, the missing piece of her. The part she'd never shared with me.

'It's such a pleasure to talk to you at last.'

Words I would never once imagine coming from my mother's lips. Yet they had just been uttered by her other half.

"It's an honour to finally speak with you too," I said, unsure what words were appropriate. Kaethe must know far more about me than I do about him. He had heard every one of my mother's thoughts. He'd seen her memories of me all the way from my birth to the current day, like an intimate spy throughout my entire life.

I wondered if Kaethe had ever wanted to meet me over the years, and if he would have if it wasn't for my mother's wishes. Or are the two of them on the same page about everything?

"Can I ask why you're calling now?" I inquired politely.

"You can. I have been informed that at this moment you and Harper are both at the Academy?"

"That's correct," I said warily, looking down at where Harper was laughing with the others.

"You have to get yourself and Harper to Wellington International Airport immediately. Bags will be prepared and packed for you. Everything will be taken care of."

"The airport?" I repeated, trying to hide my incredulity. "Where exactly are we being sent?"

"New York." Kaethe politely waited for my moment of surprise to pass, before adding: *"Your mother has been named Prime Inquisitor of the Praetory. She desires for yourself and your brother to attend her coronation."*

The air was knocked out of my lungs.

The others were all staring up at me now. They'd silenced the music. They must have caught from my tone and expression that something big was happening. A momentous change which may affect all of us.

"My mother..." I swallowed. My mother, just a commoner before she met my father, who clawed her way up to the top. My mother, the zealous member of the Praetory who had, perhaps unknowingly, married an acolyte. "She's the new Prime Inquisitor?"

It was one of the most powerful positions in all of the

Praetory. This would place her at the very side of the Potentate himself. It was an unheard of ascension of power, especially considering the common blood that Mother had always feared would hold her back.

"*Yes.*"

But that would make myself and Harper...

"*We await the Prince and yourself in New York, Princess Crowley.*"

―――――

I hope you've loved *A Princess so Noble and Vengeful*. Don't worry, Book 2 of Counterpart Academy, A Princess so Noble and Vengeful, is available here.

COUNTERPART ACADEMY BOOK TWO: OUT NOW!

Princess by title, rebel by blood—my fight for justice is just beginning.

Elevated to the rank of Princess within the secretive Praetory, my life and the lives of those I love should be secure. But when extremists twist the legendary Jupiter's vision of equality into a campaign of terror, I'm tasked with bringing them to justice.

With my father's legacy haunting me and my counterpart nowhere to be found, I realise my secret link to Jupiter might be the key to saving us all—or to destroying everything I've sworn to protect.

Keep Reading for a Sneak Peek from Book Two in the Epic *Counterpart Academy* Series....

A PRINCESS SO NOBLE AND VENGEFUL

The atrium was enormous, gilded, and, in my opinion, had all the cozy charm of a maximum-security prison. It was the Praetory's crown jewel—a New York palace near Central Park that looked like the Museum of Natural History, provided you swapped the dinosaur skeletons for oppressive statues of dead tyrants.

Mother had been busy with her duties since her coronation as Prime Inquisitor. In between our various balls, dinners and mandatory social appointments, Harper and I had been left to explore New York.

Now I stood alone, waiting for Mother to appear from behind the curtain at the top of the stairs like the Wizard of Oz. Maintaining my dutiful composure was proving difficult, mainly because the man I intended to kill was also behind that curtain. Nothing said quality introvert time like plotting regicide.

The Potentate. The man who sat on the throne of the Praetory and the man who had ordered my father's murder. Every moment since learning the truth, I had dreamt of his end. He was tauntingly close, but palace security had more layers than an onion. Plus, my '*army*' was all the way back in New Zealand, and consisted of a ragtag club of student rebels who barely survived their last field trip. Without them, it was me, my prosthetic leg, and a simmering mountain of treasonous intent. Not exactly '*overthrowing an empire*' material.

The mask I wore was perfect: Princess Crowley, the daughter of the newly-minted Prime Inquisitor. Mother had no idea that back in New Zealand, I was '*Scarecrow,*' the leader of the very rebel cell she was being paid to hunt.

Footsteps echoed across the abyss of the hall. I turned to see a young human and a Shadow approaching me. The girl looked about fourteen, but walked with a stiffness that was strangely military, considering she should have been taking selfies with friends on the schoolyard. I stood and strode across the gaping hall to meet them, as waiting for them to cross it felt like a waste of a good semester.

When we reached each other, the pair came to a stop and bowed simultaneously.

"Princess Crowley," the girl said respectfully. She sounded almost awed.

Oh God, not this again.

"Please, just call me Crowley," I said, sticking out my hand like a normal human.

She flushed as if the request was inconceivable, staring at my out-held hand. Then she nodded obediently and shook it.

"Very well, Lady Crowley."

I sighed, perplexed. It was a good enough start.

The girl had an abundant mane of ginger hair that she wore in bangs. Her hair splayed out of her headband at the back like a pair of adorable floppy dog ears.

"My name is Corporal Virginia O'Hart," the girl introduced herself. "Although a lot of people call me..."

"Let me guess," I stopped her. "Ginger?"

"Oh, wow, good guess," she said, wide-eyed. Then she rallied herself. "I mean, why, you are correct, my Lady. Wow," she added, stopping to blink at me. "I'm sorry, but... you're really beautiful. They warned me, but..."

I blushed, stricken. I'd been hearing that kind of sugared, carefully calculated praise all week from sycophantic noble suitors, but from her it sounded embarrassingly genuine. I wondered what she'd say if she'd seen the gaunt, socially awkward scarecrow I was before the professional hair and makeup team went to work on me. It was amazing how 'regal' you looked when you were wearing a ten-thousand-dollar blue dress and enough foundation to hide a felony. Still, a shy smile broke out across my face.

I didn't say I was *immune* to flattery.

"If you think I'm the bombshell here, you're selling yourself short," I bowed, shrugging off my awkwardness. "Corporal O'Hart."

Ginger grinned. Her Shadow beside her looked like a humanoid dragonfly that had raided a couture runway: rose-petal battle corset, translucent wings. And me? Totally unfazed. Six months at Counterpart Academy and bug-people with fashion sense barely made the list of *'weird stuff before breakfast.'*

"This is Wasp," Ginger said, gesturing to her counterpart, who examined me curiously with bulbous, radioactive green eyes.

"Pleasure to meet you," I told Wasp, inclining my head. Shocked silence greeted me. It didn't surprise me. Acknowledging Shadows was near-unheard of among the Praetory's high nobility. To them, Shadows were to be treated as little more than impressive furnishings.

"You did say '*Corporal*' O'Hart?" I asked Ginger hesitantly, quirking an eyebrow. "Both of you are in the *military*?"

"Yes, Princess – my, um, Lady."

"If I may ask, how old are you, exactly?"

"We're fifteen," she said. "We were recruited at thirteen, and fought in the war with Shadows' Eve."

I stared, and she shrugged.

"I discovered Wasp very young," Ginger explained, "and the Praetory realised we were gifted. So... we were put through intensive training and sent to the front-lines. I've actually just returned from active duty abroad! I've been summoned back to the palace to report."

I swallowed. Welcome to the horrors of the Praetory. Literal children, drafted into risking their lives as long as they were of sufficient ability.

My own parents had wanted to give me some semblance of normality for as long as possible growing up. I may have been trained to excel at combat all through my childhood, but I hadn't been told about the existence of Shadows.

"So, have you had the grand tour, my Lady? Over there we have the East Wing... or, maybe that's the South. It's definitely a Wing. Shit. I was going to brush up on this..."

The Potentate's palace, the pearl of the Praetory, was white and ornate. The grand atrium was bustling with throngs of officials and high-ranking nobles. I gazed at the Pool of Tranquility, which sat like a black hole in the middle of it all, sucking up light and hope.

"You know, we had a group of school-kids we were showing around the palace the other day," Ginger said. "A

Shadow somehow managed to accidentally set this boy's backpack on fire. It was terrible. It triggered an emergency lockdown of the entire palace."

"What did you do?" I marvelled.

"I pushed the kid into the Pool of Tranquillity."

I lost it, my laughter ringing off the stone walls. Ginger seemed stunned by the response. But then she smiled too.

My brother Harper and I had flown to New York at the drop of a hat. My Mother, who had been a commoner before marrying a Count, was to be coronated as Prime Inquisitor. This unheard of ascension in power meant that Harper and I were, technically, Prince and Princess. Don't get excited. It was just a title granted to the children of the highest ranking Praetory nobles. The title was honorary, like being crowned prom queen.

In terms of opportunities for our rebel group, it changed everything.

At the centre of the atrium stood an enormous pair of statues. The sheer scale of the artwork was almost suffocating, as if the entire room existed to serve as a stage for this brutal display of power. It depicted the Potentate, a man who had long since surpassed the figure frozen in stone in years. His bearded face was shaped in a scowl, thunderous and eternal.

A towering being of dark majesty rose behind him, its massive form coiling and unfurling. Serpentine necks twisted upwards, crowned in the savage heads of eagles, their beady eyes gleaming with an unholy hunger, reflecting their master's own will.

"I hate this place," Ginger sighed. Then her eyes widened as she remembered who she was talking to. "No disrespect, Princess.... *my Lady.* But I'm not used to the wearing dresses and looking... pretty and stuff. My first ball here, I was told to make sure I dressed up. You know what I dressed as?"

"Um..."

"*Red Riding Hood*," she said bitterly, rolling her eyes. "I thought it was a dress-up party, with costumes. The noble girls here still laugh about it behind my back."

My hand flew to my mouth.

"Oh no."

"The first week I was here people thought I was snubbing their dinner invites," Wasp buzzed dreamily, "but I was actually just lost in the tunnels of the New York underground."

I blinked.

"I'd mixed up all my medications," the dragonfly said seriously, "and I didn't know how to get out."

"We're gifted in other ways," Ginger assured me, clearing her throat loudly. "A battlefield with a clear target to whack is much less anxiety-inducing than all this schmoozing."

"Amen, sister," I muttered. I watched Ginger adjust her heavy, ornate collar—a garment that clearly felt more like a straightjacket to her than a fashion choice.

"A battlefield has its charms," I said, careful to keep my tone casual, like someone who often traded war stories over lukewarm coffee. "At least there, you know which way the bullets are coming from. The politics in this atrium? That's the real minefield."

Ginger nodded fervently. "Exactly! Give me a trench any day."

"You would have served on the front lines," I said, tilting my head as a squad of severe-looking guards marched past—looking like they'd all been born with a permanent scowl and a stick up their collective backside.

"Ever cross paths with the Shadows' Eve cells?" I dropped my voice, sliding into the role of a bored gossip looking for a fix. "I heard stories back in Wellington... specifically about the day they finally bagged the Dark Father himself."

I let the name hang. Even eighteen months after his capture, the name of the acolyte leader carried its own gravity.

Ginger's expression hardened. "I was in training when they bagged him. We all thought the war was over once that unholy tiger was behind bars."

"And still, those acolytes keep crawling out of the woodwork," I murmured. "Mother's been so tight-lipped lately, I wondered if they were keeping him here in New York—somewhere so secure his fan club wouldn't dream of a rescue."

I kept my tone light, almost gossipy—the curious daughter excited about her mother's high-stakes work.

"Jupiter? Here?" Ginger snorted. "The Praetory has its secrets, my Lady, but they aren't stupid. You don't keep a Shadow like that in a place with this many windows. If he's still breathing, he's buried in a black site so deep the devil himself couldn't escape... and that's kind of the idea." She paused, her eyes narrowing slightly. It wasn't suspicion, just a soldier's reflex. "Why the interest?"

I laughed, using my natural nerves as camouflage. "Can you blame me? I'd feel safer knowing the boogeyman was under a very specific, *very* distant lock and key."

Ginger's face went blank—a professional mask, but somehow I saw through it. She didn't have the information I needed; it was likely miles above her pay grade.

The heavy velvet curtains at the top of the stairs parted.

"Crowley," Mother's voice rang out, possessing all the warmth of a New Zealand southerly blast.

I snapped into a perfect curtsy, the movement smooth despite the carbon-fibre prosthetic hidden beneath my skirts. Ginger and Wasp scrambled into a formal salute.

The Prime Inquisitor descended the stairs, a thunderstorm in heels. She was tall, with hair blacker than night. Her irises were icy blue and held an intimidating clarity. She was darkly beautiful, but a beauty that was so bound up with her charisma that a photo would not capture it: a crackling, domineering intensity that had compelled many, and scared off far more. She wore a long, tailored black velvet coat, the cut sharp and severe. Nothing said 'approachable leader' like looking ready to preside over a public execution.

As Prime Inquisitor, Mother was now the head acolyte hunter. She was responsible more than anyone else in the Praetory for rounding up, interrogating and killing people from the movement that I was now irrefutably a part of. How utterly would it break my mother to find out that her husband had been an acolyte himself, and that her daughter had followed in his footsteps?

I shivered. Mother and Father may have already separated before Father's death, but somehow I suspected part of her had still always loved him. Not that she would ever show it.

At her side was her Shadow. I found it hard to stop looking at him. I'd never met Mother's counterpart until this trip. Considering who Mother was, I found her Shadow... surprising.

Order 'A Princess so Noble and Vengeful', Book 2 in Counterpart Academy today.

FREE BOOK? YES PLEASE!

Download *A Warrior so Clever and Cursed* completely for FREE (a gripping and essential prequel to the *Counterpart Academy* series) and join my mail squad to be the first to hear about new book releases at:

www.sambloodauthor.com

Hi there! I'm Sam. Thanks for coming along for the adventure. If you enjoyed *A School so Gorgeous and Fatal*, I'd love it if you shared a **review** to help other readers find it:

ABOUT THE AUTHOR

Sam Blood lives in Auckland, New Zealand, where he spends his days writing urban fantasy, eating, and trying to impress his spectacular Sri Lankan lawyer wife with plot twists. He started writing the first book about magical creatures called Shadows when he was nine years old, and frankly, things have spiralled out of control ever since. Sam loves hearing from readers—you can reach him at:

www.sambloodauthor.com
www.facebook.com/sambloodauthor
www.instagram.com/sambloodauthor

Dive into the Shadows universe with my other books:

Counterpart Academy
A Warrior So Clever and Cursed (Prequel)
A School so Gorgeous and Fatal
A Princess so Noble and Vengeful
A Knight so Loyal and Broken
A Shadow so Queenly and Defiant

The Shadows Series
Shadows
Raven
Cameron

Majestic
Eclipse
Winghold